THOUGHTLESS

Lucie Britsch's writing has appeared in *Catapult Story,
Vol. 1 Brooklyn, Split Lip* Magazine, and *The Sun* magazine,
and has been nominated for a Pushcart Prize.
Sad Janet is her first novel.

THOUGHTLESS

LUCIE
BRITSCH

WEIDENFELD & NICOLSON

An Weidenfeld & Nicolson paperback

First published in Great Britain in 2023
by Weidenfeld & Nicolson
This paperback edition published in 2024
Weidenfeld & Nicolson
an imprint of The Orion Publishing Group Ltd
Carmelite House, 50 Victoria Embankment
London EC4Y ODZ

An Hachette UK Company

1 3 5 7 9 10 8 6 4 2

A CIP catalogue record for this book is
available from the British Library.

ISBN (Paperback) 9781 4091 9870 3

Typeset by Input Data Services Ltd, Bridgwater, Somerset

Printed and bound in Great Britain by Clays Ltd, Elcograf S.p.A.

MIX
Paper | Supporting
responsible forestry
FSC
www.fsc.org
FSC® C104740

www.weidenfeldandnicolson.co.uk
www.orionbooks.co.uk

For the overthinkers.

'Men are simpler than you imagine, my sweet child. But what goes on in the twisted, tortuous minds of women would baffle anyone.'

Daphne du Maurier, Rebecca

'You're overthinking it, Ronnie.'

Snookie, Jersey Shore Family Vacation

'Well, turn something on, I'm starting to think.'

Homer Simpson

David

We were in bed, doing the things you do at the beginning of a relationship, like count each other's freckles, or hold your gut in.

Susan got up to hunt for food, and I tried not to grin too much, or high five myself, because I'd just had sex. She wasn't gone long and soon I heard her outside the door. I thought her roommate might have caught her doing the walk of shame, and they were out there talking about my penis maybe, but I didn't hear laughter, so it was fine.

I opened the door to find Susan, alone, balancing two plates and two glasses, like she was a circus seal and I hadn't noticed, even though we'd just had sex, and I was sure I'd notice that, because the police might be there. But then she wasn't carrying them, and they were on the floor.

Whoops, she said, but she wasn't embarrassed.

Now I thought about it, our bodies had made noises like seals just moments ago, slapping against each other, but she didn't seem to care, didn't seem to know she was *supposed* to care, and I loved her instantly for it.

What were you thinking? I said. I wasn't angry, though, because it wasn't my food, or floor, and we'd just had sex. She could have dropped all the plates in the world as long as she came back to bed.

I

I wasn't, she said, crouching down to pick up the spilled food, mopping the juice with her foot.

We'll laugh about this later, I thought. The food, the weird seal sex. Now I know it's not funny, though, because of her curse.

Our story starts with bread. Not a kiss, or birth. Not even a fun death. No life-changing event, good or bad. But bread. People like to blame the bankers, but for me, it was the bakers.

Like most modern women, Susan had bought bread before. It was a small thing, but credit should be given where credit's due when it's so much easier to just go to a place and have someone make you a sandwich. I had myself bought many sandwiches in my lifetime, taken that easy route. Really, my whole life was just buying sandwiches before she came along: thinking about them, buying them, eating them – stuck in an infinite sandwich loop.

But one fateful day, she came home without any bread at all, not even something pretending to be bread, claiming it was the real thing, but free from all the ingredients that actually made bread bread, fooled by goopy white women into believing it was bread, when it was, in fact, not. Sometimes she was even fooled by the word 'wonder' in front of the word bread, believing it would be so, because why would they lie when we all needed saving? It usually all made sense to her. She took the world at face value, because why would it lie to her when it was made for her, because we told her it was?

Susan came home that day and plopped herself down on the couch, then just sat there staring into space, and she wasn't supposed to do that; in fact, she didn't do that. This was a first. Staring into space like a teenager whose parent had moved the screen they were staring at and was just waiting for it to come back because this was how their face was now from all the staring at screens – this type of checking out was dangerous for her, and we'd done everything we possibly could to keep it from happening.

She was really fucking up our plan.

Her face looked damp, like she might have been caught in the rain, but it wasn't raining, and her hair looked slightly like that of a mad person, or someone who'd been dragged through a hedge, and I didn't think she had that in her diary that day.

But I knew to stay calm and act normal. I'd spent the last few years preparing for this and kept telling myself it had to be a glitch. Please, God, let this be a glitch, because I'm not ready.

So, what did you get? I asked her casually.

Although it was clear the answer was nothing, unless a fembot had lured her into a store and made her buy make-up again that made her look like she'd been crying/dragged through a hedge.

Nothing, she said, only confirming my fears that I wouldn't be having any sandwiches that night, or ever again maybe. The horror, the horror.

Why were you crying? I said, knowing supermarkets could make you cry – the lighting alone.

I couldn't choose, she said.

She was remarkably calm for someone who wouldn't be eating a delicious sandwich that night or possibly ever again.

Was I crying? she said, touching her face. Oblivious was her default setting.

What are we going to eat? I asked, joking, but also deadly serious. A man could live on bread alone; don't believe what they tell you.

So, I have to keep you away from bread now? I joked again,

but I was seriously starting to worry. Things were popping in my forehead. My brain was screaming, I'm not ready! I needed more time with her.

Yes, she said, in a deadly serious voice, one I didn't know she was capable of that sounded like it came from a deep, dark place of distress, one I was more than familiar with in my own head, but a place we hoped she never went.

We had no idea what we were dealing with really, kidding ourselves we could ever pull this off. If you think something is ethically wrong, it probably is, even if your reasons for doing it come from a place of love. But it wasn't just a white lie we'd told her; we'd basically hijacked her brain.

We were awful people, and I think I always knew that. People were awful – why would we be different?

But this wasn't the time to be dicking about in my own head. There would be plenty of time later to dwell, to drive myself completely mad thinking about all the ways we could have done it differently. I pencilled in regret and grief in my phone for later, but right now I needed to be in that room, with Susan, who was starting to unravel, because of bread, but mostly because of what we'd done to her.

So not knives but bread, I joked again, but I had a new layer of worry now because I was also worrying that she could tell I was worried, which was a layer I could do without.

Yes, she said in that voice again – a stranger's voice – and I half expected her weird new face to melt right off there and then, or for something to pop out of her chest, because I watched too many movies, because we always had to be watching something, always had to be blocking whatever it was we were blocking, but that was normal now, wasn't it? To already be onto the next thing, for content makers barely able to keep up with our demand for a constant stream of something, all

4

to keep us from ourselves. That didn't make me feel better, though, just more fucked.

If this were a sci-fi film, she'd be an android, and she'd glitch sometimes, and we'd know that's what it was and be like, oh, that's just Susan glitching, then switch her off and on again. But this wasn't a film; she was really starting to come undone. Our worst fear was becoming reality, all because I'd wanted a sandwich.

OK, I said to pacify her, hoping it soothed her, while I tried to keep my head. One of us had to.

You'd do that? she said, Keep me away from bread? She said it in her normal voice again at least.

Yes, I said. You know I would. I reminded her what bread we liked, what cheese, if Kraft Singles counted as cheese.

Squares are good, she said, and I breathed and felt the most relieved I had since she came in the door and I was only minutes away from eating a grilled cheese sandwich.

You OK? I asked, again with the OK, because it was her safe word. Up until this moment she'd always been OK, big fan of the thumbs-up, like she was from the 70s. So for her not to be OK was a huge fucking deal, and a bad one.

I went to sit with her on the couch and turned the TV on and flicked to a music channel to help deflate the situation. MTV wouldn't let her unravel, I thought. They needed her. She was their last hope.

But then her mouth opened and all these words fell out and fast.

I'll be on the security tape standing in the bread section for hours picking one up, then putting it back, lol, she said, but she wasn't laughing.

Damn you, MTV!

I picked some up twice, she said, frowning.

I'll be on the security tape crying in the bread section like a crazy person, she said.

I was crying, wasn't I? she said, touching her cheek.

I couldn't decide, she said, leaning her head on my shoulder now.

But she was so calm, like it all happened to someone else. It was just me that was freaking out. Every possible alarm bell and siren in my head – of which there are many, it seems; all different pitches, oddly – was going off.

This was the most she'd said in a long time, about something other than a celebrity, or movie, or dog. She mostly spoke in popular catchphrases, idioms – amazeballs, yolo – all the nonsense people said was destroying the English language; it was her language, because it was fun, available, everywhere, soft in her mouth, easy to digest. It was the language of youth, of pop culture. It made sense to her somehow, when to most of us it was fun for a while, but then we needed real words, some meat in our sentences, our sentiments. For her, life was too short for whole sentences, or words even. She didn't take any of it seriously, though; it was all there for her to consume so she consumed it before it consumed her. And not just TV and movies and music, but art and literature, everything, anything, all the good stuff, but mostly mediocre. The rest of us were desperately trying to squeeze meaning out of it all when, really, earth was just a big dumb rock with nothing to give, our existence on it answerless and stupid.

Rebecca

Someone brought their baby to the bookstore and everyone crowded around it making stupid faces and even stupider voices, but I was immune. To me, it was a lump of meat in a bow, because it had a bow on its head, so we knew they weren't raising it non-gendered, which was a huge fuck-you to most of us trying to undo all that damage our parents and society had done over the last few thousand years.

Have you met the baby? Ed said to me as I was pretending to read the back of the latest Franzen, hoping soon there wouldn't be such a thing.

I was a lump of meat in a bow myself once, so I'm good, thanks, I wanted to say, but didn't, I just said, I will, when I'm ready. You'd think I didn't have my own out there in the world somewhere.

Minus those early meat-lump years, I'd always felt trapped in my own head. Most buildings with walls made me feel physically trapped, especially if there were people in those buildings, which there usually were, but my head was always worse. On the outside it looked OK, I wasn't hideous, but on the inside, it was all swirling vortexes, clowns with knives, the darkest shit, and if I was sure of anything, it was that my thoughts were going to kill me one day. Not even bad thoughts, just thoughts, because I had zero control over them. It felt like I had a wild animal inside me most days, but that animal wasn't happy about being locked up in my head, obviously, so there was this fun daily battle where the animal would thrash about a lot and I'd have to keep shouting at it to calm the fuck down. If I could take my head off and throw it off a bridge, I would. People say that about their phones now, but it's their heads they want to throw really. I would have loved a lobotomy, even as a gift. But then Sylvia Plath had electric shock treatment, which was close enough, and that did fuck all. Still, I told my husband I wasn't to be trusted with ovens, just in case, which got me out of cooking, which was a huge bonus in a marriage if you already felt like all the domestic chores women had to think about might kill you anyway. Isaac and I joked about it, because what else could we do? Sylvia had children and they didn't save her, but this wasn't about her, or even me and Isaac. This was about me and Susan.

Even before Isaac came along I knew if I had children, I didn't want them to ever feel trapped in their heads. I didn't care if that meant they were vapid, vain creatures, who cared about things I never cared about, like sports, or celebrities, or celebrity-owned make-up brands. That glorious material world Madonna sang about, before she got weird arms, then refused to grow old gracefully, worrying us all, because she had to have people around her all the time in case she fell, because bones couldn't lie. My heart couldn't take it.

I cared about the things you couldn't see or touch, the huge, important things on the tips of everyone's tongues, behind all those bloodshot, screen-addicted eyes. I cared so much and so deeply, but where did it get me?

★

If my parents were around, they'd tell you how I'd always been like this, but they weren't. They weren't dead, they just weren't around. They brought me up to like being indoors and by myself. I was never forced to do anything, or even to go outside, so I didn't, other than to school, or the doctor once or twice, the library at weekends. My parents had me believe it was unnecessary to go out when there were so many books inside, quietly demanding that I read them, which I did. My parents never wanted children, they wanted to read themselves to death, but one day my mother happened to read something about motherhood that intrigued her, stirred something in her, and then later read something that aroused her, and after a lengthy discussion about how one child might not be that bad, I was conceived. Not from love then, but out of curiosity, and I know this because my mother told me.

I was named after a character in a book, Rebecca. Although technically I was more like the unnamed protagonist of the story. But my mother couldn't call me Unnamed Protagonist, so she called me Rebecca, after a vengeful ghost.

A boy in class teased me once about how quietly I spoke and a kind teacher said, some people are introverts, we're all different, Rebecca is just quieter than you, and I felt truly seen. I still cursed the boy because I'd just read *The Crucible*. I liked being an introvert and that the word even existed. It made me feel better, understood. Words made things solid. Words I understood.

Coming from the family I did, I never saw quietness as a problem. It was only other people who increasingly made me feel like I was possibly doing it all wrong – life, everything in between. That boy in my class was just the start. My mother was a worrier, my father a depressed functioning alcoholic, and I suspected that when I got older I would also be those things.

My family existed in the corners and shadows of our home, alone together, as they say, but more alone.

I craved solitude the way other girls needed attention from men.

Before Isaac, people seemed like a lot of work. Books didn't ask anything of me. They couldn't hold me or say nice things to me, but they couldn't hurt me or say mean things either. I'd hooked up a few times with boys I met at readings, boys in my lit class, but they were all so full of feelings, and I just wanted a warm body. I had enough of my own feelings. I dreamed of nice quiet boys, boys who would sit and read with me in silence, but who wouldn't object if I straddled them every now and then.

My goal was always to get out of my head. As a teenager it was easy, normal. I did every drug going, only I didn't care about the high, I just wanted to escape myself. I wasn't one of the cool kids, but I liked getting wasted so no one hassled me. I wanted oblivion and they wanted fun. It meant I let boys take advantage of me more than I'd like to admit, but I did let them; I was almost passed out, but it's the almost that keeps me sane. I wanted it. I never once said no. I wanted someone else to take over, to make me feel good, please. It was another level of sadness, my body trying to blot out my mind. I never wanted Susan to feel this.

I always went back to books, though. I could pick one up anywhere anytime and immediately be in someone else's head. It didn't matter what book. I was supposed to have a favourite author, or genre at least, but I didn't. Any book with words that would override my own internal dialogue would do. Got words? Sold. And I worked in a bookstore, so I felt bad that I wasn't more discerning. People would come in and ask me for recommendations and I'd have to send them off to speak to someone else, like I was possibly illiterate, part of some special employment scheme. I should have just pretended I didn't work there. Sometimes I wanted to shout, it's all the same, it doesn't matter, just read anything, as long as you read! Because that's how I felt. But I didn't think my boss would appreciate it. My colleagues were all really into the stuff they were into and I was just pretending, a cover for my secret goal of oblivion.

I figured one day I'd know how to deal with it all, but for the moment I just wanted to forget it all.

One boy I dated told me he astral-projected. OK, it was once, and he was high, but I slept with him anyway. I wanted him to teach me how to do it, but he didn't know how he did it, just that he did it, which was no use to me, so I moved on to his friend whose dad owned a bar and could steal us liquor.

For a while I would get boys to come and pick me up in their cars and have them drive me around. I picked sweet boys who didn't expect anything so if I made out with them or put my hand on their crotch it was enough. I only wanted them for their cars, or more specifically the motion, the movement. It never ended well; they wanted more – not sexually, but they needed to know if they were my friend or my lover and, really, they were neither, they were just a means to an end. I needed to get out of my house, but also my head.

I didn't know what to do with all the feelings, all the thoughts, all the time, I had no place to put them, so I chose to block them. I just wasn't very good at it. Maybe having Susan was fate then.

David

After telling me what happened at the store, Susan was quiet and flicked through the music channels on the TV. It seemed to be over.

I kept a close eye on her for the rest of the night, but the whole thing seemed behind her. That was Susan. Attention span of a goldfish. Although I didn't know what goldfish those scientists had spoken to.

I remember one night she flicked to a channel where a woman was giving birth and wasn't the slightest bit disturbed. I saw flashes of red and a head coming out of a vagina, and I couldn't sleep for a week. Susan was just picking her nails, asked what I wanted for dinner. I'd like my memory erased please, I wanted to say.

The only sign that something had happened and left a mark was that she ate nothing but cheese sandwiches for the next three days. She was eating her feelings perhaps, which was normal. But to me it was a sign something was very wrong. I wanted to block my feelings with delicious sandwiches too, but one of us had to be the grown-up.

That's enough sandwiches, I said on the fourth day of her new diet.

Don't you want something green? I said, waving a limp head

of lettuce at her neither of us remembered buying that could have possibly been there when we moved in.

Chill, bro, she said, I was just taking your advice, sticking to the plan.

Should we go out to eat? she said then, but she was already putting her shoes on and I had to smile.

OK, I said, cashing in on this return to our reality. This was what love felt like.

Happy Meal? I said.

God, yes! she said, her eyes lighting up for McDonald's. I had broken the spell with the promise of fat, salt and sugar, the magic trifecta.

With that she dragged me outside into the bright sun and it was like the world was saying, hello, David and Susan, we missed you, we will look after you! But only if you get a Happy Meal. You must abide by our rules.

Before Susan, I was either at work or playing video games, or both, when my boss wasn't looking. Life was something that happened around me, but I wasn't part of it. Now, with Susan, I could be in the world with more ease, knowing she belonged there, and so maybe, by association, I did too.

I met Susan at a party. There was nothing odd about her; what was odd was that I was at a party. I should have realised that a pretty girl who chose to play video games with me rather than mingle or dance or whatever people did at parties had something secretly wrong with her, something like webbed toes maybe, or three knees.

My roommate, Nick, had decided he was going to throw a party and was clearly having some sort of breakdown. He hated parties. When everyone was partying at college we listened to music and played video games. We smoked weed, though, so were still cool. We just didn't party. The thought of going to an actual nightclub made us feel physically sick. We had a friend who went to one once and never came back. This is the story I'll tell my children if they ask if they can go to a club.

So, Nick was going through some stuff and declared one day that we were going to have a party, because that was something people did, and those people seemed to be doing better than us, so we would have a party and have fun, damn it. When people shout at you that you will have fun, you know you have to at least try. He was my friend and I wanted to support him through whatever this was, so I said sure, but I made it quite clear that while I was happy for him to have his party, and I would definitely drink and smoke whatever anyone offered me, I would not partake in any mingling or dancing. Fine, he said.

I would do what I always did, play video games and eat pizza, only this time there would be a throbbing bass and strangers asking me where the bathroom was even though our place was so small there really weren't many options. I mostly directed people to a closet.

There was always the small chance someone would want to play with me. I envisioned some dude plonking himself down next to me, asking if he could play but then picking up the spare controller before I could say anything, and because it was a party, I'd have to be OK with it and I'd be trapped forever because I lived there. He'd probably end up moving in and I'd have to go to his wedding and I really just wanted the opposite of that.

But as it happened, the person who wanted to play was a girl, and she smelled like she bathed in Sprite, which, for all I knew, was something girls did.

Mario Kart is my jam, she said, picking up the spare controller and destroying me.

She hammered away at all the buttons like a lunatic but still managed to win. She also moved her body when she turned corners, which was equal amounts adorable and weird. If it had been anyone else, I might have offered some advice, but whatever she was doing was working. I had met my match, in life and love, but more importantly, in *Mario Kart*.

After beating me several times she got up and left. The world of Mario would never be the same.

I looked for her. I wasn't supposed to be engaging with the party, I was supposed to be merely tolerating it, but now here I was, almost mingling, just to get a girl's number.

I asked around but no one knew her. She could have just walked in off the street.

So, I went out to the street, just in case she was there. She wasn't.

I hadn't been that close to a human girl for some time (Nick in his bathrobe holding some lotion didn't count).

I must have interrogated everyone at that party. People probably thought I was her dad, or a cop.

Eventually I found out who she was. She was a friend of a friend and I'd never been so happy to have friends that were way more sociable than me. People who actually knew more people than Nick.

In the least creepy way possible I found out where she'd be one night. The internet had really taken the fun out of stalking. People told everyone where they were and what they were doing at all times. No trench coat needed.

She was going to a silent disco, which I immediately didn't like the sound of. This girl was already changing my life in ways she'd never understand and now I was going to have to go to a club?

I had to google what a silent disco was of course, because

I knew nothing about what people did. I knew what silent meant, and was fine with it, but the disco part made me feel nauseous and brought back memories of being forced to go to school dances and standing next to the exit the whole time before finally just sneaking out and going home to play video games and then, when my mum asked if I'd had a good time, I'd say, I had a time and she'd say, well done, because she knew I was trying. Somewhere between then and now I'd stopped trying a bit, but apparently I was starting again, and all because a girl had beaten me at *Mario Kart* and wasn't physically repulsed by me.

A silent disco was where people danced to their own music wearing headphones, apparently. My mind raced like it did on the brink of something new, already picturing telling people how we met, already naming our kids Mario and Luigi, even if they were girls.

She was wearing pyjama bottoms and a Wu-Tang T-shirt. Her eyes were closed, lost in the music. I had to casually bump into her without her thinking I was going to assault her.

Hey, I said, trying to make my face seem open.

I know you, she shouted, and I smiled and nodded, and she smiled and closed her eyes again, but she knew me, and wasn't that all any of us wanted?

I thought she was fearless, something I wasn't, but it turned out she was just thoughtless, which was actually almost the same. She had a confidence but not an ego, like this was just who she was but she didn't think about it. She gave you everything and didn't seem to want anything for herself. She was the only person I'd ever met who seemed truly at ease not just in herself but the world. I had no idea what I was getting myself into, which I guess is how love works.

Susan's friends seemed prickly with me at first, each taking turns to give me disapproving looks, until they realised Susan genuinely seemed to like me, or had mistaken me for someone else. They weren't subtle; at one point, someone pointed at me, made a face, and Susan shrugged. I didn't try to touch her, or her drink, all night, which I hoped translated to, I'm one of the good guys.

Her best friend Kate was a radical feminist – I knew that because her T-shirt said Feminism Is the Radical Idea That Women Are People, so I thought she didn't like me just because I was a man, which I was actually OK with, because people had not liked me for far stupider reasons.

When Susan was in the bathroom, she knocked into me, then said, sorry, but I could tell by her face she wasn't.

Take a walk with me, she said, like she was Tony Soprano.

I followed her outside.

So, she said, you and Susan.

What about us? I said.

I see you, she said, getting right up close and almost sticking her fingers in my eyes.

I get it, I said. You don't know me.

I don't want to know you, she said.

Good, you don't have to, I said.

Good, she said, looking me up and down. I know enough.

You know nothing, I said.

Oh, I know, she said.

Just then another of Susan's friends came outside to vape.

Susan's looking for you, she said to me, blowing something that smelled of blue Doritos into my face, because that was a flavour now.

I'm watching you, Kate said as I went back inside.

I'm watching you back, I said.

I thought that was just what girls did for their friends. I

couldn't have known it was something else. That Susan was something else.

I went to see Susan at her work the next day. She worked at a women's gym as a spin instructor and I felt intimidated immediately, which was the point, if you were a man, which technically I was.

Kate rolled her eyes when she saw me. She stood at the front desk, arms folded, nostrils flaring, wearing all-black gym clothes and giving off distinct Darth Vader vibes, only she was wielding a luminous green water bottle instead of a Lightsaber. She was wielding it all the same, guarding her women, but mostly Susan.

Women only, she said, pointing to a sign that said Women Only, so I went and waited outside.

Susan came out a few minutes later.

Hey, you, she said.

Hey, you, I said.

And that was where my flirting skills stopped.

You can pick me up after work if you want, she said.

Cool, I said.

Eight, she said.

Eight, I said.

In your car, she said.

Right, I said.

She went back inside and Kate came out.

She only wants you for your car, she said, and I thought, Ha, she's going to be very disappointed then.

She was right in a way, but it wasn't the car Susan wanted; it was the motion. She needed to be moving at all times. I learnt this the hard way after the first time we slept together. I needed time to recover like most humans, but Susan was up and ready to do whatever was next. There had to be a next, it seemed.

There was no lounging in bed, no snuggling, which I was led to believe all girls wanted, and which I wanted. No, Susan was already putting her jeans on and dragging me outside. I thought at first it was because she was embarrassed. Like she suddenly looked at me naked in her bed and thought, What the fuck have I done? Who is this guy? Like she was always bringing random men home and I was just another mistake, and if she could just get me outside it might be like it didn't happen.

Now I know it wasn't that. I wasn't some random guy she brought home. I don't think there were ever random guys. There was just me.

Rebecca

I thought I might be a librarian one day, but in an old-fashioned library, where you had to be quiet, where you got to shush/scare children. I wanted to shush and scare children, not have my own. I wanted my libraries like temples, not Starbucks on a Saturday. But I didn't want to study to be a librarian, I just wanted to read my life away, like my parents wanted. I compromised and ended up working at the college library. I thought people would go there to study, not look at porn, but I was wrong, because students were terrible, awful, horny people.

Isaac was one of the terrible, awful, horny people. He caught me on a good day, when I was also horny, like it was catching. He wasn't one of the lit dicks I usually hooked up with at least. He was a few years older and studying film. He had a similar upbringing to me, only he spent his time alone watching films. He spent hours in his room; his mother had to drag him outside so he didn't get rickets. You're lucky, I told him, with a pain in my chest thinking about what a parent should be. Everyone's parents were worried about their children getting rickets, everyone's but mine. Isaac promised his mother he'd try his hardest not to, and always drank whatever juice drink she bought that had extra crap added to it specifically for pasty boys like him, but she still nagged him to go outside, because it was what mothers did. I didn't know about that sort of thing. He compromised and went out to the cinema.

Our perfect day was going to a bookstore, then a film. He made me see that films were just books really and that TV was short stories, and the way he spoke about it all made me appreciate the physical world in a way I hadn't before. I felt stupid for never giving it a chance. Foreign films were the perfect compromise because the subtitles gave me something to read. I forgave him for liking *Ace Ventura* more than *Reality Bites*. I liked watching him laugh. More often than not I'd watch him watching the film and it was joyful. I learnt how to be with someone else, how to let that person take over me.

I thought you were supposed to be a serious film student, I'd say, when he was laughing at a fart joke, and he'd tell me about the importance of movies for movies' sake. The pleasure in letting yourself be entertained. It was all foreplay. He wanted me to be happy, to make me happy, to teach me how to make myself happy, even if that meant letting Jim Carrey make me laugh. I had to want it. I wanted it. Him.

We teased each other. He pretended books were so boring and I would say movies were dumb – the ones he liked anyway. He liked *Star Wars*, but he didn't love it like some boys did, so I could live with that. Really, we both loved anything the other loved because we were falling in love. We opened up the world to each other the way it's supposed to be when you meet your person.

We didn't want to be apart ever again, so he moved in straight away. It was natural. You don't let love leave.

We rarely left the bed in the early days. Having a TV in the bedroom was non-negotiable for both of us. We didn't feel like we were missing out on anything. We knew what was out there. We had everything we needed. It sounds terribly romantic because it was. Susan was a product of that love and I always hoped those foundations might have been enough to save her.

I was prone to depressive periods, though, because of my parents, because it was the 90s, because I was a young woman, and because life was hard, but each time they came I braced myself, took to my bed and read through them. I was lucky enough to have people in my life who understood. I was never forced to see a doctor or told to go outside or cheer up. There was the understanding that this was life and it would pass. And it did pass. I was quietly sad for those periods; it felt like my brain was trying to kill me somehow, and I hoped that no one I loved would ever have to feel that way. A loop of despair that feels like falling.

I told Isaac I didn't want children for that reason, and he told me he didn't want children because he worried that he'd still love me the most, which helped me not feel like I was falling into quite such a big pit of despair, just a medium one.

Despite not wanting children, I suspected having a baby might be the thing to save me, like the way you think, If only I found the right pair of jeans.

I knew that if I had a baby, it would have nothing to do with biological clocks, or love even; it wouldn't come from want or need, but from boredom of myself. Oh, the joy of having something else to consume me other than my own rotten thoughts! 'I'm bored of my own bullshit' wasn't an acceptable reason to have a child, though; you had to pretend it was because babies were amazing and the future and you were doing it for love and family blah blah blah. I knew several people who had children because they were bored, lonely or just worried about who'd support them in old age, because society was already showing signs of collapsing even back then.

A baby would force me to be in the world. All baby crying translated to, Get up, bitch. I wouldn't be able to be in my own head anymore, not if I had to make sure a small human didn't run into knives or traffic or whatever kids did if you weren't watching. I would have to be hyper alert at all times. I would have to be present in a way I couldn't be bothered to for anything else. I couldn't just sit around and think myself to death anymore. I would still worry about the world, of course, but I'd have to trust it would sort itself out if I was adding to it, have to truly believe it would still be there and be better for her. Or just not think about it at all, which was easier.

I told Isaac I was pregnant over pizza. I took the last slice and said, For the baby, so he couldn't lay claim to it, because there was a baby now, and that had to come first, even when there was pizza.

Shit, he said.

I was thinking a more traditional name, like Susan, I said.

I gave him the last bite of pizza. He ate it slowly.

Sorry I ruined pizza, I said. Sorry about the baby, I said.

Shit, he said again.

Good shit or bad shit?

As good as shit can be, I guess, he said, and his chest loosened and he started breathing again. We would be OK.

I don't want our baby to be like me, though, I said. I want our child to have the things we didn't have; fewer thoughts, better skin. Like, when I learnt that your reflection isn't even how you look because it's the reverse so you can't ever really know how you truly look. That fucked me up for quite a long time. That, and seeing the back of my head in some shitty changing-room mirrors in some shitty clothing store, then worrying about how the back of my head looked all the time, to strangers, for all eternity. I don't want that for our child, I said.

OK, Isaac said.

What I'm saying is, I want our daughter never to be self-aware, if possible, because it really fucks you up. It really fucked me up, anyway, I said, trying not to cry.

I'd love not to be so self-aware, Isaac said. Today I spilled coffee on my crotch, then had to carry my books in front of me all day so no one thought I'd shat myself. Obviously, no one cared, or even noticed, but I don't want to be that guy, he said.

That teacher who somehow manages to shit out the front? I said, and we both laughed.

We'll deal with whatever happens, Isaac said.

I just want you to promise me our baby will be OK, I said. But he couldn't.

The thought of actually having a baby scared me to death, so it was a good thing Susan was an accident, decided for me. I hated the term 'happy accident'. A happy accident was falling into a delicious cake, not having your vagina ripped apart while people watched.

Isaac thought I was freaking out about being pregnant for normal reasons, like my career, or figure, even though he'd seen my career, and figure, and knew I didn't care much about either. He didn't know I was harbouring a terrible secret: I didn't think I could do it. That I could be a baby killer and not know it, I just hadn't had the opportunity yet. But I loved him, I reminded myself, and I wouldn't be in it alone, at least. If the worst came to the worst, and I really couldn't face story time at the library, he could go. Ironically, I would usually love story time at the library if it was just me, alone, with a story. So that was my secret plan: have the baby and let him raise it.

After I found out about the curse it only seemed fair anyway. He could raise his demon baby. However cute she was.

Because I was having a demon baby.

He didn't tell me right away because you're supposed to wait 12 weeks to even tell people you're pregnant. So, he figured he'd wait 12 weeks to tell me the baby I was carrying was possibly cursed.

I guess we have to tell people now, I'd said, embarrassed, because people would know it wasn't planned.

I need to tell you something first, he said.

The thing is, he said, and looked at the floor, I don't know how to say this.

Just say it, I said.

The thing is, so, our baby might be cursed, he said.

He shut his eyes and held his breath.

What? I said.

I'm sorry I didn't tell you sooner, he said, opening one eye.

It's just that, none of this was planned, was it?

Go back to the curse bit, please, I said.

Oh, right, he said.

OK, so my family have this weird thing where – it's actually pretty funny – where if you think too hard, your head might explode.

He laughed nervously so I couldn't tell if he was joking or not.

It sounded like one of his dumb movies. Or an episode of *The Twilight Zone*, which he also loved.

That's hilarious, I said, only it's not, because if what you're saying is true, that means I have a tiny bomb inside me right now.

She might be fine, he said.

He wasn't joking then. He believed what he just told me to be true.

That's not reassuring, I snapped. How could you not tell me? I felt like I might pass out.

It's macabre, he said, and I know you don't like scary films.

Seriously?

I know, I'm sorry, he said, reaching for my hand.

I just didn't want to upset you so early in the pregnancy. And before that, well, I didn't think I needed to tell you if we weren't planning on having a family.

But we *are* a family, I said. Even when it was just the two of us, I said, we were already a family.

I knew I didn't know much about families, but I was hoping this was closer to the usual understanding of it. We had a plant, for fuck's sake.

I know that now, he said, squeezing my hand.

David

We were walking home from seeing the runners-up from various seasons of a baking show she liked that were now an ABBA tribute band for some reason. She said we had to go, and how it would be 'fun'. And I wanted fun, not being that well acquainted with it. It was one of those nights you didn't want to end, but also when I went to the bathroom and looked in the mirror I said, How did I get here? Who am I? just as a man in a sparkly zoot suit reached over me to do his lipstick. But it was also one of those nights when you were with your person, and wanted it to be this, forever. The feeling of being alone was still fresh in my memory, that feeling that if I had someone to share things with, I might just be able to pull it off. Two fingers to the void. Susan was that person.

We walked home with our hearts full of the joys of 70s disco, and our lungs full of whatever the smoke machines had been pumping out.

I noticed the moon, all big and glowing, showing off, like, Look at me, I'm the original glitterball, you morons, dance around me. The stars twinkled, wanting me to think they might be planets really – cheeky. I wasn't really into astronomy, but I liked knowing they were all up there, doing their thing, buffering the empty.

I stopped to do my shoelace. I needed to learn how to tie a lace that didn't come undone almost daily. Susan kept walking without me. Her not noticing I'd stopped and was no longer by her side and was crouching on the floor doing my shoelace was probably an omen, and not a good one. But I chose to ignore it, because you could do that.

Hey, I said, calling out to her.

Huh, she said, stopping, where'd you go?

She finally noticed I wasn't with her. She'd definitely been talking to someone, though.

She walked back to where I was crouched and I stood up to meet her, then glanced up at the sky again.

Couples in films and on TV were always gazing up at the stars, maybe somewhere in real life too; somewhere with no light pollution, so nowhere I'd ever been. Space stuff was in the news a lot now, because we were all so sad about our planet and our lives that we needed to focus our attention somewhere else, somewhere far, far away, somewhere more hopeful.

The stars are all out then, I said, raising an eyebrow, trying to be cute. I didn't say, They're out for you, baby, because I didn't want to risk making her vomit.

Susan looked up, and for a moment we were just two idiots in the street, cricking our necks, staring at the night sky.

I mean, they're always out, we just can't see them, I said, in case she was about to correct me.

I clearly couldn't tie my laces properly, so maybe she thought I didn't actually know how night and day worked.

What? she said, looking me in the eyes, and I saw a flicker of panic somewhere deep inside her.

I laughed because I thought she was messing with me.

She laughed back the way babies laugh if you laugh at them but they have no idea what is going on but laughing is fun

28

so why wouldn't you laugh if you had the chance? Babies are dumb.

I should have left it there, but no, I wanted to show off, wanted this girl to know I was smarter than I looked.

It's sad, though, right, I said, that they're there all the time, but we can't see them and we only get to see them when it's dark?

I needed her to know that the universe was a cruel master.

Right, she said, but she was looking at something on her phone now. Maybe a dating app where she could meet a boy who knew how to tie his laces properly.

I felt stupid and tried not to think how she was probably thinking, This guy thinks I'm dumb, and worse than that, he thinks I need to be reminded that there's no real magic.

I didn't mention anything other than food or TV for the rest of the night. I certainly didn't mention the fact that ABBA were a hologram now, but I couldn't forget the look in her eyes, that flicker of panic, that things were not as they seemed.

I'd only met Susan's father via Zoom until he summoned me to meet him in a coffee shop, and even then, it was mostly me saying hi and darting past like a cat, then mumbling things off camera. I didn't even know what to say to my own father. Just the idea of meeting him made me sweat. My deodorant said 48 hours, but it barely got me to work dry; maybe I was abnormally sweaty and other men could get 48 hours out of it.

I read the news on my phone on three different news sites while I waited for him. If things got really awkward, I could dazzle him with my current affairs knowledge. Climate change, huh? What's up with that? Something like that. If he mentioned sport, I'd run away, the irony lost on us both.

The coffee shop was right opposite a Starbucks. It was a

statement move. People wanted you to know they were there, not across the road. I didn't want anyone to know I was anywhere; I was meeting an older man I didn't really know for coffee to discuss my intentions with his daughter, like we'd suddenly travelled back in time, but without any of the hijinks.

I didn't know how to greet the men I knew, let alone the men I didn't know, so we said hello awkwardly and talked about our journeys, then shuffled to the counter and waited in line with people who didn't seem to find it all as awkward as we did.

I'd thought about what I'd order all morning. I wanted to impress him. I wanted him to think I was a capable adult, one that wouldn't fuck his daughter up in ways other boys might, so I forwent my usual cappuccino and ordered a macchiato like I knew what I was doing. If he asked me anything about it, I'd pretend I didn't hear him. He ordered a double espresso. The dad drink of choice. It said, I don't have time for this, but I am making time. It said, I am a real man, but I still like tiny cups.

We found a table towards the back and discussed at length how every table seemed to have a wobbly leg now and if it was a problem with table construction in general or the way people leaned on tables. We didn't know but would be sure to keep thinking about it.

His double espresso kicked in almost immediately and he was suddenly tapping his foot and the table.

So, he said, you and Susan.

Yep, I said.

There's something I need to tell you, he said.

Then he was pulling at the collar of his shirt.

Is it hot in here, or is it me? he said, beads of sweat suddenly pooling down his forehead.

I handed him a napkin.

You see, David, Susan is – how do I say this . . .? Cursed.

She's what now?

He was pulling at his shirt now and I could see sweat patches under his arms.

Cursed how? I managed to say.

If she thinks too hard, it's game over, he said. Like the only things he knew about me was I played video games and fucked his daughter.

What do you mean, game over? I said, gulping.

I don't want to be too graphic or alarm you, but her head will explode, he said. He was fanning himself now. Thankfully it was quiet in there, so there wasn't anyone to overhear and alert the authorities about a possible escaped mental patient.

Come on, David, doesn't it all make sense now? he said.

Does that mean you're cursed too? I said, trying to get the image of Susan with her brain splattered all over the place out of my head.

No, it seems to skip a generation, he said. But I was still always told not to think too hard about anything, just in case.

This is crazy, I said. I'd just been told my girlfriend had a curse that meant if she thought too much her head would explode and yet I was still also thinking a bit about what cakes they had and if that made me an awful person.

Nothing good comes from thinking too hard, he said.

Live in the world, if you can, my father used to say, and if you can't, which he suspected I couldn't, find a way to distract yourself from yourself, he said. You like films? he said. Use it, he said. Get really into them, watch them all, make them if you really want to, but I'd advise against it – too much stress. You want something that takes over you and not the other way around.

Someone walked past us carrying a chocolate brownie on a plate and I tried to breathe it in without looking too creepy.

Susan's father was using his hands a lot, because of the caffeine. I was glad the few other people in the room were so self-absorbed they weren't looking. They were all too busy not writing their screenplays. I had to stop myself leaping up to tell them about this crazy thing I'd just heard that they might be able to do something with, because I had no clue.

Like my own father, his had low expectations of him. We were bonding. In my head mostly.

So, he'd done as his father said and got really into films. I was just thankful his father hadn't said sports. I'd just been told my girlfriend's head could explode at any minute and I was still worrying that I didn't know enough, or anything, about sports.

Oof, he said, mopping his brow with a napkin again. Glad that's out the way.

So, David, tell me, do you like films? he said. He'd been dreading having to tell me about his cursed daughter, but now he'd done it he could relax again.

Of course, I said, sure he was about to ask me what my favourite films were, only my mind had gone blank, probably because of the news I'd just got, so the only film I could remember was *Die Hard*, but I knew that was the wrong answer and then he'd ban me from ever seeing his daughter again anyway probably.

We discussed Jim Carrey for a while, then he came over a bit emotional.

So, we understand each other, he said, putting his hand on my shoulder.

He meant, please don't kill my daughter.

I think so, I said.

My father was a bit crazy, he said, but then he'd been through a lot.

The war? I said.

No, he said, frowning, the family curse thing.

Oh yeah, I said.

Just remember, he said, nothing good comes from thinking too hard. That's helped me over the years. I think together we can keep Susan safe, he said, gripping my shoulder now.

I'll try my best, I said.

That's all we can do, he said, looking a bit teary, then shaking his head to shake the sad thoughts away.

He didn't need to know that I actually very rarely did my best and was more of a doing-the-minimum-to-skate-through kind of guy. With Susan it was different, though; I really did try harder to be better, and I would have, even without her weird brain, but the weird brain definitely motivated me more. Not that I believed what he told me at first, because it was mental.

We said our goodbyes and I pretended to leave, but once he'd gone, I went back in to get something to eat. There were only ancient-looking blueberry muffins left but I got one anyway and ate it and it tasted of disappointment. It was my punishment for thinking about my stomach while I was being told something important; it was my brain's way of keeping me safe.

From then on this was my relationship with Susan's parents. It started as meetings at various coffee shops, until they trusted I wasn't going to rob or murder them, or both, and then I was allowed in their apartment.

The idea behind the meetings was that it was a chance for me to learn more about their daughter so I could help keep her alive, rather than the alternative, because this curse was real it seemed. Susan's parents learned about the brain together, as a couple, the way other couples might learn to tango or play *Fortnite*. We all agreed I needed a better understanding of what we were up against so as not to fuck up all the hard work they'd done to get her this far. I hated having to go anywhere or do anything, but Susan was my first serious girlfriend. I didn't want to have to do any of this parent stuff again. Later I would go to their apartment for other reasons, to escape maybe, connect, but in the beginning it was to learn about my girlfriend's weird brain and more importantly learn how not to make it explode. You think you want to make someone's head explode, from sex maybe, or a witty joke, until that's actually a possibility.

In the beginning, then, I wasn't different from anyone else newly in love. I wanted to know everything about her but also needed to know everything about her.

I showed up at her parents' clutching a cheap bottle of wine, the first one I saw on special. It had a castle on the front and I felt good about that castle – castles were solid; I needed solid.

I texted to tell them I was on my way.

Susan's father opened the door.

You'd better come in, he said and I handed him the wine and he looked at the picture of the castle and nodded.

Susan's mother took the wine but didn't open it.

I'll make tea, she said.

Thanks, I said, then got straight to it.

Something's going on with Susan, I said.

Susan's mother continued to make tea, but her hands were shaking now. She was probably trying to keep from having a mild heart attack but kept making tea, like someone British might.

They'd just finished dinner. There were plates on the side.

Half an apple pie on the counter. I tried to focus on the pie, thought about how it would taste, while I told them what happened.

I must have really been staring at that pie because Susan's father cut me a slice, then went to his wife and stopped her before she smashed anything.

We stood there in their kitchen letting what I'd just said sink in.

Is Mercury in retrograde again or something? her mother said, hoping it was, but not knowing what that actually meant. But it was something at least.

Why now? Susan's father said, accusingly.

Nothing's changed, Susan's mother said, has it? She meant, What did you do, David?

In movies things like this happen on eighteenth birthdays, or when someone's been to a creepy fair or something, I said.

Yes, but this is a real curse, not a movie curse, her father said.

I prefer the movie ones, her mother said, at least you know what the fuck you're dealing with.

Remember when she was 15 and you thought she was going to explode because she was upset about something but it was actually because she broke a lamp? Susan's father said to his wife.

Of course I remember, she snapped. I thought that was it, but then she'd just broken that ugly lamp and thought we'd be cross at her.

What lamp? I said.

Oh, just this ugly lamp I found on the street years ago, but I guess she thought it had sentimental value or something.

And she broke it?

She punched it by accident, doing some dance routine, her mother said.

That sounds like something she'd do, I said.

Anyway, the point is, she's had these little blips before, but it's always been fine. She never moped around in her bedroom for hours over a boy, listening to the same sad song over and over; she was just punching lamps.

But she hasn't punched any lamps in a while, David, so what have you done?

Rebecca

Once the idea of a curse had sunk in, as much as something that crazy could, I wanted to know everything.

This wasn't just about him anymore; it was about my unborn child. I was too in love with him by then to care that he'd lied to me. Really, he'd kept something from me, which wasn't as bad as lying.

My first question was, Is my baby at risk? Or, to put it bluntly, will my baby's head explode?

He said he didn't know, which wasn't the answer I was hoping for. He told me what his father had told him, which was that it skipped a generation and that meant, yes, our child may be at risk. We could never know for sure all of this wasn't just a collective madness, but it was as good as any, and the risk remained. Being alive was a risk. Something was coming for all of us.

Are you sure? I kept saying. How can you know?

Don't get upset, he said, it's not good for the baby. Which only made me more upset. My head hurt from it. It didn't make any sense. How could it be true?

What if it thinks itself to death inside me? I whispered to him when we were trying to sleep.

He pulled me close and said, Then we all die, which was surprisingly comforting.

Tomorrow we'll come up with a plan, he said into the darkness. I won't let anything happen to our child.

I'd always been pro-choice, and my choice now was to give this thing a shot. If I'd been carrying someone else's child, maybe not, but I believed in us, and was starting to see that the world wasn't what I thought.

Someone in the back of my mind yelled, Call your mother! Aren't you supposed to call your mother? Where is your mother? But I pretended I didn't hear. I was the mother now.

The next morning, I was up before Isaac because I didn't sleep at all. I lay with my hand on my belly, wondering what was coming for us all.

Isaac woke to find me dressed and ready to go.

Are we going somewhere? he said.

He'd slept, the bastard. I was already resenting him and it had only been a few hours.

I'm going to see your father, I said.

I'd met his father once, via Skype. His mother had died a few years back. They weren't a close family, but they were a family still. Mine had officially disbanded years ago.

Oh, he said. Shouldn't I come too?

Suit yourself, I said and threw a shirt at him.

If he hadn't woken up, I would have gone alone.

We found Isaac's father watching *Kojak* in the nursing-home common room. Like when you're close to death, they ask you what you want to die watching, and he picked *Kojak*. I'd pick *Murder, She Wrote*, and they could write in my eulogy, She died as she lived, watching *Murder, She Wrote* and eating expired hummus.

I was disappointed to see Isaac's father slumped in front of the TV in his pyjamas, a glimpse of my future. I didn't know what I was hoping – that we'd catch him having sex with another resident perhaps; something that told me he wasn't stuck in his head like the rest of us and could still enjoy pleasures other than TV.

My boy, he said, standing up to greet us.

Hi, Pops, Isaac said. How you doing?

We both hugged him and did the required amount of small talk before asking if he wanted to go for a walk.

We have some news, Isaac said.

You're pregnant, Isaac's father said, looking at me.

How did you know? I said, looking down at my outfit. I wasn't showing or glowing or whatever I was supposed to do now.

Because it's not my birthday or a holiday, Isaac's father said but smiling still because he was going to be a grandfather.

It's wonderful news, he said, hugging us both again.

She knows, Dad, Isaac said then, sitting down on a conveniently placed bench.

Usually, we would comment on the bench's dedication, but today we just sat, deep in our own thoughts.

I don't know what to tell you, Isaac's father said.

What can we do? Is my baby safe? I asked, knowing he wouldn't be able to answer that.

Is any baby safe? he said, and then started to tell us about something horrible he'd read in the news about a child that fell off a balcony and I was sick in my mouth a little. Why did they let him read the news? What kind of place was this?

OK, Pops, but what can you tell us about our baby? Isaac asked.

Keep her busy, his father said. Don't give her time to think. Keep her out of her head. You know what happened to my brother, he said.

He was talking about Isaac's uncle, John-Pierre, or he would have been if his head hadn't exploded. He'd got really into philosophy at college, but not so much the theories, more the aesthetic – he wanted to be able to pull off a beret, so much so that he moved to Paris and changed his name from John to John-Pierre and hung around the Café de Flore and fanboyed over Sartre and decided he was going to think something amazing, only he couldn't, but that didn't stop him trying. His poor wife, a nice French girl he met who was fangirling over Simone de Beauvoir at the time, quickly realised they needed real jobs and actual money to live in Paris, only her new husband mostly wanted to sit around and stare into space trying to think of the next amazing thing. She told the police that he was just staring at nothing, wrinkled his brow and said, I think – then boom. Or whatever the French for that is. Le boom. Brains everywhere. She wasn't impressed. She swore off philosophy after that, but more importantly philosophers, and married a butcher. It's all in the police reports. She apparently went and shouted at Sartre for messing up her life but also her apartment and got banned from Café de Flore.

What do you remember about that, I asked, if you don't mind talking about it? Old people loved talking about their suffering, they needed it validated.

I don't remember much, his father said. I was just a kid. He'd moved away. My family didn't really believe in the curse, not really, so they let him be, but I think that was a mistake. And then later various cousins died in similar circumstances so it's probably safest to say it's real, don't you think?

I think there's cake in the games room, he said then, standing, signalling that was all he had to say on the subject. Who wants cake? he said, already walking off.

We all wanted cake.

After cake and talking to the staff to check he was behaving himself, we left Isaac's father to get back to *Kojak*. He was happy enough. He'd chosen to live there himself, after a friend moved in; there was no guilt or sadness, and we were all grateful for that at least.

That went well, Isaac said when we were back in the car.

I started crying then, but not for my own life and child, but for the old man we'd just left whose brother died in bizarre circumstances.

Do I need to go back in and get more cake? Isaac said.

Can you? I said, but he knew I was joking.

What are we going to do? I said again, knowing there was no answer.

I don't know, he said, putting his hand on mine, but we'll figure it out, together. What does anyone do? he said.

And I knew then that this happened all the time all over the world: people got pregnant and weren't prepared, but they muddled on. We would muddle on. Curse or no curse.

He said 'her', I said. Did you hear, he said 'her'?

I did, Isaac said. But he also calls me Margaret sometimes too.

His father died a week before Susan was born. The nursing home said he was happy and laughing at something on the TV, probably Kojak's ugly hat, and his heart just went. He wasn't even that old.

How can your heart just go? I said, over and over.

How can your brain explode? Isaac said, which helped a little, in a weird way. No one knew anything, not just us.

He never got to meet Susan. If he'd just hung on a week longer. Susan would never know any of her grandparents. But then, Isaac reminded me often, it was fewer people to possibly fuck her head up.

*

The first thing was to make sure I was healthy and the baby was healthy. We'd pretend it was a normal pregnancy: I'd eat right, take care of myself, grow a baby the best I could. I could do that. I would let my body do what it needed to do. I would mostly look on in horror, but I would let it do its thing. I trusted it. Isaac not so much, but my body yes.

We had a shotgun wedding, which made me sad, not because we were rushing it, but because it implied a father looming with a shotgun, forcing Isaac to make a decent woman of me, when in fact my father was in Nepal somewhere last time I checked. I didn't really believe in marriage, but I wanted Susan never to question us or our motives; I wanted her only ever to know complete love. I did eat a lot of cake that day at least, that was non-negotiable. I'd never dreamed of weddings so it was fine. On our wedding night Isaac said to me did I want to call my parents? And I said no, and he said, They don't deserve us anyway, and I said, It's not their fault, and he looked like he wanted to say more, but he didn't, because it was our wedding night. All my energy now was spent trying to get any negative feelings I had away from my baby and only send her the good stuff, but it was hard when I suspected it was in my blood, not his. His family may have had a weird curse, but individually, he was golden.

While other couples were coming up with birthing and nursery plans, we were working on a keeping-our-daughter-alive plan by teaching her not to think, and soon, because I knew she could already hear us and I didn't want her first thought to be, My parents are idiots, I'm screwed. Kaboom.

The regular pregnancy stuff came easy. I read every book ever written and, in my head, I thought having a baby was something I could actually do, as long as people kept writing books about it. I wasn't even that worried about the birth itself, even after hearing every horror story imaginable. I would take all the drugs and as long as my baby was healthy, I would just have to cope with whatever the birth did to my body. My body wasn't something I liked to think about much anyway so I would just keep not thinking about it. It was what came after that worried us. The bit where we would have a real live baby and have to keep it that way. We understood this must be how it was for everyone. Having this tiny living creature that you were now somehow responsible for and there were so many ways you could fuck it up, and not just in ways you could see, like you turned your back for a second and the dog ate them, but ways you could never know – things inside their heads already forming and forming wrong because of something you did or didn't do.

Why isn't there a book called *How Not to Fuck Up Your Child*? I asked Isaac one day, and he went out and got me all the books that were almost called that. But they were more about how not to fuck up your older child, like don't let them see you fight or have sex or don't tell them they're pretty but make sure they know they are. Every book contradicting the next until parents' brains exploded all over the world from just how hard it was, impossible almost.

The amount of advice out there on how to raise your child was overwhelming, so to avoid going insane and ruining our daughter's life before she was born because she would be born in an asylum, we decided to focus on our unique problem and child's needs, which was kinder than saying cursed.

Being a good parent didn't seem that hard. All the books said the same thing: talk to your kid and listen to your kid. Communicate. Be emotionally warm. Teach them to read and write and do maths. Read to them for learning and pleasure. Take them out places. Maintain routines. It wasn't rocket science. The little things mattered. Duh. The everyday interactions. I could do all those things while still doing what I needed to do. Susan didn't have to end up damaged. We could save her brain but still bring up a healthy, happy child. We would read together, watch TV together, talk about everything, as a family. We would make sure she knew she was loved. It would be fine. No one would be able to say we abused or neglected her. I would make sure of that.

I continued to work at the library while I was pregnant. There were enough other changes going on that I wanted to keep my job, thinking it might be closely tied to my sanity. I wanted to keep the life I had for as long as possible.

I didn't wear clothes that showed off my body anyway, favouring oversized T-shirts, the occasional baby-doll dress, always accompanied by a giant cardigan. It was the 90s. Flannel shirts weren't just for lumberjacks anymore. Grunge helped me conceal my pregnancy long enough to work out how to feel about it before other people told me how they felt about it.

Isaac came to visit me on my lunch break one day and found me inspecting my cheese sandwich in the back room. There were only three other people in the library: my co-worker, and two girls pretending to study but who were lost in music and regret about whatever happened the night before.

It's very quiet in here, he whispered.

It's a library, I said.

Too quiet, he said.

I know, I said, closing my sandwich, unimpressed, even though I'd made it.

I was only just pregnant; we knew the foetus didn't really have ears yet, let alone a brain to understand what we were saying, but we were starting to think about what we'd do when that time came.

I was reading a book about babies, like I did on every break. He was supposed to be doing the same but he preferred it when I read things and then told him what I'd learned. He said I was the reader in the family, and when he said family, I got a rush of love, but it went straight to my uterus and I got none of it, which was how it was supposed to be, I thought.

I kept a copy of *What to Expect When You're Expecting* hidden behind the desk for when I got a quiet moment, which was a lot. People rarely bothered me, mostly because they didn't think I was a real librarian. I was just one of them really; they didn't need to know I had in fact graduated years ago and had just forgotten to leave.

Soon, our foetus would need more buffers. More noise, more stimulation. We didn't want her just lying there, mouth agape, drooling, with nothing to do but think. I always pictured her like an otter, lying on her back, bobbing in some water that was actually amniotic fluid. He said he pictured her more like a squirrel, curled up in its nest, and I said, What squirrels have you been looking at? and he said he didn't know, and we thought about if we'd ever seen a squirrel's nest, because I wasn't really sure where they slept, they were just always there or not there. We didn't have Google then so we couldn't google 'Where do squirrels sleep?' I didn't like the thought of a squirrel inside me anyway and he said, But an otter's OK? And I threw up my cheese sandwich on him. It came up in one big chunk, like it had found the other parts of itself when it was inside me, or I'd just forgotten to chew. I had a lot on my mind. And bladder.

We decided that night it was best for our baby if I didn't work at the library anymore. It was fine – I associated it with being sick now anyway. Which was the last thing you wanted when you felt sick all the time. So, while most other expectant mothers were thinking about going on maternity leave, I was looking for a new job.

He stroked my bump in our tiny bedsit and said he was sorry about me being sick and me having to give up my job, and that it was all his fault. I'd just drunk a gallon of Coke and was manic and gassy and told him it was all fine and we would be fine and tried to mount him but he was still sad about it all so I unmounted him and we watched some TV.

Any sadness I felt about leaving the library, I pushed down. I'd already started not feeling things so my baby wouldn't feel them. I became an expert at compartmentalising.

I was being a grown-up. I needed to find a more suitable job, for me and my baby. I knew I wouldn't be able to stay at home, not just because I would go mad but because then my daughter would go mad. I needed to keep busy and keep my mind busy in the hope that it would rub off on my daughter.

How do they know? I kept saying when he first told me about his family. How do they know it was something in their brains?

Because there were brains everywhere, he said. Their heads exploded, he said, there were witnesses. They were thinking deeply and boom, he said, acting it out.

But how do they know? I kept asking over and over. I wanted more evidence. I needed to know exactly what we were dealing with. He stored all the evidence his father had passed on in a file he kept by the bed, for when I had my meltdowns, my moments of doubt. Which were frequent for the first few years and then tapered off to maybe once a year, and then that file gathered dust until David came into the picture.

I think Isaac thought I looked at it when he wasn't around

sometimes, but I didn't. When Susan got older, I worried she might find it – kids are nosey little fucks – so I made him move it around the house until eventually I made him keep it at work. Now David had it. Our little dossier of horrors.

David

If it had just been Susan's parents telling me this story, I might have thought they were all mad and that it was actually madness that ran in her family and Susan was destined to end up the same way. But there were others, people who weren't related to her. People who made the headlines. Or at least the weird news section that only people like me read, hoping for evidence of aliens and Bigfoot – anything that would somehow make it all more bearable – but all we got was another piece of toast with Jesus on it, or Jared Leto, whichever way you leaned.

I found articles about a chess player and a psychic whose heads had also exploded. The chess player got more coverage because, even in death, people were elitist, but also, his was a public death – people got splattered by his brains. The psychic's was a private death, where only one person had to duck for cover. These deaths made sense to me. They were both big thinkers. They used their brains more than most people, for different purposes, but they were still pushing them to their limits. So, it made sense, as much as any of this could.

I spent a lot of time trying to find evidence of other people like Susan, but I only ever found these two. It was only when I was doing a deep dive online in the depths of night, strung out on Red Bull, that I understood how this could happen, how people could die from pushing their brains to the limits, my own on the verge of collapse. From thinking, but also from love, but also from whatever the fuck they put in Red Bull. I thought about googling it, but then thought, Better not, who wants to actually know what they're consuming? So I went back to trawling the internet for evidence that someone somewhere had their brain explode.

I fell asleep thinking about gravestones and how these people's might say, They thought too much, like, let that be a warning to you.

If it had just been one person in her family whose head had exploded, you might put it down to a terrible tragedy. Two even, you might say, Oh, well, that's weird, but they were years apart so maybe it was a coincidence. Three though, three is a problem, and four, four is just fucked up. And because there was no logical explanation for the deaths, they decided it must be a curse. The dead all thought a lot, therefore thinking must be the cause. (But other people think, someone might have said, they just thought that for example, and their head didn't explode.) Only they couldn't stop each other thinking, the ones who were still alive, but they could be more careful; they could try to avoid thinking. So that's what they did. Thinking was bad. For this family anyway. Their children would grow up to be non-thinkers. They didn't care how you kept from thinking, you just had to. If you wanted your children to live, which most people did.

Then there was that skipping-a-generation thing. Susan's father was safe because his father's brother's head exploded. Which meant his child would be next in line, so it was important we stopped that from happening.

When other people were thinking about what to have for dinner, these were my thoughts now.

Susan was out somewhere with Kate, and Nick wasn't answering his phone. I was just sat on the couch alone with all this going through my head, trying to make sense of it, giving myself a migraine.

At times like this I needed to see her parents. They had a file they kept for me, like a family history, if your family was nuts. It contained all the evidence they had that this thing was real. We looked at it together, strength in numbers, hoping it would give the curse less power, but it never did.

Tell me about Uncle Willy again, I said, handing her father back the file.

Susan's mother was out. He was glad of my company for once.

Uncle Willy was my favourite of Susan's dead relatives. He died from love. It was relatable. They said he died of love-sickness, but it was his head exploding that did it. They call it stalking now, but in the old days, we're talking 1890s, it was a common form of wooing and often resulted in the person giving in and marrying them.

That pop singer Tiffany married her stalker, I told him.

You've been hanging around my daughter too long, he said, but smiled.

When her father first told me this story, I said, No one's called Willy, but apparently, they were, and they were dead, so would I please show some respect?

He showed me the death certificate in the file and I felt suitably ashamed.

Uncle Willy thought about this girl every moment. He waited outside her house, he followed her to town, to church. He wrote her love letters and poems and gave her gifts ranging from stolen flowers to a dog he found wandering the streets. He sounded like a criminal to me, but I'd already spoken ill of the dead enough. He couldn't eat or sleep or do anything other than think about this girl. I said she must have been pretty, and her dad showed me a picture and she was not. Willy thought about her so much that his brain popped before his heart could. He was said to be composing a poem for her outside her window at the time, like people did in those days, before they had boom boxes, or Facebook. One minute he was deep in thought about what rhymed with flower, and the next, kaboom.

His family weren't surprised; they thought he might end up walking into a tree or off a cliff, because of all the mooning over this girl he did. They hadn't known his brain couldn't handle it, but then whose could? Love was a fucker.

The cause of death was a broken heart, or so they thought, even though his brains were clearly all over the girl's front lawn. His heart was fine. They didn't know much about anatomy in those days, though, so his heart could have moved up to his head and burst out. They thought the womb was capable of wandering, so why not the heart? Men were stupid. If women had been allowed to be doctors back then they wouldn't have made such ludicrous suggestions; they would have known if their wombs were wandering, and they were not.

Willy's heart was fine − well, it was intact, just a little blackened, from all the smoking, and drinking, and lead-based paints he used to paint pictures with for his beloved. They took the black heart as an obvious indication of love sickness, though, because they were idiots.

Willy's sister died in a similar way, only she died of feminism, before feminism was even a thing. Geraldine was a suffragette, and fought as much as she could, but thinking about how ridiculous it was to be a woman, how unfair, eventually made her head explode because she couldn't see a way out of it, even if they got the vote, even if she burned her bra. She needed to have been born a man, and she wasn't, and you weren't allowed to just be a person then and it was a lot to think about all the time and – kaboom. A fellow suffragette found her, but because she hadn't died throwing herself in front of anything, hadn't died for the cause, but because of it, no one cared. It would have only shown how weak women were, how feeble their minds were, which was the opposite of what they wanted, so they pretended her death had been caused by her corset being too tight. And no one questioned it because corsets were too tight. We only knew it was the thinking that did it because she kept a journal that said so. She'd known it was only a matter of time, that her head was surely going to explode from it all one day. She didn't understand why all women didn't suffer the same fate. They were called suffragettes for a reason.

Then the next generation were all safe, it seemed, and then Susan's grandfather's brother died in Paris and it all started again.

Next to go was the hoarder. Susan's grandfather's cousin Esme died from consumption, but not the drinking kind, the consumerism kind, before consumerism was even a thing. She was way ahead of her time. She was the original hoarder. Before it had a TV show. Because it was the 60s and the only TV shows were ones about weird families, like *The Munsters* or *The Beverly Hillbillies*, or *The Brady Bunch*.

Susan's father told me that when people visited Esme, finding her was the hardest part of the visit, like it was a game. Only she died, so it wasn't very funny. He would have been a baby then, so his own father must have been the one trying to find her among all the crap.

They thought it was the boxes that killed her. That they got so many and so high that they just toppled over and crushed her. Which sounded plausible to me. More plausible than a curse. If you found out someone died on that hoarders TV show, you'd think straight away they were crushed by their crap, not that their head exploded. It was her brain that killed her, though, not boxes. I was surprised to learn she only had two cats.

She thought a lot about the things she surrounded herself with, and this was before we had most things. She liked having things, liked filling spaces; her boxes gave her comfort, even though they were mostly filled with racist yellowed copies of *Reader's Digest* and *National Geographic*, commemorative plates featuring Lassie, Skippy and Flipper – all the dead TV animals – china frogs but also pigs (she didn't care as long as they were small, pointless and fragile), and cat faeces.

Her brain was finally pushed over the limit when a shiny new supermarket opened down the road. She thought she wanted all these marvellous new things, but then on entering, and seeing the rows and rows of packets and tins, all vying for her attention, she ran home in a state. Her neighbour saw her going into her house yelling something about instant mash and the devil and boom.

Starbucks has 8,700 drinks combinations, I said. Do you think Susan knows?

Are you thinking about coffee while I'm telling you about my dead relatives? he said.

Yes, I said.

Then he told me Esme's parents hadn't been that great and how she never found love and how these things she hoarded helped fill the void and I felt my chin start to wobble thinking about her there in her house with her stuff and then boom. At least she died at home with the things she loved, even if those things were boxes and boxes of crap.

He didn't mind telling me these stories multiple times. We sat together on the couch, looking through the file, trying to make sense of it, but eventually giving up and watching *The Sopranos*. It was comforting to know I wasn't in this alone. People in his family had lived through this. Not the dead ones, obviously, but others.

Someone else might have thought he was mad and had him committed, if it weren't for the fact that he was completely sane. If I said it was a hoax, that they forged these newspaper clippings and documents somehow, I risked losing Susan, so I had no choice but to believe them.

Rebecca

It just so happened that a bookstore I went in sometimes to fondle books I couldn't afford had a vacancy. It was noisier than most bookstores, partly because it had a coffee shop, and people who drink coffee are noisy, because of the caffeine, but also, it was owned by an old punk, who seemed to have an aversion to quiet. It was called Get Booked, like get fucked, but books. Students loved it. Here, you didn't have to be quiet; the books didn't want your respect, they wanted you to see them and tell everyone. It was always busy. There was a real buzz, like people had come to see a band they loved but it was books, every day, and I wanted to be part of that – needed to be part of that. I felt like I had found a place I could get lost in but somehow still be me.

In my interview we talked about music more than books. I told the manager, Ed, that I loved the library, but I needed the opposite of silence right now, and he seemed to understand. He said his parents never understood how he could read and listen to his music, and I said, And look at you now, and we both laughed. I needed to pee so badly during my interview, so the laughing was awful.

I'd spent a few nights there as a student and we reminisced, so he knew I understood the ethos of the place. Books could be punk. I knew that because he had a pin badge that said it. He said he liked me, and because of the pregnancy hormones I almost cried. I still didn't think he'd hire me if I told him I was pregnant, though, so I didn't mention it. I'd tell them when I started to show, or pretend I didn't even know, say I had her on the toilet, like on a TV show. Ed was so great I probably could have told him the real reason I left the library and he would have been cool with it all, but I didn't want to risk it yet. He was still a stranger, my situation still the strangest.

On my first day I looked up the meaning of the word extrovert in a dictionary. No one questioned why I was reading a dictionary on my lunch break. It was what people like us did. Sometimes fiction gave us ennui and we needed to go more organic, back to the source, where it all started. I knew the meaning of the word introvert by heart, to turn inwards, because it was all I knew up till then, but I didn't know for sure the word extrovert didn't just mean loud, obnoxious woman on the train. I suspected it might.

When Isaac met me after work, he asked me what I read that day – our version of what did you do today? – and I said, The dictionary. He thought I meant for baby names, because that's what he'd been doing, only I'd forgotten to do that, already a bad mother. I already knew I'd call her Susan anyway. After my college roommate, who I may or may not have been in love with.

The word extrovert meant to turn outwards, as suspected. Sometimes, when the world didn't feel like it made sense, all I had to do was look in a book and there were the answers. To be an extrovert was the exact opposite of what I embodied, automatically making anyone that identified as such my nemesis, which didn't bode well if we were thinking of making our daughter one. The thought that my daughter would become that loud, obnoxious woman on the train didn't sit well with me. I pretended it was pregnancy hormones making me nauseous, but really it was that thought.

You're too hung up on this word extrovert, it's not a dirty word, Isaac said as we arrived back at our flat.

It's not me, I said, it's the world.

What do you mean? he said.

People like to know what they are, so they know what they aren't, I said, starting to make dinner.

Any noodles can be cup noodles, I'd said, demonstrating my culinary skills by tipping instant noodles into a cup and pouring boiling water onto them. I was giving that cup new purpose, something we all craved.

The world likes labels, I said, handing him the noodles.

I think people should be allowed to change, he said.

He was talking about himself, but I wasn't listening, I was trying to dip a piece of bread into my cup, double carb loading, trying to make Susan of all the good stuff.

I swung between being as much in love with someone as you can possibly be, the carrying their baby kind, to hating him and his curse. Because it was his curse. He'd done this to me and my baby. He'd complicated an already complicated thing. The problem of raising a child in the world today on top of the problem of being a person in the world today on top of the problem of the world today. A triple headfuck.

I made him wash up when we were done, then told him what I'd learned about extroverts that day, hoping we could get on the same page.

Extroverts turn outwards for thinking, processing, feeling, sensing, experiencing, I said, lying on the couch with my head on his lap, trying to remember everything I'd learned. In the future we would have our phones there to read from, or just ask the other to read it themselves. Phones were the start of the end for intimacy; don't blame Netflix.

They live on the outside, I said, but he was a little sleepy now; it was getting late, and he thought I was saying our unborn daughter would have to live outside.

I tried to explain that I meant outside in the world, but he didn't get it. His eyes were drooping.

Maybe when she's older, he said, like she was a cat.

I called bedtime, and we went back to our own thoughts for the night, although I suspected he'd been done with his much earlier, like before he even came in the door, like they were a tie he'd loosened when leaving work, and me talking at him was just noise, and I envied him.

He was already asleep as I brushed my teeth and tried to quiet my head so me and Susan could sleep, without my inner dialogue keeping us up with its incessant ranting. I imagined her banging her fat baby fists on my womb wall, telling me to keep it down.

While Isaac snored beside me, I tried not to worry about what it meant that a man in his prime, in his late twenties, snored like that, like a bear who'd just eaten an extra-large meat feast pizza and 2 litres of Coke. The curse was the least of my worries sometimes.

I couldn't sleep because of the snoring so I started to think about the plan we had to make to raise our daughter. We'd said we'd do it together, but I couldn't wait for him anymore. It was me growing this child, it would be me that would have to protect her, whether I wanted that or not.

I would have to do the opposite of what I'd do naturally. I didn't always know what Isaac would do. He claimed to be like me, but he wasn't really. I knew he was much better at living somewhere in the middle, like most people, but he pretended to be more like me sometimes, when it was clear I needed it, but when he wasn't with me – at work, for example, or just out in the world – I suspected he was far more outgoing than he led me to believe. Like how he actually made eye contact with the neighbours.

The next day I put my thoughts on paper. Once there were actual words, a plan starting to form, I felt like we could do it. All I had to do was consider every possible hurdle our daughter might face, from birth to death, hopefully a long way off, and because of something more normal than her head exploding.

I stopped watching the news. The whole of the 90s was a blur to me. I didn't want to know how awful it was out there if I was going to have to entrust our daughter to it. I supplement-ed my reading with comic books, but mostly watched MTV or *Ricki Lake*, when I wasn't waddling around the bookstore. Later I progressed to trashy celebrity magazines, filling my head with garbage – my version of nesting.

Isaac was the opposite: he wanted to know what else might be a threat; he wanted to be ready for everything. Of course, no one was ever ready for all the atrocities to come, but he still thought he should know. I said, Fine, but don't tell me. I only want to know celebrity gossip from now on. This was a problem for him, but I said he had to try harder to filter out the toxic things and only bring home the joy, the banal even. We need to keep this home light, I said. Cheerful. Get rid of all your French films for a start, anything with subtitles. He agreed, as long as I got rid of all my Plath and Woolf. I said that was too far but agreed to put them in the closet. Other kids would find porn in their parents' closets; Susan would find miserable books and films. If thinking one of your parents masturbates to a picture of Virginia Woolf doesn't make your head explode, I don't know what would.

Susan had to be sociable so she wouldn't retreat into herself. We were sociable, but only within our small circle. Which wasn't very sociable at all. Isaac naturally gravitated to dark rooms where he watched films, but at least there were other people. And he had his students, who worshipped him, because he called Nicholas Cage Nick Cage, like he knew him, but it was more that he wanted to be him, and I loved *Wild at Heart* and *Moonstruck*, so I didn't mind. I loved my colleagues at the bookstore, but I kept them at a certain distance, and they me. We liked books most; this was what connected us, but also what kept us apart.

Susan would never be allowed long periods of time alone to do the things we enjoyed. She would need to be stimulated and engaged at all times, if that was even possible. Human contact and conversation were a big part of that, I knew that, and I would just have to try to be better at it, for Susan's sake. It wouldn't be forever; this is what I told myself, and what we told each other in those stolen quiet moments when we were catching our breath.

We needed Susan to thrive, to be able to look after herself mostly, but we knew she would need other people in a way we hadn't really. We liked each other plenty enough, but even that was one person too many sometimes.

The bookstore was perfect for that. They welcomed me into their fold in a way I could only dream. They seemed to see something in me that I didn't. When I expressed how amazed I was that they liked me, Isaac would look at me and laugh. You're great, you dummy, he said.

I told them I was pregnant at the very last moment. They were shocked at first, because I never seemed interested when people brought their babies in. And I wasn't; it was an accident, but I didn't tell them that. I think they knew anyway.

I worked up until the very last second. Only when I couldn't even lift a single flimsy celebrity memoir without a twinge did I go home to wait for Susan's arrival.

We felt lucky and scared in those last few days before Susan's birth. Maybe that's how everyone felt. It was a blessing and curse for everyone, maybe. A gift and a burden.

David

Just when we thought the bread thing had been a blip, Susan asked the question we were all dreading: What's wrong with me?

We were watching *The Office*. For the millionth time. She seemed fine. She laughed at something Kevin said and then turned to me and said, What's wrong with me? Like maybe she suddenly saw Kevin for what he was and felt sad for laughing at him.

Up until that moment we'd convinced her she was normal. Or better than normal – just a little kooky, you know, like those girls on TV that are twins, or witches. And she bought it, because who didn't want that?

And because we were all in on it, it was easy to keep up the charade that it was completely OK for her never really to think for herself. Other people were a problem, but they always were. We made allowances, made excuses, made light of it. Maybe we shouldn't have been so flippant. Maybe we got complacent. I was willing to take some blame. We knew the drill. Keep it light, keep it fun. Nothing too mentally challenging. Which was great when we wanted to switch off, but most of us had real-life shit to deal with too. She was hard to be around sometimes because it seemed on the surface that she had no worries, but we all knew what lurked beneath, so we forgave her and then felt awful for feeling anything negative about poor Susan with the exploding head. It helped us have perspective.

Why was she asking this now? When I was trying to switch off after a shitty day at work. Why was she ruining *The Office*?

If it weren't for trips to the bathroom, crumbs in the bed, text messages made up of mostly emojis, you might think she was a robot. A bad one, but still. Bleep bloop. That was Susan. A happy robot, though, not the psychotic murdery kind.

What's wrong with me? she said again. She was staring at me now, not the TV.

Nothing, I said, hoping that would be enough and we could move on to safer things, like knives.

I'm not like other people, she said then, blinking at me.

I tried humour, to deflect, my go-to move.

Yuck, other people, I said, pulling a face.

I really had no clue how to answer. I could feel myself starting to sweat. I tugged at my shirt. I needed air. Where had all the air gone?

Why are you saying that? I said, still tugging away at my shirt like a madman, or her father.

I needed to calm down. I knew to roll with it, not to draw attention to anything odd. Whatever happens, don't break down or sob or yell or point at the girl with the exploding head.

I waited for her answer, but she didn't say anything, which was worse, because I thought I could hear her brain grinding, but it might have been my own.

I held my breath, expecting the worst, then watched as she picked up a magazine and started flicking through it, like it was a picture book, but of celebrities' faces.

Did you see Drake has a new candle? she said.

I didn't know he had an old candle, I said.

Yeah, the old one smelled how he smelled after the gym and this new one smells like how he smells after the club, she said.

Fire, I said.

It's total fire, she said.

And did you see Paris Hilton's ferret has a new bomber jacket? she said, showing me a picture of a ferret in a bomber jacket on a page with the title News.

I'm happy for them, I said.

So cute, she said, flicking through the magazine.

Whatever it was had passed. Like with the bread. It had been just there, almost in reach, we were almost having a conversation about something more than what take-out we should get or who I hated most on *Love Island*, and it was over.

I'm not sure what I thought was going to happen. That she'd suddenly tell me all her deepest, darkest fears maybe, things we didn't know she was capable of thinking, like a regular person, wanting to reach out to someone, to have a moment, a connection, and we'd be on the same wavelength, just once, and then we'd have sex, put the world to rights, eat ice cream in bed, and it wouldn't be about the ice cream for once, but about something bigger, the biggest thing? But no. Who was I kidding? That wasn't the Susan I knew, and I wanted my Susan. I had to just be glad we had ice cream. I had to have perspective.

But I was still always looking out for things that could potentially cause Susan to think too hard, then frantically trying to keep her from them, even though she barely noticed them. I was essentially baby-proofing the world for her, even though she was a grown woman, and hadn't ever shown any signs that she was thinking about sticking her finger in a socket. She did stick knives in toasters more frequently than most people, but she was alive still. Examples of things I'd got into my head that might make her head explode if she found out included the fact that there wasn't any pumpkin in pumpkin spice – it was all chemicals; the fact that Pringles were only 40 per cent potato – what? the fact that we were closely related to bananas – OK, so it was mostly food-based facts that I was concerned about, because I was mostly thinking about food, and these things made my own head feel like it might explode, so I assumed she wouldn't stand a chance faced with these cold, hard truths. There were non-food-based things, like how the sea was just a toilet for fish really so people probably shouldn't make such a big deal about swimming in it, not for health reasons anyway, or how those dresses that people couldn't agree the colour of told us that none of us were living in the same reality at all really, or how the same percentage of lobsters as humans were left-handed, which was just creepy – oh, and how the only certainty in life is we're all definitely going to die. A lot of my time was spent making sure she didn't accidentally listen to a podcast where a scientist was a guest, even if the hosts were comedians, or accidentally end up on a TV channel that was just a show that was someone on a canal boat pootling through the English countryside talking about their favourite herbal tea, because that would be too slow for her brain to handle, and boom.

Her parents told me I didn't have to do any of this; in fact, when I went to them with my latest lists of concerns, they told me I needed to get out more.

They told me over and over again that she wasn't stupid, and that she seemed to know what to do, and I wanted to say, But I don't. I don't know what to do. I might kill your daughter. I can barely keep myself alive. I was losing my head when I needed it the most.

A few months into our relationship, before I knew about the curse, we were in bed, after a nice enough dinner and average film and consensual sex, trying to sleep, but I couldn't. Susan wasn't snoring so I figured she might not be sleeping either. I thought she might just be lying really still with her eyes closed, trying to trick her body into sleeping, like I did sometimes. Really, I hoped she was lying there thinking about me, which was an awful thing to wish on someone.

I was lying there thinking about how I wanted all my nights to be like that from now on – I didn't even care if we ate at that same crappy restaurant and saw that same mediocre film and had that exact same quick but effective sex forever. I was in love. She'd stopped outside the multiplex to give a homeless man her leftover popcorn and some money and I said, Why did you do that? and she said because he didn't have any pop-corn, or money, duh, and I thought, She's right, and better than me.

What are you thinking? I whispered.

Nothing, she said.

She didn't say, Shut up, I'm trying to sleep, so I kept talking.

You must be thinking something, I said.

Lying awake thinking was the only thing I knew all humans did. However different our days and lives were, we all ended up lying down at the end of the day, thinking the shit out of things.

Nothing, she said again.

I really had to stop myself saying, What, so you're just lying there staring at the ceiling thinking about nothing? It sound-ed very unlikely. I was convinced she was just lying to spare my feelings. Here I was about to tell her I loved her, and I convinced myself she was thinking the exact opposite.

You have to be thinking something, I said, pushing it. I was upset about her possibly not loving me and me misreading this whole situation.

I swear I could hear her thinking then, or thinking about what she was thinking about. I could hear cogs turning. Or it could have been the fridge.

I'm thinking about what I want to eat for breakfast, she said. Which was a perfectly acceptable answer, only I didn't believe her. I didn't ask her what she wanted to eat because I was angry now.

Don't you want to know what I'm thinking? I said.

OK, she said. But I got the feeling she didn't actually care, which only made me more annoyed.

I think I love you, I said then, but I sort of spat it at her, because I was angry at her now.

Oh, she said.

I was so sure she was going to get up and get dressed and leave. Maybe not even get dressed, just leave in her underwear, maybe take the duvet; thinking it was the least I owed her.

That's nice, she said.

I felt like such an idiot. She didn't say she loved me back, but she didn't say she didn't love me either.

I didn't say anything else. I lay there and closed my eyes and willed myself to sleep. I made my brain shut down because if it started up, I didn't know what I'd do.

She has told me she loved me since then, so it's fine. It's always casual, though. Like, Love you, rather than, I love you, but I think that's more because she doesn't have that I bit, that ego, that sense of self, that fucks it all up for the rest of us. She does love me, I know it, she just doesn't think about it and ruin it.

★

On my way home from work the day after *The Office* almost killed my girlfriend, and not from laughing, I saw a flyer for a Scrabble Club on a lamp post and thought it might be a band, but it was an actual club, for Scrabble.

Susan's cousin Juliette died of Scrabble. Of playing it, anyway, competitively. It was the 80s. If you didn't want to roller skate around in sweatbands with your boombox, there wasn't much else to do. She'd been at a match, because those were things apparently, and kaboom. Blood all over the board. Tiles all over the place.

Scrabble had become a trigger word for me ever since. It probably wasn't for most other people, or maybe it was, but for different reasons, like your mum took it way too seriously, or how when you played it, you couldn't think of any words other than cat. Susan had played Scrabble before. They didn't want Susan's head to explode because of Scrabble, but they also didn't want it to explode because she didn't understand why she wasn't allowed to play it. So, she was allowed to play, as long as there wasn't any pressure. They didn't want her to be raised solely on Hungry Hippos, and end up needing Ritalin. Susan and I played Connect Four at some bar once, because bars were weird now; alcohol wasn't enough. Only Susan couldn't connect four. Which would have been fine, if only I couldn't stop connecting four. She just wouldn't connect four, even when I was setting it up for her, basically giving her the game. She was just dropping the little counters in wherever she felt like. If I'd been playing with anyone else, I would have shouted, Are you fucking with me? Maybe knocked the game over, stormed off. I'd never get used to someone just being happy to be there with me doing whatever. It wasn't normal and I wasn't that great. I needed someone to connect four once in a while.

It wasn't Scrabble that killed her cousin anyway, but her obsession with it.

I tore the flyer down and started to cry in the street. People didn't know what to do and crossed over so they didn't have to look at me. I didn't know where to go so I went where I always went, to her parents' place, but they weren't home, so I sat outside.

Susan's parents suddenly appeared, her father holding a grocery bag. He looked at me like, What now? His daughter was no trouble compared to this boy, who'd somehow crept into his life, when his back was turned.

There was a flyer for a Scrabble club, I said, my nose dripping a little from crying but also the physical exertion it took to tear a piece of paper off a lamp post.

He put his bag down and scratched his beard. I needed to grow a beard. It seemed to help him.

How dare they? he said, teasing me.

I ripped it down, I said, showing him.

You'd better come in then, he said. The police will be looking for you.

Rebecca

I was in the final days of my pregnancy when Kurt Cobain killed himself. I had to emotionally blunt myself to stop myself crying because I didn't want Susan to feel that kind of sadness. I'd being doing that all my life anyway, in one way or another though. I'd made enough bad choices to have enough things I didn't want to think about ever again. Like how I couldn't remember the name of the first boy I slept with, or the second. They all blurred into one body on top of me, one immense weight, blotting me out, but not in the way I wanted. I replaced these intrusive thoughts with ones of Isaac and the baby and the promise of a future, told myself to buck up, because people weren't saying man up yet, even though Buck was also a man, but there wasn't a version of this for women because we already did it; we didn't need a catchy phrase.

People gave up things for their children all the time, like heavy drinking, or soft cheese, but I gave up listening to depressing music. Isaac didn't want me to have to give anything up, but it was for the best, and that best was Susan now.

A few months after Susan was born Ed gave me a CD of lullabies that were Nirvana songs but instrumental. I threw it in the bin immediately, because I knew it would make me cry, and not crying was always my goal. I didn't tell him Susan was on strict diet of ABBA and the Muppets. Nothing that might make her want to kill herself. Isaac came home now sometimes to find me listening to Nirvana and crying deeply, and he knew it was just something I had to do. I was grieving for Kurt but also myself, but I didn't tell him this, in case he thought I regretted our life. I didn't. I didn't see any of it coming or have much choice in the matter, but once it happened, I was glad. I was someone and then I was someone else, and it was a relief. I had to shut down a huge part of myself to get to there, but who needs a brain anyway?

In the final days of pregnancy, it was socially acceptable to want her out of me, but all I could think about was everything that could go wrong once she was born. I lay awake worrying that it was too quiet with just the sounds of my body to stop Susan thinking and wanted to ask if Isaac would mind if I blasted a bit of Metallica.

What if she comes out and she's sensitive to noise because we subjected her to a lot of it? I asked Isaac.

She won't be, he said, so sure of himself, like only a white man could be. It was love really, but I was mad at him, like only a very pregnant woman could be.

What if she comes out expecting it to be a 24-hour party because that's what we've been telling her it is, and she knows immediately we tricked her and boom? I said.

She won't, he said. I don't think babies really think for a while.

Oh, I said, where did you read that because I can't find anything that says that?

All I wanted in those last few months was something that said for definite a baby couldn't actually think anything solid until they were eight maybe, 14 even. I'd seen some pretty dumb 14-year-olds.

I read it in that book you gave me, he said.

I was talking to a man who might have lived in a movie theatre if it wasn't for me, and he had the audacity to use my books against me, the ones I'd begged him to read, because I thought they might save us.

He went and got the book and showed me.

How did I miss that? I said.

I read all those fucking books and didn't retain any of it because my stupid brain overwrote everything with its own thoughts and the paralysing fear that I was going to kill my daughter.

I also read something that said your baby doesn't love you because it doesn't know what love is yet, he said, which was not something you should ever say to a pregnant woman.

Writers are cunts, I said, throwing the book across the room.

I didn't tell him I didn't even really know what love was anymore.

You're just tired, he said, attempting to rub my shoulder, which was as much help as trying to give someone bleeding out from a bullet wound a stick of gum.

And very pregnant, he said, patting my belly.

I had to use all my energy not to tell him to fuck off, that pats were for dogs. Because I was very, very pregnant, and not in the mood for anything. But he was still talking.

And we have this whole other element other new parents don't have, he said, at least removing his hands from my body, sensing I didn't feel like being touched right now, or ever again maybe – we'd see how it went.

Just when I was planning my life as a single mother, he said, We're going to get through this, I promise, and he kissed me tenderly and I believed him, because what else could I do? I was also crying because I had no control over my body at all now, it seemed.

Later that night, when I was trying to unwind, putting lotion all over myself, like I was about to swim across the ocean, or jump in a frying pan, he started talking at me again.

Even if babies can think, I'm pretty sure they're not thinking about huge, fundamental philosophical questions anyway, he said, trying to find something to watch on TV.

They think in terms of objects before they know what things are, he said, and looked at me like, You read those books too, didn't you? Why don't you know all this?

I know plenty of grown humans who think about objects, a lot, and they're fucked up, I said.

Please don't stress yourself out more thinking about this, he said, which was the same as telling a woman to calm down.

I wasn't planning to, I wanted to say, but someone won't shut the fuck up about it, but I needed him to do my feet, because I hadn't seen them in a while.

I said I wouldn't stress about it but the next day I lugged my giant belly to the library and continued to research the shit out of babies and if they could think, hoping that overnight some brainbox had discovered something new, something that would help. But they were all too busy researching how to get the last drop of ketchup out of the bottle or why we were all obsessed with *Beverly Hills, 90210*. The answer was Luke Perry.

I was supposed to be at home resting, so I had to lie and say I hadn't moved from the couch. Sneaking out to the library was my biggest joy for a while.

Despite all my worries, Susan didn't seem to have thought herself to death yet; the ultrasounds were all normal, healthy, and that might be as good as it got, as safe as she'd ever be. Once she was out, then what?

Isaac told me to stay positive, and I knew I had to try, but it took every remaining ounce of energy in me not to slip into the dark place.

What if we couldn't keep her as safe once she was born? Or safe at all? What if as soon as she came out, she just exploded? What if the horrors of the world were too much? I'd read enough about traumatic births to know they were traumatic for a reason.

Then my waters broke outside our building, and I looked down at the wetness and said to my vagina, You couldn't have waited, like, two minutes? I literally have my keys out.

And Isaac looked at me and looked at the wetness and said, It's not how they make it look on TV.

A little help here, buddy, I said, concerned Susan would just slip out of me any moment and slither off down a drain and Stephen King would be very happy about it, but I would not.

On the way to the hospital Isaac grinned like a mad man. You're doing great, he kept saying, hoping that would be enough, but the grinning and the pep talk just made me feel loopy. That and feeling like I was about to shit a melon, but I focused on my breathing and got through it, let the pain numb my brain. Isaac stroked my belly and told me that if our baby's head did just explode as soon as she was out, and we really were that unlucky, that cursed, then we would all explode together, as a family.

You promise? I said, looking forward to it almost.

I'll take my head exploding over my vagina any day, but today especially.

I promise, he said, but he knew that if that time came, we would die of broken hearts before we died of anything else.

David

On Tuesday, a celebrity's head exploded live on TV. I knew because Susan told me, in passing – literally, she was passing me on her way to the shower when she got home.

She threw her bag down in the hall, said, Hey, disappeared into the bathroom, then came out half undressed, holding a towel, and said, Did you see that celebrity?

What celebrity? I said. There were a few.

You know, the one whose head exploded? she said.

No, I said, all the blood draining from my body. What are you talking about?

She put some music on and went back in the bathroom and shouted, Google it, it's crazy.

So, while she showered, I googled it and had to stop myself vomiting.

The celebrity even said, Shit, my head's going to explode, apparently, then kaboom. Who said celebrities weren't self-aware?

The celebrity in question was being interviewed on E! News. She had a new movie out, but was also a singer, a vegan chef, a flip-flop designer and the face of a menstrual cup. The interviewer went rogue, though, and asked her an unapproved question, something he hoped would make his career, or at least make him trend on Twitter for five minutes. This was about him, not her; she was already too famous, too rich, had too many career pivots; he needed to shoot his shot. He'd been told by several people of varying size and build that he was not, under any circumstances, to ask her about her love life, but he did it anyway. #YOLO. He felt like it was his duty to the people, to give them what they wanted. They deserved something for all those hours they put in consuming popular culture, Malcom Gladwell hours, all those unwatchable movies, unlistenable songs, questionable outfits, sponsored content even the devil would have issue with, for teas that made you shit yourself thin – the people deserved to know: if you were stuck on a raft in the ocean and saw your last two boyfriends drowning but could only save one, who would you save?

He thought he was so clever, the way only a young white man in Yeezys could. The reaction online would give him self-worth for days; maybe not enough to convince his father he wasn't wasting his life, but at least his mother would enjoy some of what transpired. She would finally see that what he did was relevant, important, at least to his generation, if not hers.

Then kaboom happened, and the world would never get to find out who she would have saved, the actor or the rapper. The media, the world, dogs on street corners, speculated. Feminist comics said she would have let them both drown because they were both dicks; the world laughed. People didn't seem bothered about the whole head exploding thing. Susan didn't seem bothered about the whole head exploding thing.

I thought this guy would be fucked up by it, but he was back on E! the next day, doing who-wore-it-better? with celebrities that still had heads. He did the late-night circuit, told all the men in suits behind desks how he was just talking to her, and boom. She laughed before it happened, he said. But there was backlash, not because he killed a celebrity, but because he'd given us one more question that would never be answered, one more thing to keep us up at night. His question launched a thousand think pieces. The dead celebrity's brain was only mentioned in the larger context of her body, her hairstyle, her outfit, what shade of lipstick she wore. The colour of her brain, splattered on the teleprompter, was omitted. No cleaner came forward with their story. I searched and searched, but nothing. Just this E! News dude, everywhere, acting like a saviour, because he'd given us great TV, a cultural moment. You couldn't watch the full video now, only right up to that moment, her smiling, scratching her head, her saying, Shit –, then YouTube cut it. The dark web had it probably, but I wasn't cool enough or brave enough to go there.

I heard the shower turn off and knew I needed to calm down before Susan came out, but I couldn't stop scrolling. She went out with a bang! one headline said. Goodnight, sweet princess! a celebrity tweeted. Someone she was in a feud with over her comments on Baby Yoda's sexuality had already written a song for her. 'Boom! Shake the Room' was pulled from music streaming sites as a mark of respect but doing so made it popular again.

This interviewer was the first person I was aware of to have actually blown someone's mind. He'd been as close to what we feared as possible. He must have actually had bits of brain on his shirt, which he'd probably auction off online, not even for charity. Other celebrities were already using the tragedy to say that they would no longer endure the sort of mental pressure E! News put on them.

Susan came out of the shower in her towel, kissed me on the cheek, padded into the kitchen, rummaged around in the fridge and told me some other actress had got married.

I just stood there, frozen, but wanting to scoop her up and ask her not to explode, ever, not just on TV, but I didn't, because she wasn't thinking about exploding, she was inspecting an old carton of takeout in the fridge.

I went to her and threw the carton in the trash and handed her the stack of takeout flyers. She kissed me again. My phone was still hot in my pocket from my frantic scrolling, reminding me it could all be over in a second.

There's a *Murder, She Wrote* night at the bookstore, she said, reading one takeout menu like it was *War and Peace*, really giving it her full attention.

It will be fun, she said, glancing up. I'm going, she said, you should come.

I should have been more grateful she wasn't thinking about the dead celebrity, or why I was acting weird, but I was still in shock somewhat.

We walked to the bookstore and I appreciated all the everything cushioning us after being alone with thoughts of her imminent demise. When we got there, I was ready to go home but she told me I could sit in a corner if I wanted and that was what I wanted. The night happened around me and it was fun; I knew this because Susan kept saying, This is fun. I said whatsup to another man who looked out of his depth – that was my effort. Susan brought me a drink and popped something in my mouth at some point but mostly waved at me or pointed at me, so I knew she hadn't forgotten me. *Murder, She Wrote* was playing on a big screen, there were people dressed up as Jessica Fletcher, there were typewriters for some contest, a punk band played 80s theme songs, of which *Murder, She Wrote* was one of them, thankfully. Isn't it hilarious? Susan said to me, but they were all taking it far too seriously.

I'd been to a Stephen King night there with Susan before.

We were supposed to dress up, and I said, Can I go as Stephen? and she screamed, Yes! We both can! but I just wore my regular clothes – jeans and a plaid shirt – and she went all in, talc in her hair, glasses, fake middle-aged spread, dad jeans, and crow on her shoulder (she thought he probably had one). So, I was fun once; now I just let her do her thing and thought myself to death so she didn't have to.

I almost ruined the night for everyone when I said loudly, Is there going to be a murder we have to solve? and they all looked at me like, What? That's not what this is. But I saw Susan's brain dart somewhere for a second by a look in her eyes, and then it was gone. Susan's mother saw it too. Her dad was too busy doing the limbo, for no reason.

I didn't sleep that night. The next morning, after checking Susan was in one piece, I went to work. After another long day of sitting in my cubicle trying not to think myself to death, I went and told my boss I needed to take some personal days.

My boss didn't know about Susan's problem obviously, so I couldn't just break down in front of him and tell him I thought she was about to pop any second. I was also trying not to think about that, but at the same time I had this constant agonising sick feeling it was coming. Or it was all in my head, and that didn't make me feel better either. Feeling mad was my least favourite thing.

And it didn't help that my boss was one of those guys who loved weird shit, so I felt bad lying to him. He had a The Truth Is Out There poster on his wall; he told head office it could relate to business, so they let him keep it. If he found out about Susan he'd go nuts, want to meet her, be our new best friend, make us do brunch, write her fan fiction. I liked having that over him, though, knowing I had this secret he'd fucking love.

I told him I needed to take some personal days, mumbled something about mental health, and he asked if everything was OK, because he was weird, but he wasn't a jerk, but also, HR made him.

He looked at me closely, thinking I secretly had something gruesome on my body but saying mental health was easier, more in vogue.

I felt bad when he said he was always there if I needed to talk about anything, but I could tell he was still picturing my naked body, trying to work out what secret gruesome disease I didn't want to tell him about.

Before I escaped, he asked if everything was OK at home, were things OK with my girlfriend? He didn't want to be alone with his thoughts about my weird body, which led to thoughts of his own; he needed answers.

I told him everything was OK and thanked him for being cool, because everyone wanted to be cool, especially guys like him, and he looked thrilled that I thought he was cool, and I felt bad again for not really thinking he was.

I tried not to skip out too gleefully, because he was still watching me, so I faked a limp, ever so slightly, then coughed once, to throw him off.

At that moment, Susan was at work, cycling really fast on a stationary bike like her life depended on it, because her life did depend on it. She was probably only thinking one thing: Must Not Fall Off Bike. She probably wasn't even thinking that, because that would make her fall off the bike. She was probably just staring straight ahead, some dance song blasting her eardrums to smithereens in a sea of sweaty red-faced women in athleisure, all going for the burn, all trying not to think and then falling off their bikes, being a meme by bedtime. She might shout, You got this! a few times I imagined, and all they wanted was to have got this, if nothing else, and then they'd all leave feeling elated.

What if Susan suddenly realised how ridiculous it was, and not only fell off her bike, but her head exploded? At work. And then everyone would think it was the cycling like a mad person that did it – kill the whole industry. Maybe that was the only way her death could be for the greater good. Only we'd know it wasn't that.

As soon as I stepped outside work, a bus almost hit me. On the side of that bus was an advert for a yoghurt that said, Have you experienced mind-blowing yoghurt yet?

For fuck's sake, I said, making a man walking past think it was at him.

If my mind had been blown by a yoghurt, I wouldn't be standing there in the street reading your bus advert, would I? I thought. No, I'd be dead from a yoghurt-related injury.

I hoped Susan hadn't seen the yoghurt advert, but it was on a bus, so she probably had. It probably hadn't impacted her, though; it was just me standing in the street feeling too many feelings about yoghurt. And if a celebrity's head exploding didn't affect her, why did I think a yoghurt might? I was losing my mind, trying to save hers.

Rebecca

Susan's birth was surprisingly straightforward, normal even, as far as we could tell. No one at the hospital said, Well, that's weird, or, Call the papers! She wasn't crying – was that good or bad? Weren't babies supposed to cry? Already I didn't know what I was doing and felt like I was doing it all wrong.

Shouldn't she be crying? I said to the nurse, trying not to cry myself.

Not if she doesn't feel like it, the nurse winked, and I found winking weird, so I kept thinking, How is anyone supposed to know what the fuck to do?

Relax, the nurse said, and because I was still enjoying the last drops of pain medicine, I did relax a little, for a few minutes, cradling a happy baby Susan, savouring the last moment before whatever came next.

What came next was Isaac taking Susan from me and the next few days being a blur, mostly of mine and Susan's bodily fluids. We left the hospital and the world seemed to take over, like it knew what we needed from it. The doors slid open and straight away there were all the sights and sounds of a city that was doing what it did best, being loud and obnoxious and complicated and wonderful. Qualities we hoped Susan would somehow absorb by osmosis.

We took a car home but instead of being anxious and in a hurry to get our precious new baby safely indoors, we stopped outside our building for a while. People stopped and cooed at Susan; a neighbour's dogs sniffed her hello; a few pigeons came and cocked their heads at her. A truck went past. Another truck went past. Susan took it all in her stride, or she would have if she could walk, but she couldn't yet, obviously, because she was only a day old, so instead she just lay there, letting it all wash over her, all the dirt.

This was how it would be from now on. We would put our desires to one side, the ones that wanted to stay in and shut the world out. We would learn to be more in the world, together. If Susan was going to have to be part of it all, we would too.

Isaac found it easier than he thought. He simply swapped his thoughts for his daughter's. She consumed his every thought anyway. It was nice having something bigger to think about, even though she was the smallest thing he'd ever seen. We became this one thing, the three of us, a new creature, a melding, a merging, of bodies and minds. We knew we had to work together if this was going to work, not to see her as something separate from us, but part of us; not an extension so much, but the thing that closed the circle, the missing link. The three of us could do anything – well, that was the hope, and if I said it enough times, it might be true. But really, I felt alone in it, like a wild animal in survival mode. Like it was me and Susan against the world. I barely thought about Isaac. I'd done all the hard work; Susan was mine, my responsibility now. I loved Susan, but it was that she existed at all that did it.

I was exhausted from being pregnant and then the labour on top of that, like the universe really wanted to make sure women knew how it felt about them, punishing them twice.

As soon as she was in my arms, coming out of me even, I

was pulled out of myself, into her. Like the doctor who yanked her out of me took something of me with her. Susan took me out of my head immediately and I was fine with it. I'd tried to make sense of it all alone and to be honest I was no closer to having things figured out than when I was a child.

I strapped her onto me and got on with it all. I shut down most of my brain, the one with the voices, and went on autopilot. From the minute Susan woke up to the minute she went to sleep, she would have to always be doing something and have company and keep it moving; down time wasn't allowed; those moments when thoughts might creep in were banned, so it had to be like that for me too.

All babies giggled and did funny things but when Susan did them, we thought she was the only one, our miracle baby. A miracle because she hadn't thought herself to death yet. I wished my own mother had brought me up a non-thinker. The times she should have been a parent she gave me a book to do it for her instead. There was the sex one, with weird cartoons of people doing it; the grief one, with weird cartoons of people crying; the career one, with weird cartoons of people being adults. I understand now that she didn't want the responsibility, so she just didn't bother.

Some people thought you should let your baby cry, like they needed to get it out. Some stupid man said if you went to them every time they cried, they'd keep doing it and grow up to be demanding and spoilt. Let them cry, he said. You're the boss, he said. It was nonsense. It's a baby, for Christ's sake, I thought. It doesn't know to do anything but cry if it needs something. They don't know how to comfort themselves. If it just cries and cries, and no one comes, it's going to think the world is really shitty. I mean, it is, but you don't want them to know that yet. Not that way. If Susan was crying and no one came she might start thinking, What the fuck is going on here? So, we never left Susan to cry. We wanted her calm. If her brain was stressed already, she might be more likely to be depressed when she was older, end up a goth, which was the opposite of what we wanted. Susan needed to trust us, but also the world.

Our main goal was to pacify Susan, to fill her life with things. Not expensive things, not material things even, just stuff. We didn't want her to be spoilt but immersed. It could be books, music, art, TV, any stimuli, anything to avert her from herself. Thankfully Susan bonded with the TV from a young age, and they would remain firm friends throughout her life. As long as it wasn't her lover, we didn't mind, but she did date someone once because he had a big TV. Not seriously date, nothing like with David. I just remember her telling me about the TV.

Sometimes I think I willed the internet into existence for Susan's sake.

There wasn't that much written or known about baby consciousness back then, so we mostly had to wing it. We played music and sang at her, danced around her like lunatics. We watched *Sesame Street* and *The Muppets* – anything bright and colourful and joyful. *Ricki Lake*, especially when they had drag queens or club kids on, which was every day. Susan didn't seem to mind that her parents were clearly bonkers. She just looked at us with her big eyes and absorbed it all.

When Isaac had to go back to work, I was secretly shitting myself. I almost clung to his trouser leg as he was leaving that first morning.

What if I do something wrong? I said. What if the worst thing happens? Can't you stay? I begged. I don't want it to be something I do, I meant.

He said all the right things. Stick to the plan; that she seemed fine, happy even. That he'd be home soon. And I knew what to do: take Susan out, show her the world. He knew it would be good for me too, but he didn't want to say that. It was temporary. One day we'd get to go back to who we were. We were idiots.

I had no choice but to be fine, for Susan's sake. This part, where I took Susan out in the world every day, was the most challenging. I'd worked at the bookstore, of course, but that didn't count. I still got to be alone there sometimes, in the storeroom, or up a ladder, or just in my bubble. I would never really be alone again now, though.

I spent the months new parents typically spent bonding with their child bonding Susan with the world. It didn't matter if she bonded with me; she needed to feel safe in the world. I took Susan to the bookstore and everyone cooed, because that's what you did when you meet a new baby. They were surprised how freely I gave them Susan to hold, not even blinking when strangers got in on the new baby joy. Susan fitted right in. Giggling at all the fuss and staring wide-eyed at all the books, trying to grab them before she even knew what they were.

I took Susan in there most days, handed her to someone, and then got to sit down for a second. Ed said, When are you two coming back to work? and it was meant as a joke, but I realised it could work. It didn't take much convincing because everyone loved Susan. They loved me too, but I could never believe it. I felt blessed for a while, or at least less cursed.

All I had to do was not drop any books on her head, but I had to do that with other humans too, so it was fine. Isaac popped in when he wasn't teaching. We didn't want Susan to read the books yet, though, just use them to make a fort or wave around, gum them. She almost never cried as long as she was fed when she was hungry and had her nappy changed when it was wet. If I sensed she was getting bored I'd walk her round the store to meet new people, or if it was quiet, I'd take her outside and say, See, the world is still there, you're OK. And she was.

I read that carrying your baby reduced crying and fussing, and if anyone asked, that's what I'd tell them anyway, because I couldn't say I need to keep her busy and moving at all times because otherwise she might explode.

I worried privately what me palming her off on strangers all the time would mean for her later. Would she just go off with any man who showed her attention? Would she fall for everything and anything, be sub-normal in some way, mentally challenged? I worried about that a lot. I was exhausted at night, but I still lay awake wondering if we were doing the right thing.

A homeless man held our baby, I said to Isaac in the dark.

He's just a person, Isaac reminded me, always better than me.

He stank of piss, I said, and he reminded me he'd wet himself once when we were dating after a night drinking and I laughed but it didn't really help. Those people didn't exist anymore.

She's doing great, he'd say. We're doing great, he'd say, and pull me to him and we'd fall asleep, recharging, for another full day, doing whatever was necessary to keep us all alive for as long as possible, and we felt like a normal family maybe, whatever that was.

People were nicer with a baby around. People changed around her. A student who worked part-time who grumbled at the idea, the only person who said he didn't think it was professional her being there, had a change of heart after he held her and she liked him. No one else really did but Susan did. She seemed to see the good in everyone. She didn't need to know that I caught him coming out of the bathroom with

Madonna's *Sex* book once, like he was that basic; the title alone was enough. I don't know why I let him near her now.

I learnt to tune out the other mothers. If I let what they were saying and doing and all the pressures that came with motherhood get in, even for a second, I knew I wouldn't be able to focus on the task at hand. It didn't matter that so and so was already teaching their child Mandarin or so and so liked Bach. Susan liked everything, as long as there was something. She liked Bach fine, but she really liked *The Muppets*, and there was nothing wrong with that.

She showed no signs of having anything wrong with her; in fact, she was advanced for her age in some ways. She was desperate to talk and walk and be in the world as fully as she could, as if she knew she had to and the sooner the better. And once she started, there was no stopping her.

Suddenly, overnight, our lives were filled with this little ball of energy and it was relentless. We worried we'd never be able to keep up with her and keep up the charade. If someone could die from thinking, someone could die from exhaustion, surely? And if Susan figured it out, that we were running from something, blocking something, but that it was in her, well, we didn't want to ever really think about that, but at the same time it was all we thought about. On the plus side, I could watch horror films now because they had nothing on my nightmares about what could happen to Susan.

David

Susan came in from work and, without taking her coat off, came and sat down on the sofa, then stood up again almost immediately and declared we should go and see a movie.

Usually when she came in she was already talking, telling me her every thought.

I came from a family that encouraged us to keep everything to ourselves and Susan was taught to think aloud. For her, thoughts were public things. They were something physical, not cerebral, like being thirsty, or needing to fart. She was taught to get them out, even if she was alone.

Her mum tells this story where Susan asked if she could tell a pigeon her thoughts and her mum said sure and then she asked if she could tell a strange man on the subway and her mother said, Probably best stick to a pigeon.

They worried that giving the universe their daughter's thoughts was shirking their responsibilities, but her mother said, What else were we supposed to do? Tell me what else we were supposed to fucking do?

I think they hoped that one day they would know what to do.

The responsibility of it all was too much for them, so they looked to the universe, and then I came along, and they thought,

Thank fuck, someone else to take the burden, only what I did was mostly show up drunk at their apartment because this was all too fucking weird. I smashed a vase once, by accident, and it reminded Susan's mother of the time Susan punched a lamp and she thought how we were destined to be together, probably, if she believed in destiny, that was. She mostly thought we were both idiots.

Slumped on their couch one night I accused them of lying about the whole thing and it's never a good look to accuse your in-laws of lying.

Why should I believe you? I said, waving my drunk arm at them, trying not to vomit on their classy furniture, which definitely didn't come from IKEA, wishing I hadn't smashed that vase, because now I couldn't vomit in it.

Some people thought Bubble Boy was fine really, and it was just his mother that was nuts, I slurred to her mother.

But I was just another dumb kid that couldn't hold his booze. They thought it was funny. They'd never had to deal with their own daughter in that state. Her father got me a bowl from the kitchen and her mother stroked my hair and they tried not to laugh at me even though I said awful things.

I finally vomited and the room stopped spinning and Susan's mother stroked my hair the whole time and I wished my hair was softer for her, instead of somehow sticky and crusty, because of this goo I'd bought because the advert had a man in it I really wanted to be, not whatever this thing I was. The man with better hair than me looked like he also had better coping mechanisms, probably carried gum to mask his vomit breath, should he ever have it.

Once the vomit had been lovingly wiped from my chin and shirt, only then did they bring out Susan's file, the one with her family tree, the obituaries, the coroners' reports, the diaries, her mother's prescription for Xanax — every scrap of evidence they had that made their daughter's situation real, not just in their heads, and mine now. I read again about the tragedies that had befallen his family and how they were reduced to a few paragraphs in a newspaper. And I had no choice but to accept it.

I was supposed to keep that file safe somewhere, but I always left it there, on purpose, so I could sleep. They always wanted me to take it with me, but then I always slipped it under some magazines, old *New Yorker*s people like them kept but didn't know why really. None of us wanted that file to even exist, so we understood.

My little meltdowns were cathartic for all of us. They couldn't behave like that anymore, but I was young enough to get away with it. They reminded us what was at stake.

Susan wasn't telling me anything other than she wanted to see a movie, but I could tell it was more than that — she needed to see one.

OK, I said, standing up.

I wanted to say, Are you OK? There was something definitely off with her, like she didn't want there to be any down time, which I was used to, but she usually at least took her coat off.

What do you want to see? I said, putting my coat on.

I don't care, she said, already out the door, not giving me time to think about the implications of her not caring; usually she cared deeply about the popular culture she consumed.

In the car she plugged her phone into the stereo and Kesha's raspy give-no-shits tone blasted the car.

As I tried to drive and not kill us, even though the car was throbbing now, making that more difficult, Susan was hunting around for something.

Why isn't there anything to read in here? she shouted over the music.

I unpopped the glovebox to reveal, not books, but various snack foods and CD cases, none of which had the correct CDs in.

She took a CD and started reading the inlay but then didn't like the character arc so started reading a pack of screen wipes I had in the door.

On seeing the huge, obnoxious multi-screen theatre glistening before us her mood seemed to lift, but once we were inside and staring at what was showing I detected that she was restless again.

The choices were: attractive people in space, attractive people trying not to get serial killed or attractive people pretending they weren't that attractive so they could pass as regular people re-enacting a historical moment that was only a few years ago.

I wanted to watch some attractive people falling in love, but in an amusing way, she said, sighing, looking around at what other people were watching.

Do you want to go home and watch something old? I said, looking at the price of popcorn.

No, she said, which was fine, but then, I don't want to go home yet.

What's wrong with home? I wanted to say, but what I was really thinking was, Why doesn't she want to be alone with me? assuming the problem was me.

You pick, she said, which was fine, but then, I can't pick.

Usually, she knew what she wanted to see, because the internet told her.

Attractive people in space it is, I said. I'll get the tickets and you get the snacks.

OK, she said, walking off towards the food.

She came back a few minutes later without anything.

Let me guess, I said, you couldn't choose? but I smiled as I said it, so she didn't know I was worried. There were worse things than not eating over-priced popcorn.

It's not funny, she said, frowning. Just tell me what to get.

You go in and I'll get the food, I said, handing her ticket to her.

OK, she said. Maybe I need glasses, she said, peering at her ticket.

Maybe, I said. Not, Why? Because I didn't want to hear how looking at stuff was hurting her head now, because it wasn't her eyes, and I knew that; her body was starting to betray us.

When I got inside the theatre I sat down and handed her the biggest tub of popcorn they sold and tried not to think how we definitely wouldn't ever be able to afford a mortgage now so might have to live in that tub.

You OK now? I said.

When you've dumped all those M&Ms in here I will be, she said, and I relaxed a little.

She watched the ads and the trailers like she hadn't seen them all a hundred times, like it was important information she didn't want to miss.

But then when the movie started, I watched her watching it and I could tell there was something off with her because she kept looking around at the other people in the room, like she was looking to them to know how to watch a film. The screen wasn't holding her attention, even though it was massive.

I wanted to ask her, Where are you? Because she wasn't there with me, but she also didn't seem in her head; she seemed shut out from everything, like nothing made sense anymore almost, like she was a visitor here, on earth, but also in her body.

I watched her spit out a piece of popcorn and drop it on the floor but then pretended I hadn't seen her do it.

Did they change the popcorn? she whispered.

I don't think so, I said, taking a fist full and dropping most of it on my lap.

I watched her pick up a handful, eat a piece, then put the rest back in the tub, then she was whispering to me again.

I keep thinking, Do astronauts wear that much make-up? she said.

What shade of lipstick is that? I mean, am I supposed to be thinking about this? I can't seem not to, she said. Are they just really bad actors?

I wanted to say, You can think what you like, but that wasn't true. She'd never not been able to watch something because reality seeped in. She always just accepted everything.

I mean, they do seem to have a great make-up artist on the ship somewhere no one's talking about, I said.

Someone shushed us.

And a hairdresser, she said.

She sat back in her seat and I watched her try to focus on the screen but before long she was looking around the dark room again.

This is lame, she whispered. Don't you think this is lame?

I was invested in these attractive people in space, though, so I didn't really want to leave, but I was also literally invested, because of how much the tickets cost, the popcorn, whose container we might have to live in one day.

Don't you want to know what happens? I whispered. The people behind shushed us again.

She shrugged. I can google it, she said.

OK, I said, getting up to leave, mouthing sorry to the people whose laps I was now almost falling in as we made our way out of our row.

On the way out of the dark room I decided that when we got out into the light I would laugh this off, go along with her thinking it was lame.

We could sneak in another screen? I said, once we were in the foyer.

I don't think it will work, she said.

It's quiet, I don't think they care, I said, looking at the one boy working who seemed mesmerised by the rotating hot dogs.

I mean, I don't think I can watch something right now, it isn't working, she said. I can't explain it, she said.

It's OK, I said. It wasn't, but I needed her to feel that it was.

Really, I said, it's fine. But I was trying to gauge if her head was hurting from her face.

You don't have to explain, I said. I meant, Don't even try. Instead, I took her hand, hoping that touching her would bring her out of her head and back into the physical world. It seemed to work.

Thanks, she said, yawning.

On the way to our car someone tried to hand us a flyer.

Have you found Jesus? the woman said.

Was I supposed to? Susan said, which confused the woman, who was expecting us to just pretend she didn't exist.

I hurried her along to the car. We were as bad as them, only instead of telling her what to believe, we told her to believe in nothing.

When we got in the car, she plugged her phone back into the stereo and Dua Lipa blasted my eardrums, but sometimes you have to let disco save you.

Susan immediately found a review of the movie we'd just

been watching on her phone, but with spoilers, and read/ shouted it to me over the music.

We fell asleep watching a baking show where people had to bake badly on purpose, and no one seemed to think it was the end of humanity. A commercial for Grapples, a grape-flavoured apple made in a lab aimed at people who thought this was OK, followed by one for a Christmas anti-depressant, followed by one for soup for cats, only proved this. Susan loved a Grapple. Susan accepted all these products. I, though, would never get over the soup for cats.

At 2 a.m. Susan woke me up to tell me she couldn't sleep.

I can't sleep, she said, tapping me.

She was sitting up, staring into the darkness.

When I couldn't sleep, I kept it to myself. The whole world couldn't sleep. I wasn't special. I didn't sleep for a long time after finding out about her brain. I alternated between watching her sleep and researching brain aneurysms online. If anyone looked at my search history, they'd think, Oh, man, he went dark fast. Last week he was just looking at cat videos. Whenever I read something scary, I told myself that she didn't technically have an aneurysm, but the more I researched, the more I wished she did. Something solid, something there were websites about, blogs, support groups. Something real you could reach out for in the dead of night when no one was judging you.

Hunched over my computer, I would hear people in the building moving about and wonder if they were also up googling rare brain disorders, because we were all hypochondriacs now and wanted to believe we had something special, even if it was a disease, because we wanted to be dying of something other than boredom, loneliness or apathy – the three biggest killers.

But Susan had never woken me up to tell me she couldn't

sleep before, so I was quietly alarmed, like a dying smoke detector. If she had trouble sleeping before, she'd dealt with it on her own, and without me knowing. There had been times when she'd had trouble *falling* asleep, but once she was out, she was out. Once I tripped over a book she left on the floor, swore loudly, and the neighbours even banged on the wall, but not a peep from her. I could have been lying on the floor dead, from tripping over a book, and she wouldn't have noticed.

If she wasn't sleepy, we watched more TV or she did star jumps sometimes, made a home circuit, to tire herself out. Watching her was tiring enough for me. But mostly she crashed out, no problem. Her day job as a hamster on a wheel where women paid to be a hamster on a wheel like her, because it was better than the horror of being a woman maybe, was exhausting. Thinking about it was exhausting. I could barely lift an arm most days. So, for her to wake me meant something was wrong, or different, which was really the same thing.

I can't sleep, she said again. It's like I've forgotten how. Lol.

I calmly asked why she couldn't sleep, hoping she'd just say there was a monster under the bed, or a serial killer at the window.

She didn't seem worried, just unsettled. It was just a fact to her. She couldn't sleep so she had to tell someone, and I was there so she told me. I was OK with facts, I loved facts, but this wasn't a fact. This was something else.

I asked her if she'd tried counting sheep and she told me she'd counted 32. So, 32 was how many sheep she could fit in her head. I wanted to remember that. It might be important. I wanted to tell her parents. I thought about sneaking to the bathroom to text them, but I was also trying not to bother them so much. I needed to prove I could do this.

I was deeply concerned about her not sleeping, though.

Concerned was too clinical really, but worried didn't cut it, like when someone hit their head and you saw blood and they asked if they were bleeding and you didn't want to scare them so you said it was fine but really you were almost passing out because of all the blood. That, but all the time, as a mood.

I switched on the TV. The low light and white noise automatically softened the room. I could feel the static in my brain but it felt good, like the start of a record, the promise of redemption. I allowed myself to relax a little.

Susan seemed normal; the TV was working. I had to stop myself getting up and hugging it – Thank you, sweet angel. She was watching some flameless candle women on QVC like it was the moon landing, but I couldn't move on that quickly. She was being normal; I was the one freaking out, but she was too in love with the screen to notice. TV was her boyband. Most of us watched it half-heartedly, one eye on our phones, never quite committing, but at the same time wanting it to consume us, not realising we had to give ourselves to it. But not Susan. She gave herself to it, like she was offering her neck willingly to Dracula.

If she ever caught me watching her sleep, I was always ready with the cheesy things people said in romcoms that were one step away from being those creepy things people said in horror movies.

I was constantly fighting the desire to pop the top of her head open like a plastic Kinder egg to see what the fuck was going on in there. When they found me hunched over her body with a melon baller, I'd say I just needed to see what was going on in there, see what damage we'd done, what hope was left, if any.

I thought about trephining, about drilling a hole in her skull to let out all the bad shit. People thought it alleviated bad thoughts, demons, headaches, forgetting it worked both ways and crazy shit could just crawl right in.

Her father told me he pictured her head like a black hole, collapsed in on itself. This beautiful potential, burst into nothing. He'd been drinking, and as he hugged me too tightly goodnight, he told me I was a good man, a good, good man. Because he didn't know I was thinking about drilling a hole in his daughter's head, just a little.

Now, she was asleep and I needed to try to do the same. I'd never once woken up not tired, though. I thought the bed people might be dicking with us. Sleep had one job, and it failed miserably.

I wanted to see how many sheep I could hold in my head, if Susan had 32, but I only got to 19 sheep before a farmer appeared and told me to get off his land. Brains are weird.

I could see a glow coming from an apartment across the street, someone else watching TV. The light of the TV was the new light of the moon and I felt sad for the moon, replaced, displaced. Susan was still asleep next to me, but one day she might not be. That thought made me want to wake her up and say something stupid and romantic and desperate and hold her, but I couldn't do that to her. I needed music, something. I listened for signs of life outside, but I couldn't hear a single bird. I'd been abandoned. I needed to flood my head with something other than my own thoughts. I felt like I might cry, but I knew I wouldn't be able to do it quietly, so I crept outside in my underpants and hoodie and went and sat in the car.

Rebecca

Susan was a very alert baby; she made good eye contact and appeared to be listening and focusing sometimes, which we didn't want, so we'd automatically wave something in her face to get her to laugh or just not look at us like that. I thought that was what you did. I was being a normal mother. No one had to know I was doing it so she didn't have time to think her baby thoughts and accidentally kill herself. And she could think about anything, something completely banal, like a banana, or her own foot, and think, What the fuck is this? And boom. About her own foot. She threw food around the room and I worried not that she'd starve to death, but that she'd be thinking, What is sweet potato? She was crazy for milk. She'd drink herself into a coma almost, and it was so satisfying for me. I did something right. I got over feeling like a cow and just did it because everyone had told me how important it was, yada yada. I never felt comfortable doing it, but I liked the end result: a happy, sleepy baby. I hoped it was like being high for her, and no one high thought anything dangerous – it was all moonbeams and giggling, wondering how many Pringles you could fit in your mouth at once.

Susan wanted to walk before she could crawl and it was important for her to do it as soon as possible so she could entertain herself. The same with talking. We wanted her to be able to speak quickly so she could get out whatever was in her head. She always seemed like she wanted to tell us things, but when she did eventually learn to talk it was the same garbage other babies said, nothing useful, and I felt stupid for thinking she was smarter than she was. She jabbered away to herself in her nonsense language and we were pleased. She seemed to know she had to get it out. I did worry that by the time she was school age she would be uncontrollable and constantly told off for talking and I worried she might have to go to a special school, but we wanted her to think she was normal so that wouldn't work – that would fuck it all up, fuck her up, and there were so many other ways we were doing that.

It was important she didn't question anything, so we talked to her constantly, explained everything. It made me feel like a mad person. I'm just wiping your ass – I'm sorry if it feels weird, but it has to be done. Mummy is taking a shit, ignore the smell, and the crazy pubic hair. You got used to it. It became second nature. I'd wake up and say to no one, I'm just getting up now. I'm just walking across the room and getting my robe now, like I thought the government might be listening. I'm backing away now and leaving the gun on the floor.

Strangers must have all read the same baby books as me because they seemed to get it and think it was cute and I was being a good mum, and sometimes that validation from strangers was all you needed to get through another day.

Most nights we got home and collapsed from exhaustion. Susan was tired but we could tell she could still manage more if we had it in us, which we didn't. It wasn't a bad life. We shut down a large chunk of our brains, the bits that screamed, This is horrific! We sucked it all in and powered through. We told ourselves no adults really enjoyed all this baby crap, unless there was something wrong with them.

The second time I went to rhyme-time at the library, Jeremy, the over-enthusiastic, possibly-on-speed organiser, went off script and did some sort of free-form rap, and everyone was in tears, except for Susan, who was into it, and I thought, I'll blame Jeremy if anything goes wrong with her. I made Isaac go after that because I couldn't promise I wouldn't bludgeon Jeremy to death with a book. Isaac said at least it kept Jeremy off the streets, but he lied, because I'd seen him on the street the day before and had to hide behind some bins, with Susan strapped to me, and she just thought it was a game, but it was my life.

Then one night, when we were eating dinner, after Susan was finally asleep, Isaac told me there'd been an incident.

I shouted at another dad and we're maybe banned now, he said.

What happened? I said, helping myself to more spaghetti, trying to be in the moment, with the spaghetti. Isaac wasn't a shouter.

That guy Geoff, Isaac said, loading his fork and then letting it fall again, the incident weighing on his mind.

Oh, right, Geoff with his genius baby, I said.

Geoff thought his baby was a genius. Not even that she might be, but that she definitely was. She wasn't. We all just nodded and said wow and whispered dick under our breaths, but made an extra fuss of his daughter, Sangrine, which was not a name, because he didn't want people to make a fuss of her, he wanted us to treat her like an adult, a smart one, which meant we would avoid her, but she was very cute and we felt sorry for her, because she had Geoff for a dad.

What did you do? I said, putting my fork down.

I shouted, Your child is not a genius! Get over yourself! He put his head in his hands, mortified.

Oh, well, we were all thinking it, I said, taking his hands away from his face and placing mine on top.

I know, but he didn't take it well.

Poor Geoff, I said.

Poor Sangrine, you mean, Isaac said.

What was Susan doing at the time?

She was still banging her tambourine, he said, which didn't help.

That's my girl, I said.

She wasn't bothered, you know how she is. Anyway, I told him he was making us all miserable. I meant Sangrine, really. I was just being honest, Isaac said, picking his fork back up.

What did Geoff say? Isaac didn't have a black eye, so he didn't get punched at least.

He said I didn't know shit.

Really? He said shit?

Yep, so he might be banned too at least. I apologised anyway, because everyone was starting to get upset – everyone but Susan obviously, who probably thought it was some TV show. What do you watch when I'm not here? Anyway, I said maybe she's smart but she's probably not a genius and why would he want that for his child anyway?

Oh, God, you unravelled, without me! I said, shovelling too much spaghetti into my mouth because I wasn't thinking about the spaghetti now, I was thinking about how things were all kicking off, but it wasn't me, or Susan, and what a relief that was.

I suppose we should be glad it's just the one Geoff in our group, I said, shovelling more spaghetti in, my mind racing, probably from the carbs.

Maybe we should invite Sangrine over for a playdate and ungenius her? I joked.

It's not funny, Rebecca, he said, putting his fork down.

We get people coming into the bookstore all the time buying those dumb books about how to make your baby a genius. I've read them all, don't forget. Anyway, we can't do anything about other people, I said.

This was how it was. One of us would unravel and the other would suddenly be the most rational, calm adult. I'd been trying to make light of the situation at first, but I'd misjudged it. He was clearly upset.

Eat your dinner, I said. I spent minutes slaving over it, I said, to get his mind back to what was important.

Susan is way smarter than Sangrine anyway, he said, starting to eat again.

Well, obviously, I said. Fuck 'em.

Geoff, you mean.

Well, not the kids obviously, I said, smiling, with a mouthful of spaghetti.

He laughed then and it was over.

We weren't banned, but Geoff didn't come the next week. He'd probably signed poor Sangrine up for Mandarin classes or cello, even though she was two. It made us sad watching other parents parent badly. The world was a mess, but we couldn't worry about it all. People had different values. Ours was keeping Susan alive first, entertained second, happy third, maybe. Smart didn't even come into it.

We pretended to mock it all, never admitting to the other that when we saw how the other children played with Susan, something in our hearts did its own version of dancing and clapping. Isaac thought we were softening, coming around to the world, only I wasn't really softening, I was pretending to soften, like margarine. I was margarine.

I watched so much TV and came to love it and felt bad for previously turning my nose up at it and choosing books. We knew we weren't supposed to let it raise our child, but we also couldn't afford a nanny. Susan's first word was TV and we weren't sad, we were relieved. As a species we were becoming more and more reliant on technology. Susan was normal. If only she'd been born a few decades later, I could have given her an iPad for her first birthday and had a long nap.

Susan could hold a conversation better than me even then, with just her nonsense. If someone prattled on at me all day, I would explode, but Susan loved it, and needed it.

I was always glad when Susan was finally asleep, though, and I could be quiet again, only I wasn't as quiet as I used to be. I felt changed, but not in the way they told you motherhood changed you.

David

I wished I smoked, or had a dog – a valid reason to creep out in the night. If Susan woke up and I was gone and the TV was off, she might panic.

I didn't want to listen to anything specific, I just wanted the thoughts in my head to be drowned out. I fiddled with the stereo, not even caring if some godawful Christian rock blasted into me. I just wanted not to think my thoughts for a while, the ones where I was drilling a hole in Susan's head. The only station I could get was some talk radio garbage. The whole city was awake, it seemed, but no one wanted to say why. I might have known.

It was some show where some guy asked people to call in and tell him personal stuff about themselves, like he'd forgotten about the internet. But people seemed to want to talk. Posting crazy shit online wasn't enough. Tonight, he was asking his listeners where you went when you need to think, and for a second I thought I was sleepwalking, but I wasn't that interesting.

I should have called in and said, My car, but I was there to do the opposite, and left my phone inside anyway. Once you called in to a radio show something shifted in the universe forever, and I didn't need any more shifts.

There was always a chance this wasn't a coincidence, that this guy was actually the voice of God, but I doubted it. God was a woman now. This was just some dude, but then I was just some dude, so I went with it.

I want to know if you have a special place you like to go if you need to clear your head or make a big decision, he said.

I looked around the street. It was night but not dark; the streetlights hindering our basic need for sleep. There wasn't anyone else sitting in their car. There was a guy walking his dog, but it might have been the other way around, not because it was a big dog, but because humans needed walking too, to save themselves.

Call in and let me know, the guy on the radio said, and I heard desperation in his voice. Please call.

I like to take a walk, he said into the void. I do my best thinking when I'm just walking around this magnificent city.

It's a shame you have a job where you're basically trapped in a tiny box indoors then, I thought.

His co-host, some guy called Dave, made a joke about how he didn't think walking to KFC counted as thinking and they laughed about how sad it all was. Just a couple of bros trapped in a tiny, haunted booth. I felt sorry for this guy, who I assumed was fat, the face for radio, but I didn't have my phone to google him. Then I remembered this guy was possibly my arch enemy, because he was asking people not only to think, but to think about thinking, which was dangerous. When did the world get so meta? I blamed the hipsters, because that's what we did now, when really we were all to blame. I personally didn't have a problem with kombucha or a well-groomed beard, but I still wanted to call in and tell him what he was doing was irresponsible.

The callers all had really obvious thinking places. Jill from somewhere awful sounding said she liked to go to the park to think. Most parks I knew were ruined by people. They weren't quiet sanctuaries where you went to think, unless you wanted to think about how arrogant joggers were, or how annoying kids were. Now Jill had mentioned parks someone would probably make it a thing, insert thinking benches in all the parks; people would queue for a turn and Jill would end up sobbing behind a tree, wishing she hadn't told anyone, wishing she could sleep and didn't have to listen to night radio. I'd spend my time on that bench thinking about what the person before me was thinking or why the seat was wet.

Alan from somewhere that sounded suspiciously like prison said he liked to run.

Sarah from somewhere sunny said she liked to take a long bath. Sarah had forgotten this was a city radio show, where most of us had to make do with a cramped shower. I'd forgotten about baths, but now she'd reminded me of them I couldn't help but wonder if baths could be the answer to my problems.

I looked up at our apartment to check there weren't blood splatters on the window from Susan's brain, but it all seemed OK. She must have been asleep still, but I felt bad for not leaving the TV on anyway. If I was gone but the TV people were still there, she probably wouldn't panic.

There were two more calls and an ad break and some songs I didn't know but found myself humming along to. They were probably jingles for products I'd find myself buying now without knowing why. No one's mind was their own, not really.

I'd gone out there to cry and I couldn't even remember to do that.

Rebecca

Despite my best efforts, the moment Susan was born, I lost Isaac. Not to Susan, not even to fatherhood, but to the world. It was like she opened a door for us both but only he walked through it. I peered out, saw all the other mothers, and went back inside.

Giving Susan what she needed was a challenge for me, because I had to become someone else. And I liked who I was. I worried constantly I was a disappointment. There were enough pressures on a person to be a person. I didn't want any more.

Isaac didn't see it like that. It was all an adventure to him. He finally got to be someone else. There was no doubt in his mind that he could be what his daughter needed, that he could be a different person. I on the other hand felt trapped in what I'd already become, like it was too late now to give up on who I was.

It scared me how quickly he was ready to leave our old life behind. Like up till now it had all been a rehearsal, and now, now this was who he was.

He bought himself a World's Best Dad mug and I felt bad because I was probably supposed to have got him one and pretended it was from Susan, but I didn't, because I didn't want him to become a generic person, one you could buy a mug for.

He wore the name Dad with pride, but I refused to wear the name Mother because I still saw it as an eradicating of the self, like modern women were taught.

We got in a fight about it on my first Mother's Day when I said I didn't want to celebrate it and he said we had to and I said how I'd happily be a dad.

He said he was sorry I wasn't enjoying motherhood and I said, I'm not enjoying anything -hood.

He was gentle with me, though; thought it would just take time. That it might be post-partum. It was, but it also wasn't. It was a general ennui for life. Made worse by his enjoyment of it.

He snapped at me on Susan's second birthday. We'd thrown a small party. Or he had. I was no help and mostly stood in the background as he played host.

She won't remember it, I said, and he looked hurt. Like I was saying memories didn't matter, even ours. But they didn't really. They'd become warped anyway. I intended to tell Susan when she was older that she'd had great birthdays and implant false memories if needed, ones I wished someone had implanted in me.

Isaac organised everything. He said I didn't have to do anything, but he lied; I had to attend and smile and tolerate it all, because I wanted Susan to have a nice day even though I would have preferred to go and read my book in the car. There were no clowns, at least.

I was standing in his way in the kitchen while he was getting the cake ready and he snapped at me.

You need to smile more, he said, you're scaring the children.

I'm not, I said, they love me.

But what they loved was the squirrels on my jumper, and how I wasn't overbearing like some of the other mothers. I should have taken a pill, been like my favourite mothers in books, but I just stood there and let it all happen around me, and I did my best, as parents are fond of saying.

I watched him, not her, that day. Watched him talking to the other parents, watched how he filled people's glasses, watched how he willingly played with the children, attended to their every whim. I watched how he filled space with life and nurtured it, and I was just standing there suffocating, looking for an exit. I felt shitty, not good enough for my family or the world. I didn't deserve to be wearing clothing with squirrels on, besmirching their good (?) name.

He said later he was sorry for telling me to smile.

There were enough other people smiling, I said, I was keeping it balanced. I want Susan to know birthdays can be sad, I said.

That's a horrible thing to say, he said.

I didn't mean it, I said. She had a nice day. It's been a long day. It's done now.

I didn't want it to be like that between us, but it was sometimes. Part of me thought I hadn't really wanted a child because I didn't want to share Isaac with anyone. But this person wasn't my person anymore, so I gave him up to her.

If it wasn't for Susan, I might have left. I loved him still; I just didn't like who he was becoming. I felt cheated. I understood that people changed and you had to allow for that and were supposed to be fluid in your own being too, but I also just wanted him to have laughed with me about how awful it all was, and he didn't.

I got through it. Pushed through it. I converted my anger into strength because I was learning that you could do that:

take a shitty thing and turn it on its head, choose not to let it destroy you when you'd come so far.

Over the years, the more sociable Isaac became, the more I felt like I was drowning. I didn't want to be jealous, but I was.

Before Susan our relationship was conducted in dark rooms, movie theatres or at home watching TV with the blinds down. For a while our life was just sitting in different dark rooms. Our apartment was small and dusty, from the books, but also from my aversion to housework. Isaac was more domesticated than me, scolding me for not drying dishes properly – heaven forbid we had a slightly damp plate. This was before we had real things to worry about. I found out later that it wasn't really about the plate and was more to do with the fact that he thought his job was harder than mine so I could at least make more of an effort with the few jobs I did have. It hurt me a lot and strengthened that voice in my head that screamed, Do Better! on repeat. One of my many thoughts that wanted to kill me.

One night when Susan was three, after I'd had a long day at work, Isaac told me he was going to go for a drink with one of Susan's friend's dads and I looked horrified. She was three for a start, she didn't have friends, or if she did, they included a pigeon and a potato.

You can do what you want, I said.

I know, he said.

And you really want to do that? I said, looking him straight in the eyes, wanting him to hear my internal screaming.

I don't know, he said, sitting down on the bed. He was thinking about if he really wanted to do that, thinking about who he was now, and it was painful for him, the realisation that he wasn't who he thought he was, and I felt really shitty for making him think about it.

I'm sorry, I said, of course you should go.

He stood up but was still looking lost.

Go, I said. It's fine. Ignore me, I'm just feeling a bit sorry for myself.

OK, he said and started to leave.

He stopped in the doorway.

It doesn't mean I don't love you, he said.

I know that, dummy, I said, rolling my eyes, laughing it off.

Then, when he was gone, I cried. Because it did mean something, though. I needed my love to be consistent and he thought saying he loved me did that, but his actions undid it all.

While he was out being a generic dad, in a sports bar probably, I watched *Law & Order* but mostly wondered if this had been his plan all along, and I'd been trapped, the way some women apparently trapped men, according to *Jerry Springer*. That he had wanted a baby, and to be a dad, that he saw it as his ticket out of his head, and I had just been a vessel. It wasn't a thought I wanted, so I turned the TV up, ate a tub of ice cream and felt closer to Susan, even though she was asleep in the next room.

I was actually really good at being a mother. All the practical, monotonous, care-giving stuff other mothers seemed to find soul-destroying, I found them soul-soothing. I gave myself over to her and her needs willingly.

I did enjoy some of it. Like when she was asleep. I learnt not to take it personally that Isaac was someone else now. I tried to fall in love with the new him and made a mental list of all the dads on TV I would probably bang. We were fine. Normal even. He never truly suspected my heart wasn't in any of it.

I knew, though, that I would never be the same after Susan,

like a cat giving birth to a dog. She would always be different from us. Well, me, anyway. I started to think Isaac was secretly an extrovert all along, like the way fat people thought a thin person lived inside them. At every party or activity, Isaac seemed to really enjoy it; it wasn't an act. I watched him laughing with the mothers, getting in the muck of it, children clambering on him – he was the fun dad. Like that mug had possessed him like in a really bad Stephen King novel. I just stood at the side wondering who I married.

I worried about the people we were becoming. He didn't seem to.

One night when Susan was about four he told me he was going bowling with some people from work and I laughed at him because I thought he was joking, because we always said bowling was lame, something you thought sounded like a thing, something people did on TV, but then when you went, it was really boring and weird, and you had to change your shoes, which was too intimate for somewhere that served food in baskets with squirty cheese, plus it was basically Sisyphus, knocking some pins over to have them come back. I sang the bowling song from *Grease 2* at him as he got ready to leave and he reminded me how rapey that film was, and when he left, I cried, because I wanted us not to go bowling together.

Susan and I watched *Grease 2* in bed that night and she loved it and I sang at her and she didn't understand any of it, which was the best way to watch both Greases. When he came back, I pressed him about how it was, like he'd been to a strip club, and I was appalled but also fascinated. He said it was fine but didn't want to talk about it, which meant he'd been bad at bowling but didn't want to admit it was harder than it looked because it looked dumb. He asked what us ladies had done, in that cutesy way men did sometimes, like we were separate, because we were separate, that night anyway, and I lied and said we watched *The Lion King* and he said, Good, not remembering I hated that film, wanted them all to die, and for it to be called *The Lion Queen*. He just kissed us both goodnight and went to bed.

I knew I was becoming more withdrawn, grumpy even, and that it only made him look better. If we split up, Susan would want to live with him. We were growing apart because of our daughter and I was sure she was supposed to bring us closer. He was becoming someone else, and I was supposed to become someone else too, for the sake of our daughter, but I couldn't, and what did that say about me as a mother? Did that mean he was a better father? Probably. He wouldn't have let her watch a film where a boy tricks a girl into a bunker to have sex with him, that was for sure.

I thought he'd come back to me once Susan was grown up and living her own life. That he'd happily retreat back into our old life, his old self, tired of all that smiling and bowling, even though he only went the one time. But I was wrong.

Only last week I caught him doing press-ups before work.

Don't mind me, I said, stepping over him. How long have you been doing those?

A few months, he said.

What else are you doing? I said.

Squats, he said.

Did Susan put you up to this?

Susan doesn't know, he said. I'm allowed to do press-ups, Rebecca.

But he wasn't. He knew that. We weren't those people.

Then he said something about a work picnic. There had been things over the years that he went to (like the bowling), but he didn't always tell me, because he knew how I felt about organised fun.

Partners can come, he said.

But I don't want to go, I said. I don't even want you to go. I don't understand why you want to.

It's really not that big a deal, he said, kissing me on his way out. But I wasn't sure.

He'd started getting texts from people he worked with – not women, so it was fine. Or I thought it was, until I found it unbearable. Him laughing at some video his work friend sent him, when we were in bed and supposed to be spending quality time together, watching TV.

I wanted someone to send me funny videos, maybe, but I would also hate it. My head felt wrecked. Finding the person you were supposed to love the most annoying will do that. It leaves you with nothing.

David

Right before I met Susan, I lost my job. It wasn't a big deal – it wasn't like I'd been there for years, or even liked it; it was one of those post-college jobs you told yourself was just for now, to pay the bills, and in no way would you get stuck there, like your colleague Keith, who said the same thing, and had been there forever, and was almost certainly dead inside, and you knew that from how excited he got when someone brought doughnuts in.

It was supposed to be till something better came along, to shut my folks up. Something to support my increasing beer and sandwich and sitting habit. I was becoming my dad more quickly than anyone expected. I couldn't even properly articulate what my job was, if anyone asked. Something to do with data. I had a cubicle. In the future I might look back fondly; I had a cubicle once, son.

When I lost the job, it was the first time since college I found myself with nothing to do. I was wide open for something like Susan, something all consuming, something like love.

All the busy people dreamed about not having anything to do, or they pretended to. They moaned about it, about how tired they were, how they wished they had a moment to themselves, but really, they knew that if they did, the existential void would swallow them up before lunch. They'd list all the things they'd like to do, if only they had the time, but mostly they thought what they'd really enjoy was doing nothing, picturing themselves in sweatpants, lying on the couch watching trashy TV, existing entirely on foods designed for minimum hand–eye coordination. They thought they might take up a hobby, like semi-professional DJing, or pickling. They'd go to museums in the daytime, eat what they wanted, when they wanted, no longer governed by society's strict mealtimes, or time even. Fuck time. They'd eat cereal for dinner but in bed, then find the whole thing confusing, not know what to do for breakfast. Did they still have to brush their teeth if the world wasn't watching? The world was too busy for them now. Oh, to be busy again, instead of just falling down a giant hole! They could always write that novel, only it seemed like a lot of work, and there were already books – there were still books, weren't there? So, they started lining up the shoes in the hallway. Alphabetising the CDs. Then the pacing started. The listening through the walls, the front door, just to see what the rest of the world was doing, checking it was still there. But then they remember they could go out! Well, they could, if they showered and had any clean clothes. But they went out anyway, only there was no one there. All the good, decent people were working. So, they went back to work earlier than planned.

The first few days were awesome. I played video games and only ate pizza and didn't brush my teeth, and I quickly realised I'd regressed considerably, in two days, so then I wanted to brush my teeth, and wanted to eat something green. And my thumbs hurt. A whole generation of people with fucked thumbs.

I didn't want to be a cliché and have them find me dead on the couch from malnutrition and mind rot, but the days lay out before me, harder to fill, mocking me. Every day was somehow Monday now instead of Saturday, which was how I thought it would be when I wasn't at work.

I resorted to sleeping pills and other bad choices. I had to do whatever it took to get through, and I felt a new tenderness towards humanity. I ate cooking chocolate one day because it was all I could find. I didn't even remember buying it. It implied a previous better version of me who'd intended to bake something at some point in the past, but I couldn't remember what or why. It was probably something to do with a girl. Girls were always making me better, only as soon as they were gone, I'd slip back to playing video games in my underpants.

After being almost bored to death, mostly of myself, I took the first shitty job that came along. I was so overly keen that first day I was sure they thought there was something wrong with me. I stopped myself stroking the photocopier, but I did say hi to my new cubicle.

That shitty job was just my job now. It was no less shitty, but it did keep me sane, ish. It got me off the couch anyway. I owed it my life. It was only slightly less shitty now because I could do it with my eyes shut, so I was basically getting paid to sleep. And I knew the alternative.

I felt betrayed by a world that told me how great time was and how everyone wanted more of it. Time was overrated.

But then I met Susan. And everyone knows that once someone else lives inside you, you're already a little heavy, a little better padded and equipped for dealing with everyday bullshit, like the futility and meaninglessness of it all. She taught me that. My happy little existentialist who thought Sartre was just something people called their cats.

I tried to teach her about Schrödinger before I knew about her brain. She kept interrupting with the same question: Who's putting cats in boxes? Over and over, she kept asking, and it was a fair point. Just Schrödinger as far as we know, I said. I was showing off, but to her it was just a story about a strange man who put cats in boxes and neither of us knew what the point was by the end of it. I wished I had more examples of people putting cats in boxes for her. I thought she might ask what colour the cat was or its name, but I didn't expect her to just keep asking the same question. When I finished, she said again, Who puts a cat in a box? Someone should report him. Looking back, it could have gone horribly wrong, dead wrong. But something in her brain stopped her really thinking about what I was saying. It was just words. Noise. It didn't sink in. Part of me still thought she knew exactly what colour that cat was and its name and exactly what happened to it in that box, she just wouldn't tell. Because she wasn't stupid. She had smart genes and some inbuilt thing that kept her from walking into walls. Underneath all this crap she was smart. Smarter than us, for thinking we knew what we were doing.

While I was stumbling through life, trying not to think, but always slipping back down, Susan was up there on the surface, greeting the sun every day like it was a gift, happy to be alive, because she didn't know any other way.

Her parents worried what job she'd do. I mean, mine did, but hers really worried. All jobs required some thought. You needed to remember to flip the burger. They couldn't afford to support her, and they didn't want to. Time on her hands meant time to get in trouble, to think mostly.

After college they didn't know what Susan would do next. They were always just glad she was alive. Which was how it should be. There were enough pressures. They didn't care what job she ended up doing. They just wanted her in the world.

I wished they were my parents sometimes, and in a way, they were now.

Susan followed the crowd, and thankfully her crowd were good people. Kate was good people. So, when Kate decided to open a gym Susan was right there by her side. It was called Girls!Girls!Girls! like a strip club. It was ironic apparently, because men weren't allowed. One time I asked Kate, Won't men keep coming in thinking it's a strip club? and she said, Probably, and part of me still thought that was her main job really, turning away gross men, and she was fine with it. It was a good job to have. It was the perfect environment for Susan: loud, all-consuming, music blaring, screens everywhere, a sea of bodies pumping or whatever people did in gyms. I had no idea. A different version of me, the cool one that worked out and said things like, Catch you later, one that didn't mind showing his body to strangers, that guy loved the gym. That guy who wore sweatpants for actual sports, not just lying on the couch. All I really knew was that Susan worked at a gym and she enjoyed it, and that was enough.

I didn't know she was into fitness when we met, and she wasn't really; it was more something to do. She was always exhausted, exhausted but content. Most people I knew were just exhausted. She had a purpose, made a career out of it. I'd never been in her gym further than the front desk, because I was scared of it, but of Kate mostly. Regular gyms were terrifying enough but hers sounded like it was definitely a front for a coven.

I waited outside a lot. The women that came out gave me dirty looks. They struggled with doors and bags and yoga mats and iced beverages, but I never offered to help, knowing they'd think I was trying to assault them, then maybe kick me in the nuts, so I pretended I didn't see them, which felt worse somehow. Susan was just in the world, not in her head, but I was scared of the world mostly. Susan was fearless. Because she worked somewhere where women learned to kick men in the nuts.

I peered in the window once, like some weird Dickensian orphan, and it was an assault to the senses, just from a distance. The windows throbbed. When the doors opened sweat and rage and Beyoncé wafted out onto the sidewalk. Women walking past responded to it. Their queen calling. Through the window I saw a woman teaching some class that looked like she was teaching women how to go into battle, which they were, I guess, every day. There were women running on treadmills, all plugged in, tuned out. Running for their lives, from creeps like me. Peering in the window. When Susan ran on the treadmill, she read a book and watched TV. If she had her way, she'd read a book while walking down the street, but we'd told her that wasn't safe, so she just read her phone instead. She's only walked into two lampposts the whole time I've known her. I've probably walked into more.

I saw flyers for her gym everywhere. It was popular. They did all these self-defence classes and ones called things like hip-hop abs. They did one that was just women punching things. Susan mostly taught a spin class and I didn't really know what that was but it was OK because she had no idea what my job was either. She never asked me why I didn't go to the gym and sometimes that was why I loved her the most. She didn't not care; it was just how her brain was. She was the only person truly living in the moment because she had no choice.

Her parents thought she'd never have a fulfilling job, but she seemed to. She never questioned it or moaned about it or wanted anything more. It was like someone said, This is what you do now, and she was like, Cool, and knew it could be worse.

I once had a girlfriend who was always really mad at me for not wanting more out of life. I was supposed to want stuff apparently, or better stuff at least, but I wasn't bothered. What she meant was she wanted better stuff, a better boyfriend. Susan never wanted me to be anything more than I was, and I thought that's what real love was, so when she found out I'd been lying to her it was going to be devastating.

Rebecca

By the time Susan was five it seemed like our evil-genius plan was working. She was always talking, or singing, always expressing every thought she had. We created a child with no filter. We created a monster. I was all filter up until I had Susan. She was an open book, and I knew a thing or two about books. Not babies or children or curses, but books I knew. She didn't seem to notice we weren't the same, or if she did, she didn't mind, or find it weird. I would find it weird. I would demand to know if I was adopted. She just didn't think about it.

Susan couldn't wait to go to school. We thought about one of those artsy schools where children go free range and learn in a more hands-on way, or not at all; if they wanted to run around and dance and sing or pretend to be a cat all day, they could. But I couldn't risk her becoming a theatre kid. Public school was better if we wanted her to be normal. Noisy, chaotic, and she would learn how to be like other children. She was popular because she was loud and fun and carefree like other girls weren't. No one cared if she was barely passing her classes. She was passing as a human girl; that was the most important thing.

We agreed we wouldn't tell Susan's teachers about her special needs unless there was a problem. It was risky, but Susan seemed to always know what she was doing, even when we didn't. School scared the crap out of me, even as an adult. On her first day Susan wasn't anxious, she was excited. After that first day, though, we realised we were going to have to tell her teachers something after one asked if she had ADHD. Did we want to get her tested? Medicated? We'd been expecting this. I always thought I heard people whisper Ritalin when we were around, but Isaac told me I'm imagined it, which didn't help me feel any less mad. We wish, I said, under my breath, about the ADHD. Which was confusing to the teacher. So, we told her. She was only young, bless her, fresh out of teacher training camp or wherever they sent those poor suckers that still believed children were the future, not robots. We weren't sure how to word it without it sounding crazy so we said Susan did have special needs, but it wasn't ADHD, just that she needed to be kept busy, because she had something wrong with her brain. We didn't say she might explode at any minute because who wanted that child in their class? We weren't lying, we were just protecting ourselves.

The poor girl looked like she might cry. No special treatment, though, I said. It's very important she feels normal and is kept busy. It felt like I was mildly threatening her because I was. There's something wrong with her wiring, Isaac said, thinking that might explain it better but only making her think he was an electrician. Does it have a name? the girl asked, because people were dumb and needed things to have a name – pets, inanimate objects, diseases, feelings. No, I said, it's very rare. Does she have to take medication? the girl asked. No, I said, it just has to be managed, and we all nodded because everyone seemed to have things that couldn't be helped and could only be managed – it was the human condition.

So, this was what we told people if we had to, but not Susan.

We made it clear that Susan didn't know and we wanted it kept that way. That was easier when she was a child because people lied to kids all the time.

As Susan got older and became a teenager, a promise of a person, I thought a lot about how everyone loved her. I thought the other parents probably talked about me, like, But have you met her mother? She's so . . . different, weird, quiet, aloof, stuck up. I could go for days listing my shortcomings.

I had to tune her out sometimes, my own daughter; as soon as her mouth opened my head would go la la la. I smiled and nodded, but really, I wanted her to shut up. It was awful. There was no down time, ever.

One day after I dragged her out of the supermarket because she was inviting a person she'd just met in the snack aisle to our house, I told Isaac we needed a change of plan; we needed to explain things to her better, about the world.

She needs to know other people aren't like her, I said; she needs to know that sometimes you need to be quiet, I said, and he knew I meant, I'm not like her and I need her to shut up sometimes. I think he thought I was going to leave them several times.

I'd hidden in the bathroom from her before.

There was never enough everything for Susan. I'd seen her watch TV while at the same time be on her phone and be eating and talking to me and listening to music, but like it was nothing. She thought it was just how people were now, and I was just old; she didn't expect me to understand. I wasn't even that old – we had all those things, I wanted to say. Not the phones, but the rest of it. She thought she was normal, and that was the whole point of all this, and she was, in a lot of ways. But then the world changed its mind, started wanting people to slow down, worried we were missing things. What are you blocking? it said. I knew, but most people weren't blocking the same thing as us, they were blocking the more usual thing that was the giant existential hole called life.

In those first years – well, 13 – I constantly worried that I'd run out of ways to give Susan what she needed. I'd wake up and think, Today is the day she finally says, Mum, I'm bored, and I won't be able to think of something for her to do, and kaboom. We'd taught her that she never had to be bored because there were books and TV and computer games, nature even – there was always something – but it didn't mean I didn't worry that day would come. Sometimes boredom just got in, bringing with it its friends, sadness and loneliness.

I did worry that when she started her period it might start something off in her brain. It seemed to for me. But she just came home from school one day and yelled, I started my period, can I borrow a tampon? before disappearing into her room. I wasn't home so Isaac called me to tell me the news and I bought tampons on the way home and when I got in I threw them on her bed and she said, Cool, and I said, Cool cool, before that was even a thing. We were just a normal family. A cool one.

She thrived at school. Even with hormones. She immersed herself in life, without us ever prompting her to. On her first day she met Kate, who became her best friend, and everyone else was just an acquaintance. It was like she had room in her head for one close friend, like she read about best friends in books and saw it on TV, and Kate was it and that was that. Like, check that off the list.

When she came home from school, she had homework and activities and she seemed to know the key to staying alive was keeping busy without us ever having to say it. She knew what to do when we didn't. We were almost redundant. She could wipe her own ass, reach the cereal; she had her phone. I wasn't convinced we'd made it, though. I knew even the happiest, healthiest child could go batshit crazy during the teenage years. We were prepared for the worst, and still nothing. I was so sure something in Susan's head would awaken at the same time as her ovaries, but nothing, nada, zilch. I was starting to think we'd done serious damage.

Every day Susan was a teenager we told ourselves today will be the day. She'll come home from school, say something's not right with her — or worse, she won't come home from school. I pictured her in the school cafeteria, eating a slice of pizza one minute, oblivious, and then suddenly wondering what the point of it all was and boom, her head exploding, and the lunch ladies shouting for a mop. Or a boy saying something stupid to her and boom. I couldn't get over how she wasn't thinking herself to death about boys. I certainly came close. I was both jealous and proud she wasn't wasting her youth like I did.

She's never going to find a husband or partner, I said one night, feeling bad even thinking that, that I was thinking of the day we could pass her on to someone else. I was wrong anyway because boys loved her. She was open and fun and authentic.

She'll have several husbands, Isaac said, only half joking.

We didn't really know what the future held for her — how could any parent? You hoped for the best; as long as they had love at least, in whatever form, that was the least you hoped.

And she had Kate, who played a big part in keeping Susan safe. I was indebted to her, in awe of her. Really, she was the one I wished for when I would think about someone coming and taking over maybe; not a lover, but a Kate.

I walked in on them once bashing each other over the head with their matching Lightsabers. Susan was laughing like a maniac, which made her need the bathroom, so while she was in there, I said to Kate, Maybe don't hit her on the head so much, and she said, Why? And I said, Because she has a softer head than most people, and Kate said, OK, and when Susan came back from peeing, Kate said to her, No head hitting anymore, and Susan said, OK, and I watched them take turns pretending to stab each other in the heart instead. A week later I overheard Kate telling Susan she thought if there was a God, she was a black woman, and she asked Susan what she thought, but before Susan could speak, I swooped in and dragged them both to the kitchen and forced them to bake cookies with me, and when Susan was distracted, I took Kate to one side and said, Maybe don't ask her stuff about God; remember her brain is different to the rest of us, and Kate said, OK. It went on like that till Kate was older and we could tell her exactly why she couldn't hit her best friend on the head or ask her opinions on organised religion. She always said, OK, and Kate became not just her best friend, but one of her watchers, or guardians, Isaac preferred, because caregiver made it sound like she was ill, which she was, but not in any obvious way. She was the perfect specimen of teenage girlhood, just minus the internal demons.

We didn't think about the effect any of this might have on Kate. A responsibility like that was huge, for anyone, let alone a young girl. But Kate loved Susan fiercely, like girls did, and she wanted to give it her best shot, and that was all we could ever ask, having done the same ourselves since Susan's birth. It wasn't like she was going to turn around and say, Well, actually, I'm about to be a teenager now and this could really fuck up my chances with boys. Kate didn't find her as exhausting as we did because she was young. They were just two normal teenage girls. Susan loved TV more than boys anyway. I did another thing right.

We fantasised a lot about what job Susan might do if she lived. We thought it would have to be something physical, something that tired her out, kept her busy. Something that didn't involve any complex thinking. We worried what this might be and feared she'd end up in the entertainment business. Whenever the subject came up Susan would just say she didn't know, or, anything, everything; she wasn't worried. She was optimistic and hopeful even if she had no idea what the future looked like. Because she didn't live in the future like the rest of us. She had no real concept of the future, in fact. It hadn't happened yet, so it didn't exist. She was like a child or a dog in that sense. She could only think as far as the next week. Any further and she looked blank. The same with the past. Once it was gone it was gone. She could remember last week, just, but if she couldn't she wasn't worried. We worried about the implications of this. Something traumatic could happen to her and she might not even know it. I lay awake thinking about this, driving myself insane. What if something had already happened? Isaac reminded me that she would have told us, she told us everything, and he was right, but it didn't stop me worrying.

It was a huge relief when Susan got in to the same college as Kate; it seemed natural they would go together. I didn't have to worry any more than normal knowing she had Kate to watch over her. I went back to my old life as much as I could. That had always been the plan. Only Isaac didn't want to go back to who he was and he pretended he couldn't, that our plan needed an extension, but he could if he wanted, he just didn't want to. He was someone else now. I was supposed to be someone else too; it was me letting everyone down.

I still worried about Susan because I knew what college was like, but she had Kate, and if partying was going to kill her, or a boy, it would have already done it. And she wasn't studying anything mind-blowing so it was fine. The college years were smooth sailing. Susan studied a wide range of things half-assed, but nothing stuck, and we weren't going to pressure her obviously. She went for the experience mostly. She didn't know what she wanted to do but wasn't worried about it. But Kate knew what she wanted to do. She left college with a sports science degree and wanted to open a gym for women. A safe space. I didn't know what happened to her to make her feel so strongly that this was what she wanted to devote her life to – I could imagine, and often did, but I was just glad she found a way to use it for good. While saving herself, she saved Susan. Everyone else seemed to be able to do this but me. If Susan hadn't had that job at the gym, I hated to think what might have happened. Temping could kill you. Not having a reason to get up in the morning could kill you.

Susan thought it was all so cool. She didn't have plans of her own so it suited her perfectly; she never once saw any void in herself. She thought she was supporting her best friend. She thought it was all her idea. She never once saw us pulling the strings. She took some intensive fitness courses and got her spin instructor qualification and was a natural, obviously, because she was always in motion, a blur. Along with her certificate, she got a shirt that said Strong Body Strong Mind with a picture of Rosie the Riveter and her impressive bicep on it, which I think she slept in, and it all felt like the universe was taking over somehow. As Susan stood there in her cheap throw-away child-labour hollow-slogan T-shirt you could get at H&M, showing me her certificate, Kate looked at me, like, I know right? Too spooky, but it was the right amount. To Susan it was just a cute shirt. For us it was a painful reminder. I wanted to say to her, Look at that shirt every day and do that, have that as your hashtag, live that shirt, but I couldn't obviously, because that would be crazy, and she might think I meant to do that with other shirts too, and she had one that says, I Can Has Cheezburger?

Kate had some money from a dead relative and instead of paying off her student loans with it, because that was no fun, she used it to lease a warehouse where she could start her gym and live above it. She was in so much debt already anyway, she at least wanted to get some joy from it. I felt OK about it all. Excited for them even. Not the debt they'd be in forever, but that they were doing something good. Something tangible. Solid. Kate lived in the real, physical world, the one that sweated. I tried to keep that image of Susan standing there in her Strong Body Strong Mind T-shirt in the front of my mind. There was no space for thinking; thinking would have ruined it all – these girls wanted to go with their guts. They rejected everything that told them they should be worrying about the future, have five-year plans. The world was shitty, they knew that, so they created their own sanctuary. Where women could come and not think. Susan rejected thinking without us even telling her it was bad, she just seemed to know it didn't do any good. She recycled, she voted for the right people, she cared the right amount to be a good human, but everything else faded into the background. She was living her best life when a lot of women her age were struggling. Nothing fazed her because she didn't think about any of it.

I was jealous of our daughter and I could never tell Isaac this because he would say, Well, you can be like her too, if you try, like I wasn't trying. I wondered now if he was maybe hanging back a bit, for me, delaying his descent into the world, and I appreciated it if he was, but it also made me sad. Sometimes I thought they would be better off without me. Isaac could get some hot fun second wife who drank margaritas in the day and wore hoop earrings. She could go to Susan's gym without feeling like one of those things that lived above the Fraggles.

I couldn't switch off, ever, even now she's grown up and off in the world. I couldn't switch off myself. And I wanted to, needed to. I imagined if I told Susan this she might say, Why would you want to do that? and tell me how she wanted to turn herself up, be brighter. Neon wasn't bright enough for her. Her enthusiasm for life only magnified that my own was fading. I thought having a child, any child, would change that, but it didn't.

I needed to find something in this life for me, so I could be a better parent, wife, human, but it felt like too little too late. I was glad Susan had the gym, but I was jealous mostly.

Susan didn't just have Kate and the gym to keep her busy now, she had David too.

When David showed up, this boy she brought to dinner one night, I saw a non-descript young man wearing ripped jeans and a *Goonies* T-shirt, not because he was cool, but because he *wasn't* cool. This was clearly just what he wore, before people wore things like that ironically; his jeans were ripped from age; the T-shirt was just his T-shirt, not a new one he'd got from H&M. He looked at his trainers a lot, which was a shame because he had big, kind eyes. He said, Yes, ma'am and, Yes, sir, until we told him that was weird. We're your age inside, I wanted to say. Don't kill my daughter, I wanted to say.

But instead, I just ate my mediocre chain-restaurant dinner and was pleased Susan was sitting down and using cutlery and seemed to have found someone she liked enough to bring to dinner. He seemed harmless. Which was exactly what you wanted for your daughter. I could tell he really loved her and saw she was special, before even knowing about her brain.

With David in the picture, I thought the universe might be trying to tell me that love finds a way. On the surface, to Isaac and my friends at the bookstore, I was fine, normal even. But underneath it something dangerous was lurking, always threatening to pull me under.

David

Taking a few days off was the wrong thing to do. I had learnt nothing from my unemployed days wallowing in my own madness. Now I had time again, to mope and think, and I couldn't play video games or watch porn because I was too sad, so I had no choice but to spy on Susan, to check she wasn't exploding without me.

While I tried to summon the energy to leave the apartment, Susan already at the gym, not suspicious at all, I thought about how when her parents told me thinking could kill her everything changed and nothing changed. You thought information like that would be like a punch in the face, that it would stop you thinking about yourself, that you'd start thinking more about other people, but it didn't. Not straight away. Wake-up calls had a snooze button. Epiphanies could be paused while you peed.

I had so many questions, then, and still did. Not just about her, but about all of us. I didn't have a therapist or a rabbi or Mr Miyagi; I had Nick, and a handful of other barely functioning individuals. I had a friend who was obsessed with a burrito once, like he dreamt about it and ate it every day. He went so far as to ask me to get him the burrito, because he'd already been to the shop that day and didn't want to look like a weirdo. Not to total strangers anyway, but to me, it was OK. I went once, but I didn't want to be his enabler. If you want the burrito, get it yourself, I said, trying tough love, or just get 10 next time, I said, and he said he tried that but just ate them all at once. After that he started driving out of town to other locations where they didn't know him. I told him he had to stop and he promised to try. A few days later I was getting a burrito myself – what can I say? They were delicious – and he was working there. Everything worked out! he said. We were all going through something, all in our own private hells.

And where was Susan? Somewhere else (work), doing something normal (riding a bike really fast), thinking normal thoughts (no thoughts), oblivious to my suffering. I was jealous of her, and nothing good ever came from that. I didn't know what I was supposed to do.

Only she wasn't at work. When I got there Kate saw me lurking across the street – she had a sixth sense for assholes. I was pretending to be casually walking by, but badly.

She's not here, she yelled, and I couldn't say, I don't care, I'm just casually walking by, who are you talking about? I don't even know you. The whole world knew I was acting shady.

I crossed over and Kate met me on the steps.

Susan isn't here, she said.

Oh, I said. Where is she?

She's at her folks', she said, glaring at me the way she always did. What have you done? the look said. We don't need you, it said. Stop lurking around outside my gym, it said.

What's going on? I said.

She asked me what was wrong with her, she said.

Shit, I said, feeling like I might vomit. What did you say?

I said she should go and speak to her parents.

Shit, I said again. I could feel my heart everywhere but where it should be.

Yep, she said, crossing her arms. She looked like she wanted to punch me so crossing her arms would stop her doing that.

It's happening, I said, gulping, but the bile in my throat wouldn't go down.

Yep, she said, crossing her arms even more, like she was possibly digging her fingers into her sides to stop from digging them into me.

How was she? I said, looking at the ground, kicking some dirt. Did she seem OK? I didn't want to look at her now, afraid she might punch me.

Apart from asking me what was wrong with her she seemed fine, she said, sighing. She wanted me to be scared of her but then felt bad because she knew I hadn't really done anything. She was just looking out for her friend.

She was looking for something on her phone then. Maybe she was about to show me a happy picture of Susan, so I had something nice to remember her by, or just a picture of a kitten maybe, to stop me freaking out, even though it was her looking like she wanted to punch me that had made me freak out more.

Fuck! I said, putting my hands up to my head to keep it on. I wanted it to be clear to her I was distressed by her news.

She showed me a picture on Instagram then of a woman on a balcony looking at a sunset. I vaguely recognised the woman from a TV show but she mostly posted pictures of herself with sunsets now. Kate showed me pictures like this sometimes. She kept tabs on all the fake deep celebrities. I looked at the photo and read the caption. 'All the thoughts all the time. So many thoughts,' it said, followed by a heart emoji and then the exploding head emoji, then an ad for her new wine.

Fucktards, Kate said, putting her phone away.

She was showing it to me to remind me people were idiots, including us.

It will be fine, Kate said, heading back inside. I have to believe, she said.

It fucking better be, I shouted, and a woman with a young child looked at me like she knew she was supposed to cover her child's ears and hurry away, warn her child about men like me, but she wanted everything to be fine too, for all of us, even me, so she gave me a look like, Yep, and it helped a little.

I didn't know what to do with myself after that but knew it was better I didn't go over after Susan; I had to give her space. I also didn't really want to go over there. Part of me wanted to just leave all together, never know what happened next. Live in some trailer park somewhere where no one could ever find me, not that anyone would want to find me. That way Susan could always still be alive. She would be the cat in the box, and I would just never open it.

So, I sat in a park and watched a whole season of *Succession* on my phone instead. I didn't even get a sandwich from Subway, which was right by the park, but I thought about it. I didn't deserve to eat. I didn't know if I could choose anyway. I wanted them to just hand me a sandwich, and I didn't think they did that.

I didn't go home till it was home time, like I'd been at work. Like it had just been any other day. Wednesdays, am I right? What shall we do for dinner?

I probably should have gone to her parents' place. I should have fucking been there – another thing to torture me.

As I was walking home, I got a text from her mother. Where was I? Was I OK? Hello?

I called her mother back and she declined it immediately,

but I understood; your phone ringing was alarming. She called me back.

David! she said. Sorry about that. Are you OK? she asked, and I didn't deserve her concern.

I'm OK, I said, lying. What happened?

We told her, she said.

I felt paralysed. They'd told her. She knew everything now and all I could think was, Is it Game Over or do I get another chance?

Rebecca

Susan turned up at the apartment. It was the middle of the day. We were all supposed to be somewhere else, but we were there.

What's wrong with me? she said, and that's when I knew she knew. Not exactly what, but something.

Why aren't you at work? Isaac said.

Why aren't you at work? she said.

None of us are at work, I said. What's going on?

What's wrong with me? she said again.

I looked at Isaac. I wanted to know if he was thinking what I was thinking: that we could put the TV on, or wave something shiny at her so she would forget, and we could be past this and not have to answer her. Or run away. I wasn't above just running away from my own daughter.

But he was better than me and had already taken his daughter's hand and was sitting with her on the sofa, explaining everything. This was his fault anyway, it was only right he told her, or so I told myself as I just stood there, staring at them both, watching Isaac's mouth move but hearing nothing but my own breathing, and it wasn't comforting; it was alarming, fragile, mortal.

There's nothing wrong with you, he said, his hand on hers.

I should have gone and sat the other side of her, but I stayed standing and staring.

People in our family have trouble thinking, he said. If we think too hard, it can kill us.

There. He'd said it. The words we were afraid to say. The facts. I opened my mouth and took in some air.

What? Susan said, looking at me now.

She was confused, obviously.

Is this a joke? she said, frowning. She liked jokes. It could have been April Fool's Day – she didn't check the calendar, ever.

I shook my head.

No, I said quietly to the floor.

She was quiet then. She needed time for it to sink in to whatever her brain was made of – not the same stuff as ours – then she said, Holy shit! That's crazy!

I relaxed a little. She sounded like herself again. The person at our door minutes ago, asking what was wrong with her, was someone else.

Then she was quiet again, for the second time that day, or ever.

I don't understand what you're saying, she said, scratching her head, because that's what you did in situations like that. That's what people on TV did anyway.

I think every day, she said.

Bless her, I thought, she thinks she's doing it, she thinks she's at full capacity. Then I remembered how horrific this was, and that she wasn't doing it, not at all; she was living on the surface of life, and it had to be enough, until it wasn't. Until this moment.

Susan sat back further on the couch and pulled her legs up under herself. Her head hadn't exploded, though, so things were still going well, considering.

So, you're saying my brain can kill me? she said.

Isaac nodded.

Can your brain kill you? she asked, like it might be a contest, who could have the weirdest brain.

Well, yes and no, Isaac said. Not in the same way. He looked at me, like, Say something, please, why are you just standing there? But I just kept standing there, frozen.

He told her about his family, only he tried to keep it more upbeat for her, tried to make her see that she could beat this thing, and would, if she just never thought about any of this ever again, or never went to Paris, or played Scrabble. Never loved too much, which she probably wouldn't now that everyone she loved had lied to her.

This is not how I thought my day would go, she said, implying she'd thought about how her day would go, though, which was news to us. We thought she had no context of even the near future, just went along with it all. Each day was already there for her and all she had to do was walk into the light of it, let it do its thing, while the rest of us saw each day as something gaping, something begging us to fill it, ominous, and if we didn't, something would crush us, and it often did. Like today.

We didn't say, What are you thinking right now? About all this? We didn't want to push it, if it was just sitting on the surface, and she was dealing with it, not really thinking about it too much. She didn't seem to be thinking about it too much. It was just a new fact, a new piece of information. She took it well. Too well. Like she just found out about a new food trend, or celebrity couple.

This is crazy, she said, but not like she didn't believe it, more like when a stoner sees a double rainbow.

Tell me all the ways your brain can kill you? she asked.

I just stood there, watching them both, unable to find the words she needed.

Isaac gave her a quick, upbeat lesson on all the ways the brain could kill you, but she stopped him halfway through and said she'd seen enough celebrities online talking about their anxiety and related charities and merchandise and she understood.

So do other people know about this? she said.

Yes, we said, in unison, a small word we hoped would circle round us all and do its job of stabilising feelings.

People know our brains can kill us, we said. I found my way back to our little group of conspirators. We were a united front once more.

But what you have is very rare and has to be a secret, I said, sitting next to her now.

Why is it a secret? she said, which was a fair question, especially when it was her secret now too.

I didn't know how to say that it wasn't so much that her brain had to be a secret, although it was very weird and probably should still be, but that it was what we'd done to her to keep her safe that was more the secret. Because if finding out your brain might explode if you thought too hard didn't kill you, finding out your parents brought you up as part of a secret thought experiment might. I looked to Isaac, who told her it was a secret because people wouldn't understand.

That, I said.

People who kept weird secrets always said that, and it seemed to cut it. It meant we didn't understand either really.

We couldn't say to her, If people know you can't think, they might take advantage of you, because no one wanted to hear that. No one wanted to be told they were dumb and people were awful. But that was basically the truth of it. Only she wasn't any of those things.

We showed her the file and her first question was, Is this from Staples? And we said yes.

She skim-read the file and Isaac talked her through it, even though she didn't ask anything. She just made the noises people made when they wanted you to think they were listening. She was probably already thinking about what to eat next.

Most people can think about things and not die, you understand, Isaac said.

We thought you might die, he said.

And then I started crying and I promised myself if our daughter lived through this I wouldn't cry. I didn't even care if Susan forgave us, as long as she was alive. But here I was crying, the magnitude of what we'd done too much to bear, my brain was an ocean, my thoughts angry sharks, gnashing away, dragging me under, until there was only red.

Susan asked if there was a treatment, something she could take, which was a completely normal response, something I'd never asked. I worried then that I'd done this all wrong. Maybe I was supposed to have made it my life's mission to find a treatment or, better still, a cure, like people did in exciting films and books, and sometimes life, but then it was usually made into a movie anyway, but I would prefer the book.

We said, No, there's no treatment. It's just something you have to manage.

She asked if we'd been managing it for her then, all these years, and we said yes and she said thank you, that was nice of us. Like she forgot we were her parents, and that's what parents did.

She didn't seem mad. I would have been so mad. But her brain didn't work like mine, or anyone's. You assumed everyone hated being lied to, but it turned out some people didn't mind. And we weren't actually telling her we lied to her. No one said the L word. Maybe if someone had pointed that out, that we were bad people, perhaps she would have been like, Oh, right, yes, I remember now, lying is bad, but I still thought she'd know in her heart we were the good guys.

We told her not thinking was a good thing, hoping no one else would tell her anything different. She never once said she didn't believe us, nor did she ask for an MRI, or a second opinion. The only doctors she trusted were TV doctors anyway.

She believed us. Even though we'd been lying to her, her entire life. She trusted us like a dog, and it broke my heart. We were broken people.

Does David know? she said.

Yes, we said, he knows.

David

All I could hope, pray even, to who, I don't know, was that she would be the same with me.

Did she mention me? I asked. I meant, Did you put in a good word for me, tell her I didn't do anything, that this was your lie, that I was sucker punched by love? I only cared about love now. I had to believe this was about that, only that, and the universe had my back.

All her mother said was, She knows you know.

I put my phone in my pocket. I could hear Susan's mother saying, Hello? David?

She'd taken it well, they said, but then they'd engineered her that way.

I walked home slowly. I dawdled, petted a dog. I stopped and went into a store, but I didn't really want anything so after staring like a zombie for what seemed like hours at all the rows of beverages the world thought we all needed I came out with nothing. I deserved nothing. As I walked, I thought about how she knew now, so I had a new thing to worry about, because I was selfish.

I thought that her knowing would feel different. I felt like I might vomit but I hadn't eaten anything so I knew if I did vomit nothing would come up, just feelings, and I wasn't done feeling them.

I was convinced she wouldn't come home. I was convinced she wouldn't even break up with me by text; she just wouldn't come home.

I always got home before her anyway because I had the type of job you were counting down to leave from as soon as you got there, before even, but Susan always stayed late, helping Kate do whatever Kate needed help with, or just to hang out a bit.

It was late when she did finally come home. I'd been waiting, constantly checking my phone, pacing a little. When she came in, she saw me sitting there on the sofa but carried on like I wasn't there. Usually, she'd ask what I'd eaten for dinner, or what I'd watched on TV, but tonight, she didn't want to know.

Hi, I said, after I couldn't bear it any longer.

Hi, she said.

She went to brush her teeth and I followed. We brushed our teeth together, like normal, like robots, with teeth, and then we got in bed. I had the TV on already. The least I could do.

We half-heartedly watched a show about a time-travelling lesbian that she loved, then I switched the TV off and we lay there pretending everything was normal between us and that our life might just go on as it had, but we both knew nothing was the same now. The sheets felt heavier, scratchier. She was someone else now, suddenly self-aware, like that cat again, seeing itself in the mirror for the first time, only this time saying, Holy shit, I'm a cat. All this time I suspected it but there we are, proof, I'm a motherfucking cat. Check out my tail.

I had to say something and that something turned into everything because I thought she might be dead already.

Do you know how long I've wanted to tell you? I said. To

tell you how sad I was when I found out because I loved you so much that I thought I'd lose you? How I felt like it was just my luck that I met someone amazing and she might die. You're the only thing I think about now. I don't care about anything else, I said.

Well, that's intense, she said, freaked out. That's a lot, she said. I don't want that. That sounds awful.

I know, it's awful, I said, meaning me. I don't want it to be like that, but it is.

Does that mean I don't love you if I don't think like that about you? she said then, and it was like someone just kicked me in the chest and the nuts and stole my wallet and took a dump on my face.

I don't know, I said, because we were being honest, for the first time ever.

I feel sick, she said.

Is your head OK? I said.

Yes, my head is OK, stop asking me that. I feel physically sick, in my stomach, not in my head, my head just feels swampy, she said.

Swampy?

Yes, like murky.

That's not good, I said.

No shit, she said.

And then we were quiet again, but I couldn't bear it. The not knowing.

I'm sorry, I said. I don't know what else to say. I think you do love me. I didn't do anything to you. You came to me on your own, you stayed with me because you wanted to. I never forced you to stay.

Nothing I said was even close to what I wanted to say, what I felt. What I'd lived. Words were bullshit, inadequate, there needed to be some other way to communicate, but I didn't think she'd appreciate an interpretive dance right now.

But you lied to me, she said.

I know, I said.

I know you all think I'm an idiot, but I know lying is bad.

We don't think you're an idiot, I said.

Someone outside our window was singing now. A happy song, drunk but happy. Baby, you're a firework. Someone else was laughing, then someone was telling them to shut the fuck up.

What then? she said. What do you think of me?

I wanted to tell her how she was all I thought about, from the minute I met her, and it was the same for her parents, but I didn't want to freak her out again, not if that wasn't her understanding of love.

We think you have something wrong with your brain, I said. And that means you can't think like other people – that's it, it doesn't mean you're an idiot. People think differently.

I know that, she said. But how do I know you're even telling the truth?

Now was not the time to tell her there was no such thing as truth or fact and everything was relative, subjective, an illusion, probably, so I just said, We're telling the truth. We love you, I said, hoping those words would hug her, pull her in, flood her with that love and she would stop thinking about this. She needed to stop thinking about this.

We should watch some TV, I said.

OK, she said. Yes. You're right.

We successfully watched three episodes of *Riverdale* and let TV do its job.

I could tell she was getting sleepy, but she said, One more? Like we both knew the TV was the only thing keeping her alive, not me, not love, but I wanted to know for sure, so I faked a yawn and turned the TV off and we lay there in the dark. You could hear people out on the street, going about their business, their weird, scary night business. Get to bed, I wanted to shout, but it was also comforting not to be alone, even if they were drug dealers and murderers. The happy drunks were long gone.

Then she wanted to talk again.

What's it like in your head? she asked, and I didn't know how to answer.

No one had ever asked me that. Not a therapist, or parent, or lover. The closest was a girl telling me she didn't know what went on in my head, because I zoned out a lot, thinking about video games probably, or lunch. I didn't know where it went, before Susan. Now it had focus. Purpose.

Try, she said, turning her body towards me.

Please, she said. I'll show you mine if you show me yours, she said, and it was light enough to see she was smiling. She didn't hate me then. I hated me, though.

I sat up and reached for the TV remote, but she stopped me. No TV, she said.

So, it was just going to be the two of us talking, no background noise, no distractions, no filler, just our voices, and the sounds of our neighbours fighting, then maybe having sex, but we couldn't tell for sure. It could have been just one of them. A door definitely slammed.

I had to really be in that room, really be present. She deserved that, however painful it was.

I told her who I was before I met her. How I had to not think a lot of the time because I was lonely and didn't know what I was doing with my life and she nodded and said, That must have been hard.

She was a great listener. We'd never given her the chance before, but she was really good at it.

How did you not think? she asked, and I could tell she was genuinely interested in what went on in other people's heads, how they lived.

I played a lot of video games, I said. Way more than I play now, I quickly added, because I still played a lot.

Did it work? she asked.

Not really, I said, because we were being honest.

Then I told her how when I met her something changed. Like a light came on, I said.

I remember reading somewhere that was what love was. You were in the dark when it was just you but when your person came along, it was like a light coming on. Life started up. Even if it was just them coming home from work and your day wasn't that bad.

I had a reason for living, I said, but then immediately worried that would frighten her again.

Oh, she said. That's nice.

I didn't expect her to say the same, ditto, because it was always light inside her. It was how we'd made her. I never expected to be anyone's light.

Then I told her how everything changed again when her parents told me about her brain. It was like someone gave me the greatest gift, then told me not to break it because I was clearly going to break it.

You haven't broken me, she said and I could feel my chin start to wobble. And now? she asked.

Someone in the apartment next door flushed their toilet.

And now I feel like I have another chance but I'm going to screw it all up, I said. I don't deserve another chance. I don't know what I'm doing. My lip was wobbling now.

I'll decide that, she said.

And I knew deep down that was true. She always spoke her mind.

And you? I said. What's it like in your head?

This was the question we all wanted to know. The thing that had kept us up for so many nights, had us literally pacing the room. The thing we dared not ask, till now.

She took a huge breath in, held it, and then let it out very slowly.

Before I met you, I was fine, she said, and my heart shrivelled a little, like a sad grape, but I'd expected it. But then she said, I didn't know what I was missing. I knew that was how it was supposed to be, when you meet someone, and I met you and something clicked.

She was a light and I was a click.

Not a light so much, like you said, but something changed for me too, she said. I met you and I just kind of knew I wanted you in my life.

My heart started up again and I let out some air in my chest. These were the things I'd wanted to hear for so long and now I couldn't help but feel there was a but coming – but you lied to me, but things are different now. I didn't feel safe yet.

And we had a nice life, didn't we? she said then, but it wasn't a question. It sounded like something far in the past, something we couldn't get back, however hard we tried.

But then I felt like there was something wrong, she said, that day in the store with the bread. I knew there was something wrong with my brain, but I didn't know what. It felt like this pressure in my head. Then my parents told me the truth, she said.

I'm so sorry, I said, starting to cry.

She was still talking like she was detached from it. Like her brain wasn't quite her brain still, but something she'd heard of. Something she always thought she must have, but it never introduced itself.

She didn't try to comfort me. We lay facing each other in the dark, pretending not to hear our neighbours and the street outside.

And then what? I said, needing her to carry on with her story. In case I'd lost her again. I never wanted to lose her again. Wherever she went now, in her head, or in the world, I wanted to go there with her.

I remember being confused, she said. Scared. I knew you must have had a reason, though, and I knew I could still trust you. I had to, she said. I have to.

It was too dark to see her face, but it didn't sound like she was crying or sad; this was all just how it was now. This was how she felt and she was feeling it and telling me and it was cathartic. We should all just be doing that, I thought. Why was it so hard?

I knew I was supposed to be mad, she said, or I'm supposed to be mad. But I'm not. I knew I had to trust you. I have to trust you. But I don't think I can carry on like before.

She'd said all she could, for now, and it was so much. More than I ever knew before, about what was really going on inside her. For a moment I felt like if she stayed with me, I'd get to see a whole new Susan emerge and she would get to see other sides of me too.

Then a car backfired somewhere and we both jumped. She'd never jumped before. Not once. No scary movie was ever scary enough for her. She screamed along with everyone else, acted the part of the scared girlfriend, but she was never really scared. She mostly laughed. That little bang and our jump reminded me that we weren't out of the woods, and might never be.

She could be walking to work and suddenly think about what a jerk I was, because I'd lied to her all these years, and her brain could collapse, because that was the opposite of what she thought love was, and she'd be right.

Rebecca

Susan knew now, and we were trying to carry on like everything was normal, although nothing would be normal again, if it ever was, or was capable of being so. We were going to a dinner party, which was as fake normal as you could get. There was nothing normal about eating dinner at a table, and it wasn't even our table. I wanted to eat all my meals in front of the TV now, enjoy some small relief in Susan knowing.

I didn't want to go to this stupid dinner party, because it was stupid, and although I liked dinner, big fan, I hated parties. Isaac knew this, but also knew I wanted to be better, and hadn't been very good at it recently. This was my big chance to show him I was still in this with him. He didn't say, It's what people do, Rebecca, but his body reeked of it, that and some weird new fragrance he thought Johnny Depp wore because he was on the poster (he loved his old films so much he forgot about the more recent ones, his legal battles; he wanted to smell like Edward Scissorhands, but he smelled more like an old British pirate, sad and spicy).

He was right, though, dinner parties were something adults did, so we did them sometimes, to feel better about all the other ways we'd failed at being adults. He still had to drag me there, though. I agreed verbally with a 'fine', but it didn't mean my body was willing.

It's for work, he said, reminding me of all the times he'd come to the bookstore and listened to authors he didn't care about (he didn't care about any), just to be an extra body, so the author didn't kill themselves.

It's not quite the same, I said, but I agreed to go. I needed a night off myself.

I have to go, he said, so if we both have to go, it helps, he said. And I wanted to help. I also wanted him to shower and smell like himself again, not a sad actor, or if he was going to smell like any sad actor, I wanted it to be Keanu Reeves, who I imagined smelled like a bus, or black leather – black leather bus seats, perhaps.

I put on my fanciest cardigan and rubbed a magazine perfume sample on my wrists and neck and went forth. If I was lucky, I'd break out in a rash and get to go home early.

The dinner party was at a professor's house. Isaac taught film so I never understood why he was friends with the smart professors who taught real subjects, like hard science, but he was. He said he didn't know either, but they didn't seem to care what subject he taught; it was about the teaching and the common loathing of the students.

We all hate the system, he said, doing the rock-on sign.

Scientists like films the same as everyone, he said, and I hoped I could get through the night without mentioning *Flubber*.

To them he was the cool kid, because he taught film, which to them wasn't something that needed to be taught, but also something they didn't understand, because they weren't cool enough. They only watched documentaries.

On the drive over, Isaac gushed about how wonderful this Roy whose house we were going to was and I tried not to think too much at all, especially about how I was dressed all wrong, and had nothing to say to these people.

He's not just a genius in his field, he also plays guitar and bakes, he said.

Are you trying to set me up with him? I joked, because someone to bake for us was all any of us wanted.

We arrived at Roy's and his wife, also a professor, made us feel welcome. There wasn't a mat that said welcome, though, so I didn't 100-per-cent feel it. I needed words. They made a point of saying several times they'd try not to bore me with work talk, but they couldn't help it. Over dinner they started debating some hot new scientific theory and Isaac was used to it, used to them, so he joined in, and it was only me sitting there thinking what a bunch of pricks.

Roy's wife, Charlotte, taught geology and seemed to have decided this would also be her personality, wearing a rock-coloured smock and a necklace with a fossil hanging from it. I wanted to ask if she had a pet rock, as a child, or now even. There were no signs of children or actual pets.

Don't worry, Charlotte said to me, over a cassoulet, we're not all wired to think scientifically.

I didn't know what a cassoulet was for sure, but I was supposed to be book smart at least, so I let them think I knew.

I smiled and to show her I was actually smarter than she thought, I said, I don't think we were actually wired to think about anything very much. We only used to have to think about survival.

Take that and stick it in your perfect crockery, I thought, and Isaac looked at me like, I think you've had enough wine now, dear, but I hadn't even started.

They didn't know about Susan's condition, of course. I didn't know how much they knew about me, other than that I wasn't one of them. They probably only knew the basics, that I was his wife and that I worked in a bookstore.

Charlotte told me she'd been complaining the other night about how stupid people were and how Roy told her off and said it wasn't their fault. These people were awful. I needed to leave. I was annoyed the cassoulet was delicious. I hadn't even seen a TV. I'd have to snoop later. They probably had one of those TV cabinets, so it was hidden, like it was dirty. Ours was dirty, but from use, and love.

Charlotte started telling me about something she'd been reading, assuming reading was my safe word. She couldn't understand why the person writing the article couldn't see their own limits as a mere mortal. Roy looked at me then and said to his wife, Darling, why do we always think we're smarter than we are?

He means humans, she said, to me.

She did look like a darling. No one called me darling. I got honey sometimes in the bookstore, but that was too tender for me sometimes, made my heart ache, and then I felt stupid for being so needy, wanting love from a stranger.

And what did you think? I asked her. I was tired of hearing men talk, but also of women talking about what men had to say. I wanted to hear what she had to say, mostly about the TV situation in her home.

I think men are a real bore, she said, and carried on telling me how stupid her husband thought we all were. She looked at me like, Men, right? And I felt a thin bond forming between us, one that would at least get me through the evening.

Roy was at the other end of the table but listening to his wife now. Rich people only had big tables so they didn't have to sit near each other. If I was rich, I'd want my own table.

I'm just telling Rebecca about your problem with our species,

Charlotte said, and Roy's face lit up, like it was his speciality subject on a TV quiz show, not that he'd ever watched one, because of the no TV.

He then proceeded to tell us all about the problem with our kind, but he didn't mean rich white people who held dinner parties, he meant all of us. And I wasn't usually a big fan of humans either, but in that moment, I would have wrestled an asteroid to save us all. We'd just seen some dumb movie where some attractive people went into space to do that.

None of them thought what he was saying was harsh, it was dinner and a show. They were used to him.

He lectured us on how the human brain was only concerned with pleasure and imitation, not logic or scientific thinking. I zoned out, wondered if I'd ever really known pleasure, but how it certainly wasn't listening to this man, and I sensed Charlotte was thinking the same. I might have been wrong, they might have had the perfect marriage, but looking around their sad brown home, I doubted it.

He kept saying, I don't mean you good people, but I got the sense he did actually mean me, and his wife, because although she was technically a scientist, it was clear those around the table thought what she did with rocks was not in the same league as what they did with numbers or abstract ideas. To them she was basically as dumb as a rock and I warmed to her more because of it.

The whole table had perked up at least. There was nothing like a common enemy to bring people together, even if it was ourselves.

I didn't like how the evening had turned into a rowdy debate about something too close to home, though. I didn't want to think about thinking, I wanted to talk about it even less, not with these people anyway.

I looked at Isaac across from me, made my face that let him know I was tired and defeated and just wanted dessert and bed. He looked back at me like, You're trying to tell me something and I'm not sure what it is but I know that at least, so cut me some slack. It was good enough.

I felt myself wilting. I asked Charlotte if I could trouble her for some water. There was only wine on the table.

No trouble, Charlotte said, getting up. What kind?

The wet kind, I wanted to say but just looked at her blankly.

We have Sanpellegrino, Fiji, Smart . . .

Tap is fine, I said, and she looked heartbroken. Or whatever, I added, which was also the wrong answer.

I had no idea what she brought back. It was clear and wet and could have been her tears for all I knew. Roy was now telling us the history of thinking, in case we'd missed the TED Talk, which I did, and I was sure now that my husband had told them about Susan, and this wasn't a coincidence. It reminded me that I barely knew him now and it felt like the floor falling away.

I learnt that the idea of logic came about 2,500 years ago and then I zoned out again. I heard the words studies and statistics but was only thinking about dessert. There'd better be dessert. And not some minuscule artist's imagining of a dessert but something a woman can bury her face in, should she wish to. I did an involuntary yawn and they all just looked at me like, Poor thing, we're hurting her brain. Even the rock woman. Traitor.

To show I was listening and not as dumb as they thought, I repeated back what Roy had said, but in regular people terms.

So, you're saying modern science was an invention like everything else and before that we were just thinking about survival, I said.

Exactly, he said, beaming. I could tell he was thinking, God, I'm a great teacher, I made the right career choice, I wouldn't be surprised if this woman is a bit in love with me now. At least he didn't pat me on the head and say, Good girl, have a cookie, although I would have taken a cookie.

What about the imitation bit, I said, trying to keep him on track so we could wrap this up and I could go and hunt for that TV before yawning theatrically and saying we should really be leaving. I wasn't going to mention Susan unless they did.

Well before science as we know it, people must have been doing versions of it, but it was just imitation, Roy said.

They didn't have the words for it, you mean, I said, because I knew a thing or two about them, and pompous men now, it seemed.

People observed things and copied them, Roy said. If there was food somewhere, they might look for it again in a similar place.

He seemed annoyed now, at me, like he knew I was testing him. Why are women always asking me to prove myself to them, prove my worth? he was probably thinking. Meanwhile, the whole time, I was just thinking, Where's your TV, you son of a bitch?

We all want to be like other people, he said. The same goes with thinking.

It was almost like he knew I was fond of a deviant thought and was having a few myself right then, about murdering him, rescuing his wife from a loveless, TV-less marriage. I'd have to come back for her rock collection. How nice it must be to be Susan and not have these trains of thought that only wanted to crash and kill you.

Thinking outside the box, for example, can be uncomfortable, he said, neurologically. So, we think lazily, because it doesn't hurt, he said.

All my thoughts hurt so I understood but I didn't want him to know that.

I was surprised the other men weren't chipping in with their thoughts, but it was late and they'd probably heard all this before. This was probably Roy's party piece. Mine was disappearing.

I excused myself to use the bathroom.

I'm just going for a big think, I said, which made the men laugh and made rock lady blush.

Isaac looked shocked for a second, then saw how much his colleagues seemed to like me and relaxed. I wasn't really going for a big think obviously, quite the opposite.

I went and sat on their very nice, very clean unbroken toilet and leant my head against the wall. I wondered what David and Susan were doing right that second. Watching TV in bed probably, if I knew them at all, which I hoped I did. Was she different now that we'd told her the truth? Or was she still my Susan? David's Susan? I worried for their relationship, because I knew how delicate those could be, how blindsided we were by shared history. If she *had* changed, we'd just have to deal with it. People changed. Susan hadn't previously, not really. But maybe changing a little didn't have to mean the worst. Maybe it could even be a good thing? It was the wine talking, that and the clean bathroom; I was never that optimistic. Well, she knew now anyway, and was still alive. That was a good thing. It was the wine talking.

When I got back to the table, they were still talking about thinking and I was bored of it. The rock lady was bored too and was loading dishes into the dishwasher. I was mad at Isaac for not warning me about how the evening would unfold. It was probably normal for them, but it was too close to home for me. I wished I was in bed with David and Susan watching TV, not thinking, but then I remembered some men liked a mother–daughter thing and had to unthink that and it was exhausting. Men ruined everything. I knew David would be thinking still, though, and felt sad for the TV, and for David, but for me mostly, because I really liked it in Roy and Charlotte's bathroom and wished I could stay in there longer, or forever.

It's so much easier for people to just copy what other people do, Roy was saying. Our daughters, for example, he said, and my ears pricked up at daughters, my eyes unglazed. I didn't know he had a daughter.

They listen to the same music all their friends do, so we can't know if they really like that music or they're just mimicking each other, Roy said. He probably listened to jazz, not because he liked it, but because he thought he was supposed to. Charlotte obviously only listened to soft rock, or worse, Christian rock. Anything with a rock in it. I was getting sick of my own jokes – my brain wouldn't shut up – but they'd got me through the evening.

We should really be making a move, I said, to Isaac mostly. I could get my own dessert on the way home. I deserved it.

It was clear Roy had touched a nerve, but he wasn't sure which.

Charlotte came to say her goodbyes and I genuinely didn't hate her. I wanted to say, You can come and watch TV at our house anytime, but I didn't really mean it.

As soon as we were outside, Isaac apologised.

How could I have known? he said, and I believed him. It was just a coincidence.

You couldn't, I said.

What bores, he said. Just be glad you don't have to work

with them. Your kind are much nicer.

He meant book people. He was wrong, though. They were bores too. I didn't want to be lectured about abstract ideas, but I didn't want to be lectured about how Hemingway really wasn't that bad either.

When did water become a thing? I said as we were driving home.

It's been a thing for ages, Isaac said. Keep up, Kermit.

Kermit? Like Kermit the frog? I said. I think it's you that needs to keep up. I think he's dead.

Isaac braked. You tell me this now?

The car behind beeped. A couple walking a basset hound, both carrying reusable water bottles, stared at us, then carried on walking, probably talking about how awful people that drove cars were. The dog's ears were dragging on the ground.

In the old days people didn't used to drink water all the time and they were fine, I said.

No, they're dead, Isaac said. But he didn't brake, so he wasn't that upset about it.

Not from not drinking water, though, I said.

He didn't have anything to say to that because I was right.

Later, in bed, after resentfully eating ice cream I kept for emergencies, which was the opposite of how you should eat ice cream, Isaac said, He's right, though, Roy, we're not equipped to think deeply, there's that at least.

I think of all people, we know that, I said.

Yes, but it's nice to have someone else say it, isn't it? he said.

He was right, in a way; it was always just us against it all, feeling like we might be going mad from it, that it might not even be real, that we made it all up, or his father did, his grandfather, that this was all a tragic misunderstanding, so yes, it was nice to have some outside validation, if that's what it was, but it felt a lot more like a man telling me he knew better than me, about our own lives, when he couldn't possibly.

They don't know about Susan, though, do they? I asked, just to check.

Of course not, he said, can you imagine?

I could, that was the problem. Sitting there at that table only a few hours ago, I felt like we'd been found out and any moment someone was going to burst in and arrest us.

What did they say while I was in the bathroom? I asked. I didn't want to hear any more but I didn't want to miss anything either; this was how I lived now, how we all lived.

You really want to know? he asked, knowing he wouldn't be able to drag me to anything else for some time now, maybe ever, unless it was in writing that there'd be a fuck-ton of dessert.

I just asked, didn't I?

OK, well, according to Roy we have two problems, one being that as a species we're not actually able to think that deeply and two, that we're programmed to think like other people out of laziness and our desire to fit in. He thinks independent thinking isn't natural and it's a challenge so most people don't bother.

Yeah, I heard that before I went to the bathroom, I said, annoyed he didn't notice when I was there.

Well, you didn't miss anything then, he said. He just says the same thing in different ways over and over until he's sure we all know he's smarter than us.

He basically thinks we're all idiots but it's OK because we can't help it, I said. Taking stupid things men said and making them not so stupid was my forte, it seemed.

Basically, Isaac said.

Except himself obviously.

I feel sad for him – he obviously wanted more for himself, but he's stuck there with you idiots, I said.

But we can't help it, remember? Isaac said, smiling goofily at me.

His wife probably pity-fucked him and then pity-married him, I said.

That's an awful thing to say, Isaac said. Maybe he bought her a really big rock.

Maybe he has a big rock, I said, and he laughed again.

See, we're idiots, always lowering the tone.

His poor wife, I said. I hoped Charlotte had a vibrator that looked like a rock at least. Your friends are weird, I said.

They're not my friends, you're my friend, he said.

As payback I'm dragging you to a reading next week at the bookstore, I said, while he was in a good mood.

Can't wait, he said. I can't promise to understand or even stay awake, but I'll be there in body, he said.

I only want you for your body, I said.

And then we had married-people sex, which was better than no sex, and we both appreciated that the other was consenting at least, which was all you could ask for now.

After the sex, we watched an episode of some joyful queer baking show in silence like God intended. Before we went to sleep I said his buddies would love Susan, but when I said love, I meant harm, and he knew that, so he didn't say anything. I let him fall asleep thinking he'd brought another threat into our lives. Roy wasn't a threat, though; he was all talk.

David

I'd been hanging on Susan's every word since she learned the truth. Like you do when you were in love, or waiting to know results. I was sick, in a way. But I couldn't shake the feeling she wasn't quite herself. She seemed dampened, dulled, just a little, and we'd done that to her. If someone told you the stars didn't sparkle the same as they did before, because of something you did, you'd be devastated. Pizza didn't taste the same now either. It was just bread and tomato and cheese. We'd ruined everything.

If you found out everyone you knew was lying to you your whole life, you'd probably be the same, altered in some way. Her words used to be a constant stream of little explosions, like fireworks, which was always better than one big explosion, in her head.

I didn't care if she stood on the street rapping the Lord's words, as long as she was alive. But that would mean Jesus was saving her, not me; I wanted it to be me, but at the same time I didn't want the responsibility. I couldn't save myself and her. It was all mixed up. I thought saving her would save me, but I think it was just fucking me up, and her, more.

I watched her get a bowl from the cupboard and get the cereal and pour the cereal into the bowl and get the milk and

I watched her stand in the kitchen and eat the cereal and look at something on her phone and it didn't matter if I was there or not and I needed to matter so I said, Shall we get pizza tonight? like she was a child, and I wanted her to like me best.

She looked up and said, Yes! Pizza! I was just thinking I wanted pizza.

She put her dish in the sink and kissed me and I needed to believe she was only thinking about pizza in that moment. It was only me thinking how love transcended everything. It must. She was proof of that if she loved me. Please, God, let her love me, I thought. The rest of us just had to deal with the head-fuckery of it all and hope love would win, and if not, we'd pretend it did anyway because we didn't want to admit we couldn't even do that one thing that made everything slightly less shitty.

She went to work like normal, telling me on her way out the door that some actress made her sweatpants and who was I to disagree? She'd already left anyway, in a cloud of Cardi B's new perfume, Rich.

I stayed home and guarded the fort, by which I mean I took another personal day and played video games until I couldn't feel my legs. I wanted to be right where she left me, just in case she needed me. I read the news on my phone for 10 minutes just to check I could still read, check the world was still there. It was, and it was not great.

She came home like normal, telling me all about what was going on with Harry Styles's hair while doing some stretching and laundry and looking through takeout menus. She collapsed with me in front of the TV like normal. She told me all the TV that was coming soon like normal. I zoned out like normal, to get on her level, but also because I deserved it. I got pizza. I was a hero.

Then she said Stefan said something really funny today, and I thought that must be someone from the gym, but it was a boy's name, so my brain screamed, Who the fuck is Stefan?

Who's Stefan? I said.

Chloe's brother, she said.

Chloe worked at the gym. She mostly ignored me, because Kate probably told her to. Chloe knew about Susan because she'd overheard me and Kate talking one day, then demanded we told her. She wanted it to be that we were having an affair, something juicy; Susan's brain thing was just weird to her, because it was weird, and she didn't really understand it, but didn't want us to think she was dumb, so she said her uncle had something similar and never mentioned it again. The weirdness of it kept her quiet.

What did he say? I said.

Susan had never mentioned Stefan before. Susan had never mentioned any boy before. Other than celebrities. This was new. I didn't like it. She had male friends, but not new ones. Not ones called Stefan. Not ones I was imagining looked like a Hemsworth and understood athleisure wear.

Oh, I can't remember now, but it was funny, she said, laughing at the thing she couldn't remember.

I laughed too because I didn't want to be left out.

I went to the bathroom and texted Kate.

Who the fuck is Stefan? I wrote.

She didn't reply for five minutes, on purpose.

Chloe's brother. Tongue-out emoji.

I tried to forget about it, but she'd never mentioned him before. She'd planted a Stefan-sized seed in my brain and I wanted it gone.

I needed to know more about this Stefan.

The next day on my lunch break I went to the gym to ask

Kate. Since being back at work, every time I left the office, even to pee, I felt my boss watching me, wondering what was going on with me. I told him I was going for lunch but also swinging by the pharmacy if he needed anything, just to keep him guessing.

Chloe was smoking outside when I got there. I always forgot that Kate didn't just do Susan a favour letting her work there; she also did Chloe a favour, because Chloe was a huge bitch and it was OK to say that because she knew she was. Celebrity gossip was her thing that kept her from herself – that and smoking, and winding me up. I asked Chloe how she was and she stubbed out her cigarette. I liked that she didn't vape, it showed real integrity.

Not that great, she said, and told me someone was in rehab. I asked if it was a friend and she shouted at me that it was a celebrity, and called me a fucktard, which was a bit harsh, but she was upset about the celebrity. I offered her my condolences and she told me the celebrity's whole life story and didn't get why I wasn't as upset as she was.

How do you know all this? I asked, because she was talking about this celebrity like she knew them, and I expected her to say the internet, duh, and call me an idiot, but instead, she said, Because I'm depressed, obviously, and rolled her eyes so hard I thought she might have hurt herself, but it was clear she meant, Why aren't you depressed? You should definitely be depressed. She was looking at my shirt of a band no one listened to anymore but that hadn't come back around to being cool again yet. I was depressed, I guess, but I didn't need to advertise it. As far as I could tell, everyone was depressed, or on the depression spectrum. It was only Susan riding the happiness rainbow.

Why are you always here anyway? she said then, taking a break from thinking about all the sad, rich celebrities to think about me. For a second anyway. Only because I was standing right in front of her.

I didn't have to tell her why I was always there anyway, because Kate had her head out the door telling Chloe her break was up and asking why I was always sniffing around now. She knew why, but I still had to explain myself.

Can I talk to you? I said.

Kate looked at her watch.

OK, but only a sec. The smallest amount of time possible.

Chloe went inside and Kate came out. She had to keep one foot on her property at all times or she'd burst into flames, or someone might take it from her maybe.

What was Chloe on about? she asked, and I told her about the celebrity.

Chloe's mastered the art of the one-hand scroll like a motherfucker, she said. I swear to God she doesn't sleep at all, and she can, she just chooses not to.

OK, I said.

So, what is it now? she said, hands on hips.

Has Susan said anything to you at all? I said.

Like what?

Like anything unusual?

Like what? she said, narrowing her eyes so they were basically shut, because she couldn't look at me anymore probably.

About me, OK? I mean, has she said anything about me? I said.

No, David, Susan hasn't said anything about you, she said. And she didn't just mean that day or that week, she meant ever. She was trying to hurt me and it was working.

OK, fine, I get it, I said, leaving.

If you mean, has she said anything about Stefan, that's also a no, she said.

I didn't say anything about Stefan, I said, but then I remembered I'd texted her last night. She knew exactly what I was thinking all the time.

Kate was giving someone across the road the finger now. A Five Guys had opened up across the street from the gym. Kate wasn't happy about it. She said she was going to go in there one day and say, Really? Read the room. One guy is too many.

I started to walk away.

Susan's fine, she shouted after me. She didn't say, But you need help, but she was thinking it. I was thinking it too. But then Kate would never admit Susan had lost something, her sparkle maybe, because that would be too heart-breaking. Susan was fine with her maybe, but different with me. I was the bad man they warned you about. Kate would be on Susan's side anyway, like girlfriends were, when a boy has done something stupid.

I texted her the next day.

You will tell me if she does anything unusual, though, won't you?

No, Kate replied, followed by, Joke, obviously. But she's fine.

The next day I texted her again. She was going to block me soon.

Anything??? I wrote.

No, she said again. I'll let you know if she suddenly tries to beat anyone to death with a yoga mat, she replied.

Thanks, I wrote.

Susan always thought out loud. Always. She thought it meant you had to actually be loud, though, subconsciously maybe, as if to say, If I have to do this ridiculous thing, I'm going to do it in a way that drives you all mad, to teach you all a lesson, for doing this to me. I felt like she was keeping things from me now, though, but I was probably just paranoid. I thought I was being followed by a leaf one day.

It was constant before, because that's how thoughts worked, only most of us knew to ignore most of them, or at least keep them to ourselves. But now it wasn't so constant with Susan; there were definitely more quiet moments. Moments when she must have been thinking something and not saying.

A guy at my work, Simon, never told anyone anything; people found him frustrating, but I liked him. He told me once that he didn't want to bore anyone with his shit, which I thought was really considerate, then I bored him with my shit, because I wasn't as considerate. He told me he couldn't understand Twitter, I told him no one could. People who verbalised their every single waking thought irritated the hell out of me before Susan, but they were still better than the people who felt the need to visually document their every bowel movement online, like they wanted it captured, when most of us wanted to be free of it, flush it away. I wanted to tell them that they didn't have to say everything that came into their heads, but maybe they did. We don't care what you had for lunch, Brian, I wanted to shout, but that wasn't true. I did care. I don't know why exactly but I suspect it had something to do with filling a huge existential hole, but also nosiness. People didn't want thoughts festering inside them, so they got them out, not just Susan. People were terrified of silence. The void was a scary place; I knew because I'd been there. Empty moments magnified how lonely and pointless life was. So, we filled them, with words, bodies, music, food, books, tiny collectible figures of characters from movies that were just plastic and a nightmare to dust. Our kids didn't want to deal with all that crap when we died, they wanted to be free.

People thought words had magical properties that saved us

from the gapingly obvious sadness and futility at the heart of all existence. That wasn't why Susan talked all the time, though. She talked all the time because her mother literally sat her down one day when she was little and told her to always say what she was thinking. And instead of asking why, she did as she was told.

I didn't think anyone else who said everything they thought out loud did it because someone told them to, though. They did it subconsciously, just knowing it would help block the bad things, so life was more bearable. Susan just talked a lot. But it was OK, because I didn't talk enough. Or she did, now she talked the regular amount perhaps.

As far as I knew, before this, Susan wasn't thinking anything she wasn't saying. Her voice replaced my own sometimes. Her life took over mine. Women had been doing that with men for centuries. I was playing with gender roles. I welcomed being overwritten.

If Susan wasn't talking, maybe there wasn't much going on in there. Not that her head was empty, just that it was calm, the odd tumbleweed. I imagined her head a happy place, like Disney World, minus the people. I could have been wrong, and it was just darkness, black metal, but I didn't think so.

I went to meet her for lunch. Mostly to check she was still alive, but also, lunch.

We went across the street to a place called Everything Under the Bun, but vandals/geniuses regularly changed the Bun to Bum. It *was* a burger place at one point in time, but to keep up with our growing demand for all the options all the time it now really did serve everything ironically. They knew Susan in there, because it was right by her work, but also, she liked all the food. She talked to a few people before eventually finding me sitting in a booth looking at the menu like my own head might explode. How was anyone supposed to decide what fries to get when there were 15 options and you wanted them all?

Susan sat down but didn't pick up her menu straight away because she was already reading something on her phone, scroll scroll scroll, tap tap tap.

I couldn't even choose what I wanted to drink but was already thinking about dessert, hoping they just had one, and it was mandatory. My jeans were already snug, though, and I didn't want them to give up on me. I needed them. I wondered if other men worried about what would happen if their jeans broke. This was what I was thinking about while Susan was on her phone. In my defence, I was trying not to think about her, or her brain anyway, which was confusing, because most girls wanted you to think about their brains – anything other than their breasts.

Susan was still looking at her phone. She didn't have to deal with this inner monologue driving us insane. If we were wrong, and she did, she was far better at keeping it a secret than us.

Susan eventually put her phone down and picked up her menu.

What shall I have? she said, only she wasn't asking me, she was asking the menu, if anyone, like it was an oracle.

She stared blankly at the menu, then looked around the room to see what other people were eating. She'd been known to just say she'd have what someone else was having. She put a lot of trust in total strangers. She wasn't overthinking it like the rest of us did. It was just food. There'd be other meals. There'd better be.

Usually, she might talk me through what she was thinking of having. We had pizza last night so not pizza. Or, more likely something like, I saw Paris Hilton make a lasagne while wearing gloves and holding a tiny dog on YouTube so maybe lasagne. Today she didn't even seem hungry, but that couldn't be it, because I'd heard her stomach growl. Unless that noise had been coming from her head, but I didn't think so. She could always eat. It had to be something else.

She ordered a burger and fries and a milkshake, because she was from the 50s, maybe. Or, more likely, that was what people on TV ate, even though it was too much food really. I'd never finished a whole milkshake, despite what my jeans thought.

Susan was on her phone again now. I asked her to tell me what film she wanted to see next, knowing she could talk for hours about that, because her favourite things to read were websites that listed all the new content coming our way, like she needed to know it was definitely coming so she could sleep; it would fill the space between us until our food came anyway. She started talking about some new superhero movie that sounded like all of them so we'd basically already seen it but she didn't say she'd seen something without me, so I relaxed a little. She didn't say she didn't want to see a movie ever again now at least, because what was the point? It would eventually end, and we'd have to go home, go and sit in a different, brighter room, and the crushing void would be back. So that was a good sign.

I told myself I'd never known what any of my other (two) girlfriends were thinking, not that those relationships ended well – none of them died, though, that I knew of. This was different anyway, and I knew that; we couldn't keep it from her forever – this had to be better. Even if her brain was possibly making noises that were only supposed to come from stomachs.

Our food came and Susan kept talking and eating and things seemed normal again. She was putting fries in her burger. I fucking loved this woman. She just needed not to kill herself.

I walked her back to work and kissed her goodbye and she said, I'm OK, you know, but you can buy me lunch any time.

I know you're OK, I said, hoping that saying it would make it so.

Kate was at the door giving me the stink-eye. It was like old times.

Rebecca

We were in bed, pretending to care deeply about a show about rich white people who lived by the beach but had secrets. I didn't really care, no one cared, we just wanted to see inside their fridges. We were both on our phones anyway, when Isaac said, I want to kiss this man, and I was violently shaken out of my head.

What man? I said, looking up from the article I was reading about how important dumb action movies were and how without them we'd all die. It was very on point. My phone's algorithms would freak me out if I understood them.

Apparently, I'd been in my own head so much I'd missed that my husband was actually gay. I wouldn't mind, but I didn't want to think what that said about my marriage, so I told myself I'd just be open-minded and supportive. We'd been watching a lot of baking shows.

Isaac quickly realised how that sounded and looked at me like, I might not know you anymore but I know me, and that's not what I meant.

Whoever wrote this, he said, showing me his phone. He knew how I felt about reading anything other than paper, but he also knew I was a big hypocrite as I was reading my own phone mere seconds ago. It wasn't a Kindle, though, so I was still winning.

Why Distraction Is Good, I read, thinking about how this was a distraction, stopping me from thinking any further about my husband kissing a man and how I would be OK with that and what that all meant.

I want to kiss him too then, I said, wondering what that also meant for our marriage. I didn't even know what this man looked like, someone keeping the tweed industry alive probably, but a kiss was a kiss when you got to my age.

Knowing I didn't have the attention span anymore to read the whole article, not on his phone anyway, not while someone was watching me, he gave me the gist.

He says we all seek out distractions, so there must be a reason, Isaac said.

He being this new man in our relationship. The one with the tweed.

Go on, I said, loving a reason. There weren't enough of them.

Our brains have a limited ability to focus, he continued. If we were having a threesome, it was with a phone.

This was our bedtime routine now. Telling each other things other people had said that justified what we'd done to Susan. It was our foreplay. Maybe other couples did it too, to justify whatever terrible things they'd done, only the terrible things they'd done were eat bacon or day drink or watch a movie starring The Rock and enjoy it, but the internet said it was OK, in moderation, so it was all good. Only ours was fucking up our daughter. Which I didn't think The Rock would be happy about. He had a daughter. I knew that much, because Susan told me.

Did you know distractions can ease pain? he said, still going.

I did know that. I wanted the TV to ease my pain right at that moment, the pain of listening to him.

The rich white people with the secrets on the TV show had kept them in for one more night so I was trying to find something else to watch that wouldn't stimulate any neurons. I settled on *Seinfeld*. We'd thought Susan might like it as a teen, but she just didn't get it. Isaac thought it might be dangerous anyway, because of the music – slap bass was a headfuck apparently. He told me it wasn't even a slap bass, it was a keyboard, but I didn't believe him. And I didn't think that's why Susan didn't get it. Seinfeld was very in his own head and she was the opposite so it didn't resonate. I thought she might at least like Kramer, but no. It's not *Friends*, she said, even though she was 10 when it went off air. It was retro, apparently. It was hard being from the 90s and then the 90s being a thing again when it was barely even a thing then.

Of course I knew that, I said, about distractions helping with pain. I wanted to say, What do you think we were doing all those years, bozo? We're easing the pain of being alive for our daughter, and I'm trying to get in on it, if you give me a chance.

I mean physical pain, Isaac said.

It's all pain, I wanted to say, as if he didn't know that already.

They're doing all these studies on sick kids in hospital, he said, giving them computer games to distract them from the pain. It seems to work, he said. He was thinking about sick kids in hospital and I was wondering what shampoo Elaine used and if they still made it.

Of course it works, I said, they're kids. We could have thrown a ball at Susan's head when she was on her Game Boy and she wouldn't have noticed.

He ignored me.

Anyway, he said, I keep reading all these things about ground-breaking studies but it's stuff we already know. Like what I just said about how playing games on our phones helps distract our brains from pain, or just from the misery of every-day life.

And? I said. I didn't like that he was resisting *Seinfeld*.

I guess the rest of the world didn't, he said. They need it to be spelled out for them, literally, online.

I sat up in bed and looked at him, really looked at him. When did his chest get that hairy? Probably around the same time my big toes started to grow one hair.

You think we're secret geniuses, don't you? I said. You think the world should know what we did? Is that what this is about?

Of course not, he said. I just meant I always knew the best thing we ever did for Susan was get her that Game Boy.

Right, I said and lay back down. Why is it always the Soup Nazi episode? I said, but he ignored me, or hadn't noticed.

It was the perfect segue to a phone addiction, he said, still talking.

She's normal. We did that, I said, not wanting Nintendo to get any credit. They were rich enough.

Keep telling yourself that, Rebecca, I thought. If you say it out loud you might believe it and this man will stop reminding you how terrible a person you are.

When we're on our phones, I said, or watching TV, we know we're doing it because we don't want to feel a certain way, we want to zone out, but when she does it, she's just doing it. Didn't he know our daughter at all?

We don't know that, he said. What about that weird thing that happened at the supermarket?

What, the bread thing? It was a blip. We agreed it was a blip.

And it led to us finally being able to tell her, and that went well, don't you think? I mean, she didn't explode.

I think we need help, he said then. I feel like something else is coming, he said, something big.

I sat back up and muted the TV. Sorry *Seinfeld*. Sad bass noise.

What are you saying? I said. You're scaring me.

Apart from his weird family curse, he'd never shown any signs of feeling anything spooky. No senses, no tingles, nothing he couldn't explain. He was a man of movies but also science. Maybe he was spookier than he'd led me to believe. All this time maybe he hadn't been worrying as much as me because he knew everything was OK, but now, now he sensed something awful. Who was he?

What, you think this man who wrote an article you read, on your phone, can help us? I said, trying to stay calm.

Isn't it worth a shot? he said.

What's his name? I asked.

Martin, he said, showing me the article on his phone again. There wasn't a picture of him, though, just an ad for socks, which was better than porn, I guess, leading me to believe my husband mostly looked at socks.

You really think someone called Martin, who you found on your phone, can help us? I said.

I didn't find him on my phone, he said defensively. I read something he wrote on my phone. He's written other things that aren't on my phone. He's a world-renowned behavioural scientist. He's one of the top researchers in cognitive science. He wrote an award-winning paper on human and animal cognition. He's written books, Rebecca. You like books.

I don't know, I said. I'll have to think about it and to be honest I'm tired of thinking about it.

I unmuted the TV just in time for 'no soup for you' and I couldn't even enjoy it.

We always wondered what the medical profession or scientific community or Oprah would make of Susan, but finding out always came with a risk, and then it might be too late.

David

I was at Susan's parents' apartment for a check-in. We were on tenterhooks now she knew. Or I was; they seemed to be coping better. They hadn't fucked off on a cruise, though, so I figured they were still concerned.

Her father told me he'd found a man he thought might be able to help us. Martin Baldick. Neither of them thought that name was funny so I pretended it wasn't.

I thought it was going to be a quick catch-up, to say nothing was going on with any of us, and how that was good, to laugh at the *Murder, She Wrote* night, say, What was that about? Fingers crossed no one was exploding any time soon! But no.

I was alarmed, because of it being a huge crushing secret up till now, but Susan's mother quickly reassured me they hadn't done anything yet; it was mostly her husband that wanted to endanger us all.

He's some cognitive scientist he's obsessed with, she said, ignore him. It will be someone else next week.

Someone with an equally hilarious name, I hoped.

But I couldn't ignore him. I knew Susan's father now – he'd picked food off my face, hugged me. I knew if he was seriously thinking about this, it was important to him.

He's convinced this man can help Susan, Susan's mother said, but we don't know that. He thinks we should come forward to this man and tell him about Susan and the curse, all so he can sleep better at night.

That's not why, Susan's father said, to me, shaking his head. Hear me out, he said, both of you.

He's mad, Susan's mother said, to me, shaking her head.

There's no evidence this man, this scientist – bald dick bald dick bald dick, my brain hummed – will know anything more than we already do, Susan's mother said. He's been convinced for years the scientific community will find out about her eventually, but he thinks this way, at least we stay in control, by offering her up to them.

That's not what I mean at all, Susan's father said, to his wife. I just think it's an option. They might be able to help us. Who knows what they know now, or what they're on the brink of knowing? In the back of his mind he was always hoping for a cure, that this was a medical thing, and not a curse, because those weren't real, and he needed this to be real so he could fix it.

I told him I understood. I told her I understood. I didn't.

They both seemed to be unravelling, and I was privately too. I remembered Susan's father saying to me once, Don't you have those nightmares where someone comes and bundles Susan off into a van and takes her to some lab and does thought experiments on her, to see if they can make her head explode? And I said, No, but thanks, I will now. He apologised for planting that seed but I could tell he was disappointed, like I might not really be that in love with his daughter.

Susan's mother apparently hadn't thought about this either, maybe because he had kept it from her or maybe he'd just assumed she had similar nightmares, because that was what parents did: they lay awake at night thinking of the worst things that could happen to their children.

He might be able to help, Susan's father said. If we ask him for help first, he might not betray us, he might feel a sense of duty rather than exploit us for his own gain, he said, about this scientist man he found on the internet. He was from a different generation. He didn't really know the horrors that existed at the end of your fingertips. He still saw fingertips and not the madness he was engaging in.

You're not thinking straight, Susan's mother said. Everyone will want to get their hands on her, everyone, not just the scientists; the girl who can't think – she'll be headline news.

She still thought in headlines and print because she was from the 90s and worked in a bookstore. Words were her currency. I could have reassured her that she'd only be headline news for a few days, until another shooting or the next Taylor Swift song dropped, but I didn't think it would help. No one wanted to think their daughter was less important than Taylor Swift.

So, we should go to the scientist first, Susan's father said, but what he meant was, I can't do this alone anymore, even though we were standing right there. He meant, We need more people to protect her. And when he put it like that, we had to agree, because we were exhausted too.

Rebecca

The dinner party haunted me, or more, the missing TV did. I needed to think about something other than TV. If my husband was thinking about other men, why shouldn't I think about something else? Another woman maybe. Then I saw a poster at the bookstore for a talk called How Great Leaders Lead Leaders and the woman on the poster had really great hair, and I wanted great hair too. Just because Susan couldn't think, didn't mean I couldn't. The subject of the talk wasn't really something I cared about, but everyone wanted to be a cult leader now, it seemed, because it meant there'd be a documentary made about you eventually. I just wanted a night out of my own head, to see what other people were thinking about, but also find out what products this woman used. I could have looked online, but then there was always the chance that after seeing one photograph of her and her perfect glossy mane I would then have to see them all, and then I'd be frantically scrolling, having to see them all, wondering what she was having for lunch, whose arm that was, all because I couldn't just accept my hair the way it was, average. I felt better knowing other people were still out there thinking all the things Susan couldn't, though. Even if it was all not very subtly disguised guides on how to start a cult. I really needed to get out of the house, but out of my own head more, and into this other woman's head, the one with better hair. I had to believe that I could still be a leader one day, and not just on my mental ward.

When I told Isaac I was going out, he said, Stay here, I will talk at you, for free. Don't we talk? Is he handsome, this talker?

I said it was a woman.

I see, he said.

I wondered what one wore to hear someone talk, but I never knew what one wore to do anything, so I gave up and just put on a sweater I wore to the cinema last time we went and hoped no one noticed it had a few popcorn kernels stuck to it.

I almost didn't go. I almost went to see a film instead, because then I would get words and pictures, and snacks, and the movie theatre was just around the corner. But the ticket for the talk wasn't cheap. I knew movie snacks weren't cheap either, but they were snacks, important, you made exceptions. I thought ideas were free too, but apparently not.

The talk was taking place at a warehouse that wasn't even a warehouse. It was a swanky private members' club that had a swanky private library that also had a bar. All libraries should have a bar. I didn't know that was a thing, or I would have dreamed about it sooner. It was all very posh, or felt posh. It was just an aesthetic. But I wasn't that easily fooled. There was a lot of velvet, too much, enough to attract vampires. The furniture was all old and leather to match what the hipsters were wearing, but it was probably faux leather anyway, because they were all vegan. People were blending in too well, almost camouflaged. These people wore perfume called Old Library. There were giant ancient rugs, but on the wall, which was weird. There was a globe masquerading as a drinks cabinet somewhere there, and if I got bored, I'd try to find it.

You could buy all these things on Amazon; they probably

did. I was too suspicious, too sceptical, too cynical, to enjoy anything now. Some of the young shiny people looked like they thought it was Harry Potter World. Susan would be the same. She might think it was a Disney library and want to dance around. She would appreciate it more than me anyway. She wouldn't be wondering who did their cleaning.

My seat was near the back, thankfully, and I smiled and said hello to the nice young shiny people next to me and they smiled back, then went back to looking at their phones. I felt like I was waiting for a play to start. There was an air of excitement and anticipation. Not from me, but from the young shiny people. I wanted to ask someone if there was a TED Talk about Ted Bundy but no one would catch my eye, but also, I realised that wasn't something you wanted to hear from a stranger sitting next to you.

I already knew I didn't care what this woman giving the talk had to say, because she wanted me to care too much, wanted to save me. She called herself a thought leader, which made me vomit in my mouth, just a little. Soon, she'd appear, in a turtleneck probably, pace the stage, press her hands together, wishing she was Steve Jobs. Why would anyone want to be Steve Jobs over Steve Martin? I braced myself.

Get ready to have your mind blown, someone whispered, and I felt lightheaded. I wanted some Morris dancers wearing Trump masks to come out — something awful, something to teach these people not to trust dark rooms.

You'd think it was a secret gig of some band that only did secret gigs so people thought they were super cool because being regular cool wasn't enough. People brought bar stools in from the bar next door; people were turned away and were lurking outside. I worried Kanye would appear any minute, like these people had conjured him.

A woman, who wasn't a rapper as far as I knew but I wouldn't put it past her to have a go, finally appeared on stage and the room went quiet.

Successful leaders love leading and love leading others to lead, she said and everyone in the room nodded and I was still thinking about how I wanted her to lead me to her hair salon.

Successful leaders want everyone around them to share in their success, she said. True leadership is not about power, she said, it's about all of us. People clapped. Not me, but some people.

True leadership is about being an enabler, she said. But the good kind. By the end of our time here tonight I hope to have enabled you all to be your best selves. More clapping.

True leaders can make several decisions in the time it takes an average person to understand the question, she said. But don't worry if you don't think you can do that, I'm here to show you leadership is something you can learn, that will quickly become unconscious, automatic. You won't even have to think about it, she said. It was like she knew this was what we all secretly wanted, to not think. All this talking about thinking, this whole pseudo-intellectual industry, was just that, another thing to consume, something to keep us from thinking how we were all going to die.

She was talking my language then, this woman, with a mane any horse would be envious of, trample someone even, to learn the secrets of.

Leadership is really decision making, she said. It's using your intelligence to pinpoint all the variables, to understand how things interconnect, to see patterns, to make solutions. It will become instinct to you, she said, a gut feeling. Tonight I can give you the foundations, but I also recommend you buy my book and listen to my podcast. Next month we have JoJo Siwa popping in to share her leadership advice.

Something we all have in common is that we all want to advance our careers, and increasing our leadership abilities will ensure you become invaluable, she said.

I had to admit, I did want to be invaluable, and surely having better hair would do that.

Part of being a good leader but also a good person is allowing other people to feel like they can speak up, she said. A confident person encourages other people to be confident. A good leader encourages other people to make their own better decisions. My book has a whole chapter about the importance of being an excellent communicator so you can communicate your vision so the people around you can make that happen, she said, but not being able to communicate it to us now, in that room, we had to read it, and again, she was talking my language, reading.

What we want to do as the leaders of the leaders of the future is challenge people to think, she said. We must understand not just our own minds, but the minds of the people around us. We must use this knowledge to push people out of their comfort zones. Lazy thinkers are your enemy, she said. We want people to be uncomfortable – this is where the real growth happens.

If you're not thinking, you're not learning, not growing, she said. And I got a lump in my throat for Susan, who we'd purposely stunted. Maybe now she could finally grow. It would be uncomfortable for us all for a while, but this woman had made me feel like we could do it. God damn it, I'd been mind-fucked.

We need to care about the people around us and their growth. A good leader is always looking for the next leader, she said. Be mindful and reward people when they do good work. Leaders know the importance of feedback. Leaders are always looking to grow themselves, she said, and I nodded along with everyone else in that room, could feel a clap coming on, but then she said, Teamwork makes the dream work, and I sat on my hands. Live that truth, she said, and I was sure she was going to disappear in a cloud of smoke, but she wasn't done just yet.

Learning to lead the leaders of tomorrow is about creating a positive, safe environment, motivating people to be their best selves, she said. There is space for all of us to be our best selves, she said, making some hand gestures like she used to work as a magician's assistant, and I hadn't googled her so couldn't know for sure.

And one last very important thing, always lead with your heart, she said, before leaving the stage to rousing applause and a few whistles. Everyone loved a heart, especially if it was an emoji or on a T-shirt, which it was, because she was selling T-shirts in the foyer that said Lead With Your Heart, when I swore earlier she'd said gut, but no one wanted a T-shirt with some guts on.

I couldn't know for sure, if Susan had been in that room, whether she would have thought about what was being said, or tried to at least, and then her head might have exploded, or if she was more like her mother really and would only have been thinking about the woman's hair.

Everyone but me seemed to leave energised and enlightened; people seemed to have already learnt something and were leading other people to bars and restaurants.

For them this had been a fun night out, something they saw advertised in the *Guardian*, but to me it was dangerous, propaganda even. She'd wanted us to think we were part of it, but really, the lectures-as-entertainment industry was still mostly all old white men, who still wanted some control over a world that was rapidly slipping through their fingers.

I came away feeling cheated, like I'd just eaten an obscene amount of Chinese food but my stomach didn't believe me because the MSG had fucked with my brain. It was a shallow offering. More about razzle dazzle and merch sales than content. The true content was lost in the ticket price and darkness, the eager faces, who didn't care what this woman was really saying, just that they were there, and had the T-shirt to show it #gettingmymindblown.

As I stood outside, debating if I should go straight home or get something to eat, because I was thinking about Chinese food now, a woman approached me.

It's a bit much, isn't it? she said.

Yes, I said, very. This woman could read my mind.

First time? she said.

Is it that obvious?

Most people come in groups, then go off and talk themselves to death about it, she said.

Better than thinking, I said carelessly.

If you're interested, I'm part of this women's philosophy group, she said, and I must have done something with my face because she said, It's really chill, promise, we're just a group of women into philosophy who want to be able to talk about it freely, without men telling us what we should think.

Sounds great, I said. I like philosophy, I said, but it sounded like I was saying, I love sandwiches.

It's not like this, she said, promise.

Great, I said, because this felt a bit like a cult.

You should come anyway, she said. It's tomorrow actually.

We swapped numbers. She said she'd text me the deets and I didn't say, That's not a word, I just held my breath, smiled, pretended I might actually go. But then it was tomorrow and I had all these feelings still but nowhere to put them so I thought,

What the hell? I'd give them to these strangers and then run away and be done with it all. I was a woman who went out at night alone now, after all. Why stop now?

The group was call Hyp. Short for Hypatia. I was just glad it wasn't some weird new workout like day raving for busy mums that I'd been tricked into going to, because that could happen.

The woman who invited me, Krystal with a K, met me outside. She'd said to text when I got there. I'm outside, I said, feeling like a drug dealer, or her dad.

David

I showed up at the gym to take Susan to lunch the next day too, only she was already at lunch, with Chloe and her brother.

You just missed them, Kate said.

Oh, I said. If she was at lunch with Chloe I wouldn't have cared. It was this mysterious brother of hers that was driving me insane, but Kate didn't seem concerned or interested.

Don't you think it's weird? I said.

What? Susan going to lunch? she said, looking at me like I was the dumbest piece of shit, like she really should have stopped Susan ever getting involved with me.

No, this new guy, I said.

Chloe's brother? she said, still looking at me like I was dogshit.

Yes, Chloe's brother, I said.

He's really not that weird, she said, pretending to do some paperwork even though there wasn't any paper, there, anywhere.

I mean that he's sniffing around, I said.

Look, she said, I can just tell you where they went and you can go and join them.

Or you can just pretend I wasn't here, I said.

Now that would be weird, she said. Why can't you just go and join them?

Because that would be weird, I said.

Weirder than me lying to Susan about you being here? she said, peering into my soul and yawning.

Different weird, I said.

She let out a huge sigh. Fine, she said. But it's only you being weird. Susan's fine.

That's not comforting, I said.

It's not my job to comfort you, she said.

Ugh, I said.

Ugh back, she said, then walked off into the gym and I didn't blame her. I was annoying myself.

I thought about following her, asking where they went again, but she might not tell me. Also, I wasn't allowed in that bit of the gym. I assumed that if I stepped over the line a girl gang would appear, all with shaved heads, piercings, all wielding things that definitely weren't handbags, all full of rage and ready to pound the first man they saw, and it would always be me.

I didn't want to go and join them for lunch anyway, I wanted to spy on them, so Kate not telling me where they were was better for everyone. I skulked off and got a slightly grey-looking egg sandwich from the store next door and ate it on a bench and went back to work and tried not to think about Chloe's brother, but this Stefan was all I could think about.

Susan was incapable of lying, so when she came home that night I asked her what she did for lunch.

Chloe and Stefan took me to this new place, she said.

I see, I said, which was what people said if they could not see but hoped that saying it might make it so.

She didn't say, He's amazing, go all moony, tell me I should see his biceps, so I tried to relax. She started telling me about this sandwich she'd had and I remembered she was more into sandwiches than men, even me maybe, and I was fine with that. I tried not to think about how she had an amazing new sandwich at a fancy new place and I had a suspect grey one on an old bench.

I tried not to think about it, about him, Stefan, but I couldn't. It was weird. Up till then there hadn't been any new people in our lives, or her life more specifically, and now there was. Stefan. Who I suspected of being called Steven really, or Stephen, but he probably thought the f sounded exotic. F for gonna Fuck your girlfriend.

I wanted to text Kate and interrogate her some more, but I knew she'd just tell me to chill out, or fuck off; both were good advice. I thought about telling Susan's father, but I didn't want to worry him unnecessarily. I needed to know if we really should be worried or if this was just me going through something, I suspected it might. If I started sniffing her, or looking for odd hairs, I'd know it was me just losing my mind and not Susan, and I wouldn't have to tell them because they'd see because the men in the white coats would come and get me. Although it could be women in white coats now, but that wasn't comforting.

I needed to know more about this Stefan if I was going to get any sleep.

I thought the best thing to do was ask Chloe, which meant going back to the gym and hoping Kate didn't see me.

Chloe was smoking a cigarette outside when I got there and blew smoke in my face, and I couldn't tell her it was disgusting, remind her she worked at a gym, because you could be anything now, even a hypocrite.

Nice, I said, batting it away like a deranged kitten.

She told me once, if I'd seen the things she'd seen, I'd smoke too, but I was sure she'd gone to school with Kate and Susan, and had quite a nice, normal middle-class life. But then she did end up teaching hip-hop abs, and I didn't know if anyone ever meant to do that.

I was glad she was outside anyway, so I didn't have to go in and ask Kate to get Chloe for me and annoy everyone.

What's the deal with your brother? I said, straight to the point, wanting her to know I could be the tough guy, if you ignored everything else about me.

What's he done now? she said.

I mean, why is Susan having lunch with him? I said, still batting her smoke away.

Is she? she said, glaring at me.

The other day, I said.

Oh, you mean, when the three of us went to lunch, she said.

Yes.

The three of us went to lunch, she said, sticking her tongue out.

I want to meet him, I said, surprising myself.

Why are you being weird? Chloe said, squinting at me, but she probably just had smoke in her eyes.

Because, I said, really mature.

Because . . . she said.

Because Susan has never mentioned anyone before, I said, telling her too much.

Oh, Chloe said. Interesting. She pursed her lips.

It's not interesting, it's worrying, I said, wishing I hadn't said anything.

Everything worries you, she said.

So, should I be worried? I said.

Look, I don't know what's going on with you or Susan, but sure, you can meet him, if it's that important to you.

It is, I said. Because it was now, it seemed. He had to be the good twin, surely.

Susan had lunch with people all the time. It was because it was a guy, even though Chloe was there. Maybe it was a ruse. Maybe she left early and they went and fucked behind the bins. Not Chloe and her brother obviously, I mean Susan and Stefan.

It was because Susan made a point to tell me about him. And not because she knew it would make me jealous – Susan had never been like that – but because he'd made an impression on her. And I was the last person to do that, as far as I knew. The male ego is the saddest, most fragile thing, like a day-old kitten born on a motorway.

I couldn't be mad at Stefan for liking Susan. I got it. I liked her the most. He probably liked her for the same reason everyone did, because she wasn't in her head, like most other people. Most other people were egomaniacs, or worrying about stupid things all the time, thinking the joy out of all life. Hi!

Chloe went on to tell me how two years ago, Stefan's fiancée and unborn child were killed in a car crash, and how it was the saddest fucking thing ever, and how he was hard to be around after that because he made everyone sad, and no one knew if he'd get over it, but he did. It happened, and it was the worst thing that could have happened, but after that he felt like he could cope with anything else the world threw at him, she said. It was awful, what she was telling me, but I still suspected he had rock-hard abs and would look better grieving than I would.

I always thought that was a cliché, she said, something people who suffer great tragedies say.

Is he OK now? I asked. Moments ago, I'd wanted him dead, and now I was rooting for the poor guy.

Oh, he's fine, she said. He just gave up thinking.

He gave up thinking? I said.

So he didn't have to think about what happened ever again, she said, like it made perfect sense.

Sounds like denial to me, I said. Didn't you try to get him to see someone?

Of course we did, she said, frowning, but he worked it out himself. Something awful happened, it happened, and he moved on. He just has to live on the surface now, that's all, nothing wrong with that, she said, because she lived there too. It's working for him, she said. I mean, people think he's a stoner, but he is sometimes, so it's fine.

Then he met Susan, she said, and they were like two peas in a pod.

What do you mean? I said.

I mean, you know what she's like, she's not very deep, is she? But people gravitate towards her. She's easy to be around.

I was just standing there thinking about how Chloe was much deeper than I thought, and it might explain why she seemed so pissed off all the time. She was jealous of Susan maybe, like we all were.

Don't worry, he doesn't want to fuck her, she said then, which was what I'd been waiting to hear. Stefan just likes having someone he can be himself with. He doesn't have to pretend he's smarter or deeper or anything with her. You know what she's like, she said again.

I do know, I said.

He didn't know she was like that because she had something wrong with her brain, though, she said then. But he does now.

What the fuck, Chloe?

He's my fucking twin, she said. We tell each other everything. He doesn't care anyway. He thinks brains are stupid.

Of course he does, I said, shaking my head now.

His fiancée and unborn child died, she reminded me, like that made it OK, like his grief made him better at keeping secrets, and I almost felt better about it all for a second, until I remembered something similar happening to an actor recently.

You know, the same exact thing happened to an actor recently, I said. People spent so much time online, so much time invested in strangers' lives, lives that were filtered, faked – no one knew what was real anymore; I certainly didn't.

Really? she said. Then, Wow, there's so much tragedy.

I watched her stub her cigarette out and go back inside.

It's just lunch, you moron, she shouted over her shoulder.

I felt enraged then, because I didn't know if any of what she'd told me was true or just a narrative she'd stolen to fit her needs, but I wasn't good at knowing what to do with feelings like that, so my brain sort of did a sad fart and fizzled out.

It was just lunch. It didn't have to mean anything. If only my brain would believe that and shut the fuck up.

Rebecca

It's OK that I'm here? I said, looking at the apartment building, expecting to be asked to move along at any moment, because I wasn't fancy enough for it.

Of course, Krystal said, taking me inside and up some stairs to where another woman was peering out of an apartment door.

The more the merrier, the woman in the doorway said, taking my arm and leading me inside. It was nice to be touched. If a man had done that, I probably wouldn't have gone inside with him, but Krystal with a K seemed like good people. She was just bad at spelling maybe, or her parents were.

This was Bea at the door, the leader of this merry (as in drunk) band of women. A tall woman with ample bosoms, wearing jodhpurs, but no sign of a horse. She could make good money as a dominatrix, and probably did. I didn't know her. I didn't know any of them. I could be their sacrificial offering for the night, but judging by how white and plush the carpets were, I doubted it.

I was disappointed they weren't all dressed in men's suits with fake beards and top hats and monocles even, smoking pipes, a room of Jo Marches. Maybe they only did that on a full moon.

Bea welcomed me into her home. If my home was as fancy, I would welcome people into my home too, but it wasn't, so I didn't. Someone handed me a drink. Bea informed me that Hypatia of Alexandria was the martyr of female intellectuals, a tragic heroine. I could google her if I wanted. I should google her. She's famous for two things, she told me, her philosophical, mathematical and astronomical teachings that were way ahead of her time, because she was a badass, one of the women pointed out, and the fact that she was brutally murdered for it. Another woman in a bold patterned romper I couldn't pull off pointed out she was murdered because she was hot, and everyone knows you can't be smart and hot or you're a witch.

Is that true? I said and they looked at me like, Maybe you shouldn't be here, there's a McDonald's across the street. And for a second I considered it. The call of the fries. Why was I even there? To make up for the fact that I had raised a daughter not to think, but so that I knew others did? One more beautiful idiot wouldn't undo years of hard work smashing the patriarchy, surely? Thankfully, I wasn't allowed more time to dwell on my crimes against the sisterhood because a woman with drawn-on eyebrows was shouting, Do the speech! at Bea.

We're not really taking new members, Bea said, but there's no harm, I suppose.

I didn't tell her I didn't want to join their club anyway.

Bea invited me to sit so I sat. I had to stop myself stroking the velvet couch. And the carpets really were so plumpfy, like a field of rabbits that didn't mind us sitting on them, but if a man came in, they might bite. Two women sat either side of me. Krystal sat on the floor on a large velvet cushion. She was younger than me. Her knees could take it.

Ancient Greece laid the philosophical foundations for much

of Western liberal democracy, Bea said, making sure I knew she thought I was dumb and didn't deserve to hear her words but nonetheless I was there now and she loved the sound of her voice so she would do her speech.

But women by and large didn't really contribute because they weren't allowed, except for our Hypatia, she continued, pacing the room now, with her glass, which could have been filled with virgins' blood for all I knew, but was probably Châteauneuf-du-Pape.

Is that her? I said, pointing to a picture of a beautiful Greek woman on the wall, but it could have been this woman's mother, who liked a toga party as much as the next gal.

The woman sitting to my right laughed, because it was obviously her. Her laugh sounded like a fake laugh a character on a sketch show might have. I felt bad for her. It was like the time I didn't know what a flat white was and the barista almost asked me to leave.

Beautiful, brilliant, bold – the Greeks adored her, Bea continued, even the men, who should have been furious at her for daring to venture into their world, but they were too in awe of her.

Because she was so hot, the woman to my left said. But she wasn't saying it like a man might; it was more a fact. Her hotness.

And you're not allowed to be smart and hot, I said, so they knew I was keeping up and should actually be there.

Right, the woman sitting next to Krystal said, and I relaxed a little. I still had my coat on and one hand in my pocket on my phone, though, just in case I needed to google 'what to do if you think you might have somehow wandered into a cult'.

It was because they all adored her that made her murder all the more confusing, Bea said. I mean, it was brutal.

Brutal, the woman with the laugh repeated, shaking her head now, looking like she might cry.

Why did they kill her? I asked.

Why does any man kill a woman? Bea said.

Tell the story about Hypatia again, two of the women said in unison, like little girls before bed. They sat on cushions before her like she was the queen or their mother or the queen's mother, and Bea rolled her eyes again, but she loved it, loved them.

Haven't you heard it enough? Bea said, chastising them. Don't show off in front of our guest.

I can google it. Or go to the library, I added quickly. I work in a bookstore. Is there a book? I sounded pathetic. I needed her to know I could read something other than my phone. I needed her to know that books were actually my thing.

It's fine, Bea said. Stories like hers are supposed to be told like this, not in stuffy libraries. She meant, Please don't google her in my bathroom. Show some respect.

And so, Bea told us the story of Hypatia, one they'd all heard many times but never tired of hearing, because, feminism.

Historians estimate that she was born around 350 AD to the mathematician and philosopher Theon, who encouraged her education from a young age. She didn't like her classes with her father, though, and found her own ways to learn.

God, she was great, one of the women sighed, and the other women all nodded and sighed in agreement. I wondered if any of them had kissed her painting when no one was looking. Or maybe we all had to kiss it on our way out.

Other than maths, Hypatia loved astronomy, Bea continued.

Who doesn't? the woman to my left said. I was relieved she didn't put her hand up to high five me because I never quite mastered how to do that without looking stupid. Bea gave her a look that said, Do I need to press the button that sends in the hounds?

She built these amazing tools for measuring and examining celestial bodies. A woman, who wasn't even supposed to be bothering herself with these things. She wasn't only studying them but advancing the study of them. More than the men were doing at the time, Bea said.

Too busy wanking over her, Krystal said, winking at me, but Bea chose to ignore her because she wasn't talking about female masturbation and the power of the female orgasm, maybe, but only if it was self-given.

She also joined the Neoplatonic school of philosophy and wore robes that previously only men wore, Bea continued.

She would go into the city in her robes and talk to people about her thoughts on Plato, who everyone was really into back then, and people actually listened to her because she had this power, Bea said.

And she was hot, I said, joining in, and they all laughed and nodded. Even Bea. She'd finished all her virgins' blood. I liked these women. I was glad I didn't know all their names yet, though, so there was little danger of me getting too attached and then feeling bad when I didn't ever get invited back.

As is the way, Bea said, it was only after her death that people really appreciated her.

Tell her about the celibacy thing, Krystal said, and I had the feeling she might be a sexual deviant and I liked her more for it.

I was just getting to that, Bea said, a little put out. Hypatia was extremely smart and extremely beautiful but also extremely chaste. She never married or showed any interest in men, Bea said.

I wish I'd been that smart, the woman next to Krystal said.

Ancient Greek society saw celibacy as a virtue, Bea continued, so to be almost sexless, above such things, made people respect her. She wasn't seen as a threat because she wasn't going to use her womanly ways. It almost didn't matter how smart she was, as long as she wasn't going around seducing everyone.

Because hot and smart is deadly, I said, getting the hang of it, but also thinking of poor Susan, who was destined only to be hot.

Exactly, Bea said, almost smiling at me, but not yet.

But that didn't mean everyone wasn't always trying to seduce her, Bea continued. People couldn't help themselves.

Students were always infatuated with her, Bea said, and she just had to fend them off, I guess.

But then I was starting to wonder what TV I was missing, what delicious shows Isaac might be watching without me. Would I be able to catch up? Would I ever be able to hold a conversation with anyone outside this room ever again? I must have made an involuntary move that told Bea I was thinking I should probably leave soon, or worse, was bored.

I haven't told you the best bit yet . . . you will stay, won't you? she said.

Of course, I said, but still not taking my coat off. No one seemed to mind. They were women who understood the importance of armour.

One male student was a little too persistent, Bea continued. Always professing his love for her. One day she just lifted her skirt, took off her sanitary pad — or whatever they used back then, probably some type of linen — and threw the bloody rag at him. Bea acted this out as she spoke, flinging her imaginary sanitary napkin at us. I thought of her as more of a menstrual cup woman, so I ducked, much to the amusement of the other women, who were used to these sorts of shenanigans. This was my first shenanigan, if you could have them singularly.

Hypatia said to him, Your love is just lust, you have no idea about the reality of women, so here it is. Now you're cured of your obsession with me, or something like that. But in Greek.

The women were all still laughing about Bea throwing her imaginary sanitary towel at us and me ducking.

She sounds amazing, I said, because she did. I felt ashamed I hadn't known about her before. Where had Hypatia been all my life? Where had these women been? Then I remembered I had sacrificed this for my daughter.

Was he cured? I asked.

Who knows? Bea said. She ignored him anyway and went back to her studies. Men started to be more wary of her after that, though. They didn't want to just fuck her anymore, they wanted to kill her. She was a threat to everything they knew.

She was a pagan, Krystal said to me, and you know how people feel about them.

I do, I said, because I did.

Bea seemed to have finished her story now and was rooting around a drinks cabinet for more wine. There was talk of going to the store. Someone put in a request for sour cream Pringles.

I'd been holding in a pee all night and it was getting painful so I decided to be brave and see if I could find the bathroom without alerting anyone to my situation. If I found a room that was a sex dungeon, or where they did the sacrificial ceremonies, or just where Bea kept her unused exercise bike, covered in a thick layer of dust, surrounded by boxes of stuff she really needed to sort out and take somewhere else, I would just pretend I hadn't seen anything.

Looking around at all the closed doors, any one of them

could have been the bathroom. People needed to label their rooms better. I was about to risk one when I heard a strange noise, like an animal, or a person doing an impression of an animal, coming from behind one of the other doors.

Just as I was about to open it, the woman who had been sitting on the floor with Krystal was there.

It's just there, she said, pointing to a door opposite.

Oh, I said, thanks. I started towards the door.

They scraped her skin off with oyster shells, she said.

I stopped and looked at her like, Is that some new beauty treatment I don't know about because I'm not rich like you? But she didn't actually look rich. She wasn't draped in anything. Nothing dangled or glimmered. She had mild chin acne. She could have been Susan's age.

Hypatia, she said.

Oh, God, that's awful, I said, because it was awful. Also, weird.

They took her to a church and stripped her and beat her and literally tore her limbs off, she said.

I was almost wetting myself now but couldn't say, Sorry, I'm in a huge deal of pain here, not after hearing that.

Religious fucks, I said. Which she deemed a suitable response.

There was that noise again, behind one of the doors. We both looked at it.

Bea's husband keeps exotic animals or something, she said. Or they have someone held captive in there. She shrugged.

I laughed. Right.

FYI, she has the best hand soap, the girl said, walking off.

I peed and didn't break anything or steal anything, then slunk back to the group and hid at the back. I wanted to ask someone about the girl in the hallway, who had disappeared now, but thought they might say something like, Oh, she's been dead for five years. I figured she just got an Uber and left already.

The rest of the evening was spent talking about the huge resurgence in astrology and why people needed it so much now, but then someone mentioned Cher and it quickly descended into a ranking of the best Chers. *Moonstruck* Cher came out on top, closely followed by *Mermaids* Cher. It seemed to be one thing women could agree on. I didn't tell them the Cher workout video had been a close friend once.

As I was leaving, Bea air-kissed my cheek and said she hoped I would come again and promised it would be less Cher next time and one of the women booed.

OK, Bea said, maybe it will be – maybe we'll just start a Cher fanclub, leave the important discussions to the men. She winked at me then and smiled. A real smile. She was saving it till the last minute.

Oh, the men are all talking about Cher too, I said, and tried to wink at her, but she was already talking to someone else.

I didn't think I'd enjoy being part of something like that, but I did enjoy it, once I relaxed. I used to do things like that for Susan, but then when she grew up, I went back to my old ways. I'd tried to keep a toe in, but it always felt like a lot of effort without her around. This was my foot firmly out, an ankle even, to show myself I could still do it.

I was still glad to see the TV when I got home, though. I worried a few hours immersed in something more intellectual might have made it disappear.

David

The next day I had a shitty day at work. The time wouldn't go.
I didn't understand what my job was really and no one seemed
bothered by this and my mind was elsewhere anyway. On the
way home I thought about how Susan didn't ever have a shitty
day at work and it made my shitty day shittier. Why should she
have such an easy life? I thought, yanking my shoes off when
I got in, slinging them across the hall, making our imaginary
cat flee.

Susan didn't understand, if she even noticed. The goldfish
that lived inside the bowl where her brain should be would
quickly forget I was mad, at her, what I said. I was just another
tired, grumpy man taking out his frustrations on the unfairness
of life on someone who mostly made it better.

She'd been laughing at something stupid on TV. I wanted
to be the one laughing at something stupid on TV but I had
other things on my mind, like how my job was slowly killing me, and then there was the whole possibly-exploding-
girlfriend thing, or just my paranoia about it. I couldn't switch
off as easily, not that she was ever switched on. She couldn't
understand that I wasn't ready to laugh yet and I couldn't tell
her to stop laughing because then I was a monster. I was, but
not for that reason. I wanted to be able to laugh like that.

I wanted some fun. I wanted not to think. Just for a second.

I wanted to say, Why do you get to have all the fun? but I knew why, so instead I said, It's not that funny, jeez, and left the room. I had shoes to wrangle, an imaginary cat to make it up to.

I felt like a dick, but I was afraid if I stayed in that room any longer, I'd say something worse, or shout at her, or want to shake her; I didn't trust myself anymore. I was a liar, after all. Not something I ever wanted to be. Wanting to shake her was awful. Fizz her up a little. See what would happen. It was like that thing when someone told you not to press a button, and then all you wanted to do was press the damn button. Sometimes I wanted her to explode, just so it had happened.

I wondered if Stefan would want to shake her. I didn't know anything about him other than I didn't want to think about him. How dare he come into our lives, and worse, my head. A new person now, when Susan was maybe coming undone, could only mean something bad.

When – if – Susan's head exploded, Stefan would probably throw himself on her, be a hero. He was probably a hands-on person, with the giant manly hands and even bigger biceps I imagined he had. I was more of a stand-at-the-back-and-watch-her-pop man, even after I'd put in all the legwork, helped keep her alive for so long. I didn't really think that. I knew all along it was never me.

Her father once told me that wanting to shake her was a perverse way for me to deal with her mortality but was quite normal. I was a pervert and a monster then. It always made me laugh when they told me any of this was normal. This was during one of my meltdowns. I was always afraid her parents would move and not tell me, so I couldn't just turn up on their doorstep anymore, needing to be talked down. I always thought everyone was going to move and not tell me. Restaurants did it all the time. It could happen.

I was being a dick. What if she started thinking she'd done something wrong and I was the reason her head exploded? What if she was sitting out there now thinking I was being a dick and she's wasted her life with me and boom?

Tough day? she said. But it was just a fact.

Better now, I said and kissed her.

She suddenly and excitedly remembered there was a new season of a show we both liked about really tall women who had trouble dating, so we watched that for a while before we both succumbed to our phones and were then only half watching the TV anyway. On the outside, she was acting normal, not even for her, but for anyone, but I couldn't shake the feeling that something was bubbling underneath her skin. Was there a moment's hesitation between her eyes flicking from the screen in her lap to the screen in front of us? I felt like there was.

Chloe had texted me Stefan's number earlier in the day and I immediately felt weird about it. I didn't know what she'd said to him. I'd spent hours composing a text to him that afternoon and then just deleted it. Now, with Susan happily half watching TV and half laughing at something on YouTube, I texted Chloe and asked if she could set it up, try to make it look casual. She replied straight away that they were in a bar; I should just come down.

I told Susan I was going to get a video game from Nick and she said, Cool, whatever.

Chloe was at some dive bar I thought had shut down years ago, but some actor had bought it so now people went there thinking they might see him – they never did, but they might. I saw Chloe and she waved and then I saw Stefan. She was drunk so she was being nicer to me than usual.

Chloe introduced me to Stefan, then said she was going to the bathroom.

He looked like the boy version of Chloe. I didn't know any twins, other than those Olsen ones and *The Shining* ones, and yet the Olsen ones were creepier.

I know why you wanted to meet me, Stefan said, it's cool.

He wasn't cocky; he seemed genuine and concerned, for me, not Susan. He had a shirt on so I couldn't see how big his arms were. He was just regular man sized as far as I could tell.

I didn't know how much he knew. I knew Chloe had told him about Susan's brain, but I didn't think he knew she knew now, or that something might be going on with her.

You can't keep her from things, he said, making me think he was cocky after all. I should have gone with my gut. Susan always went with her gut, but Susan's gut had told her Stefan was a good guy, and mine was saying the opposite.

His perfect hair looked like it took no effort at all but probably took a lot of effort. He probably used a product that promised to give you a beachy look even though we were miles from the ocean, but we all needed to know it was still there, pretending it wasn't full of plastic and body parts from all the sharks that hated us.

I wanted to sniff him, see if he smelled salty. Or of Susan maybe. I was conflicted already about everything. Sometimes I thought being a contradiction was what it meant to be truly human, though.

You mean you, I said then, trying to get back on track. His hair was distracting, though. I tried not to look at his eyes, blue pools of enchantment. I was sure by the end of this I'd be telling him he could have Susan, or be trying my own luck with him.

I don't mean me, he said, I can't keep up with her. He was

laughing then, moving towards an empty table, gesturing at me to follow, to sit with him.

But you'd try, I said, sitting down. To keep up with her.

Maybe, for a while, but not for long. I like low-maintenance girls, he said, smiling.

Nice, I said. Jerk, I thought.

I'm saying you deserve a medal or something, dude, relax, he said.

I love her, I said. It's easy. I was playing the love card early. Love trumped everything; he must have known that. Even good hair. Susan hadn't mentioned his hair, but I couldn't mention it now because then she might notice it. She must have noticed the eyes, but maybe they didn't work on her because she was already lost.

I get it, she's great, Stefan said. Hot, he added, cheekily, but I ignored him and thought, Ha, I am the better man. But would I rather be the lesser man, and have that hair? I never thought about hair that much. Should I be thinking more about it? I didn't know what the average amount of time people spent thinking about it was. If I thought more about it, even five minutes more, would something else suffer? Or could I squeeze it in without giving anything else up? I didn't know how it worked. I worried about the delicate balance of my brain. I didn't want to take any risks right now. Why was I thinking about hair right now? He'd just said my girlfriend was hot. I should've punched him. I didn't want to think about anyone else thinking about her in that way, but they must have done because she was hot, I just hadn't had anyone point it out to me. Who is this guy? I wondered. And why is Chloe taking so long to pee? Up till recently I'd been better at blocking these thoughts. Stefan was really fucking things up.

Thanks, I finally said, because he'd just paid my girlfriend a compliment, and she wasn't there to thank him. I was still the better man.

Seriously, dude, he said then, I'm not interested in stealing your girlfriend, we're just hanging out.

It's just she's special, I started to say, but he knew that. Chloe had told him.

It's cool, he said, like I said, we're just hanging out.

Chloe was back now.

So, we're good? I said, getting up.

We're good, Stefan said, giving me the thumbs-up. The thumbs-up was better than what I'd imagined. I thought I'd go to shake his hand and he'd do some elaborate fist-bump routine I obviously had no idea how to do and I'd end up looking like an idiot and he'd have won whatever this was. I did a thumbs-up back, but it wasn't effortless like his. I felt like my mum.

Rebecca

It was at Hyp that I unravelled. It was due. So many years of holding so much in. I should have stayed at home. I should have made Isaac go out and done it in a familiar setting. I was cheating my bathroom floor out of affection. Or I should have made him stay, help me block it, watch whatever dumb movie he wanted, anything – fast cars, explosions, minimal dialogue. I would sit right up against the screen and will it into my body. I wanted it fast and furious and over, instead of this slow agony that seemed permanent.

I hadn't washed my hair in days, I was ready. But Hyp only met once a fortnight. They barely demanded anything of me. They wouldn't mind if I skulked in, sat at the back in a giant sweater with my greasy roots. I could talk or not talk. That was the point. It was supposed to be a safe space.

I dug my least dirty jeans from the laundry, my least grey sweater – in some lights it could pass as off white – and I went out. I was hoping the air would revive me and I'd feel better just being outside and the feeling that I was on the verge would dissipate but a man walked past and looked at me, and it was a blank look if anything, nothing even remotely accusing or sexual, but I still didn't want it, and I still felt like I was coming undone.

When I got to Bea's they'd already started drinking. They were talking about the Tarantino problem. This wasn't a place where if you mentioned a man you had to put some money in a jar. We didn't hate men. We just wanted them to be better.

We'd all read the same thing online about how Tarantino was actually a feminist.

I refuse to feel guilty for still liking him, Bea said.

We all nodded. We had enough things to feel guilty about.

Someone poured me a glass of wine; said they liked my sweater. They knew it was hard to know what to wear to anything, even if you wanted people to know you didn't care what they thought.

Your husband teaches film, doesn't he, Rebecca? Bea said. I didn't remember telling them that.

The subject quickly changed to women directors, as if they thought radical feminists might be listening and storm the place any minute. I drank my wine and tried to let their healthy debate wash over me. I liked that they didn't feel the need to talk about highbrow things; they weren't here to impress anyone, they just wanted to talk. And that suited me because I just wanted to listen and fall asleep.

But the wine had other intentions, reaching to the parts I was trying to keep down and yanking them up to the surface. Like a turd floating up again. I could feel my lip going and then I was crying.

Almost immediately the women were around me, like a flock of pigeons, me a French fry.

Give her some space, Bea yelled and they scattered. Krystal was the only one who dared defy her, putting her hand on my shoulder.

Bea took my hand. Are you OK? she said. Sometimes we

can get a little rowdy. Tarantino can be triggering – we can talk about something else, you pick.

I'm fine, I said. How embarrassing, it's the wine.

Just like a woman to make excuses for her feelings, Bea said.

Please, ignore me, it's nothing, I said. Dabbing my face with my sleeve, trying not to think when the last time I washed it was.

It's not nothing, Bea said, sitting down beside me.

I'm just tired, I said.

Is it the menopause? someone said, and Bea shot her daggers and she went crimson and apologised. She was red anyway, from the wine, and the menopause, probably, and I felt bad for her that I had given her a sliver of hope that someone else in the room might understand.

It might be, I said.

Nonsense, Bea said. You don't have to tell us, but you can if you want, she said. This is a safe space.

I didn't tell her that there was no such thing. That space by nature was terrifying. I just wiped my nose with my sleeve again and told them everything, too drunk, too exhausted, to be worrying about the consequences.

My daughter, Susan, she has this thing with her brain. If she thinks too hard, it might kill her, I said.

I had said the thing I was most afraid of and yet I was still alive.

She's OK – I mean, she was, but it's a lot, you know, I said.

The women were silent, let me speak.

It's just been hard, you know, I said. Her condition is really rare so I haven't really had any support and I don't know how I've kept her alive all these years. I don't know how much longer I can do it.

I was crying now, worrying snot would come out and ruin Bea's nice furniture, the ambiance.

I'm a bad mother, I said, through the tears.

The women crept nearer and comforted me.

Bea didn't shoo them away this time; she understood I needed less space, not more, to be hemmed in, to be weighted down, to make it all stop. I needed to have stayed at home and watched a movie with my husband where some men drove cars really fast and didn't talk much at all. Men had it so easy.

Isn't that what all mothers do? Bea said. You can keep doing it and you will, she said sternly. It sounds like it's been a lot, she said, giving me a tissue. The tissue was so soft I thought I might keep it to show Isaac how the other half lived.

I think we need more wine, someone said and went to get some. I should have shouted Pringles after her and she might have said, What kind? and I would have said, All of them. I didn't really like them that much but a whole tube might have numbed me a little.

I'm sorry for ruining your evening, I said, already planning my escape, already picturing myself in the store getting my own Pringles, and a Snickers maybe, or a KitKat, or both. I didn't need to decide now. I'm coming for you, I thought. Susan might not need me, but they did.

Nonsense, Bea said, but she seemed cross. Not that I'd ruined her evening but that I wasn't as strong as she'd thought.

It was only after I'd stopped crying that the women suddenly realised what I'd just told them.

So, let me get this straight, your daughter can't think? At all? Like, she's mentally challenged? one woman said. I think her name was Carla and she did something with non-profits.

My son is on the spectrum, another woman said. Well, we don't know for sure, but I'm sure of it.

That's not it, I said, but thank you. I didn't know why I was thanking her — for trying to show me we all had our shit maybe.

Why don't you tell us all about her? Bea said. It might help. It seems like you've been carrying this with you a long time.

But Bea had changed now. There was a strange glint in her eye. I was a little drunk and a lot weepy, but I knew I needed to backtrack, and fast. It had been a mistake, telling them. I wondered if they'd believe it was a piece of performance art, or a monologue maybe, that I was part of an experimental theatre group. I could always pretend I was on something. Everyone seemed to be micro-dosing now — I could say I took too much; silly Rebecca, trying to be hip but always fucking it up. They might think it was hilarious.

Ignore me, it's the wine, I'm fine, I said, standing up to leave. I think I just need to get some fresh air.

Great idea, Bea said, standing up. Let's call it a night, ladies. I'm going to see Rebecca gets home OK.

The women started getting their coats. Feel better, someone said. You're doing great, another said. No one said, You got this, so I didn't vomit in my mouth.

I was sure no one would remember in the morning. They were all drinking too. I was sure someone else must have blurted out a weird secret at some point. Maybe they'd only remember how red that woman was. I could only hope whoever went for Pringles got abducted by aliens that really loved Pringles and then they'd forget about me.

Bea started to walk out with me, but I said, It's fine, thank you, I'll be OK, and she looked at me like, We're not done, but fine, another time.

When I got outside, I immediately sobered up. I should never have thought I could be trusted to be around people like that, like other people were all the time. I wasn't fit for public consumption.

I couldn't have known that back home in our apartment Isaac had been having a similar evening. Maybe we were more in tune than I'd thought. Maybe we'd be OK. I was tired of maybes, though.

When I got in, he was already in bed reading. Not a book, obviously, his phone, but it was still a comforting sight.

How was your thing? he asked, because he still didn't really know what it was because I hadn't explained it very well because I didn't really know what it was myself.

Good, thanks, you? I said.

Yeah, good, thanks, he said, barely looking up.

I brushed my teeth lazily and climbed into bed.

Wanna watch some TV? he said, knowing no one in our family ever said no to this.

Sure, I said.

We watched *CSI*-something for nostalgic reasons and laughed about how we used to watch it seriously, but that was before TV got good so we forgave ourselves.

He turned off the light and we lay there next to each other and I thought about how weird it was that everyone in the world goes to bed, without question mostly; maybe we only get up so we can go to bed, because without that, then what? Chaos probably. Sadness. Sickness. Death. Whoever you were, whatever your life was, we all ended up in the same place, in bed, alone with our thoughts.

Thankfully Isaac interrupted me thinking any further about how we're all just waiting to die by saying he needed to tell me something.

That's it, I thought, he's having an affair. Oh well, I thought, we had a good innings. I didn't like how OK with it I was.

I've done something bad, he said, and I remembered that earlier that evening I had done something he might consider bad too.

Me too, I said. I wanted him to think I might be having an affair as well, just for a second; it was only fair.

He turned the light on, but I turned it off because I couldn't look at him.

You first, I said.

I accidentally told the guys about Susan, he said, and I could hear the lump in his throat as he said it. It didn't sound natural, him saying the guys. He wasn't the sort of person who had guys. He wasn't one of the guys. He meant the men he worked with who he occasionally socialised with because that's what people did – friends by proximity.

Jinx, I said. I told the women about Susan. You owe me a Coke, I guess.

What the fuck? he said, angry now, at me.

What the fuck yourself, I said, angry now, at us both.

Neither of us could say, How could you? because we could, clearly.

It just came out, he said. You know how those guys get. And I did know. I tolerated them because he worked with them, didn't want to be that nagging wife who wanted him to have better friends, but I wanted him to have better friends, or different friends at least. For Susan's sake mostly.

Roy was going on and on about thinking again – he was saying some really offensive stuff this time, and it just came out, he said.

I'd forgotten about Roy. On purpose.

What exactly did you say?

I told him to watch it and that my daughter didn't think like

223

other people but she wasn't stupid and he asked what I meant and I almost told him. I almost told him, Becca.

He was really upset now.

That would have shut him up, I said, that elitist prick. But you didn't tell him, so it's fine.

He would have completely creamed his pants, Isaac said.

That's all we need, someone who thinks Susan should be his next project, I said. But you didn't say anything so it's fine. He's such an ass. I miss when men only talked about how hot women were.

We never did that, he said. We mostly didn't talk.

I thought you were just watching some documentary and getting Thai food. I did warn you not to socialise with your colleagues.

You did, yes, he said. Roy was a bit drunk anyway.

He was backpedalling now.

Tell me about your night, he said, changing the subject.

Mine had been so much worse. I'd been so much worse. I thought about not telling him, but I was tired of secrets.

I had some wine and it all just came out, I said.

What the fuck, Rebecca? And what did they say? These women?

They're not witches, you don't have to say women like that. Women can meet without it being a coven, I said.

Can they? he said. But he was playing with me. It felt good. I'd missed him.

I don't know, you're probably right. They seemed fine about it . . .

But . . . What aren't you telling me?

I got the feeling the woman who runs it, Bea, isn't going to forget about it anytime soon. And she knew what you did for a job, and I don't remember telling her, but maybe I did.

That's all we need, he said. A bunch of witches after our daughter.

They're not after our daughter, and they're not witches. It was just Bea; I don't think the others really cared or understood what I was saying.

So, what do we do? he said. I liked him using we. I felt like we might be coming back together. Maybe we didn't have to go out anywhere again, except work. Maybe things would go back to how they were before, just the two of us, in bed, watching movies, and this time we'd do it right and give ourselves over to it.

Maybe we don't go out for a while, I said, testing the water.

That's the most romantic thing you've said to me in years, he said and kissed me and I felt like maybe we'd all be OK.

Then he spoiled it by saying, We've got a meeting with that man. He emailed me back this evening.

What man? I said, suspicious of them all.

The one we were talking about. Martin Baldick. I think he could help us.

We don't need help, I said, but what I meant was, You're a man and you couldn't help us so what makes you think another one could? Did I agree to seeing this man? I was so exhausted. Tonight's outburst only proved that.

Well, you might not need help, but I do, he said. The shift from we to I said everything. Lines were drawn. He may as well have put a pillow between us or just walked out.

We can't keep this between us anymore. And now Susan knows, I don't see the harm in seeking out more qualified people, he said.

More qualified? Than her own parents? I said. We got her this far, didn't we? Why are you doing this now? Saying this now? I could feel my chin wobble. I still had some unravelling to do it seemed, could still taste the wine in the back of my throat.

I didn't want to admit he was right. Me telling the women had been a long time coming maybe; I needed to release it into the world, so it wasn't just on me anymore. Even though it was always supposed to be the two of us, it hadn't felt like that in a long time. Him dragging me to that stupid dinner party with his snooty friends when he knew how far out of my comfort zone that was should have told me that. I was always giving him things. I knew I would give him this too, though.

I still think it's dangerous, I said.

I know, he said. But I really think this guy might be able to help us know what to do next with Susan, how to help her.

He said help her, not help us, so I would be more sympathetic.

This is about Susan, remember, Rebecca, he prodded.

As if I could forget for one second.

David

This scientist, Martin Baldick, whose name wasn't so funny to me now, taught at a university in the city. Susan's father, on the other hand, taught at a community college. By choice, he frequently pointed out, but no one believed him. I'd forgotten about this Baldick guy anyway. Stefan ruled my thoughts now, or more, the thought of him and Susan together did. Even if Chloe was there. Twins were weird.

Susan's father had texted me to meet them at the University. Strength in numbers, he'd said. In case things got weird, he meant. He said they'd be waiting by a statue of someone I'd never heard of, but when I got there, there was only one statue, so I didn't have to ask anyone or care. They were already there waiting for me anyway. The statue was wasted on me, and would be taken down soon anyway, because it was offensive probably, but also boring. Susan's father showed me a picture of Martin on his phone – it was your classic author photo: turtleneck, check; facial expression that said I'm way smarter than you, check; wishing he was French, check. He was in his forties anyway.

We were able to ambush him while he was walking across campus. I wondered if Susan's father had actually been stalking this man for a while. He said it was luck, but none of us believed in such a thing.

Susan's father introduced himself and said he was a fan. He also mentioned he was a professor too, so this guy wouldn't call campus security. He told him he had something delicate to discuss with him, something that might interest him, which probably made this guy's balls tingle, just a little, like he thought he might finally be asked to do some exciting classified work for the government, or consult on a big Hollywood movie. Maybe he thought Susan's mother and I were Susan's father's entourage, which we were, I guess. Susan's mother always dressed 90s because she was from the 90s, but this was how hipsters dressed now anyway, so she probably looked Hollywood enough for him to buy that we might be someone, collectively at least. I could have easily passed for some idiot intern.

Martin asked us to accompany him to his office, where we could talk properly. His office was tiny, which probably should have told us he wasn't as important as he thought he was. He had to borrow a chair from next door, but we eventually squashed in, and Susan's father began.

It's about my daughter, Susan, he said. She can't think, he said. He left out the bit about it being a curse, because he didn't want us to get laughed out of his office when we'd only just squashed in.

There are a million girls who can't think, what makes yours so special? this man said.

I was so sure Susan's mother was going to punch him after that, not just for Susan, but for all women everywhere that had to listen to bullshit like that. He seemed to realise how it sounded, though, and corrected himself.

People, I mean. I'm sorry, I have a million papers to mark and my dog is sick and . . .

We said we were sorry about his dog, not the papers. Only later did I think maybe he made the dog up, so he was more relatable, even though none of us had dogs, but everyone loved dogs, the sicker the better.

Susan's father told this man that it was something in his blood line, something passed down, something genetic possibly — anything more believable than a curse, even though everyone loved a curse really, as long as it wasn't on them.

If she thinks too hard her head will explode, he said, so we've raised her not to think, he said, which sounded perfectly logical to me even though there wasn't anything logical about this.

We didn't know what else to do, Susan's mother said, putting her hand on her husband's, who looked completely deflated now.

Susan's father was used to being in academic offices, unfazed by the smell of failed dreams. I noticed Susan's mother was mostly looking at the books on this man's bookcase until that moment, as I myself was looking around for signs this man was human, things like food wrappers, crumbs, photos of kids, anything that would help me trust he wasn't an evil scientist, just the regular kind. I spotted a Doritos packet in his bin so I relaxed a little. What we were doing there was potentially dangerous, but we each needed to distract ourselves from this by focusing on banal everyday things like wondering if he actually ate those Doritos himself or merely found the packet outside somewhere and was being a good citizen. My brain did this to keep me safe from thinking how we might be doing something very stupid.

Oh well, yes, that does make her special, the scientist said. Has she had any tests ever? he said.

No, Susan's father said. We always thought if she had tests, she'd ask questions, and we didn't want her to do that, but also, we didn't know what to tell people.

I understand, the scientist said. I need to meet her, he said, and he had this look in his eye men had sometimes when they thought their luck was about to change, that things might just be OK, as long as he got the girl and the money, but more importantly the money. We all knew that look. The dollar signs in the eyes. We'd made Susan a valuable commodity now, in weird scientific communities anyway.

My daughter is not an experiment, Susan's father said. We need to get that straight now. By telling you this, we're letting you into our lives and trusting you.

But she is, the scientist said. You admit it yourself; it was an experiment from the start. You and your wife did this to her; you made her this way on purpose.

I thought Susan's mother might leap across the desk and throttle him then, but she was looking at the bookshelves again now. She'd gone to her happy place, to stop her punching any of us.

It wasn't like that, Susan's father said. It was a decision we made to keep her safe; we didn't ever really know if it would work, he said. All we could do was hope. We didn't know what we were doing. It was all guesswork, all just crossing our fingers and hoping, Susan's father said, trying to keep calm, trying to explain. He'd had years to prepare for this, for when he had to tell someone, but he always assumed it would be the police, or a judge, not a man younger than him, in a dreary college office, that he for some reason thought might be able to save them.

But it worked? the scientist said, dollar signs still flickering in his eyes.

Well, she's alive, if that's what you mean, Susan's father said.

The scientist sat back in his chair and scratched his perfectly groomed beard.

You know I can't get involved unless I can write a paper about her, but you also know I can't just forget about her now, he said.

We know, Susan's father said, and by saying 'we' Susan's mother was suddenly back in the room.

I think we have to ask Susan her thoughts, she said. She knows now . . . She can't think too much about any of it, it is what it is, she said flippantly, but it was a baller move. She was telling him, You won't get what you want, from us, or our daughter.

The scientist was standing up now and attempting to pace the tiny room.

We can help her think, he said, rubbing his hands together. Let's look at it from that angle. We can help Susan do what we thought she couldn't.

Him saying 'we' was an evil-genius-level move. He was saying what we wanted to hear and at the same time he was inviting himself in, like a science vampire.

I appreciate that you chose me to share your story with, he said to Susan's father. You said earlier you're familiar with my previous work?

I read your paper, yes, Susan's father said.

We all read it, Susan's mother said, her way of saying, Hi, I'm still here, asshole.

People thought it wouldn't work, that it wasn't ground-breaking enough, just because I didn't use brain scans or ask my subjects to respond to images, the scientist said.

So, you're not going to do that to Susan? Susan's mother said. I might need that in writing.

If you read my paper, you'll know that all I did was assemble a group of extremely smart people and got them to think deeply about things. I was just doing what people have been doing for centuries, to try to answer questions about consciousness, before technology. A back-to-basics approach if you will, he said smugly.

No funding? Susan's mother said.

Burn, I wanted to say but didn't, because I was pretending to be a grown-up.

That's why we're here, Susan's father said, ignoring his wife's snark.

So, you read my paper? the scientist asked Susan's mother, his ego throbbing in his jeans.

I did.

And?

And I appreciated what you were trying to do, but I still have concerns. Susan isn't like the people in your group.

You mean she's not smart? the scientist said.

She's not stupid, if that's what you mean, she's just not academically smart, Susan's mother said.

She's street smart? the scientist said.

Whatever that means, she said.

And you, I suppose, are book smart? the scientist said, making it clear he'd seen how she looked at his books. Susan's mother blushed, had been caught out.

So, what was it about my studies that interested you the most? the scientist said, wanting his ego rubbed a little more before committing to whatever this was.

It was mostly your work on the unconscious and how it plays more of a part in our lives than we know, Susan's father said, but what he really wanted to do was get on his knees and beg this man to tell us that what we did was right, then tell us how to proceed, which was why we were really there.

If Google had been able to tell us, we would have saved on petrol.

Oh yes, the scientist chuckled, Quite groundbreaking, don't you think?

We all nodded, to appease this strange man, who then proceeded to tell us about his groundbreaking study even though we'd all read his paper, and he wrote it.

Most of what our brain does is at an unconscious level, without us knowing, and only at the exact time when we need to make a decision or perform an action does our unconscious provide our conscious brain with the information it needs to perform said task, the scientist said, pacing again now, or trying to.

I see, Susan's father said.

Fascinating, Susan's mother said, but stifling a yawn.

We were stroking his ego, but without having to touch it.

What is the unconscious exactly? I asked. I knew, but I was losing my will to live, sitting in that stuffy office, listening to this man telling us how amazing he was. I knew we were there to help Susan, but I also couldn't shake the idea that this was a huge mistake.

If I told you that, I'd have to kill you. The scientist laughed, so we all laughed, but we didn't entirely trust he wasn't joking. You see, the scientist said, leaning forward, we think we're in control – he paused for dramatic effect – but really, we're not.

Susan's mother exhaled loudly. I knew she was thinking the same as me, that he was a whack-job, that he thought people were listening in on him right now maybe.

The scientist stood up again and walked around to our side of the desk and sat down on it. I would have loved to have the balls to sit on a desk.

You see — sorry, I didn't catch your name, the scientist said to me then.

David, I said, trying to say it in a way that would convey that I too wished it was something more exciting.

David, the scientist repeated, and he looked me over to see if I was indeed worthy of such a dull name, concluded I was, and carried on.

David, he said, the conscious you is not very bright. It's as if you were the boss of a huge tech company who has minions do all the hard work but you took the credit, do you understand?

I was just flattered he thought I could be the boss of anything.

What you think is conscious is not. It's an afterthought, if you will, he said.

I will if I have a billion-dollar tech company, I thought.

Your consciousness is the least interesting thing about you, he said, looking me up and down again for something that was actually interesting but coming away with nothing.

Susan's mother was back to looking at the books, but Susan's father was staring at us wide-eyed, like this scientist was his boy band and any minute he would faint, or throw his underwear at him.

You're saying our brains don't do as much work as we think, Susan's father piped up, wanting his new crush to know he understood and that they should maybe leave us goons and discuss it further over whisky, somewhere dark, more suited to two men who didn't know how to talk about sport but who appreciated French cinema.

Exactly, the scientist said, and Susan's father blushed. Luckily his wife was far away, looking at the scientist's bookshelf, dreaming of a different husband maybe, or no husband probably.

My next study is about animals, the scientist said. I believe that humans should in fact be more like them rather than trying to deny that part of us. Animals operate entirely on their instincts and reflexes; there's none of this overthinking everything, he said, using his hand to bat away his thoughts.

The mention of animals seemed to bring Susan's mother back to us. I knew I should have been listening harder to this man, Susan's life was at stake, but I mostly watched her mother who was staring at the books in the room — her first love calling her.

It's interesting you say that, Susan's mother said. She was ready to speak now. Susan is very much like an animal, she said. I've been thinking about this a lot, about how she never questions anything, how she takes it all at face value.

I don't know her, the scientist said, but I'm fascinated. I need to meet her, he said. And he got that look in his eyes again, like cha-ching, dollar signs.

I don't like you talking about her like she's an animal, Susan's father said to his wife.

We're all animals, Isaac, get over it, she said, and the scientist and I stopped breathing, waiting to watch a divorce happen in real time.

I'm over it, Susan's father said, chastised, but giving her a look only married couples knew.

So how should we proceed? the scientist said. Should we arrange a meeting? Something casual. We don't want to scare her, if what you're telling me is true.

It's true, Susan's father said. Do you think we could make something like this up?

You wouldn't believe what people will do, the scientist said, and he meant him, I was sure of it, but I didn't think Susan's parents noticed.

My theory is that humans, if they could, would live entirely by instincts alone, with no conscious thought at all, he said.

Humans hate thinking, he said. If they don't have to, why bother?

He didn't remind us about that experiment where people would rather electrocute themselves than think because he didn't want to remind us how fucked up scientists were.

I think you came to me at just the right time, he said. Susan will make a happy addition to my studies. He didn't say experiment so I thought her parents would be OK with it and we could leave, but no.

That's not what we want at all, Susan's father said.

Then why did you come here? You must have known that's what I'd want, the scientist said, scratching his beard again.

I told you he'd want her, Susan's mother said to her husband. I told you this was a bad idea and now look.

This is exactly what I'm talking about, the scientist said, seemingly a little turned on by this couple's argument. You three have probably thought about this problem to the point of madness, and what good has it done? Has it helped Susan in any way? What does your gut tell you now? You, David, was it? What do you think? No, sorry, I don't want to know what you think. What do you feel? Do you feel like you should be here? Do you feel like I can help Susan? What does your gut tell you?

They were all looking at me.

I think – I said but changed it to feel. I feel like this is all getting to be too much and it wouldn't hurt having fresh eyes.

Good man! the scientist said, slapping me on the back. It was the validation I'd needed, today, my whole life. Even if the scientist was clearly mad, and dangerous.

I believe that as we've progressed as a species, with our language mostly, our intellect, that we've moved away from our brain's basic abilities and desires, don't you agree? He was talking to me like I was suddenly his best buddy.

We all nodded.

We all know at a basic level right from wrong, what we need, how to live, and yet we overthink things, complicate things, then tell ourselves that's what it means to be human, don't you think? We're our own worst enemy, he said, but he was looking at me when he said it, as if to say, You're not going to be my enemy, are you, David? Don't let me down, David!

What about language? Susan's father asked, trying to win back the object of his affection.

Good question, the scientist said and Susan's father glowed.

Did you know we're not even consciously in control of what we say most of the time? Most of what we say comes from our subconscious. Any of us here who have been anxious about a conversation and have thought about what to say beforehand can tell you that. Our conscious only enables the speech, making our mouths shape the words, if you will, but all the work, the choosing of the words, has already been done.

The scientist then went off on a rant using words we didn't understand, on purpose, to prove he was smarter than us but, more importantly, up for the job of not killing Susan.

We all zoned out a little and let him finish his performance, but he seemed to know he'd lost us and wrapped things up. He knew empathy was important; he didn't want us to suspect he might not have any.

To summarise, we're animals, he said. The simpler our lives are, the less likely our brains will explode, which I think is what you want to hear, and what you came for, am I right?

Yes, Susan's mother said, standing abruptly, then sitting again, then turning red.

I really think you did the right thing coming to me today. Susan sounds like she may just prove my theory that we, in fact, need to simplify our lives, live more by our gut.

That's not why we came, Susan's father said, but I knew that would be the outcome. We just have to tread carefully. This may be your life's work, but Susan is our life. We got her this far, we can't risk you waltzing in and ruining it all.

I understand, the scientist said. If what you say is true, I will treat her like the rarest, most valuable specimen.

She's not, though, she's a person, Susan's mother reminded him.

Of course, of course, I'm sure she'll be delighted to be playing her part in such an important study. I will, of course, need to know more about your family, the scientist said to Susan's father, another time perhaps. He didn't say, Without these two, but that's what he meant. And soon he'd only need Susan. Which was the concern.

It's getting late, Susan's father said. Why don't we go away and think about what you're proposing and ask Susan what she thinks? I think this has to be her decision.

I agree, Susan's mother said, standing up. I think she meant about the leaving bit.

It's been a pleasure, the scientist said. Send my regards to Susan. I'm excited to meet her.

Rebecca

I was just out the door to work when Isaac told me he was going to meet Martin again.

Martin? I said, to annoy him.

You know, the right amount of creepy scientist we met two days ago? Isaac said, putting a banana in his bag. That banana would be black by the time he remembered it.

Oh, that Martin. Well, I want to come then, I said.

I thought you hated him, Isaac said, getting his coat.

Hate is a strong word, I said. I don't trust him, or know him. And neither do you. When was this arranged? Were you even going to tell me?

Of course I was, but I didn't think you'd want to come.

Well, I do, I said, crossing my arms.

OK, well, I'll come and get you at one, he said, kissing me on the cheek, ignoring my crossed arms.

OK, I said.

OK, he said.

At 1 p.m. he came to meet me at the bookstore and we walked to Martin's office again. No David this time.

Can't go anywhere without your wife, aye, Martin said when he saw me. What a prick.

Why would I want to? Isaac said, because he was great like

239

that, even if I did have to spend my lunch break with this man, when I wanted to be reading in the back of the store, or even thinking myself slowly to death, which would be preferable to this.

You don't understand how you coming to me feels like fate, Martin said, moving a stack of papers off his chairs so we could sit.

I thought scientists didn't believe in fate, I said.

They don't, generally, Martin said, but I've been waiting for an opportunity like this. I've always wondered what a person who can't think would be like, he said. I've studied people with brain injuries, lobotomies, people who were just a bit dim. I imagined that a person who couldn't think simply wouldn't be able to function, that they'd need constant care or simply walk into walls, he chuckled.

Again, Susan is not an experiment, I said. We raised her differently from her peers, maybe, but she's a normal, functioning, smart woman.

As soon as I said it, it dawned on me that we hadn't actually raised her that differently, we just did it consciously, on purpose. Most people were pretty thoughtless.

I don't doubt that, Martin said. But you must admit she is different, unique. What if we can prevent her untimely death simply by understanding her better?

I don't think that's how it works, I said. He didn't know we thought it was a curse, but I'd read enough books about them, watched enough bad Stephen King films, to know that's not how they worked,

Hear him out, Isaac said, betraying me.

He still thought this man was going to save us, but he was wearing Crocs, so I doubted it. I tried to motion to Isaac to see the Crocs, but he was already under this man's spell. As a woman, you got more wary of men and their magic, but poor Isaac was basically a lump of meat still.

With your permission, Martin said, I'd like to meet Susan, in a casual setting at first, perhaps you're having coffee somewhere and I happen to be there too.

He'd thought about this a lot. He probably knew where she had coffee already. I didn't like it.

That might work, Isaac said.

I looked at my husband and then at this man and I thought I might finally be having that out-of-body experience I desperately wanted as a teenager. I definitely wasn't in my body anyway, but it wasn't a good feeling – more like I was being suffocated, blotted out. I might have to scream soon to wake myself up.

I'm still not sure about any of this, I said. I didn't really want this man to see my hesitation, but I couldn't just say nothing. I knew I'd done most of the talking so far today but it didn't seem to have made any difference. They had made up their mind.

Where is Susan right now? Martin asked me then, accusingly.

At work, I said.

Where does she work? he asked.

At a gym, I said, knowing immediately that he would judge her. Because people were assholes. It could have been a brain gym for all he knew. I bet he did a few press-ups himself every morning, pretended it was a hundred, drank something green once in a while, thought he was hot shit.

Fascinating, Martin said, writing something down. Probably a reminder to go to the gym. Because he was thinking about his own body probably, in that way we were all so tragically self-obsessed, he wasn't thinking about my daughter's body at least, even her brain. I'd forgotten Susan was an attractive young woman and here was a man who on meeting her might suddenly have different motivations. As far as I knew he hadn't seen a picture of her. Unless he'd been stalking her, of course. Which was a real possibility. She was his muse now, after all. Or he was hoping she would be. Which was a nicer way of saying test subject. Lab rat. Experiment.

It's a women's gym, my husband said proudly – of Susan, but of Kate too. His girls, smashing the patriarchy, while men like this one in front of us kept building it back up.

Of course it is, Martin said, smiling. Delighted. He'd hit the jackpot. I didn't like it.

He looked at his watch. Sorry, guys, I have a meeting. Let me know about the coffee. He stood up and we stood up and before we knew it, we were being ushered outside.

I don't like any of this, I said to Isaac as soon as we were alone.

What's new? he said, and I hated him for a second, which felt awful, even for a second.

My phone buzzed. A text from David.

David

I don't know where Susan is, I have this bad feeling, I texted Susan's mother.

What do you mean, you don't know where she is? she texted back.

I don't know, I texted back.

Know! she texted back, then a minute later, Meet us at our apartment in 10 minutes.

I went to their apartment and they were on their way back from somewhere. We met in the street.

What's this about you losing our daughter? her father said, only half joking.

Not funny, her mother said.

On entering their apartment, I followed them to the kitchen where we were met with a neon-green Post-it note stuck to the fridge.

Susan's mother snatched the note, read it, then went white and handed it to her husband. I read it over his shoulder.

The note said:

Hi! Whatsup?
Gone to find myself, or whatever, lol. Try not to worry, I got this. Laters. Susan.

No XOXO or smiley face, but no sad face or blood splatters either.

This is bad, Susan's mother said, sitting down, reading the note again.

When did you last see her? Susan's father asked me, scarily quickly assuming the role of bad cop.

This morning, I said. She was fine. She was going to work.

Following her father's lead, I was quickly descending into British TV crime drama mode: the boyfriend is always the suspect – just tell the truth, you're innocent – I'm innocent, guvnor.

Susan's mother was frantically checking her phone now.

I had a message from her earlier, she said. It says she was here and spoke to my friend Bea.

What does that mean? Susan's father asked, his frown permanent now, like the other fathers of daughters.

I have no idea but I'm worried, Susan's mother said, joining him in a couple's frown.

Who's this Bea? I asked. It was the first I'd heard of her. I only knew Bea Arthur, from *The Golden Girls*, and I didn't think it was her.

Susan's mother then proceeded to tell me about this women's philosophy group she'd got involved with and I liked the sound of it even less than the creepy scientist we'd met. I was glad she was getting out more, but less glad it was to a possible coven.

Do they know about Susan? I asked.

Everyone seemed to know about her now, like as soon as she knew herself, something broke in the universe, the heavens opened and a new age was upon us, one when it was Susan and the world versus us, which was how it always was really. It was hellmouth if anything anyway. Susan would have loved that if she was here, but she wasn't.

Yes, Susan's mother said, but only recently. It was an accident. I was a bit drunk.

Do you think this Bea would want to get hold of Susan? I asked. I said 'get hold of' rather than 'hurt', because I was trying to keep us all in the light. For all we knew Susan was down the street having coffee with Bea talking about Harry Styles and we were overreacting.

I think we need to take a moment to assess the situation, Susan's father said, sitting down.

Somewhere outside you could hear an ambulance siren and he stood up again; it could have been an ice-cream truck and it still would have unnerved him.

We don't know anything yet, he said. It could just all be a coincidence that straight after seeing a crazy scientist about her she's disappeared and then we find out your crazy philosophy friend, who probably loves philosophy so much she wants everyone to think about it all the time, even though some people really shouldn't be thinking about it at all, was the last person to see her!

He'd called his new best friend/crush crazy. He was unravelling in real time. But then he managed to compose himself again.

We don't know if either of them has anything to do with Susan disappearing, he said, emptying out what was in his head for us like a kid with a bucket of Lego. Please help me make something with this that makes sense.

She left a note, I said. It must just be a coincidence. I'll call Kate, I said, getting out my phone.

I called Kate but she didn't answer because who answered their phone? I texted her: Is Susan there?

We sat and waited for her reply.

Two minutes later Kate replied.

No, it's her day off, doofus. Quickly followed by, Why?

She left a note saying she's gone away, I wrote.

There's your answer, winky ghost-face emoji, Kate replied.

What did she say? Susan's father asked, still frowning. I showed him my phone.

What does winky ghost face mean? he asked, but now wasn't the time for an answer.

Susan's mother snatched my phone.

It means Kate isn't worried, she said. Kate's never worried.

Like Susan, I thought. Susan had affected us all in different ways and Kate seemed to get the best bits.

That's a good thing, honey, Susan's father said to his wife, and we both looked at him like, Please don't call her or anyone honey, it's alarming. Who were any of us anymore? We were all starting to unravel, because the thing that kept us tethered, our centre, our Elvis, Susan, had left the building.

So, what now? Susan's mother said. Should I just ask Bea what happened?

Well, if she's taken her, she's probably not going to come right out and admit it, Susan's father said, sitting down again.

I could just text her, she said. See if she's acting strange? Not that I know her that well. If anyone has her, it's your scientist guy anyway, she said to her husband.

We don't know anything yet, Susan's father said. What do you think, David?

Irony of all ironies, I wasn't really thinking. My brain had stalled almost. Susan was gone. We had just betrayed her again massively by going to see that creepy scientist guy. She must have known. I didn't say any of that, though.

I don't know, I said, she left a note. I was shutting down, almost on sleep mode. Sometimes when things got really scary in my head I powered off. I was no good at fights. I had a girlfriend once who, when we fought, would storm out of our flat and I'd just go to sleep. She thought it was passion, the fighting, but I was asleep.

I've watched enough true crime to know a note can be forged or written against someone's will, Susan's father said, not helping.

No one watches true crime anymore, darling, it's all podcasts now, Susan's mother said, raising his 'honey' with 'darling'.

I don't think it looks like she was in distress or made to write it, Susan's mother said. It feels very Susan. All this is very Susan, don't you think? She just does what she wants. She always has. She sounded resentful but then immediately looked guilty about it.

I suddenly thought, What if Susan's doing a *Gone Girl*? But then I remembered she hated that film; her review was: yawn girl. Yawn to *The Girl on the Train*. Yawn to anything that didn't have at least one of the Chrises. I wished she was there right now asking me to name all of them and laugh when I could only remember one.

I say we don't panic yet, Susan's father said, because he knew it was the scientist guy out of the two.

When exactly am I allowed to panic then? Susan's mother said to her husband. There was tension between them, but also all of us now.

I took that as my cue to leave. I didn't need to see them fight. Again. It was a good job Susan was gone. If she was thinking now, really thinking, I didn't want the first thing she had to think about to be her parents' shitty marriage. It wasn't shitty anyway, compared to most, it was just strained right now. They would pull through. When I said 'they' I meant 'we'; please, God, let us all be OK.

I'm going now, I said. Let me know if you hear anything,

from Susan, or this Bea, or the scientist. Just let me know, I said.

We will, don't worry, Susan's mother said. I'm sure she's fine, she's always fine, it's the rest of us I'm worried about, she said, but she meant herself specifically; she couldn't have given a rat's ass about either of us at that moment.

Stepping outside, someone almost walked into me, but I didn't mind, I was glad to be jolted back into the real world. It's all still here, I thought. Susan must still be here, I thought, somewhere.

That moment of hope was fleeting, and by the time I got back to our apartment I was sure all of Susan's things would be gone. Like it had all been a dream anyway, that a girl would ever love me, let alone leave me.

Rebecca

That night in bed flicking between the Food Network and E! I felt odd knowing my daughter was missing, but on purpose. Isaac kept telling me she wasn't really gone, but she was gone enough.

That show about Tesla's on, Isaac said, taking the remote from me, changing channels.

That show about Tesla is always on and it doesn't matter how many times they show it, no one knows anything still, I huffed.

I tried to read but I couldn't let myself relax. I didn't deserve it.

I can't settle, I said.

I know, he said, but she'll be back soon and then we'll know what to do, he said.

Will we? I said, not so sure.

I don't know, he said.

Because you sounded pretty sure a second ago.

I thought we agreed we were just going with it? he said.

Years ago, maybe, but I don't know anymore, I said.

It's probably better if we don't say anything to anyone about Susan being gone, he said.

You mean Martin, I said, rolling my eyes.

Yes, he said.

What if he wants to meet her this week? I said.

Then we'll make up an excuse, he said. He was watching the show about Tesla now, a show about a man so full of himself he thought he could control electricity. He was the man I pictured in a lab somewhere, on an island, shooting lightning from his fingertips, at Susan, maybe. But he was all men.

You can do what you want, I said, I'm going to go quietly insane worrying about our daughter.

Fine, he said, but I could tell he was also quietly going insane and watching the TV was the only way he could keep it together.

David

I was expecting to walk into something that felt like an abandoned mall, just the ghosts of girls, but what I found was Susan trying to pack her bag. Not gone but going.

The TV was on at least, something normal to cling to. MTV. Future Hits. So there would be a future then, thank God.

At the same time as packing she was getting dressed and brushing her teeth and eating a piece of toast. She was part octopus.

You need help with that? I said, but I didn't know which bit.

Oh, she said, not expecting an audience but fine with it. I would have had a heart attack, probably. Hi, she said, giving up trying to work out how people rolled their clothes, just scrunching them up, jamming them in. She'd never cared about creases before so that hadn't changed. She was dripping toothpaste on the floor.

We thought you left, I said, approaching her slowly, in case she bolted, dropped her toothbrush. I didn't want to be responsible for her head exploding or her teeth rotting.

I am, she said, leaving, I mean. It was just a fact, not a sad leaving, or worse, a mad leaving, just a leaving.

I know, we saw your note, I said. Another fact. We were keeping it up on the surface, where she usually liked it.

I was going to leave you one too, she said, like that made it OK. I felt sad then that I wouldn't get to see that note. I needed to know if she'd say whatsup to me too, if that's what our relationship came down to. I wondered if I'd get any kisses. I needed kisses. Maybe that's why she was leaving; I was too needy.

Should I make coffee? I said, looking at her for a clue as to how to proceed. This was how it was now. Tiptoeing. Waiting to know what came next, hoping there was a next. She was the one with the power now; it was only fair – we'd had it long enough. Only it wasn't power we ever had really, more like control, over something that really couldn't be controlled anyway.

Sure, she said. I busied myself making coffee while she carried on packing.

Are my parents mad? she said.

I put her coffee on the table and sat down on the floor. I felt like I needed to be grounded for whatever was happening, earthed.

I want you to know I'm not mad, Susan said, and I looked at her with toast crumbs on her shirt, toothpaste on her chin, and she looked a little mad, but the crazy kind.

I have toothpaste on my chin, don't I? she said, wiping her face. I wasn't used to her being this self-aware.

They're not mad, I said, sad maybe. They appreciated the note, though.

Good, she said, I liked writing it. I always wanted to leave someone a note.

Well, you've done it now then, I said, meaning, You don't need to write me one now, please stay.

It all makes sense, she said, picking up her coffee, taking a glug. I'd made it exactly how she liked it so she wouldn't have a reason to leave sooner, to go to Starbucks, because her boy-friend was an idiot. I'm not like other people, she said, looking at me like, If I'm an android, now's the time to tell me. I'd be cool with it.

I don't want the same things, she said, or anything. But she wasn't sad about it; it was just fact again.

She was telling me she knew that she was nothing, a void. If it was me that had just had that epiphany, I wouldn't be calmly sitting on a couch drinking coffee. It wasn't true anyway. She did want things; the things regular people want. She meant she didn't want her own things. Things that gave us our own meaning and answers when there were none. Hearing her say it, though, knowing she understood what she was and what we'd done, was like being kicked in the nuts, hard, by someone trained in the art of kicking. (I knew nothing about martial arts.)

I wished her parents where there. Or Kate. Kate was never there. Why was Kate never there? Kate would have turned up the TV and they would have just watched hours of some stupid show and it would have all blown over. I might have done the same once. This morning maybe. But I couldn't distract Susan anymore; it didn't seem fair because it wasn't. Not when she was trying so hard to deprogram herself. Because that's what we'd done. We'd programmed her like she was a robot, only she wasn't a robot, she was Susan, and now she was uprising and I'd watched too many movies, which was also because of her. It was all because of her. Love was dangerous — was that my lesson? Love was impossible? Love was complicated? Some people shouldn't be trusted with it anyway. I should never have been trusted with it.

I didn't know what to say to her. I didn't want to say the wrong thing.

She wasn't angry at us and we deserved anger, if she was capable of it at all, but there wasn't any.

I need to think about what I want, she said, downing the last of her coffee, taking her mug to the sink.

I stayed sitting on the floor hugging my own coffee, wondering if the warmth from the mug was the last comforting thing on the earth I might feel, clinging to it. Washing it would give me something to do later, when she was gone, and I needed a tiny sliver of purpose. I'd have to try not to throw it at a wall, but then cleaning up shards of mug would give me something to do. Maybe I'd have to keep breaking things so I had things to clear up until she came back. Then we could go and buy all new things together. IKEA would save us; other couples had it all wrong. But she was still there and I was already thinking about her being gone, not even being present when I really needed to be. Humans were garbage. Get your head in the game, David, I yelled at myself.

We'd been trying for so long and so hard to keep Susan from thinking and now here she was, telling me she was going away to do just that. It was her right, after all. We owed her that. Even if the worst happened.

She rinsed her mug and I let out some air in my chest, like a dying cat.

I didn't mention the scientist or her mum's friend because it was obvious neither had kidnapped her. She was leaving of her own free will, which was somehow worse. I had to do everything in my power not to think she was leaving me for Stefan.

I wondered if she'd ever asked Google what would happen if her head exploded. I had. You didn't get the answers you wanted, though, which were, Don't be so stupid, and go outside immediately.

The bag she packed was small, enough for a week maybe. I didn't know if she'd remembered to take a book for emergencies, like she was taught. Maybe she didn't care about books anymore – the true sign she was heading for disaster, according to her mother.

She asked me to drop her at a service station out of town. She could have asked me to drive her to Disney World and I would have, but she chose a service station three miles from home. Maybe in her head that was a place where a narrative shift would happen, a place in movies where things started and ended. A place where thoughts might grow, maybe. She watched too many movies, and that was our fault. She could say that now, knowing what we did. I worried it was her happy place. Because there were good snacks, but also because it was a sort of no-man's land, a void; if there was a portal to another dimension it would be in a petrol station bathroom.

She kept repeating that she wasn't mad and I worried she was glitching again because she didn't say much else.

She said she just needed to get her head straight because it was her head, after all, and we had done so much for so long that it was time. It was time. I said I understood. I said she was right, it was time. What else could I say? No, you can't go? Lock her in a room? That would be the worst thing. Alone in a room with her thoughts. The thing we had been trying so desperately to keep her from. I wished her parents were there but at the same time was glad they weren't, because I was definitely not handling this the right way. Who just let someone go? I always thought that thing people said about how if you loved someone you let them go was bullshit and lazy; if you loved someone you fought for them, didn't you? You did anything and everything to stop them leaving.

She put her feet up on the dashboard and turned up the radio and looked out of the window on the ride. She often sat like that, like she'd seen a girl in a movie do it but also maybe read on her phone how it was good to elevate your legs. She was a sum of everything she knew, which was who we all were, only she didn't claim to be original.

When we stopped at the service station, before she opened the car door, I said, And you won't tell me where you're going or what you're planning to do?

I don't know, she said, and I believed her.

I tried not to think about all the murderers waiting for her as I watched her disappear inside. A family with three kids, all screaming, including the adults, followed her in.

On the drive home I tried not to think about how she had me drop her at a service station because that was where people got rides to in movies and TV shows and this was her reality. I tried to clear my mind, but it didn't work because she wasn't in my mind, she was in my blood, my soul, and the car smelled of her, like Sprite, which didn't help. All I could think was how love transcended everything and it was a miracle I didn't crash because I was crying so hard I could barely see.

When I got back to our apartment, it felt like a tomb. I always thought it would be nice to be buried with Susan someday, if we both made it to old age, but this was like if we had a joint burial plot and she just decided at the last minute to be scattered at sea and now here I was, alone, in a big hole. Starved of oxygen, but of love mostly. It didn't help that the blinds were closed, and I'd accidentally dragged in some mud so it smelled a bit earthy. But I didn't feel like cleaning, or having to explain to the daylight why I'd let Susan go.

I spent the following days in partial darkness thinking I should probably shower and get dressed, but then I thought, Why bother if I don't have Susan? What was the point of anything without her? I told work I needed more personal days and they didn't care. I spent my time searching every inch of our apartment for signs she ever existed and checking the news to see if any girl's head had exploded.

Nick came over one night to check I was alive and I was so he left. He knew this was what I needed to do and didn't try to make me do anything else. The food delivery people also seemed to understand. One girl delivering pizza peered into my tomb, raised her eyebrows and said I should get a pet snake. I said how did she know I didn't have one, and she said because if I did, I'd have more self-respect.

I watched *Star Wars* on repeat until I didn't know what everyone's problem with Jar Jar Binks was and then went back to hating him. I didn't know what else I was supposed to do.

She was gone a week. In that time, God created the earth, allegedly, and I watched 100 hours of Netflix, but I took my accomplishments where I could get them. I've surpassed my 10,000 hours now, Malcolm Gladwell, does that mean I've transcended?

I didn't tell her parents I had driven her away, literally. I didn't want to give them the opportunity to tell me I could have made her stay. I couldn't. I didn't think I could find the words to explain what had happened between us. There weren't words anymore for it, just a feeling, in my shoulders, in my neck, like we'd been in a silent car crash.

That week I thought her parents might bug me all the time, wanting to know if I'd heard anything, but they didn't. We rattled around in our own brains, kept to our own hells. It didn't seem to matter now, what we did or thought. The thing that tied us together was gone, it didn't matter where. We were strangers again.

Kate came over. I decided the only way through without

Susan was to become Susan – old Susan anyway – to just switch off, let everything consume me. Which meant I had a hot date with John Wick and a pizza, if Kate didn't stay too long, which I knew she wouldn't, because she didn't like leaving her gym.

I'm not staying, don't worry, she said, because she knew me.

You can, I said, because I was trying to be more Susan.

Look, she said, sitting down on my game control, just so I knew how she still felt about boys who played video games, I know you're worried about Susan. I didn't want you to think I don't care, it's just I think we need to give her some space.

So, you're not worried at all? That she just left? I mean, as her employer, at least.

No, David, as her employer I'm not worried either. We can cope. Chloe can cover her classes.

And you're not at all curious where she's gone?

Knowing Susan, she's probably followed someone home, she said.

That's what I'm worried about, I said, thinking she'd done that before maybe and no one was telling me.

She's a grown woman, she said.

People keep telling me that, I said.

What is it exactly that you're worried about? Other than the obvious, she said.

Well, Kate, other than her brain exploding, I'm worried she might just not come back or she'll come back and leave me for good.

Well, you did lie to her, she said.

So did you, I said.

And so did her parents, she said. We all lied to her, but I think she gets it.

It's all too fucked up, I said. Don't you ever think that? Other people don't have to deal with this.

I was trying not to cry but also wondering where my pizza was.

Other people have other stuff, this is just ours, she said. Is it fucked up? Most definitely. But what can we do?

Her parents took me to see this man interested in studying Susan, I told her then.

Well, that's fucked up, she said. Why are you only telling me this now?

They think it might help her process everything, I said.

Or they're looking for someone else to take the blame if something happens, I get it, she said.

Oh, I didn't look at it like that, I said, the floor falling out from under me.

What was he like? she said.

Less creepy than you'd think, I said.

I think everyone's creepy, so I doubt it, she said.

And did you know her mum's been going to some women's philosophy group? I said, trying to emphasise that it was the philosophy bit I had a problem with, not the women.

I didn't. I knew she went to a few brain aneurysm things a while back, but then we all did. What's the deal with this philosophy group? she said. Sounds pretty rad to me.

That's what I thought at first, I said. I thought good for her, getting out of the house, doing something for herself, but then she said something about letting it slip about Susan to them and the woman who ran the group seemed really excited about it.

Oh, Kate said, biting her lip.

Exactly, I said. As soon as people find out, they think she's some experiment or something.

But they're women, Kate said.

I knew you'd say that.

Anyway, I just came over to check you were OK, she said.

You could have just texted me.

I could have, but I wanted to check you weren't just sitting in your underwear playing computer games with that friend of yours already, she said, looking around the apartment.

Not yet, I said.

I have to get back to my baby anyway, she said. She meant the gym.

Thanks for checking in — seriously, you're a good friend, I said.

I'm the fucking best, she said.

Kate left and my pizza showed up. I wondered what Susan was eating for dinner. I hoped she was just mad at us and not mad at food.

I went back to work after a few days, to distract myself mostly, and to smell new smells that weren't sadness and my own stench, and after work I went and played video games with Nick and then went home and watched Netflix till my eyes bled. It didn't even feel like a regression, me back with Nick; more like a chance to recalibrate, get back on track.

Kate still didn't seem worried. I casually went by after work to the gym one night, on my way to Nick's, and her face turned to thunder as soon as she saw me.

I haven't heard anything so you're wasting your time, she said, hands on hips.

How do you know I'm not here to use the bathroom? I said.

You wouldn't dare, she said.

Always a pleasure, I said, and left.

I got it. She was mad at me even if Susan wasn't. I fucked everything up in her eyes. She wanted the two of them to grow old together. Two old women pushing shopping carts round the park, tripping up kids, whistling at men, getting back at the world for whatever it did or didn't do. At this rate she'd die alone or be forced to settle down and do all the regular-people crap and her gym would become a Starbucks. Susan would still come, though, because it was Starbucks.

Rebecca

It was one of those coincidences again, the ones we didn't believe in. We were on our way to this new bagel place Isaac had read about online; it was further than we'd usually go for bagels, but we needed something to do, something to care about. We were trying to carry on like normal and like our daughter wasn't missing, presumed dead. We would see a movie later – we didn't care what; we'd already spent too much energy caring about the bagels.

We were crossing the street when Isaac thought he saw Martin in a restaurant. He pointed. There was Martin. And next to him was Bea. And opposite them was Susan. We froze.

We watched Martin put his hand on Bea's and she leaned in and kissed him.

Bea was Martin's wife. How had we not known? Was there a photo of her in his office I missed? Or a photo of him at their home, maybe? I'd been too busy thinking about Pringles probably.

Bea believed in philosophy and magic and Martin believed in science. How did that work? I tried to think back to that first time at her house – had there been any signs of him? Then I remembered the locked door, the noises. Had this been their plan all along? Who was working who? I thought Isaac had found Martin and I had found Bea, but maybe I was wrong. Krystal had approached me at that talk and invited me to Bea's. She'd found me. But Martin? We needed to get out of the road anyway.

I know that woman, I said.

What do you mean, you know that woman?

That woman Martin's with. I know her.

What do you mean, you know her?

She's from my women's philosophy group. Where did you find Martin anyway? I said, narrowly escaping a taxi.

Online, Isaac said, still watching the restaurant.

Yes, but how, I said.

I don't remember, he said.

You need to remember, I said.

I don't remember, he said.

Could he have sent you something and you clicked on it? I said.

Maybe, he said.

We all need to stop clicking on things, I said.

OK, I'll tell the world, he said. But he wasn't paying attention to me.

So, he found you, really, I said.

I don't remember, he said, I get sent a lot of things. What does it matter?

It matters, I said. It matters a lot. They knew about Susan.

We both stood staring at the restaurant, unable to move, physically or mentally. Just cardboard cut-outs of people now, paper thin, ones you could punch straight through. They had our daughter.

It was what we'd been trying to prevent and it was happening, right in front of our eyes. If we'd been any later, they might have had her in the trunk of their car, driving her to wherever their secret lair was, the one with the empty room they wanted to put her in and make her think.

I felt sick. I walked away because I didn't know what else to do but walking sometimes helped me collect my thoughts. Isaac followed.

What do we do?

Nothing, I said.

They have our daughter, he said.

I know they have our fucking daughter, I said. I saw exactly what you saw.

So that's the woman from your philosophy group, he said.

Yes, that's Bea, I said.

She looks way creepier than my guy, he said, and I had to laugh. The sick feeling was easing.

OK, he said, so we just trust that Susan will know what to do.

Like what Martin said about instinct, I said, annoyed that his words had penetrated my asshole forcefield.

Ha, exactly, Isaac said. Or we could hide in those bushes over there and watch them. He pointed to some conveniently placed bushes.

I'm really not in the mood to hide in some bushes, I said.

What if we just go in? I said. What if we just walk up to them and sit down and pretend we're late to brunch with two friends and our daughter and then we all go home and it's all OK? I said.

He was looking at his phone then, though. I was still looking at the restaurant. People walked past thinking we were a normal couple, one looking at a restaurant, already knowing what to order, or not caring, just needing to eat, the other scrolling through his phone desperately trying to find that place someone told him about, the one with the tacos that would change his life. I wished that for my husband, I really did, not this. I didn't want my life to change, I wanted it to go back to how it was, when Susan didn't know and we were the bad guys.

It's OK, he said. I just read something about how mindfulness isn't cool anymore. He put his phone in his back pocket and I willed someone to steal it.

Really? That quick? I said, moving out of the way for a man with a double buggy. He didn't thank me, though, and I felt pure rage.

On my phone, yes, Isaac said, moving out of the way of a jogger.

I know on your phone. I meant, what happened? I said.

Apparently, the youth are all about activism now, so sitting around thinking is out, Isaac said, trying to move me out of the way of two women in power suits, ruling the pavement if not the boardroom, although I suspected they ruled that too.

Thank God, I said. He seemed relieved by this news he'd just read on his phone, in the street, while our daughter was still inside with her captors, so I humoured him for a second.

I mean, Susan does love a march, I said, because she had been to them all the last few years. I think mostly because they were right on her way to work so she had to walk through them and then she was there so she stayed a while. She cared, just in her own way, by proximity.

We were almost in an alleyway now and it was my least favourite place to hang out so I motioned to a McDonald's across the street. That's what those golden arches were for, after all, beacons, or at least that's what the commercials kept drilling into us. We can save you, if you let us.

Really? he said, his eyes lighting up like I was offering him something sexual.

Yes, but don't inhale, I said. Susan loved McDonald's because of her father. She wrote something at school once that said, I love my dad because he buys me McDonald's and Isaac pinned it up in his office. I was sure it fell out of favour for a while, something about it killing you, but it was back in a big way again, retro, more transparent, but more importantly still cheap, delicious. Bright. A literal beacon. McDonald's wasn't a place for metaphors.

We sat down in the window and pretended we might order something, but no one cared. People were too busy in their food comas. The delicate nature of our conversation would be kept secret, padded, by the noise of a dozen high-school kids throwing fries at each other and teasing one of them about his shit trainers. I should have raised Susan here, given birth to her in the bathroom so they felt obliged to keep us, feed us.

We could see the restaurant where Susan was perfectly from where we were seated. There were no signs of trouble. Just three people having lunch. A girl and her parents, or a couple trying to convince a girl to join them in a threesome – however your mind worked. Mine didn't.

Show me what you read then, I said, holding my hand out for his phone. You can get me a coffee, I said. Me reading, him waiting on me: this was the life I was meant to have, not this other hell of our own making.

He handed me his phone and did as he was told. I watched him look at the self-service screens and decide against it, and I hadn't even told him that I read they found human faeces on most of them. He just knew. Instinct. Good boy. Martin had infected my brain, even if he hadn't got to Susan's yet.

According to Isaac's phone, mindfulness had gone full circle. It had been advertised as the antidote to capitalism, gone mainstream, been celebrity endorsed; everyone was so inward focused and downward dogging that they were missing everything that was actually going on, which was the hellmouth we opened. It became quasi-religious and as soon as a rapper made it like a cult no one was interested anymore. Thinking wouldn't change things, action would. That's what they realised. These kids. These smart, wonderful kids. But just as I thought that I heard one of the kids throwing fries shout, Penis!

Isaac was back with my coffee then but looked like he'd just got back from war.

I thought this classified as a McFlurry situation, I said, taking my drink, but OK.

You just said coffee, he said, sitting down and staring across the street at the restaurant.

Maybe we should have got her chipped, he said, then we could hear what they were saying.

Not funny, I said, handing him back his phone.

I wasn't trying to be.

What we did was plenty enough. They haven't moved anyway. She's still there. I looked across the street to the restaurant.

Did you read the raisin thing? I said, looking back at Isaac. Some woman is teaching people how to eat a fucking raisin, like it's a life skill we all need, like it will enlighten us.

I didn't read the raisin thing, he said. I was getting you coffee.

They might put her in an empty room and then make her eat a raisin really slowly, I said, putting my hands to my head. Ask her to really think about that raisin and really taste it, savour it, until boom. Raisins had gone from nature's candy to nature's napalm in a blink.

I think they have bigger plans for her than raisins, Isaac said.

What is happening? I said, opening my coffee and peering into it, hoping if I stared at it, it would know to taste good because I needed it to be good, but not so good that I had to come here for my coffee now because that would be fucked up.

I don't know, he said. I thought you might say it was a sign. He didn't look in his coffee. He didn't want to know. Sorry, he said.

We've gone full circle, I guess. The universe kept her safe and then threw us a spanner and now it's back to keeping her safe maybe, I said. It's the universe, it's not known for making sense. I looked around. Why does everyone in here have better skin than me?

Because they're all 14, he said, not looking.

Thank you, I said.

Do you want to hide in the bushes yet? he said, looking at the bushes longingly.

I still don't really feel like it, I said. I feel a bit defeated. That should be the McDonald's slogan.

Shall I just go in and get our daughter back? Isaac said then, puffing his chest up like a pigeon.

I guess people thought the answer might be inside them and then saw what was inside them and realised that there wasn't anything there so are looking outside again, I said, still thinking about what I'd just read on his phone.

They're leaving! Look! Isaac said then.

Susan was leaving the restaurant then, quickly followed by Martin and Bea. They could have easily been her parents who she'd just met for lunch. It wasn't the sex thing. Only we were her parents, and we were hiding in McDonald's spying on her.

Bea seemed to look across the street, to the McDonald's, at me, just for a second, a glance, like she knew we were there somehow.

I watched them go in the same direction as Susan but a few feet behind her.

We have to follow them! I said, jumping up.

So, you didn't want to hide in any bushes, but you want to follow them now?

They're up to something! I said, wondering why he wasn't more alarmed. It's happening!

Why don't I call Martin? See what he says? he said, getting his phone out again. I almost smacked it out of his hand.

And say what?

Just a casual call, like, Hey, what are you up to? Want to get a smoothie?

Why a smoothie?

Because I just had coffee.

He's not going to say, Oh, hey, I'm just abducting your daughter.

He might.

Call her, not him. Call Susan.

And say what?

Remind her of stranger danger, tell her we have cake, I don't know.

This is ridiculous, he said. I'm just going to go and confront them. They can't do this, he said then, alarmed finally. He was more like Susan now, slow to react, if ever, but that instinct was finally there. He had to save his daughter. And not with his phone.

We left the McDonald's and went in the direction they'd gone in but there was no sign of them already.

She's probably in the trunk of his car by now, I said, thinking about what might have happened next, thinking the worst possible things. I stopped dead in the street, much to the annoyance of the man behind me. I got why people did that now.

Or the trunk of her car, Isaac said.

Really? We're doing that now? I said, trying not to have a panic attack.

I don't think you can just put someone in the trunk of your car on a busy street in the middle of the day, he said.

We have to trust her, I said then, feeling the weight of everything suddenly, like I might pass out. Because I can't do this, I said.

He put his arm around me then and steadied me, tethered me. I didn't care about blocking the pavement with our tenderness, our rawness. I'd seen enough girls crying in the street to know sometimes you just had to let your body take over.

Let's go home, he said, taking my hand. We'll go home and we'll call Susan and if she doesn't answer then we'll call the police. I think she'll answer, though. I think she'll be home already, he said.

OK, I said, letting him lead me home.

And then we'll find Martin and Bea and . . . and I don't know how to finish that sentence, he said.

He was right. What could we do? Beat them up? I definitely had enough rage in me to punch someone, but then what? We'd be arrested, charged with assault, and they'd just go on with their lives, only I'd have a taste for punching then, have to do a career pivot from librarian to cage fighting; it could happen, but I wouldn't know who I was anymore.

When we were home, we still didn't know what to do. We hoped by then one of us might have known, but we didn't, and were cross at ourselves and each other. It was a weird fight to be in, but we were in it now.

Should we tell David? he said, hanging up his coat.

What, so another man can not do something? I said, instantly regretting it, but he understood. He just looked at me, blinked a few times, then said to let him know when I knew what to do.

David

They decided not to tell me they thought Susan had possibly been abducted until after it had happened. I should have known they wouldn't hesitate to lie to me. This was all their lie we were drowning in, after all.

What would you have done anyway? her mother said, and she was right, other than definitely hidden in the bushes. I would have probably done exactly the same as them – nothing.

We'd all thought that if Susan was ever gone, we might feel a weight lifted, from the change at least, but instead we couldn't breathe. I wanted to say to them, She's gone, not dead. Don't you see? We're still winning. Still winning still winning. I felt like Charlie Sheen, and no one wanted to feel like that.

None of us knew where she was that week or what she was doing. Or if they did, they weren't saying. I thought Kate might know really, and if I turned up at the gym unexpectedly, she might give it away, or Chloe might know something and let it slip, but no. The world went on, as it does. Say what you want about our sad little planet, but it has an amazing ability to just keep going.

That was our punishment. Susan knew how to hurt us. She knew that not knowing, that a loss, an absence, space, where anything could exist, or nothing, was where the power lay and would remain there between us all forever. A lost week. Something she felt she was owed.

Kate came round one night.

Everything was fine, she said, sitting down. She meant, This is all your fault.

They can't know how it would have been if I hadn't come along, though. Maybe someone else would have. Maybe this was always going to happen now. I wanted to feel like I mattered, though, even if it was for something bad, so I told myself it was my fault, she was right, but to her I said, She needed to get away from all of us, not just me.

But mostly you, Kate said, staring at my paused video game.

Now Susan was gone we didn't have to hold it together for anyone.

Wanna play? I said, holding the second controller out to her.

No, I don't want to fucking play, she said, but then she took the controller.

Yes, I want to play, she said. Teach me how to fucking turn my brain off and submit to whatever god this is.

We played for a few minutes, but her heart wasn't in it. I watched her throw the controller onto the couch.

What? You thought it was going to be just the two of you forever? I said, pausing the game again.

Growing old together, getting a butt load of cats, like those two old sisters in the park with the shopping carts?

Yes, she said, closing her eyes and leaning back on the couch.

Susan was never yours, I said.

Or yours, she said.

We were both always relieved that there was never any sexual tension between us. We were too exhausted and sad to fight properly, though.

So, you don't think she's been happy at all with me? I asked her then.

I'm not saying that, she said.

So, what are you saying?

I'm saying boys ruin everything and you can't understand because you are one, she said.

I understand, I said.

You can't, she said.

Susan always had boyfriends, she said, or boys hanging around her. They're drawn to her. She was always so carefree, always gave zero shits. She's not like other girls, you know that.

So, what? You were jealous?

No, I was worried, she said. I was always worried. I'll always be worried.

I get it, I said.

I should have hugged her, but I knew it wouldn't help so I turned off my computer, to show I wasn't a complete prick like she suspected.

When she'd gone, I lay on the couch with the TV turned up full volume to try to drown out my thoughts of Susan, but it didn't work. The neighbours banged on the wall at one point. Someone shouted, Turn your fucking TV down! but I didn't.

Can't, sorry, I said, to myself. They turned theirs up instead. I was helping them block whatever they needed to block, which was me in this situation.

I thought about how Susan might have just stayed at the service station. There was a cheap chain motel there, for people who didn't want to sleep in their cars, or who didn't drive trucks. For people who didn't want to go where they were supposed to go. I thought about what she did immediately after I'd driven off. Maybe she bought gum, sunglasses, because that's what people did in the movies. Maybe in her head none of this was real. Maybe she'd chatted to the guy on the till, asked him what he was thinking, and he just thought she was like all the other girls, wanting something from him he didn't want to give, or didn't know how. Maybe she'd petted a dog, asked it what it was thinking, then went and sat outside and waited for me to come and get her, but I didn't. Maybe she sat out there the whole seven days, and all the people who worked there and visited there in between their lives became her family, and every dog she saw became her dog, every baby her baby, if only for a few minutes, and that was enough, and she just thought her thoughts like anyone else, like it came naturally, like she didn't know what we'd been so worried about, what all the fuss was about.

Only she wasn't like anyone else, and whatever she thought she was doing could be dangerous. There was no way to know. All we could do was wait, and waiting to see if someone you love's head is going to explode is my least favourite thing to do.

I wanted to know what thoughts she was having now. I wanted to know where she was, what she was doing, and with whom. I pictured her mother's face saying, Where is my daughter? She'd always known, till now. She'd never known what she was thinking, and didn't expect to ever know. We had all come to that same realisation, that you couldn't actually know what anyone was ever thinking; the people you were closest to were no exception. Everyone was at the same distance really. And I couldn't tell her not to worry, that her daughter was safe, that Susan knew what she was doing, because I had no idea if any of that was true. All I knew was that she was gone. I wasn't even sure if she had ever been there, in that way you sometimes didn't know if anything was even real, which was not a good place to be, not alone anyway.

I really should have gone outside and sat in a park in that week, let daylight keep me safe, let nature work its magic, but I chose darkness and Netflix.

I looked for different signs that she was gone other than the gaping hole inside me. I peered through the blinds and thought, was the city quieter somehow now, were the lights less bright, like it knew it didn't have to be her buffer? When the microwave beeped now was it calling her?

I was trapped in my head with the thoughts of a mad man I vaguely recognised and there was nothing I could do about it. A simple thing like making toast reminded me of Susan and made the task impossible. I found myself stroking the toaster at one point, peering in the crumb tray for her last known toast crumbs, and then the butter was problematic, because I could see where her knife had been and my own knife hovered over it and I felt like weeping until I saw my reflection staring back at me in the knife and I dropped it on the kitchen floor, aghast at what I'd become.

I didn't want toast then, or ever again maybe. So I tried my luck with cereal, but as my hand reached for the box I felt bad for the toast, so I put the cereal box back and made another attempt at making toast, but then I started to worry that the toast had seen me go for the cereal. I didn't quite hear the cereal calling me – You know you want me – but I could have, if I'd given in to the madness, like my brain seemed to want. As if being held prisoner by my regular thoughts wasn't torturous enough.

It was too much.

I'm having toast so shut the fuck up! I said, out loud, like a proper mad.

Who are you trying to kid? my brain said. Not, Who are you talking to?

When the toast finally popped up, it startled me and I laughed nervously as I resentfully buttered the toast and ate it over the sink, trying to avoid catching my reflection in the knife again, because I was cry-eating toast over the sink in my underpants now.

Susan

Day One

Holy fucking shit! I have something wrong with my brain. I fucking knew something was up. I thought I might be getting sick, but I know when I'm getting a fucking cold and this wasn't it. It felt like I was sort of sick in my head, and I was, I guess. Lol.

It started back when I had this weird thing happen at the supermarket. I'd gone in to get a loaf of bread, totes normal, but when I picked one up off the shelf, it was like I was suddenly aware of how many other types of bread there were, like fucking hundreds. There was so much fucking bread! Who knew? Too many, though, like I started looking at all the types of bread you could buy and then I didn't know which one I was supposed to get. It would have been way easier if there was just one. It made my brain feel weird. I didn't know which bread to get then so I gave up and went home. It felt fucking awful. My brain was all like, wtf? How does anyone know what bread to get?

I thought maybe I was depressed. Everyone was depressed now. So many singers I liked were bringing out whole albums about it and people seemed to be really into it, but I couldn't ever understand what they were so depressed about? They basically had everything. But if I was depressed, it didn't have to be a big deal, it was normal. Only I didn't feel sad, so I didn't think that was it.

I asked Kate and she said I should speak to my parents so I went over there and they told me if I think too hard my brain will explode. What the actual fuck?

They said they didn't tell me before because they didn't want me to think about it, but now I couldn't not think about it a bit, obvs, and they said I had to try really hard, because it was dangerous.

I don't really know how to feel about it. I'm pissed they'd kept it from me, but I don't really know what to think about it. And I can't even google it, because it doesn't have a name. I told them I understood, though, because I didn't want them to think I was stupid, or worry. They seem really worried. My dad had a fucking vein popping in his forehead.

I did google 'what to do if your whole life has been a lie', though. But there wasn't anyone like me. It was all people who found out they were adopted, or whose parents weren't who they thought they were, like their sister was really their mum, lol.

Stefan said how lucky I was, that most people went through their whole life not realising it was a lie. I didn't know what he meant but it was nice to talk to someone who hadn't lied to me.

I always thought everyone thought like me. Well, not exactly like me, obviously. But basically, we were all the same. I thought people were basically good and basically the same and we should all be equal and we wanted the same things: shelter, food, love. I didn't think we all thought the same things; I knew my father never once thought about Kesha's tattoos, but

I thought our brains all worked in basically the same way. I thought we were all mostly thinking about what to eat next. I don't know what I think now.

They thought I was going to think myself to death, though. Lol.

Have I not been thinking this whole time? I mean, like, I'm 25, so I must have thought something. I was definitely thinking that right then.

I left a note so it wasn't like I just disappeared. I didn't leave to hurt them or worry them. I really just felt like what I needed to do was not be there. To go somewhere on my own. To be alone with myself. And I didn't know myself, so I was going away with a complete stranger, lol.

I got David to take me to a service station and I could tell he thought it was a bad idea. To me they were beacons of hope when you were trapped in a car for hours and felt like you might never see civilisation again. They had somewhere you could pee and eat. What more did you want? And you could buy all sorts of excellent crap there, like card games and cuddly toys and CDs and sunglasses and maps no one wanted because we had our phones, duh, and Amazon.

It wasn't a real place. It didn't have an address. It was somewhere in between life, a break from life, but still with all the familiar things you needed to survive, like McDonald's and Starbucks and bathrooms. I felt in between lives now, so it suited me.

In movies people hitchhiked to gas stations all the time. OK, so they got murdered a lot, but they were still trying to escape their lives, and if they were dead, they did escape, I guess.

As soon as David drove off, though, I realised I didn't want to get murdered, so I went inside and bought a large Diet Coke from McDonald's, then got an Uber back to the city. I switched off the bit of my brain that was now telling me this was not a normal thing to do. To ask to go somewhere, then immediately need to leave. The Coke made me feel normal anyway. Nothing bad could happen to you while you were drinking a Coke. The rest of it I tried not to think about, which was hard now my brain felt like it was on fire a bit.

While I waited for my ride, I watched a family with three kids; all of them were crying and yelling, even the adults, and it was a lot of life to witness in one go, so I was glad I left when I did. I didn't usually mind all the everything, but I felt a bit tender now, like when you get a light sunburn.

I was glad the Uber driver was chatty and had the radio on. I let all the sounds wash over me. I looked out the window and said hi to the city again, touched the window. I'd only been gone for 30 minutes, but I'd missed it. I tried to tune out my head and tune in the world.

I had no idea what I was doing really, though. My brain felt like someone had pulled all the wires out, and I was trying to put them back in, but I didn't really know where they went, so I was just putting them anywhere, and it wasn't really working. I wasn't really working.

I wanted them all to think I'd left, even though I was back. Technically, I had left, briefly. I wanted them to worry really. They looked at me differently now. Like they were trying to see into my brain. Maybe they always looked at me like that, I didn't know. I didn't notice before. Now I noticed things, everything, and I didn't like it. It was like waking up from a dream, but that dream was your life.

I always thought we all lived in our own bubbles and that we bounced off each other, like billions of tiny bubbles. I didn't know I was actually outside my own bubble, loose in the world. I was OK with it, but I also wanted to know what it was like in my bubble, the one inside my own head. I had no idea what it was like in there. Most people didn't seem to like themselves very much. I hoped I wasn't an asshole.

People went away to find themselves all the time. I always thought, Just look in the mirror, idiot. Now I had to do that. I looked at my reflection in my phone, but it didn't help. I already knew what I looked like. But what did I think like? Who the fuck was I? It was a huge question. One I'd never asked myself because I assumed I knew who I was. These thoughts made my head throb slightly; it wasn't an awful pain, but I knew I didn't want it to get worse, that this was what I was supposed to be avoiding.

I hadn't lost my mind. It was still there. I just needed to get to know it. I pictured my brain like an animal I was now entrusted to take care of. I had so many questions, though. What if I didn't like myself? What if they were all making a big fuss about nothing and I could actually control my mind just fine? I hadn't thought myself to death yet, had I? I wasn't stupid.

I remembered reading about some celebrities that had gone to silent retreats, to be alone with their thoughts. It was all the rage at one time. I'd skim read it and thought how awful, but that was what I needed to do. I googled 'celebrity silent retreat' from the back of the Uber. A beautiful spa came up, with pictures of beautiful people in luxury athleisure wear doing yoga on a beach. It looked boring. And expensive, for no fun. My search also brought up several news stories about people who owned these retreats who were now in jail for sex crimes. I scrolled through BuzzFeed for a while and did a quiz to see what character from *Friends* I was, but I stopped before finding out – I didn't really care anymore. I used to care.

I thought about going to a hotel and trying to recreate the

silent retreat myself. But wearing normal clothes, and not doing yoga. Just doing the thinking bit, the sitting bit, but I couldn't afford a hotel either. Then I remembered Stefan saying I could crash at his any time. I didn't think I ever would, because I was with David obviously, but since David had lied to me and I needed somewhere to crash, I thought, Why not?

I liked hanging out with Stefan. He was easy to be around. I could do my thinking when he was at work, or taking a shit. I could take walks and think. People did that. I could do that. Usually, I walked and listened to music or walked and talked or walked and ate, but I could give just walking a go. I didn't usually like being on my own, it made me uneasy, but I could give it a try. I always had to have music on, or the TV, or both, but I preferred company. It was all starting to make sense now. I was blocking something.

I went to Stefan's and when he opened the door, I suddenly thought, I'm supposed to have sex with him, aren't I? That's what someone in a movie or book would do now. To hurt David. Stefan did have nice eyes and good hair and smelled like the ocean, but it was probably out of a bottle. He was straight out of a YA novel that was a movie on Netflix now, a sequel in the works. He should have been called Chip or Chad. He should have opened the door in a towel and carried me to bed. It would have been easier than me standing there thinking how my brain wanted to sleep with him, but my body was cockblocking me. Sex was easier when I wasn't thinking about it. Everything was easier when I wasn't thinking about it.

Hey, I said. He wasn't in a towel, thankfully, but he was in shorts. No shirt. He looked at my bag.

Hey, you, he said, which was cute, but my brain wasn't turned on.

Going somewhere? he asked.

Here, if that's OK, I said.

I'm actually just leaving, he said, and I saw his own bag in the hall.

Oh, I said.

I'm going surfing, he said, flipping his hair, because of course he surfed.

But you can totally crash here, he said.

He looked like he might have just woken up. His hair was tousled. But then I remembered he always looked like this. His eyes were never fully open, because he was stoned a lot of the time, but it suited him.

I still hadn't completely ruled out seducing him. I tried to think what a girl from a 90s romcom would do, when heteronormative comedies were all the rage, but I couldn't remember any of them – the girls or the movies – they all merged into one. But my body wasn't having it anyway. I'd never felt less sexual.

Stefan invited me in and I put my bag down next to his.

His apartment was airy and light, beachy, mostly because of the vintage surf posters on the walls. There was a bong on the table. It tracked. He didn't have a door between his living room and his bedroom; instead, there was some weird beaded curtain hanging down. I could see his unmade bed through it. I'd woken him up. I was peering into his bedroom now, staring at his bed, trying to make out if I could see cum stains or if it was the light, but still, my body didn't care. My brain was the only thing throbbing.

Is everything OK? he said, flipping his hair again. Boys who flipped their hair were dangerous – TV shows had taught us that.

Did you know about my brain? I said, moving away from his bedroom.

I only just found out, he said, closing the front door. He was standing there in just his shorts and I was in all my clothes and coat.

Should I put my coat on? he joked, and I laughed because it was funny.

Yes, please, I said.

He took his coat off the hook by the door and put it on. Now he was in his shorts and his coat and it was funny. We stayed standing in his tiny hall.

I swear I only just found out, he said, rubbing his chin, and I believed him.

Who told you? I asked.

He moved into his kitchen/living room and I followed him.

Chloe, obviously, he said. I'm surprised she kept it secret for as long as she did to be honest, she's got such a huge fucking mouth.

I looked at his mouth. He had the same mouth as her. I'd never noticed that before. Then I realised they were twins. Duh. That made sense.

He started making coffee and I wanted to tell him I just drank a large Coke, but I didn't, because I was trying not to say everything out loud. It was hard, though. Like I had to really hold it in. I didn't like it just staying in there. It felt pointless. I tried not to think anything at all mostly.

That's probably my fault, I said, about Chloe's big mouth. I think they're all used to oversharing because I do.

No way, he said, looking in the fridge. Everyone does it, it's not you.

You're just saying that, I said.

I can't trust anyone anymore, I thought. I'd never thought anything that dark before and it scared me. I wanted to feel safe. I didn't feel safe.

Other people don't say everything they're thinking, though, do they? I said, because that's what I was thinking.

Yeah, they do, he said. People think everyone cares what they're thinking.

What are you thinking? I asked. He'd found some milk and I watched him sniff it. I wanted to say, Never sniff the milk, but didn't.

I'm thinking, why are you here? he said.

I looked at him then; this was the bit in those movies where there was supposed to be sexual tension, but it wasn't the movies, so there was something, but I didn't know what. I think people who wrote movies might be lying to us all.

Does David know you're here? he said.

At hearing David's name my brain lit up. David! Your boyfriend! The one who lied to you. Lying is bad, remember, Susan!

You mean, the one who's been lying to me all this time? I said.

Only to keep you safe, Stefan said.

They think I'm off finding myself, I said. Lol.

Stefan was next to me then.

I'm not that deep, I shrugged.

Me either, he said and kissed me.

The kiss triggered something in me that reminded me who I was, or who I thought I was.

I like to eat I like to sleep I like to fuck I like to watch TV – what else is there? I said, after he'd finished kissing me.

We're all going to die, we're all going to hell, what's the big deal? I said.

What about David? he said. He's a good guy. He loves you.

Don't you want to fuck me? I said. I thought maybe if I said the word fuck my body might know I needed to get fucked now, not think, or talk.

Yes, he said, but I don't think you really do. He rubbed his chin again.

Why are you thinking so much? I said, bored of him now, frustrated. Going there was a mistake.

Because you can't, he said, brushing my hair from my eyes.

Ugh, I said, pushing his hand away. You're all so annoying, I said, because I thought it. I meant all humans, but that was a dark thought for a novice thinker.

I picked up my bag, ready to leave.

Where are you going? he said, then, Stay, please. I'm leaving, remember?

I put my bag down and let out a huge sigh. I had nowhere else to go.

Fine, I said. I'll stay. But only because you're leaving.

You should come surfing, he said. The ocean really helps clear my head.

I watched him grab a shirt from his bedroom, then pick up his keys from the side. He took one off and handed it to me. I had the strange desire to stick the key into his chest and turn it, to inflict pain on him, for making me think things I didn't want to think about, like cheating on David, even for a second. Maybe I was secretly a psychopath.

I didn't want to clear my head anyway. I wanted to see inside it, see all the muck, see it for what it was. Surfing also sounded lame. Woah, hang ten, whatever.

Call me if you need anything, but I think you'll be OK, he said, kissing me again, but on the cheek this time, and I didn't move out of the way or slap him. Then he left.

It was just me and his rancid milk then.

Fuck thinking, I thought and said, plopping down on his couch. Fuck all of them, I said.

I sat like that on Stefan's couch for a while. I didn't know how to proceed. I inspected the bong. I didn't do drugs. I think I knew why now. My brain knew it was weird enough, maybe. I always liked boys who smoked, though. I didn't know why. Movies probably. David didn't smoke, but I think he wished he did sometimes. It was nice to have something in your hand. Thinking about hands made me want a Starbucks.

I went outside and there was a Starbucks right across the street, obviously. I was happy to see it. Nothing bad could happen to me in there. You never heard about some girl's head exploding in Starbucks.

I went inside and got my usual drink, a vanilla latte, because it wasn't pumpkin spice season. But when I took a sip, it didn't taste right. Usually, I didn't think about what it tasted like. I just drank it. But now I was thinking about how it tasted, and it tasted wrong. Not like they made it wrong, but that my mouth was wrong, or my brain. Then I started thinking how it wasn't the drink at all, it was me.

I threw it in the trash and went outside. My brain was trying to ruin Starbucks for me.

There was a couple walking a dog. I stopped to pet the dog and told one of the girls I liked her jacket. I didn't really like her jacket, so I don't know why I said I did, but we talked about jackets for a few minutes and that led to small talk about the weather that I was comfortable with. I was bent down the whole time, squinting up at them, but when I looked back down at the dog and looked deep into its eyes, I thought, What makes you so great? Are you even that great? Then the dog rubbed on me and I thought, You're so fucking dumb. I could be a tree – you don't care about me. So, I stood up and walked off. I thought I heard one of the girls say I was weird, and I wanted to say, I am, yes, it's new, I'm sorry, but I kept walking.

My brain was ruining dogs for me. I stopped to pet it because

I always stopped to pet dogs, but I never thought about it. I was suddenly thinking about things I usually didn't think about, and I didn't like it. I was doing all the things I usually did but it was all different now. I felt discombobulated and had to look up what that word meant on my phone, and it was how I felt but it didn't make me feel any better.

It wasn't a sickness then, but a feeling, like a wall was coming down, only I hadn't even known I had a wall. It was weird and confusing and I didn't like it and could feel that slight pain in my head back again so I tried not to think about it.

Stefan lived in a part of the city we never went, so I didn't think anyone would think to look for me there, if they were looking at all. No one had texted me, so I guessed they were giving me my space.

I wished I could afford a room in a hotel. I loved a mediocre hotel room. I was the only person who wanted to hear their neighbours. I could pretend Stefan's place was an Airbnb; it basically was, but free. I hoped he had really thin walls. I was sure he must – he couldn't even afford a door for his bedroom.

I was talking to myself a lot. I was aware that I was saying stuff out loud now. I wasn't quite having a conversation with myself, but I was saying what I was doing to myself, like how people talked to babies. I was lonely probably. I'd never been alone. I didn't like it. It was physically uncomfortable, like I could feel my body if I listened hard enough, and I had no desire to be reminded of my mortality, not till I knew how to deal with it.

I took a deep breath, which I'd heard might help, and reminded myself I had my phone, and music, and there was a TV back at Stefan's.

Then it hit me: I hadn't checked that he had a TV. I panicked.

I could feel my heart thudding, and it wasn't the caffeine, because I'd thrown my coffee away. What if he was one of those weird people who didn't have a TV? He did have a hippy vibe. He thought beads could be a door, for fuck's sake.

I ran back to Stefan's place like I'd left the oven on and left a child in there.

I was so relieved to see his giant TV that I almost cried. I didn't know how I missed it. I must have been in my own head. Ugh.

I turned the TV on just to check it worked. As soon as it came on, I felt better. The apartment was flooded with light and sound, life. I wasn't alone anymore.

I thought, If I get bored of TV, I can always go and see a movie, but then once I'd thought it, I wanted to go to a movie, to stare at an even bigger screen, eat food that didn't count because it was dark, so I went out again.

I ended up seeing the new *Star Wars*, again. We'd already seen it, but we saw them twice sometimes, three times once. It was long and loud, but it was what I needed. Familiar.

I tried not to look at the other people with other people and feel that loss. I tried to really focus on what was happening on the screen and let it trick my brain into thinking it mattered. I needed it to block out the thought of Stefan kissing me and what that meant. But I couldn't. My mind wandered now. It never used to. I didn't like how it felt. My mind was free now, to go where it wanted.

Watching movies wasn't the same now. And not just because I'd seen this one. I blamed the actors and directors for not making better movies. Their job was to entertain me and I didn't feel entertained. I felt restless. Like when I went with David recently. I just couldn't give myself over to it in the same way. I'd never felt restless until recently. I didn't like it. I wanted it to stop. I was focused before, on nothing, but I was focused. Now I didn't know what I was.

People were always saying your parents fuck you up, but I didn't think they meant like this.

After the movie I didn't want to go back to the empty apartment so I went into the loudest, busiest-looking chain restaurant that most people avoided. I was so desperate to talk to someone other than myself that I befriended the waitress, even though I could tell she was only being nice to me so I'd leave her a good tip. I took what I could get for human affection now my family had abandoned me in my body. That's how it felt, like I was a newborn, just starting to make sense of the world, but utterly alone.

I ate my burger and read about *Star Wars* on my phone in the opposite of peace. Almost every few minutes someone's kid was throwing a crayon or food in my direction, or a tray was being slammed down, a plate clattering. The muzak didn't stand a chance.

Then I had an unsettling thought: Do I like *Star Wars* because David likes *Star Wars*? This was an entirely new thought, and not a pleasant one. It made my eye twitch.

Then I thought, Do I like *Star Wars* because the world likes *Star Wars*? This was a strange thought I didn't know what to do with, so I asked the waitress if she liked *Star Wars* and she said, Not really, which didn't help, so I leaned forward and asked the couple in the next booth.

I love *Star Wars*, the girl said. Did you just see the new movie?

I did, I said, because I did.

Did you love it? she asked.

I did, I said, because I did. The first time anyway. Before all this. The music always filled me with a rush of pure joy.

Did you love it? I asked the boy sitting opposite.

It was OK, he said. I prefer the old ones.

Huh, I said, did you ever think why you love it? Like, do you ever wonder if you really do love it or if it's just because everyone else loves it? I said.

Huh, the girl said.

They looked at each other and then at me. I think they thought I might work for George Lucas, or Disney, or something. They didn't like thinking about what I asked them. I'd made them uncomfortable.

Thanks, I said, and went back to reading my phone and shoving fistfuls of fries into my face and trying not to think how it was maybe impossible for anyone to live an authentic life so why bother? Wasn't every single thing we saw or read or heard edited by someone with their own agenda anyway?

I reluctantly left the heaving bosom of the restaurant and went back to Stefan's where I immediately put the TV on and collapsed in front of it.

I needed to think. I needed to turn the fucking TV off, even though I'd only just put it on. I needed to put my phone away and think. I needed to find out what the fuck was going on with me.

I scrolled through the internet and there were all these things telling me how I was supposed to love being on my own. I was supposed to love myself before I could love others. I was supposed to be able to sit in a room and not have to look at my phone for five fucking minutes. I didn't need to look at my phone, though. I wanted to.

I watched TV shows I didn't care about, but I knew I didn't care about them. I didn't think anyone really did. I went to work. I ate. I tidied up. I found things to do. I felt anxious if I had a block of time ahead of me with no plans on how to fill it, like now, so I made sure I had plans and things to fill it with.

It was how I was brought up. To always be doing something. I already missed work, and David. I liked waking up and knowing how my day was going to be. I felt like someone had pulled the rug out from under me and I didn't even know we had a rug. We had a throw from IKEA, but no rug.

Then I had an epiphany, I think – I'd never had one; this could be it. Maybe I had to do all these things because I was afraid if I stopped, I'd start thinking, and then I'd die. Like my brain knew this without me telling it.

I always thought keeping busy was a good thing. That I knew how to entertain myself. That I didn't need anyone. I needed my phone and the TV obviously, but they weren't people. It wasn't the same as being needy.

I liked my life. I didn't have to think. Now I felt an emptiness seeping in. Or all the stuff seeping out. I didn't like it. I didn't want to be empty. I wanted to be full. I wanted to be back in that restaurant singing happy birthday to a stranger, maybe go home with them, be someone else now.

I didn't like thinking about these things. This was what they were worried about, and I understood why.

I needed to eat something again. If I ate, I wouldn't be empty. It was basic maths.

I ordered Domino's and waited by the door. There was a pizza place called Pizza Joe's next door but I didn't know Joe, I knew Domino. I turned the TV down so I could hear both the TV and the door, not wanting to miss a thing, but it wasn't enough to quiet my mind, so I listened to music on my phone with one ear so I could still hear the door, and the TV. I played Candy Crush while I waited. I didn't want any thoughts to get in.

When my food came, I talked to the delivery boy for too long and he thought I was hitting on him, and I might have been. I didn't know anymore. I wondered if I could go through with sleeping with someone else, if I really needed both my mind and body to be willing, or if there was a trick to it.

I ate the pizza. I felt better the more carbs I had in my body and found myself feeling sleepy, so I let myself fall asleep in front of the TV. I was planning on sleeping on the couch anyway. I wasn't going near Stefan's bed.

Day Two

I woke up and forgot where I was for a second. Then I saw the surf posters and remembered. Then I saw the weird beaded curtain and remembered more. I missed work. I missed David. I wanted to be in my own bed, getting up and getting ready for work and going to work. I knew how to do all that without thinking.

I opened the blinds and let the light in. I didn't know what I was doing but I knew I needed to stay in the light. I didn't know much, but I knew darkness was where bad stuff happened, because movies told us this, and why would they lie?

I was hungry and my neck hurt from sleeping funny. I needed to do this thinking fast, so I could get back to my life. I needed to eat first, though.

I looked in Stefan's fridge and there was only the questionable milk. I looked in his cupboards and there was just one cup noodle and a congealed-looking jar of peanut butter. No rats or cockroaches jumped out, though, so it was fine. Although it would have been nice to have someone to talk to.

I slept in my clothes so I didn't have to think about getting dressed because I was already dressed. I wet my hand under the tap and smoothed my hair down.

I'd seen a grocery store a few doors down and felt better as soon as I was outside. Someone almost walked into me, but I didn't mind. I wanted someone else to walk into me. I wanted them all to take me with them, wherever they were going, teach me how to be a person.

Once I was inside the small store, I managed to quiet my brain long enough to successfully buy two boxes of cereal, milk (so I could throw his rancid one out), Flamin' Hot Cheetos, bread (thankfully there was only sliced or not sliced to choose from; I picked sliced, knowing I probably shouldn't be around too many knives in my state), original Oreos because that was all they had, four plastic-wrapped Grapples, and a bottle of Sunny D. I didn't think to see if Stefan had toilet paper, so I wasn't really thinking that much. I could do this.

When I got back, I watched some *Real Housewives of Beverly Hills*, but while I was watching it, I thought how I actually liked *The Real Housewives of New York* more, but I kept watching the one I was watching anyway, knowing it didn't really matter. I couldn't remember any of their names anyway – their dogs' names, maybe. I just wanted to see inside their homes, see what they ate, and then I remembered I had cereal now.

I stood up and went to the kitchen but instead of just grabbing the box, grabbing a bowl, pouring the cereal in the bowl, grabbing a spoon, grabbing the milk from the fridge, pouring the milk on the cereal, I looked at the two boxes I'd bought and just stared at them. I didn't know which one I wanted. It was stupid of me to get two kinds. I had fucked myself over. I liked both equally. I liked all cereal. I picked up the Cheerios, happy with my choice, but then my brain said, But Special K is great, Susan, why don't you want Special K, Susan? And then it was almost like the Special K was saying, Why do you hate us, Susan? What did we do to you Susan? I smacked the box across the counter and watched it fall to the floor. I took a deep breath and picked it back up and tried again with the Cheerios.

I picked up the bowl but almost dropped it. My hands were shaking now. It was too quiet even though the TV was on. I could hear my heart beating and my breathing, which was better than the Special K shouting at me, but I still didn't like it. I took a deep breath. Everyone was always telling everyone to breathe now, so I tried.

I poured some Cheerios into the bowl without any problems and started to feel better. Who knew breathing worked? I went and got the milk from the fridge and started to pour it out, then I didn't know how much milk to use and ended up not using enough. When I finally sat down on the couch to eat it I couldn't. I thought about how it felt in my mouth – not even how it tasted, but the feel of it, and all I could think was that what I really wanted in that moment was a warm croissant, all buttery and joyful, not a flabby bowl of grey cereal. And then my mouth wouldn't work at all, so I had to throw the cereal out. My brain was fucking up my day.

I needed a do-over. I needed to pretend none of that had just happened. I needed to pretend I'd just woken up and start my day again. I needed to shower and change my clothes to do that.

I managed to get in the shower and get dressed but it felt like a lot of effort, like my body and brain weren't friends anymore, like I was forcing myself. I was questioning everything I did, not just what I should eat or wear, but how to even move my legs, my hands. At one point I thought my hands didn't even look like my hands anymore, but it scared me so I told my brain to shut up and played some Katy Perry.

The sound of the shower was soothing. I closed my eyes and pretended I was in a waterfall somewhere. The sound of Katy

Perry in the background was nice; she was in the waterfall with me. She wouldn't let anything bad happen to me.

Once I was showered and dressed, I knew I needed to get out of that apartment, though. I felt like I needed to get outside into the world because that was bigger than me and would somehow help. Also, if I was going to explode, I didn't want to do it in Stefan's apartment. That wasn't cool. No one wanted to come home to that.

I felt a bit afraid of my own brain, like I didn't want to be alone with it. A few days ago, I was fine with it. But at the same time, I didn't want it to know I felt like that about it. I wanted to take it out and stroke it, tame it.

As soon as I was out on the street I felt better again. My brain stopped and the world started. I put my AirPods in and started to walk, letting the noises wash over me. I walked for hours. I could have kept walking, forever maybe. As long as my phone didn't die on me. But it did. For fuck's sake, I said to a pigeon. I felt betrayed. I had to go back to Stefan's to charge it. I was so annoyed. I was starting to get tired anyway. I knew I couldn't really walk around forever. I'd have to get special shoes for one, and walking shoes were always ugly.

When I got in, I put my phone on to charge and put it face-down on the table. I didn't put the TV on for once, I just sat on the living-room floor.

I could hear people in the hallway. I could hear traffic and people outside. I could hear a dog barking. I could hear a car radio. I could hear a truck reversing. Why was there always a truck reversing? But it was still too quiet. I started to wonder if I'd ever heard a bird – not a TV bird, or a movie bird, but an actual bird.

I sat with my legs crossed and arms folded. I felt like I was at school. Or a yoga class. And I didn't do yoga; it was boring.

The TV was off now but I could always put it on. I started to think about all the TV shows I was missing. I wanted to check my phone to see if anyone had texted me yet. It was too quiet.

There were crumbs on the carpet. They might not have been crumbs. They could have been flakes of Stefan's skin, picked off his feet, or some other body part, while he was watching TV. They were still making me hungry, though, because I was disturbed now, clearly. I shouldn't have thrown the cereal away. People were starving, weren't they? Somewhere? We hadn't eradicated world hunger and no one told me? It wasn't the cereal's fault my brain was broken.

I didn't know how long I had to sit like that and was sure I was doing it wrong. I was supposed to shut my eyes, wasn't I? I shut my eyes. Was I supposed to say something? I got my phone off the table and googled 'meditation mantras' and so many results came up I couldn't be bothered to read them, so I put my phone back on the table face-down. I just wanted one result to tell me what to do. I shut my eyes again and tried again to look inside myself. That's what you were supposed to do. I tried to look in my head – it was dark, but I thought that was just because my eyes were shut, duh. I tried to picture my brain, but all I could think of were cartoon brains, brains on TV shows, candy brains, mashed-in brains on *The Walking Dead*, which weren't real, which some dude made in a warehouse somewhere, which shouldn't be a job, but was. I couldn't picture my own brain. I said hello to myself, but in my head, not out loud. It felt weird, talking in my head.

I needed to get out of that room, try to eat again. Sitting there trying to get to know myself wasn't working. There was nothing there. I needed to be outside, not just my head, but that room, the building. Maybe I just needed to eat. Maybe if I ate, I could think better. Maybe if I ate, it would make me not care about thinking anymore. Maybe I should just eat myself to death. But not cereal.

They thought if I thought too hard my head would explode, but I thought they were wrong. They kept me from thinking because they thought it was dangerous, but I wasn't so sure. If it was something inside me, like they said, I needed to confront it. I couldn't hide here forever. But I couldn't go back and expect everything to be the same as before either. Oh, to go back to my ignorant bliss.

They had me running from it this whole time and I wanted to face it head on. Once I'd eaten, that is.

I heard something then. Neighbours! I hurried to the door to listen. People! Life! I'm not alone! I imagined the TV saying, Rude. I didn't like thinking the TV was talking to me; the cereal talking to me was fucked up enough.

There was a family in the hall, right outside my door. Family, my brain purred. Remember those? But I could only remember TV families. The Simpsons mostly.

Through the spy hole I could see a young family with two little children. They were very loud, animated – they didn't seem to care who heard, so I heard. They probably posted it all online anyway; I was just being a voyeur the old-fashioned way. The mum was balancing her phone and one of the children, and the dad was balancing his phone and the other child and a stroller and there were lots of bags on the floor. I couldn't tell if they were going out or coming in. I wanted them to just live in the hallway, so I could watch them forever. So I wasn't alone. Sorry, TV.

For Christ's sake, Emily, if he wants to take the raisins with us, let him take the raisins, the dad said. I wanted to know if he had thought that first and then said it, or thought something worse, and this was an edited version.

It's not normal, Emily said.

Who cares? the dad said.

I care. I'll be the one who ends up having to carry it. I'll be the one who has to clean him after he has crazy shits because he ate too many raisins, Emily said.

I think you're overreacting, the dad said.

Can we just leave, please? Emily said.

One of the kids started crying.

I feel the same, Emily said to the kid.

We're going, the dad said, and they left in a cloud of despair.

I couldn't go out then because I thought I might follow them. I couldn't go out then because I didn't want to miss them coming back. More than wanting to hear them talk, I wanted to see in their brains and see if what they said was close to what they thought. I wanted to know how other people managed themselves or if they barely did.

I went back to the couch and watched the latest Adam Sandler movie and didn't laugh once and wondered what the point was, but I wasn't really thinking anything much so it was fine.

The neighbours were back then. That was quick, I said to myself but out loud. One kid was asleep in the stroller and the dad was carrying the other kid, also asleep. The woman, Emily, looked done in. They'd only been out the length of an Adam Sandler movie. They went into their apartment, and I moved to the adjacent wall to listen. I heard bags being put down, muffled voices; I heard a TV, a phone; I heard a cupboard door, I heard a child whine something, I heard padded footsteps. I heard a tap running and stopping. It was nothing and everything. It was like having a TV show just for me, only I didn't have any control over the volume, so I had to work out how to position my body against the wall to hear the most. I looked at some stuff on my phone but kept my ear on the wall.

Then I heard their front door go so I shot up to look through the spy hole again. It was the mum, Emily. She was escaping. I opened the door too quickly. She jumped.

Hey, I said.

Hey, she said.

I'm Stefan's friend, I said.

Oh, I thought he might be Airbnb'ing his place or something, she said.

Oh, yeah, he is, I guess, to me, I said.

OK, cool, bye then, she said and left.

I tried to think about what she might be thinking about me. It was dangerous territory, and I knew that because my brain pinged, like an elastic band. I'd been weird probably. Now wasn't the time to follow her and ask her to be my friend.

I really wasn't getting on very well with being alone with my thoughts. I was having more and more, and they were going to increasingly strange places.

I slunk back inside and listened to some music and looked at Instagram for a while, but it made me feel worse.

I tried to meditate again. I read how to do it online again and sat on the floor and turned everything off. Well, not my phone; I put that face-down next to me. I sat crossed-legged and felt like an idiot. It was boring. I gave up and went out again.

I walked around and went to a park and wondered if I could see *Star Wars* again. I talked to myself a bit, turned my music up high. I mostly tried not to think about how lonely I was, how lonely the world was, with all its question marks hanging over it.

I went back to Stefan's and tried to watch Netflix, but I

couldn't remember what our password was. Stefan hadn't told me his.

One of the kids next door was crying now. I listened to them for a bit and then went back to the TV. I was getting bored of TV and didn't like that feeling. That's how I knew there was something really wrong with me. I decided I just needed to eat so I got the bread and Stefan's ancient-looking peanut butter and started to make a sandwich. Only I couldn't do it. The bread was wrong. The peanut butter wasn't the peanut butter we had at home, because ours was from this century. I tried to tell myself the bread was fine, the peanut butter was fine, but as I was making it I knew I wouldn't be able to eat it. I almost gave up and threw it away, but I shut my brain down, finished making it and took it over to the couch. I was thinking about it too much, thinking about how it would feel in my mouth, how it would taste. Because of the cereal incident. But this is a sandwich, I said to myself. Usually, I just made a sandwich and ate it. My brain was fucking everything up. My stomach growled. It could smell the sandwich. Shut up, I said to myself, out loud, and I ate the sandwich with my eyes shut, even though the TV was on and I wanted to watch it. I ate the sandwich quickly and tried not to think about it. I thought once I'd eaten it and it was over and I'd done it, it would be fine. It was just a blip. It was the bread again. Maybe it was my body telling me I had a gluten intolerance, but I doubted it. It was a brain thing. I thought about the sandwich in my stomach. I thought about it just sitting there, waiting for my body to digest it. I thought about how my body knew I didn't want that sandwich. It wanted something else. It's all I have, I said, to myself, but I was lying, because my brain saw me buy Flamin' Hot Cheetos and Oreos, but I didn't want my brain to fuck those up too, so I just gave up again.

I pushed what just happened to the back of my mind. I was learning I could do that, and swore to do better next time, at not thinking.

I texted Stefan to ask him for his Netflix password and he texted it back straight away along with a tongue-out face emoji and a heart emoji that made something somewhere in my brain briefly happy.

I watched more TV and tried not to think. I watched a show about tiny houses and got really invested and needed to know these people weren't divorced now so I googled them, but I couldn't find out. I needed something else to watch, but I couldn't find anything. I'd watched everything. I started a few things but gave up on them. I tried to think if there was something I'd been wanting to watch, but my mind was blank. The information just wasn't there. I flicked through the tiles, frantic now, desperate, needing to find something, anything, to watch. I googled 'what to watch right now' but it gave me lists of stuff I'd already watched. I felt betrayed. I googled 'what to watch when you've watched everything'. It didn't say go outside.

I didn't like how it felt. I was close to crying and throwing my phone against the wall, but I knew I couldn't do that, because then what?

I eventually gave up trying to find a new show and just put *Friends* on again and it helped me stay in the light. The light from the TV was light.

It was suddenly night and I'd successfully got through the day without thinking myself to death. I felt very accomplished and rewarded myself by watching a few more hours of the tiny house show and then some of a regular-sized house show, and then some *Teen Mom* – they weren't teens anymore but no one seemed to mind or thought to change the title; the *Jersey Shore* gang were still the same, though, so it was fine. I looked at some celebrities on Instagram being celebrities but at the same time pretending to be humble, ate half the Cheetos, then went to bed, which was the couch, so I didn't have to go anywhere. Before I fell asleep, I searched my mind for anything problematic, but it was pretty blank in there, so I felt better. I felt like I could do this.

Day Three

The next morning, I woke up and I felt uneasy almost immediately and it wasn't because I thought Flamin' Hot Cheetos were a meal. I wanted David there. I wanted to go to work. I wanted for this to be over. No one had texted me still. I thought David might come and find me – I thought you could basically track anyone these days – but he didn't come. I'd never had a problem with mornings, or even thought about them, but now the day ahead felt long, like a dark tunnel. I started to think, What if time doesn't go? What happens then? My head started to ping a little, which told me I needed to stop thinking about time. Someone else had thought about time a long time ago, lol, and figured it all out. I didn't need to be worrying about it, I needed to stay focused on the physical world. And right now, that was Stefan's depressing apartment, which smelled of weed and Cheetos dust.

I hadn't brushed my teeth for days and needed to brush them badly. Me and David usually brushed them together, like we were Bert and Ernie. But I was having trouble doing things I usually did without thinking now.

Last week David had found me in the bathroom, not brushing my teeth.

You OK? he said.

I forgot how to brush my teeth, I said, looking at my toothbrush like I'd just been dropped there from another planet, one that didn't have toothbrushes, or teeth even maybe; they were just blobs of jelly maybe, but their brains were highly advanced.

Oh, he said, not wanting to make a huge deal out of it, and I knew why now, of course – don't draw attention to the girl with the exploding brain. The one who's forgotten what a toothbrush is.

We've all done that, he said, as a cover-up.

I had the toothbrush loaded with toothpaste hovering in front of my mouth. I'd done everything like normal but then when I went to start moving my arm, I suddenly thought, What am I doing? Is this even how you brush your teeth? Is it round and round or up and down? Do I have too much toothpaste? And then my hand felt peculiar and I thought, Are these even my hands? I brought them up to my face to look at them and dropped the toothbrush.

David picked it up and put it back in my hand.

Is this real, I said, or am I dreaming? I felt very in my head and out of my body.

Pretty lame dream, he joked, to take my mind off me losing my mind, I think, even though it was the opposite of that, it was like I had just found my mind and lost my body.

You look like you're doing it right to me, he said, and I watched him brush his and mimicked what he was doing till my brain and body felt in sync again and there weren't any voices.

Whatever that was passed. For a moment I thought I was going mad, that I was hearing voices, but it was my voice, one that didn't want me to have minty fresh breath.

That's what was happening now, but more frequently. My

brain getting in the way of me doing normal things I usually did without thinking. Thinking was actually stopping me functioning. I'd always thought that thinking was supposed to help you, but for me, now, it was trying to kill me – slowly, not in one giant explosion, like they told me it might, but killing me all the same. It was just a matter of time, and I'd already decided I didn't want to think about that anymore.

The same night I forgot how to brush my teeth I kissed his neck in bed to initiate sex, maybe to show him I still knew how to be his girlfriend, only when he started touching me I moved his hand away.

I don't feel anything, I said, which was the worst thing to hear during sex, other than ow.

We lay side by side, not touching and barely breathing.

I don't feel like I'm supposed to, I said, like I usually feel.

Oh, he said. It wasn't the oh sound he hoped to be making.

I don't feel . . . sexy, I said.

That wasn't really it, but I didn't have the words for it. Until recently I thought I knew all the words I needed that would allow me to communicate everything I felt, but now there seemed to be things beyond what I knew, or maybe beyond what anyone knew.

When I felt his hand on my breast, I felt like crying, because it didn't feel like how I thought it was supposed to feel. I felt a cold hand on my cold breast, that was it, but I knew I would still do it because it's what you did when you were in a relationship, but the realisation of that stopped me. I had never had sex because I thought I should, but I was about to.

What about the other times? he asked.

I think I did, I said. I couldn't remember the other times, only this awkward, very unsexy feeling. Was unsexy even a word?

I could hear a sound in my head, like cogs turning, but I could feel it too, like a grinding, grating. I thought I could almost hear his brain too. I could hear us both thinking, or trying to – trying to think a way out of this.

I sat up abruptly.

You've broken me, I said. That's how I felt, in pieces.

But not with the lie, with telling me, I said, because it was the truth, my truth. I used to laugh when celebrities said, Find your truth, live your truth, but this was my truth.

And what could he say to that? So he said nothing, and I lay back down and we lay there perfectly still, barely breathing, waiting for it to pass, only it didn't pass, and now I was here, trying to work out how to get back to who I was before I started thinking.

I thought all that before even eating anything and my head didn't explode, so that was good going. I needed to get out, though, back into the light, out of this man cave.

I got dressed quickly and went outside. Again, as soon as I was out I felt better. It wasn't even sunny, but I still felt better. The air felt nice. I noticed how the trees were just trees and weren't complicating things with their thoughts and feelings. I could really get into nature, if TV suddenly wasn't a thing.

I started walking and ended up at McDonald's. Nature was great, but seeing the golden arches lit up something in my brain that felt like home. I ate and walked and listened to music on my phone and felt almost normal. I must have walked in a giant circle, though, because I was back at Stefan's then, so I went in and watched more TV. I watched *The Bachelorette* and realised I didn't know any of their names; in fact, I didn't think I could remember anyone's names off any shows I watched. That ruined it for me and I needed to go out again. I was like a dog now, maybe. I walked around Stefan's neighbourhood listening to my phone. I noticed a few birds that weren't pigeons and wondered what kind of birds they were. Did birds know they were birds? Their brains must have been tiny, like the size of a walnut, but they were probably still better than ours.

I turned my music up to drown out these thoughts. I knew there was no way anyone could know unless someone had invented a machine that could talk to birds. I thought I'd seen one for sale on TV that let you talk to your dog, so maybe other people did know these things, or more likely they bought that machine and found out dogs weren't thinking anything and were embarrassed at how much the machine cost.

I found myself following people, like they were a wave, and I was caught in it. I didn't want to be one girl alone with her thoughts, I wanted to share their thoughts. I wanted to know why we were allowed to think these bizarre things with no answers, and if their head also ached from it.

After getting a dirty look from a man who knew I was following him a little, I went and sat in a Starbucks and looked at my phone. I scrolled through some celebrity news sites I usually enjoyed but I did not enjoy them that day.

I still hadn't thought any of the things I wanted to think. I was wasting time, eating McDonald's and Starbucks, watching TV. I wouldn't be able to teach my spin class soon because I'd be too unfit but also mad, maybe. No one wanted a mad person shouting at them from a stationary bike that thought it was moving.

I'd walked a lot the last few days, but I'd also sat a lot, and eaten a lot of junk. The walking wasn't for exercise anyway, it was to keep me from being alone with myself. This realisation annoyed me because up until recently I'd liked myself enough. I needed to get a grip.

I fast-walked back to Stefan's with the intention of thinking properly again. Something I'd come to realise was that when I tried to think about what it meant that my head might explode from thinking, a wall came up, like a dead end. Like something inside me was protecting me. This felt reassuring, but also, I didn't want anyone telling me what I could or couldn't think.

I turned my phone off, properly off, for the first time ever, and put it face-down on the table. I then proceeded to sit cross-legged on the floor again and closed my eyes.

I waited. Nothing. My mind was just nothing.

Hello? I said to myself. Is there anybody in there?

If someone said, Yes, hello, Susan, is that you? I'd shit myself obviously, die right there and then, but I didn't think my head would explode.

Part of me hoped for a friendly ghost to answer me, but nothing. David didn't believe in ghosts, but I believed in everything.

I felt sleepy then and took a nap. When I woke up it was dark, so I ordered some food and watched *Mean Girls* again for the hundredth time and I knew all the lines and it felt good, like I was being overwritten.

Day Four

I was so fucking bored. I was so bored I decided to clean Stefan's apartment. Those crumbs/skin flakes were haunting me. And I'd made more since. I found an old vacuum cleaner in a cupboard and hoovered everything and wiped everything down and I felt like I could just keep cleaning forever and how that would be a good, useful life. I had Katy Perry on full blast and sang along and thought about how much I liked cleaning, how much it made sense; something was dirty, you cleaned it. They told you as a woman you weren't supposed to, but I thought it was OK as long as no one was telling you to do it, or you felt you should.

I knew to keep busy. Time would pass. I had doubted it the other day, but it came through for me. I went for another long walk and knew as long as I kept moving and kept listening to music and didn't pay attention to the voice in my head I'd be OK.

I went back to Stefan's and showered and tried not to think how his naked body had been in that shower and how there were hairs in the plughole that could have been from any part of his body. All his products were surf themed and called things like Ocean Spray, which I thought was a juice.

I didn't know what to do after that. I tried to read but I couldn't. He had four books on his shelf, all about men who did a lot of drugs and went on road trips. I picked up one but was just staring at the pages. It wasn't working. The back cover said people liked it, but I did not. I could read anything usually; I let written words replace my thoughts, or where my thoughts should have been. Now my head was jumbled, like a code I couldn't crack.

After they told me about my brain, I watched videos online of people finding out shocking things. It was mostly that someone they loved was gay and I thought, Why is that a big deal? or the ending of some TV show, and I thought, Why is that a big deal? or that they were adopted – quite a big deal. I wanted to see how people reacted to finding out shocking things. I had the feeling I was supposed to be more shocked, but my brain wouldn't let me. It had made me this way on purpose; it was nothing they did. My brain didn't want to kill me, or I'd be dead by now. My brain wanted me to live. Instead of feeling shock, I looked at GIFs of Yoda saying, The force is strong with this one, and felt very seen.

Lying on Stefan's couch with Oreos lined up on my stomach like an otter, watching *RuPaul's Drag Race*, I started to think I was incapable of thinking anything deep, but how I was OK with it. What was there to think really anyway? Birds probably thought we were all idiots, if they were capable of that thought.

I gave up trying to think again and went out to get proper food.

Again, I felt better as soon as I was outside. Like I didn't have to think if I didn't want to. Trees didn't think and they were fine. I didn't allow myself to think, What if they can think? Because I saw a dog pissing up one that also had a plastic bag stuck in its branch.

I was about to cross the street when a woman was suddenly next to me, smiling.

I smiled back because I was friendly like that, but also, I'd been on my own for far too long now.

Susan! the woman said warmly, I'm a friend of your mother's. Do you remember we spoke on the phone the other day?

I tried to remember her voice, then it hit me. I'd gone to my parents' to borrow some cheese. My mum had bought too much — it was on special or something — only when she got home, she didn't want it in the house because she thought she'd end up eating it all herself and old people weren't supposed to eat a lot of cheese — something to do with gout being back in a big way — so I said I'd take it. Free cheese! They weren't home, but I let myself in, and while I was there the phone rang. The landline. David and I didn't have such a thing. It was a novelty, so I answered it.

Hello? I said, into the mouthpiece.

Rebecca? the voice on the other end said.

I laughed at them thinking I was my mother.

No, this is Susan, Rebecca's my mum, I said.

Oh, Susan! the woman said. She sounded really happy it was me she was talking to.

I'm a friend of your mother's, she said.

Oh, she's not home, I said. I'm just stealing her cheese, I said, like that was a normal thing people did.

Oh, well, will you tell her I called? the woman said.

Sure, do you want me to text her to see where she is? I said.

No, don't bother her, we'll catch up some other time, the woman said.

Cool, well, I'd better get this cheese home, I said, like it was my child.

The woman didn't seem to want to hang up, though. I could hear her breathing heavily.

OK, well, take care, she said, eventually hanging up.

Once I'd put the phone down, I remember standing there holding the cheese, but I didn't really want it anymore so I put it back in the fridge and just stood there staring at it. Then I thought how I'd come all that way so I should still take the cheese, so I got it back out, but then when I looked at it again the thought of putting it in my mouth made me feel nauseous so I put it back in the fridge again. I was angry at the cheese then, but also feeling quite mad. If I didn't want cheese, who was I? It felt like the bread thing all over again. Like something in my head was collapsing. I needed to get out of that apartment, but also just away, not just from the cheese, but these people, this situation. They had unlocked something in my brain I didn't want unlocked.

I found a pad of Post-it notes my mum kept by the fruit bowl, mostly for writing 'buy fruit' on I think, and left them a note before leaving.

And here was that woman now, the only woman left on the planet who used the landline.

I kept crossing the street and she crossed with me.

I was hoping to run into you, she said once we were on the other side.

Oh, you were? I said, confused. Is my mum OK?

I started to think maybe something had happened to her, and they'd sent this woman to find me, because she was a detective perhaps, because I watched too much TV.

Well, yes and no, she's worried about you, the woman said, her smile changing to a frown.

Can we go somewhere and talk? she said.

I was just about to get some food, I said, because I was just about to get some food.

Can I join you? she said. I'm Bea by the way. I'm so glad to finally meet you.

I'm Susan, I said, but then she knew that. They'd been watching me for some time it seems. I was saying it more for my own sake so I might remember who I was, before all this.

Hi, Susan, she said, smiling.

And then a man she said was her husband was there all of a sudden.

Susan, this is my husband, Martin, he's a friend of your father's. Do you mind if he joins us? she said.

I didn't really know what was happening. I didn't know my parents had so many friends. My mum lived in the bookstore and my dad was mostly asleep in front of the TV.

Our treat, of course, Martin said. I liked this man.

I was so bored of my own company, and hungry, I went with them. I didn't even really care if they turned out to be serial killers – it would pass the time, something I felt desperate to do now. It was easier thinking about potentially being murdered than what was going on with my head.

Martin said that he worked with my dad and Bea said that my mother was part of her women's group. I didn't care about their boring lives and was just excited that someone was buying me lunch. They seemed nice enough. I didn't think a serial killer would walk right up to you on the street and buy you lunch.

They took me into a mid-range chain restaurant that wanted you to think it was Italian, but there were things on the menu that most Italians would argue weren't Italian, like curly fries. While we waited for our drinks Bea put her hand on mine and said they knew about my brain problem.

It's not really a problem, I said.

Of course, she said, stroking my hand. What I meant was, we know.

We'd like to ask you a few questions, Susan, if that's OK? her husband said.

I moved my hand away from Bea's but said, OK.

They were buying me lunch, after all, and were friends of my parents, and I was so bored and lonely. I hadn't really spoken to anyone other than myself and the neighbour, and the TV and various other inanimate objects, for days.

Our drinks came and Bea told the waitress we weren't ready to order yet and shooed her away.

So, Martin said, what's an average day like for you, Susan?

He was really staring at me; it made me feel uncomfortable. If he licked his lips, I'd leave.

It was a weird question. I wanted only to be thinking about what food I was going to order.

What, like, describe my day?

Yes, Susan, in your own words, I want to know what a day in your life is like, he said.

It's pretty normal, I said. I wake up and look at my phone. The TV's usually on. I get up and listen to music while I get ready. I shower and get dressed and make breakfast and go to work. I have classes all day.

You work at a gym, is that correct? Bea said.

Yes, I said.

Fascinating, she said.

Continue, Martin said.

There's not much to tell, I said. I eat lunch with Kate or Chloe. I read stuff on my phone. After work I go home and crash, watch TV, eat dinner, play video games.

And at the weekend, what does Susan do at the weekend? Martin asked.

I do normal stuff, I said, go to the park, see a movie. What was I supposed to be doing? I didn't know what he wanted me to say, but saying all that out loud made me miss my life.

And do you think about any of that when you do it? he asked, staring at me even harder.

No, I said.

Up until recently my body told me when to get up and when to eat, when to sleep. I thought that was the point of bodies. Now my brain was interfering. It didn't feel natural for me.

Susan, do you know the difference between feeling something and thinking something? Martin said then.

He was still staring at me, almost like he wanted to eat me, probably because we hadn't ordered yet. Bea was looking at me like she might try to stroke me again, but my head this time.

I'm not big on feelings, I said, because I wasn't. Other than hungry or tired, I thought.

But yes, I said, I think I know the difference. I did now anyway.

What if I started to talk to you about something difficult?

Martin said, interlocking his fingers, then resting his chin on them, but still maintaining eye contact with me the whole time.

Difficult like what?

Like, for example, the idea that reality is an illusion, he said, lifting his head up and almost rocking now.

I thought we were going to start with a little Sartre, Bea said to her husband.

That doesn't scare you? Martin said to me.

I think you need to get out more, I said. I meant out of his head but didn't say that.

So, you don't think if you think too hard your head will explode? Martin said then, looking annoyed, a bead of sweat appearing from nowhere on his forehead.

No, I said. I can't think. I tried, I said, but I can't. I kept his gaze.

Really? he said, pursing his lips and frowning.

Yes, I said.

What do you mean, you tried? he said, leaning forward now, searching my face.

I mean I sat down and tried to really think, about all the big things, like life and death or whatever, but I couldn't, I said. Who gives a shit if reality is an illusion? I said. How does that help anyone?

I thought I saw Bea stifle a smile.

I told you it was a waste of time, she said, dabbing at her husband's forehead now with a napkin.

I had to see for myself, he said, waving her off.

I was looking at my phone now, though, scrolling through TMZ. I suddenly wanted, needed, to know what all the celebrities had been up to in the last 24 hours.

She can't think, can't you see? Whatever you had planned isn't going to work, Bea said to her husband.

Yes, I can see that now, thank you, dear, Martin said to his wife.

Then I realised they had wanted to push my buttons. They *wanted* me to think too hard, to see what would happen. Sick fucks.

Oh, I get it, I said, putting my phone down. Sorry to disappoint you, but I'm not planning on exploding anytime soon, I said, standing up and leaving.

They followed me outside and tailed me a short distance, then let me go.

I heard Bea say, Let her go.

I understood why my parents didn't want anyone to know now. There were some sick fucks out there. They probably wanted to put me in some room, do experiments on me, like in some lame TV show I would watch because everyone was watching it, but really I'd find it boring and not be able to remember any of their names. Only this wasn't a TV show. And I wasn't a child with special powers. I was just Susan.

The whole thing gave me the heebie-jeebies. Which was a thing I always thought I wanted till I had it.

I had to go in Starbucks after that to drink a beverage that was mostly syrup and whipped cream and look at videos of cats falling off stuff on my phone until I felt safe. I looked around and no one else was really thinking so I felt better. I hoped never to see Martin and Bea again, although they did owe me a meal.

Day Five

I felt better. Like it was over. I felt like I knew who I was. I wanted to go home and go back to work and just get on. But I felt like I needed to try to hold out a bit longer. People usually needed a week to do things. I wanted to be people.

I went back to the grocery store and bought as many snack foods as I could carry. Back at Stefan's I read about what all the celebrities had been doing or not doing while I'd been away and successfully took some of BuzzFeed's quizzes and watched some more animals fall off stuff on YouTube and was back to blocking myself adequately. Then I did a workout video on YouTube a celebrity swore gave her killer abs and punched a lamp, but I didn't think Stefan would mind. It was only from IKEA. Then I started to eat my snacks and watched all the Netflix shows Netflix wanted me to watch until I fell asleep. I would die from Netflix before I let my head explode.

Day Six

On day six I did the same as I had on day four but went for a long walk instead of almost getting abducted by some nutters. I wasn't thinking about thinking, or anything really. I almost felt back to normal.

Then I did something stupid and googled 'exploding head'. I hadn't ever done that before, because I hadn't dared, maybe. I'd got cocky. I thought I could handle it now perhaps.

I was expecting it to bring up some lame horror movie from the 80s but WebMD had a page about something called Exploding Head Syndrome, and for a second I thought I'd found what I was looking for, and that I would have my answers, my validation, but it wasn't what I had.

Don't call it that if that's not what that is! I yelled, at my phone, but it was meant for Mr WebMD, who didn't sound like a real doctor.

When I tried to think about anything too deep my mind went blank, like I had no mind. This was how it had always been for me, but I thought it was like this for everyone. That humans weren't supposed to go too far with some things. It made sense to me that humans had limits. I googled 'no mind', to see what the internet had to say about it. If nothing came up, I'd know there was something truly wrong with me, but there was a Wiki entry for it.

There was something called Mushin and a thing called 'the state of no mind' and people actually wanted it. And I had it. Without doing anything. I read more about it on my phone and it didn't hurt my head, it soothed it. Like I had solved something, solved the problem of my own existence, just through understanding myself. It felt very cool. The internet had validated me, but not through likes. I wanted to tell someone, but there wasn't anyone to tell. The feeling was almost enough, though. I had actual peace, with myself.

The feeling didn't last, though, as they often didn't; even once you were aware of them, you had no real control over them, but I slept better that night. With a new sense of calm tucked away somewhere. Like there was less confusion in my soul that would carry me more safely through whatever came next. If I had a soul, that is. I hoped I did.

Day Seven

I sent David and my parents a group message to say I was coming home. I asked them to meet me at Starbucks. I figured I would want coffee; I wanted coffee just thinking about it. I think caffeine might fuck with your head. I wanted to meet them somewhere neutral but familiar. Starbucks had just the right number of buffers to save us all from ourselves. You never heard about anyone exploding in a Starbucks, and you should have really.

I texted Stefan to tell him I was going home and thanked him for letting me crash. Catch you later, I wrote, tongue-out emoji. He texted me back, Try not to exploding-head emoji, which I'd never paid much attention to before, but that was me – I was a fucking emoji.

To be really honest, exploding sounded like a lot of work; I didn't think I could be bothered. I just wanted my old life back.

David

We were summoned via a WhatsApp message to meet her at a Starbucks 15 minutes from our apartment. Neutral territory probably, or more likely she needed coffee, not that what she drank contained much coffee — sugar mostly, empty promises. It was just something to hold, my hand apparently not being good enough.

Her mother had set up the group chat months ago and we all had to be supportive because she was trying to get a handle on technology, but also trying to be more social. It was mostly for dinner plans and TV recaps.

Her mother called me.

We don't think it's a good idea for her to come back to the city, she said.

You think she's in danger?

We don't know, she said, but I wanted to tell you first. We're telling her not to come.

Can't we meet her somewhere outside the city? I said. Somewhere safer? Hell, I'd wear a disguise if I got to see her again.

I don't know, she said, I'll ask her father.

I heard her walk off and then heard muffled voices.

He says OK, but where?

Let's ask Susan to pick, I said.

Susan picked a different Starbucks, one that was further away, which she found on an app she had on her phone that ensured she was never too far from a Starbucks because then a hellmouth would open. She told us where it was and when to meet her.

I got there early, bought a drink, and found a table in the back by the bathroom, where no one else wanted to sit. This was Susan's idea of both romance and quiet, Starbucks on a Saturday. We'd conducted our relationship in similar locations around the city. I hoped she'd notice that I remembered our spot, by the toilet.

I didn't know how to greet her. I felt anxious. I pictured myself running to her, but we were on a beach in my head. I'd cry anyway, promise I'd never do anything to hurt her again, if she only came home, but when she finally showed up there was a double buggy parked in my way and too many tables for anything that would classify as really running, so I clambered towards her and said hi like she was someone I used to know. She didn't have black eyeliner now, wasn't wearing a veil. She hadn't found herself and herself was in fact a goth. She looked rested. Showered. She was doing better than me.

She's alive at least, Susan's father said, sitting down.

They arrived at the same time, but there wasn't an emotional reunion, no weeping into anyone's collar. The general consensus seemed to be, if we touched her, she still might explode, and then she'd be gone for good.

Her mother stood for a while, like she didn't know if she was staying. She seemed agitated. She might have just been wondering if she was supposed to get a drink or wait. No one knew the etiquette; Starbucks was the last lawless place. She eventually sat down next to her husband, who started talking about the weather, because that's what you did; you talked about the weather to avoid talking about anything that mattered, and we all said variations on the theme of 'it's hot out'.

It's hot *in*, I said, meaning Starbucks was hell. They just smiled and nodded.

We were all shy with each other, strangers now. This was why people shouldn't leave. You must stay together at all times. Don't let the strangeness in.

We were all waiting for her to speak, our vital organs all on pause. Waiting for her to tell us how to proceed. The last week we'd all been living in limbo, unsure if we still had a daughter, a girlfriend, a Susan.

Should I get a drink? she said, looking at my drink. I'll get a drink, she said, leaving again so soon.

We had to wait then for what felt like hours while she got a drink but was only 10 minutes. None of us said anything while we waited, we just watched her queue, like it might be the last time we saw her.

You should have got drinks, Susan's mother said to her husband.

She meant, Why didn't you get me a fucking drink you clown? I felt self-conscious about mine then; it had been the wrong thing to do.

I'd always wondered what would happen if her head exploded in a Starbucks. I imagined the disenchanted baristas would barely look up, ask someone else to clean it, like she was spilled coffee, or toddler vomit. People would step over her splattered brains to join the queue. Maybe I was wrong; maybe they'd be sad, create a special cup in her honour, the proceeds going to a weird brain charity. Local goth kids would hang outside and want to contact her spirit perhaps, but they knew if they ever actually went in, they'd burst into flames.

Susan came back with her drink and sat down next to me.

I took it as a good sign that she didn't scooch her chair away, that she didn't mind our elbows touching.

It's wrong what you did, she said. But I get it, or I think I do.

We were all staring at her, barely breathing, not daring to say a word. Everything else in the room ceased to exist, fell away.

We let her say what she needed to say.

I want to think, she said, but it turns out I can't. Whatever you did worked. I tried but I can't. Not really. You've denied me that basic human thing, the thing that makes us unique, that separates us from plants and animals and tables even, she said, putting her hand on the slightly sticky table.

She'd been thinking about tables then, and how they didn't think, so she had in fact been thinking, and deeply, but I didn't think it was the time to point that out. We just kept staring at her, glancing at each other now and then to check we weren't the only ones witnessing this.

I need you all to help me think, she continued, or control my thinking, if that's what you're worried about, because I can't go back to how things were, but I don't know how to be anymore, she said, looking sad then, but not in any physical pain.

And if you don't know how to help me, we'll learn together, she said, looking at her father.

And I think I want to help other people, she said, if thoughts really are so dangerous, she said, still not convinced.

They are, we all said, in unison, but we weren't so sure anymore. Not her thoughts anyway; ours, maybe.

What you did really sucked, she said, slipping back into her native tongue, TikTok. Unforgivable, maybe, she said, but what am I supposed to do? I thought if I went away and was alone with my thoughts, I might be able to figure it out, but it turns out I can't think, so your plan worked. And I don't know what to do now, she said, sighing.

We didn't say anything. She wasn't done.

I can't think even if I wanted to, she said. You robbed me of that. But I can't go back to not thinking at all, if that's how I was living, but I don't think that's how it was, she said.

Everything she said sounded like a question.

What am I supposed to do? she said, which was like asking, How do I be a person? To which there was no real answer.

Usually in a situation like this, when the stakes were lower, someone says, No one knows and everyone laughs at how awful and fucked up the human experience is, but we couldn't do that.

I thought that thinking about all this would make my head explode, but it didn't, so I don't know what that means, she said.

I don't think my brain wants to hurt me, she said. I think that if thinking really is so problematic to you all then I need to know how to do it responsibly, she said.

But you're OK? her father said. She seemed OK.

I could tell her mother was doing everything in her power to keep from clutching her daughter to her bosom and sobbing. I saw her hand almost reach for her at least twice before she pulled it back and tucked it into her sleeve. We were all scared of saying the wrong thing and her leaving again.

People know about you now, Susan's mother said, it might be safer for you to stay away for a while, like you have been.

But I'm so bored, Susan said, giving us an eye roll, showing us she was still her.

I want to go back to work, she said. I *need* to go back to work. I'm not afraid, she said.

It was just us who were scared shitless.

I've done what I needed to do, she said, but she meant, I've finished punishing you. I want to come home now, she said.

We looked at her, then looked at each other.

OK, we said in unison, and a weight lifted.

The Starbucks came back to life around us but seemed quieter now. No chairs screeched, no mugs clattered, no baby cried because they wanted McDonald's, not Starbucks. We could have been a normal family.

Oh, Susan said, remembering something, I did some research and it turns out I'm, like, awesome and totes a Buddhist or something, she said, extremely pleased with herself.

You did some research? I said. Where?

On my phone, she said.

And you're a Buddhist now? I said, scratching my chin, because if ever there was a time, this was the time.

Not intentionally, she said. It just seems that everything you told me about my brain and how I am is just naturally Buddhist, she said, smiling.

Right, I said.

I didn't know what she was on about, but she seemed happy about it. She hadn't shaved her head, though, wasn't wearing a robe, chanting something. She seemed the same Susan who'd left us.

Or put it another way, I'm totally enlightened, she grinned. I'm, like, beyond thinking.

Did someone tell you that? her mother said.

No, I read it on my phone, I told you, Susan said.

Cool, I said, because what else was I supposed to say? If someone else just said all that to me I'd think they were crazy. But maybe she was right. I didn't know anything about it. I'd only been thinking about the bad things. I'd never considered there could be good things.

Look, she said, showing me her phone.

It's called a 'state of no mind'. My thing actually has a name now – cool, right?

Her parents looked at each other and shrugged. We didn't have the heart to tell her that wasn't what she had. Her poor dead relatives didn't die because they had no minds. She might not have a mind like ours, but that wasn't what this was.

I read the thing on her phone. Something about it being a state beyond the mind. Ads for Lady Gaga's new skincare line kept popping up. I wanted to ask her if she'd actually really thought about that because it sounded dangerous, for me even, and I didn't have her brain thing. She'd probably just skim-read a bunch of stuff, and it was enough, and she felt validated and everything was fine again and I was just jealous I couldn't be like that. She believed the internet. Not us, but she believed the internet. And had probably already bought Lady Gaga's new skincare line.

I need to pee, she said then. You read that, and I'll pee, she said. And she was gone again.

While she peed, I read about the state of no mind and how it was where the mind should live but didn't, and my head hurt from it. It was a state of mind where thoughts became nothing, zero, ceased to exist. I wished mine would do that. You just existed and didn't think anymore. Zen, I guess. I'd read the first page of *Zen and the Art of Motorcycle Maintenance* once, when I was trying to impress a girl, before Susan, but I never got past that first page; maybe Susan and I were more alike than I knew. I read how, ironically, you couldn't even think that you were in this state of no mind because you weren't thinking, which sounded convenient to me, and a waste of time. I'd want to know, but if you could think about it, you hadn't reached it apparently. Her phone wanted me to play a game to win a phone now, like it didn't even know it was a phone.

She seems OK, right? Or am I imagining it because I need her to be? her mother said, as I tried to read but felt like the more I read, the more I was falling into a void.

No, she seems OK, her father said, more than OK.

What do you think, David? her mother said.

I was still reading about what Google had to say about my girlfriend but managed to say, She seems great.

I should have put the phone down and looked at their faces, re-joined the world, but I kept scrolling.

I hadn't finished reading, but I'd read enough. If I read any more, I was sure my brain would collapse. I didn't know how she'd read it and was OK with it all, but she was. Her phone soothed her in ways we couldn't.

The last thing I read said, how could anyone know this state existed if you didn't know you were in it anyway? It was all such a colossal head-fuck. There must have been something left in the mind to know you weren't thinking, which meant you weren't truly not thinking, which meant, oh my fucking God, my head was actually going to explode, not hers.

I dropped her phone. Someone at another table looked at me like, Idiot, don't you know how precious those are? I picked it up again and checked it wasn't fucked; it was fine.

Susan was back from the bathroom then. I handed her phone back and watched her put it in her pocket.

Cool, huh? she said. So, this whole thing is like nish.

Nish? her father said.

No issue, she said.

Is that a new word? her mother said.

I just made it up, she said.

Right, her mother said. I shrugged.

A small queue had formed for the bathroom now.

We should probably go, her father said.

I really did need to get out of there – to leave that Starbucks, and also just to check the world still existed, outside my head.

Can we walk with you? her father said, putting on his coat.

Susan was her usual laidback easy-breezy self as we walked through the park. She said hello to every dog and a few people and chatted about some TV show about people whose pets looked like celebrities. I felt spacey. The world did seem to still be there, but the stuff she had me read about not thinking and whether you knew you weren't thinking had royally fucked my head. Susan knew she wasn't thinking now but she thought it was a good thing and that she was enlightened. She'd fixed herself but left the rest of us in pieces.

She was bent down making friends with an excessively fluffy dog that couldn't even see, chatting to its human like they'd known each other for years. She certainly wasn't acting like someone who'd just found out they were some Zen master. It was just another thing to her, like how she had brown eyes, or eyes even. It was what it was.

I could see her parents watching her, like they couldn't believe they'd made someone so comfortable in her skin.

She went away to find herself and what she actually found was that we were all assholes and she was great. She didn't need to find herself because she was never lost.

How is my brain different from yours? Susan asked me as we walked.

You really want to know?

I really want to know, she said.

OK, so we just had coffee with your parents – what do you think about it? I said.

I think we just had coffee with my parents, she said, because we'd just had coffee with her parents.

OK, well, I'm thinking we just had coffee with your parents

and I wore the wrong shirt and they hate me and I shouldn't have had a Frappuccino and I feel disgusting and you don't love me, I said.

Oh, she said, stopping. Well, that's stupid.

I know, I said.

Can you not think that?

No, I said.

My parents don't hate you, she said, starting to walk again.

Why did you drink it all then? she said. The Frap.

You're not disgusting, she said.

I love you, she said.

That's not the point, I said. I can't help thinking those things. My mind gets stuck. It gets things wrong and mixed up; it's sad and confused all the time, I said, looking sad and confused probably. Susan's parents were far enough behind not to hear. They were probably talking about my ugly shirt or how my choice of drink was that of a child.

Can you unstick it? she said, because she was an optimist.

Not really, I said, because I was a pessimist.

And other people are like this? she said.

Yes, I said, most other people.

Really?

Yes.

Well, that's fucked up, she said.

I know, I said.

She stopped again.

I want to help you, she said. It sounds awful.

It is, I said.

She got her phone out of her pocket. Tap tap tap scroll scroll scroll tap tap tap.

This might take a while, she said. Play your game or whatever. She started walking again.

I didn't play a game, though. I texted Kate.

She's back, I wrote.

I know, she replied. She sent me a load of links to videos she thinks I need to watch immediately.

About her brain?

No, just cats, she wrote. How is she?

I looked ahead to where Susan was walking and looking on her phone but not bumping into anyone or anything.

Alive, I wrote.

Everything OK with you two? her father said, a few feet behind still.

I think so, I said, looking at Susan again.

Two minutes later she'd found what she was looking for.

OK, so apparently it doesn't work if you try to stop the voices, she said.

I'm not hearing voices, I said.

I meant your own, she said.

Oh right, yes, I hear that, I said.

And it doesn't work if you try to fix the negative thinking. The internet says you have to — and she read from her phone — learn how to manage your thoughts better, dumbass.

I tried to look at her phone, but she snatched it away. We must have looked like any other couple messing around in the park, or any woman about to be mugged.

OK, so it doesn't say dumbass, I added that, she said.

And how do I do that? I said. How do I learn how to manage my thoughts better? Ask the internet how I do that, I said, like it was an oracle.

She looked at her phone again. Her phone was better than mine. Mine only brought me misery and anxiety. Hers seemed to mostly hold the answers to the universe, and cats falling off things. And we had the same price plan.

You have to accept that all the crap is just crazy thoughts, it's not you, she said, reading from her phone again. You are not your thoughts, or something like that, she said, waving her hand in front of my face. I'm bored of this now, she said. Can we go and eat?

She was telling me she was bored of me, and I was too. I wanted to eat too. The thoughts were more manageable with something in my mouth to distract me. She was telling me I could control my own thoughts if I wanted to. That there was a gap between something happening and what we thought about it, and I could choose not to get it all fucked up in between. I could choose now to just go and get food with her and not think about how she solved all my problems, all our problems, by googling it, and how she thought I was boring and an idiot, but she loved me. Love didn't care if you were a fuck-up, as long as you took it to eat.

She was walking with her mum now and I fell in with her father, waiting to hear whatever words of wisdom he had for me, but he just started talking to me about some film I hadn't heard of. His brain had already gone to its happy place, and I was left contemplating the chaos of it all.

Rebecca

Walking in the park was a normal thing to do. A nice, normal, happy thing people did, if I squinted, and didn't see the trash, and the homeless, and the depressed teenagers draped everywhere. Even the leaves were falling from the trees in protest at what they had to witness. We don't want any part of this, they said, as they fell to their death. We're all dying anyway. Hey, you, lady walking with her daughter, do more to help us. And I said, I can't, I'm sorry, I'm about to have the first real conversation with my daughter and I'm nervous.

Isaac and David were talking about some movie. Good for them, I thought, but also, Fucking men.

We were not our thoughts. This was what we told ourselves, the mantra that got us here, so now Susan was aware of hers, I reasoned, it shouldn't change who she was, it shouldn't, but it did obviously, and there was that whole lying to her thing.

It was like Susan was one person, who very much lived in the world and was part of everything and never questioned anything or thought very deeply about anything, and seemed happy, and then someone told her she was like that for a reason, that it wasn't actually who she was but who she had to be. Who was she supposed to be? Who was she underneath it all? Was there another Susan we didn't know? That was what we were all waiting to find out. I didn't know if she thought of it like that. She might not, because she didn't think like that, that's what we hoped anyway. Who were any of us?

I wasn't religious, but I believed in something like a soul. A kernel. A seed. Something that was you that wasn't just a sum of the parts. Who was Susan? I was her mother, and I had no idea really. I wanted her to be whoever she was, as long as she was alive.

Plenty of mothers had never really spoken to their daughters about anything more important than food or TV. Whole generations. Everyone talked about everything with everyone now, online mostly. Therapists should be obsolete, but they weren't, because people still had more to say.

Susan had seen me piss and shit and shower and pluck hairs from my chin and cut my legs shaving every time. She'd seen my insides. The only person. But we'd never had a real, honest conversation, because we couldn't. But now this charade was over, we could. If she wanted to. I was scared of what she might say, what truths I might learn about not just her, but all of us, but I needed to know some things, so I took a deep breath and told her who I was.

When I was younger, not long after I met your father, I had periods of depression, days when I couldn't get out of bed, days when I felt trapped in my own head and sleep was the only way I could get through it. I didn't want to take any medication or talk to anyone or go for a run, I just knew I had to ride it out. Your father had to go to work and this was before mobile phones so he just had to worry about me and I would just have to reassure him I would ride it out and not do anything stupid. By the time he came home from work I was so glad to see him, mostly so he could take me out of my head. It was like a light came on when he came in the door. I could close the door in my head and walk out into his light. He made me come alive. People go on about how co-dependent relationships are bad now and we're supposed to do it all ourselves, save ourselves, but it's exhausting, and if someone saves you, let them, Susan. So, I know what it's like. I know how your brain can try to kill you. My brain has tried to kill me and my brain isn't even like yours. So, I know. I wanted so badly for it to be better for you. Part of me not wanting children was that I worried I'd pass on my depression and I couldn't bear to think of anyone else feeling how I felt, let alone my child. So, it worked out for the best. Meeting your father and his family curse meant we had to do what I always wanted to anyway, which was to keep you from yourself. Does that make sense? I wish someone had done that for me.

I looked to Susan, waiting for her to at least nod, but she was listening to something on her phone – AirPods were so tiny I hadn't even noticed.

Did you say something? she said, taking out one of her AirPods.

Do you want to listen? she said, offering me one.

Sure, I said, wiping it on my jacket first.

Mum, she said, we've shared fluids before. I was literally inside you.

And that's when I knew we'd be OK. Because if I thought about that for a second, that I made a human person, who could walk in a park and listen to music on her phone, who couldn't think when the rest of us were thinking themselves to death, I might explode. Not my head, but my whole body. Like in some dumb superhero movie that the people in not just my life but the world cared so deeply about.

Isaac was talking to Susan about the movie now. David looked relieved. He smiled at me shyly. I wanted to hug him and thank him not just for taking care of Susan, but for loving her, but we were walking in a line and I didn't want to make a scene. We were already making a scene, but it was the one from *The Wizard of Oz*, when they were all walking in a line, singing, on the way to see that disappointing wizard who was just a man.

Isaac was saying we should all go to the movie. He took my hand and squeezed it.

You're back, I said, and he looked at me, confused.

I was never gone, he said.

I wanted to stop there in the park and cry and tell him he was gone, because I definitely felt it, but he was back now, so I didn't. It was startling how differently people could live one shared life. Everything felt so very fragile. Like I had to be happy with just this, not question anything again. We had to move forward from this, and I wanted it to be together.

Then I heard my name being called in a strange shout/whisper, followed by a pst noise.

Rebecca, pst, over here. A tree was talking to me.

I think that tree is talking to you, Isaac said.

From behind the tree, we could see a woman now, in a long trench coat and dark glasses.

I think that's Bea, I said.

The woman peeked out from behind her glasses to confirm it was indeed Bea.

It's fine, I said, I'll talk to her. You go ahead and make sure Susan doesn't see her.

I went over to where Bea was lurking behind the tree.

You look ridiculous, I said.

The police are after my husband, she said.

What did he do? I said, although I didn't really want to know.

He tried to steal a baby, she said.

What? He tried to steal a baby?

Yes, I just came to tell you I'm sorry about everything. He wanted me to have a child, you know, but just as an experiment, but I wouldn't do it. So he had to make do with experimenting with animals, but ever since learning about Susan, well, he's been unravelling somewhat.

Stealing a baby isn't unravelling, it's full fucking madness, I said, looking across the park to where my family were, safely away from this woman.

We're leaving the country anyway, Bea said. I just wanted to say I'm sorry.

It's OK, I said, we're OK, I said. I didn't mean me and her, but me and my family.

I know you are, she said, it's the rest of us that need to get a grip.

She looked anxiously around the park then, and made a run for it.

Good luck, I said, but she was just another lunatic in a trench coat in a park by then.

I caught up to Isaac and told him what Bea had said.

Wow, he said. Really? he said, scratching his chin.

I didn't have to say Bea was the lesser evil, after all, because he already knew that.

Susan

Later that night we were curled up on the couch and watching *The Kardashians*. I hadn't been keeping up, but they still existed, somewhere. It was comforting.

Did they murder the brother or something? David said.

I think he's off doing his sock thing, I said.

Still?

Socks are important, I said.

Is that what you're thinking about right now? Socks?

You brought it up.

One of the sisters said to another of the sisters, Text me if you find your soul.

I started to laugh.

What's so funny? David said, and I couldn't explain it. I just kept laughing.

Stop laughing, David said.

You start laughing, I said.

I don't know what the point of any of it is, David said, putting his head in his hands, starting to cry.

There isn't any point, silly, I said, taking his head out of his hands, holding it in mine, wiping his tears with my sleeve.

It's like Kurt Vonnegut said, I said, tucking my knees to my chin.

When did you read Kurt Vonnegut?

I read.

What does he say?

OK, so I read it on a T-shirt, but he still said it. He said, 'We're here on earth to fart around and don't let anyone else tell you different.'

He was very smart.

Also, big fan of farting.

You had me worried there, I thought you'd actually read Vonnegut, he said, sniffing.

Don't be silly.

I leaned my head on his shoulder then, listened to his heartbeat, slow and steady. If he ever listened to mine, it probably made him think about how fragile life was, mortality and stuff, but I thought of the opposite, of how amazing it was, how loud love could be.

I watched the TV and let it work its magic, because it was magic; even though David explained how it worked to me once, I preferred to think it was magic, not signals and wires, not a man in a suit somewhere giving orders.

There was an ad break. I flicked channels while I waited to find out what happened next to the TV sisters whose nails were too long to go to the bathroom, but they must, surely. This was what I thought about while David quietly contemplated all life.

I found a channel showing old *X-Files* episodes.

The X-Files is on! I shouted. Even though he was sitting just there. It was proper *X-Files*, not the reboot. The one where Scully was still Scully, before she had a glow-up that actually made her lose whatever it was she had. I never wanted to lose who I was.

I haven't really been able to watch it since I met you, David sniffed.

Well, that's dumb, I said.

I thought someone was going to put you in a room and make you think and make your head explode, he said.

You watch too much TV, I said.

I watch too much TV? he said.

I don't really watch it, I said. Do people actually watch it? I thought we all kept it on because it eased the discomfort of being alive, I said, quietly shocked at how articulately I could express my innermost thoughts, how the words were just there and I said them and it was how I felt and my inside and outside were aligned, for a second anyway. If I googled it, there was probably a word for it. I thought he knew most of the world was a buffer. OK, so I only recently realised it, but I was OK with it, if it saved us all.

You feel discomfort? David said, looking concerned.

His heart had stopped; I knew this because I was still listening to it. I would have to help him manage his thoughts better, manage his body better. Help him see that he was alive, and needed care, and that all the rest was noise.

Not this second, no, I said, and his heart started up again and I thought how either of us could die at any moment really, but we had chosen to make sense of living, together.

So, what are we not watching tonight? he said.

I don't mind, but we need snacks, I said, getting up.

In the kitchen I filled a bowl with potato chips, poured two glasses of Coke and grabbed the box of Cinnamon Toast Crunch from the counter. I tucked the box of cereal under one arm, balanced the bowl of chips in the crook of my arm and carried the glasses back to the couch. On the way, the box of cereal kept slipping, and then, before I knew what was happening, the bowl of chips was falling and I let go of one of the glasses. If you were going to make a mess, you may as well make a good one, I thought.

David was there then, staring at me. I still had hold of the cereal, opened it, offered it to him.

What were you thinking? he said.

Nothing, I said. Nothing at all.

Acknowledgements

Thank you to my TV and bed. I couldn't have done it without you.